THE RIVER'S EDGE

A gripping crime thriller full of stunning twists

JOY ELLIS

DI Jackman & DS Evans Book 10

Joffe Books, London
www.joffebooks.com

First published in Great Britain in 2023

ISBN: 978-1-80405-939-5

This book is dedicated to the memory of two wonderful friends.

Patricia Ann Warren
23 July 1947 to 22 April 2023

Dearest Pat, from school children to young women going out into that big world, we laughed and cried together . . . although it has to be said, it was mainly laughter! You were the kindest, funniest, and most loyal friend ever. We were inseparable for so long, but life has different ideas. It swept us in different directions, and although I never forgot you, and spent years looking for you, we were never to physically meet again. The happy part, is that thanks to your sister Wendy, and my books, we finally got back in contact again. I am so thankful for that. We never got that promised hug, and sadly I never met Roger and Beccy, but we were in each other's lives again, and that means such a lot. Every memory I have of you, makes me smile. Rest in peace, my lovely friend, Pat.

and

Woody
Springer Spaniel
18 January 2010 to 22 March 2023

All dogs are special, but some . . . well, they tug just a little harder on your heartstrings. If ever there was a faithful friend; it was our lovely Woody. We never once heard him growl, and he simply loved everyone. He would come into the office when I worked and settle in his special bed, and there he would stay; listening to me muttering about time-lines and plots. Now he's gone, and the office seems very empty, even though several of our other dogs often join me. Sometimes, late at night as I type away, I find myself saying, 'What do you think, Woody, my old mate? Should I kill off the bad guy?' And I swear I see him sitting there, wagging his tail, and telling me . . . 'Yeah, Mum! Just do it!' We miss you, Woody, and we always will.

CHAPTER ONE

'Marie Evans?'

The voice sounded vaguely familiar, but it had an edge to it that flashed a warning.

'Yes. Who is this, please?' Marie said.

'It's Douglas Marshall. Dougie the Dreamer, remember me?'

A picture of the young rookie copper with whom she had started her training rose into her mind. 'Of course I do! This is a bit of a surprise, Dougie. How are you these days?'

Ignoring her polite query, he said, 'I need to talk to you urgently. Can we meet?'

Now there was no doubt about that edginess. Marie knew not to press him for answers over the phone. 'Where? When?'

'The Lincoln Arms in Brewer Street in half an hour?'

Marie exhaled. This must be serious. 'Okay, Dougie, I think I can get away. But just tell me, are you in trouble?'

She heard a grunt at the other end of the line. 'More like in danger, I think, so, yeah, I'm in trouble. Big trouble.' Then the line went dead.

DS Marie Evans looked around the CID office. Everyone seemed to be either missing from their desks or

1

deep in conversation on their phones, so she decided to go and see DI Rowan Jackman and ask him what he made of Dougie's call.

Jackman looked older now. Losing his partner, the well-respected force psychologist, had hit him hard. Indeed, Laura's sudden death had sent shockwaves through the entire division — she had been a dear friend to many of them, including Marie herself. Three months down the line, it still felt raw to her, so who knew what Jackman must be suffering? He now worked harder than ever, which was something Marie understood all too well. She too had immersed herself in work after her husband had been killed in an accident on his precious motorcycle not long after they were married.

So she and Jackman were bonded through more than mere friendship. They shared loss, grief, and sadness. However, Marie had come through it, and had found someone else to love. She could look back at the years she had spent with her husband and smile at the good times, while Jackman was still engulfed in the impenetrable darkness of his heartache. It was no use telling him it would pass, no good offering the usual platitudes about time healing all wounds. It just had to be endured. All Marie could do was be around and provide a shoulder to cry on.

She tapped on his door. 'Boss? Got a weird one here. I need to slip out for a while.'

Jackman tilted his head. 'What? Something to do with one of our cases?'

'Actually, I haven't the faintest idea what it's about,' she said with a laugh. Frowning, she told him about the brief call, the voice from the past.

Jackman shook his head. 'I don't think I know this Dougie, do I?'

'We joined the force at around the same time, so you wouldn't have met him. He was a really bright young probationer, good at all the textbook stuff. I reckon he learned Butterworth's Police Law by heart, but he wasn't tough enough. Poor Dougie imagined he could talk his way through any situation. One day he tried to reason with a drug dealer who broke his arm so badly that he had to leave the force. He came back as a civvie, and then left and got a job with the Police Federation. Personally, I think it suited him a whole lot better. He was still up to his neck in policing, but wasn't out there at the sharp end.'

'And now he's in trouble.' Jackman pulled a face. 'Want me to come along?'

She shook her head. 'Not this time, Jackman. I'll test the waters and see what the problem is. I won't be long; the Lincoln Arms is just up the road. I'll report back as soon as I'm finished.'

Marie made her way to the pub on foot. It was a ten-minute walk, certainly not worth taking a car.

The Lincoln Arms was busy and, since it was a hot day, the outside tables were full. She scanned the faces of the occupants but didn't see Dougie Marshall. She went inside and stood for a moment adjusting her eyes to the gloom. Maybe he hadn't arrived yet, maybe he'd changed his mind. Then she saw him, sitting alone at a small table in the corner. It took her a few seconds to decide if this man really was Dougie Marshall. The change in Jackman she had been so concerned about was nothing compared to the change in her former colleague.

Dougie's boyish appearance had earned him a load of teasing from coppers and criminals alike. Not only that, his face took on a faraway, dreamy expression whenever he had to consider a complicated situation, which had given rise to his nickname. Now, Dougie the Dreamer seemed to be in the grip of a nightmare.

She hurried across to him, composing an expression that didn't reveal her surprise at the change in him. 'Dougie! Good to see you.'

For a moment his face shone with relief and pleasure at seeing her again, and she saw the bright young copper she once had known. But within seconds it took on the haggard look of consternation she had observed from across the room.

Two coffees sat on the table in front of him.

'I knew you wouldn't drink on duty,' he said, 'So I chanced that you still liked your coffee the way you did back then.'

Marie sat down opposite. 'Yes, some things never change.' She paused, looking him in the face. 'Others do. Forgive me for saying this, Doug, but you look like shit. What's the matter?'

'I daren't stay long, so I'll get straight to the point.' He leaned closer to her and lowered his voice. 'I think there is a serious crime going on. Something big. But the problem is, I have no proof, not one iota.' His eyes darted around the bar, as if to make sure they weren't overheard. 'My department at the Federation was approached by a film company. They were looking for a police consultant on a new crime drama series. As I was due some leave, I volunteered, and I joined them for a two weeks' shoot in Warwickshire.'

Again, he glanced around the bar, his fear almost tangible.

'Go on, Dougie,' she said. 'I'm listening.'

'I got really into it,' Dougie admitted. 'It was interesting trying to find a middle ground between authentic police work and good television drama. I got friendly with a lot of the people involved — you know, scriptwriters, directors, actors, and crew. I really enjoyed it . . . at the beginning. Then I began to catch an undercurrent. It was subtle, like conversations suddenly stopping when you were in earshot; sideways looks and conspiratorial glances between people, comings and goings at night after filming had ceased. You know what I mean — when you've been around policing in one form or another for years, you get to be able to read the signs.'

'You more than most, mate,' Marie said, smiling. 'We took the piss, but that dreamy look always meant something worth looking into.'

The ghost of a smile played on his lips, and then it was gone. 'Marie, there was something very wrong on that film set. Something was going on beneath the filming and all its trappings, and somehow whoever is responsible saw that I'd picked up on it. I've been warned off, not directly, but so many bad things have happened recently, like accidents that could have been serious, and threatening phone calls in the middle of the night. They can't be coincidence. Now I'm afraid for my life.'

He wasn't joking.

'Then are you safe coming here and talking to me?' Marie said.

He shrugged. 'I'm supposed to be in a meeting in Greenborough today. I drove there, left my car in the car park, then got a taxi here. I used the back streets to get to this pub, and I'm certain I wasn't followed, but even so, I'm being cautious.'

'Have you told anyone else, Dougie?' she asked. 'Surely, you've reported it?'

'No. For one simple reason. The police will find nothing, and all that will happen is that I'll have shown myself to be the source of the leak. Then, dear Marie, it will be curtains for the dreamer. The moment I smelled a rat I looked deeper. Believe me, the shit going down on that set, whatever it is, is bloody well hidden.'

'What's your gut instinct tell you? What kind of crime is occurring?'

'Well, naturally I suspected drugs to begin with, but nothing actually pointed to that. I soon crossed off all the usual crimes, but the bottom line is . . . I sodding well don't know.' Dougie looked thoroughly miserable. 'And I know how crap that sounds, but whatever it is, I'm dead certain it's serious enough to want me out of the equation.'

'But how can I help you?' Marie wasn't sure where this was going, and vaguely wondered why he had picked her to tell.

'Because it's about to become your problem, I'm afraid. The same company are shooting another new police procedural drama, right here in Saltern-le-Fen. The director asked me to be an advisor again, but I had an anonymous midnight call that convinced me that taking up his kind offer would not be a good idea.'

'A threat?'

'Oh yes, and it wasn't exactly subtle. Put it like this: as I'd like to make it to my retirement pension one day, I've graciously declined.' He rubbed hard at his chin. 'The reason I want you to know this, is that the man who is going to act as consultant is a retired detective called Frank Rosen, and I happen to know that he's an old mate of your boss, Jackman. No one will expect him to know anything at all about what's going on, so if he's given a brief of the situation before he even starts, there's a chance you guys can nail whatever is going down.'

'I see your point,' murmured Marie. 'And when is this production supposed to kick off?'

'As soon as they have all the locations sorted and the relevant permissions have been granted. They won't hang about, it's far too costly. Liaise with Frank Rosen, he'll be fully updated, like I was,' Dougie said bitterly. 'If I could give you more, I would, but as far as discovering what the hell is going on, I failed miserably. All I have are a few names that might be worth checking out, and that's it.' He passed her a folded sheet of paper with the names and two mobile numbers scribbled at the bottom. 'The top one is a burner phone, emergencies only. I'm going away for a while. I have found somewhere safe, but it is probably best if no one knows where it is.' With a final glance around, he stood up. 'I'll ring when I can. Good luck, Marie, and please sort this out. My life may depend on it.'

Marie was left staring after his departing figure.

* * *

Alistair Ashcroft sat at the table in his room — they called them rooms now, rather than cells — and stared at two names written on a sheet of paper. Next to the paper lay a single visiting order request. Which to choose? It was vital he make the correct decision. He was fortunate in that he had an extra slot this month, awarded for recent good behaviour. Normally, he was permitted just two visits per month.

He needed to act fast on something, and one of these two names could be the answer to his dilemma.

Hazel Palgrave. Reuben Winter.

Both had all the right attributes and skills. He simply needed the one with the most conviction. Which of these two was the most loyal and dedicated disciple?

Trying to decide, Ashcroft wheeled himself slowly up and down the small room. His new prison was one of the few that had a dedicated unit for prisoners with additional needs. Not only did it have wheelchair accessibility and physiotherapy, it also offered considerable benefits to those prisoners who qualified to take part in a specialised, high-intensity, psychological study programme. As part of this programme, he had been given the choice of a dormitory-style sleeping area that afforded prisoners the chance to associate with others, or a single room. Ashcroft, who only liked company under his own terms and if it was useful to him, hadn't even had to think.

He returned to the desk, his mind made up. He drew a firm line through the name Reuben Winter and, with a slow smile spreading across his narrow features, began to fill in the VO to Hazel Palgrave.

* * *

Dex made his way across the parking area to one of the neighbouring mobile homes.

'Is there a poker game tonight?' called out Ken, one of the film company's sound engineers.

'Yeah.' Dex laughed, 'One day I'll learn to say no and save myself a few quid.'

'Any spaces around the table tonight?' asked Ken hopefully.

Dex shrugged in apology. 'No, mate. Full house, I'm afraid.'

He walked on, beneath a cloudy night sky. He couldn't help feeling a bit anxious, although by now he should have got used to Lance's summons. He put it down to excitement, because what he'd be asked to do heralded a considerable deposit into his depleted coffers, and fear, because it was risky work, and not something that he particularly liked doing. He was no main player, but his contribution was vital to the smooth running of Lance's operation.

Four of the others were already there when he arrived. Only Craig was missing, and he was always last. He was the only member of the crew whose wife travelled on location with him, and she was a less than avid fan of the regular poker games he attended. Lance had admitted to a slight concern that Craig might be a weak link but he had skills that none of the others possessed, so they were forced to tolerate his presence.

Ten minutes later, Craig hurried in, apologising as usual, and threw himself into the only empty seat with a loud har-rumph of irritation.

'Okay, well, now we are all here,' Lance glared pointedly at Craig, 'I've got some news, and some dates for your diaries.'

They dealt the cards and arranged the table with shot glasses and a 'pot' of bets, so that any unexpected visitor would see nothing but six guys at an evening's poker game.

Lance looked around, staring hard at each of them in turn. 'We are heading for the Lincolnshire Fens a week next Thursday. We start filming at silly o'clock the next day. It's the new crime series that we've been waiting to hear about, *Fen Division Five*, and we've got some heavyweight actors coming in.'

Dex wasn't sure if that was a good thing or a bad. A high-profile cast caused a lot of hype, which was a pain, but it could also take attention from other things, things like their illegal sideline.

'Now this is one place I've been itching to get to,' Lance continued. 'I've already got contacts there, and oh boy, is it the perfect location! It's a dream, lads. Right on the coast, with a tidal river, a route out of the Wash, across the North Sea straight to Holland.' For a moment, his tight lips relaxed in a wicked smile. 'This is going to be the big one, no question.'

'Will there be any comeback on that, er, slight hitch from the last job, Lance?' asked Craig suspiciously.

'Don't you worry, Marshall's history. We have a new consultant for this one, and from what I hear he'll be a pushover. He's in it for the kudos, wants to see his name on the credits. He's over the hill, retired a while back, probably spends his days watching *Tipping Point* and *Bangers and Cash*. Plus, I've heard he can do with the dosh. Another thing is that he has no known connection with his nosey young predecessor. No, I don't foresee a problem with Mr Rosen at all.' The smile vanished again, lips tight as a drawstring. 'However, everyone watches him, okay? Even if he is a dinosaur, he used to be a copper, and he'll be with us for a while, so keep your eyes peeled.'

The 'card game' went on for an hour and a half. When it was over, they drifted away one at a time. Dex walked down to the lake, some 500 metres from the end of the park, and sat for a while on the pontoon the fishermen used. As before, he experienced mixed emotions. Part of him loved the adrenalin rush of the illegal. As a younger man he had almost become addicted to computer games, in which you pitted yourself against an enemy, used clever tactics and won the prize. Another part of him dreaded the consequences should he get caught. He had no police record, but he'd already been involved in half a dozen of Lance's illegal activities, and if he were not a compulsive, and not very successful gambler, he'd be pretty well-off by now.

He kicked at one of the wooden planks and cursed himself for being so weak. He was no fool: that last caper had been close. The police advisor had smelled a rat, even if he hadn't discovered anything concrete. If Lance hadn't come down hard, they would have had to throw in the towel, and Dex would be in a different kind of trouble . . . with loan sharks. It was his gambling losses that forced him to continue. Unless he found a way to ditch the gee-gees and the scratch cards, he'd never find a way out.

'Dex?'

He turned around and saw Craig approaching through the gloom.

'Can I ask you something?'

Dex shrugged. 'All right. If you must.'

Craig sat down beside him and sighed. 'Look, I know we are all in this up to our eyeballs, and don't get me wrong, the money is something else, but . . .'

Dex waited. 'Come on, man. Spit it out. Whatever it is it won't go any further, don't worry.'

'Don't you ever suspect that something else is going on here?' His brow wrinkled in concentration. 'I mean, something deeper, maybe more dangerous than what you and I are involved in?'

Dex said nothing for a while. Craig had just voiced something that had bugged him since their first job. Dex had always believed that because he was a small cog in the wheel, he quite understandably wasn't told everything. But he couldn't dismiss the suspicion that there was more to it than he knew. Finally, he said, 'Yes. As it happens, I have considered that.'

'Thank God for that! I thought I was going fucking mad.' Then Craig groaned. 'But in a way, this makes it worse, 'cause now it's real. Do you have any idea what's going on, Dex?'

Dex shook his head. 'None at all, and what's more, I don't *want* to know. I'm going to do this Fens job, take the money — which I badly need — and scarper. I'm going to get a job somewhere a million miles from this crew, maybe I'll even get out of the industry. With my skills I can work on anything that involves lighting and electrics. I might even try exhibition or event work again.' He surprised even himself with the certainty of his wishes. He had only vaguely thought about getting out before Craig confirmed his fears. Now his mind was made up.

'I need the money too,' muttered Craig bitterly. 'I'm in debt. My wife . . . she's kind of extravagant, and . . .'

All at once, Dex was consumed with an angry resentment at the way he'd been used by the syndicate. He hated himself, too, for the position in which he found himself. 'Look,' he snapped. 'I don't want to hear your fucking sob story any more than you want to hear mine. Just tell me, what are you going to do about it?'

Craig looked startled. 'Nothing, of course! What can I do? I have no proof, just a feeling, and like it or not, I have to do this Fens job, or the bailiffs will take my motorhome and everything in it. One more big job and I'm free of debt.' He pulled a face. 'Then I reckon I'll do the same as you, and the missus and me will do a runner.'

Dex sighed. 'Sorry, mate, I didn't mean to snap. We're in the same boat, ain't we? Neither of us wants to get caught up in something we never signed up for, but we must, or I, for one, could find myself in deep, deep shit.'

'And another thing. Maybe we are missing out.' Craig gave him an aggrieved look. 'What if we are getting paid peanuts for helping Lance make himself some seriously big money?'

'Good point,' said Dex. 'I still want out though. One thing is for sure, we need to watch our step and keep what we suspect to ourselves.'

'And keep each other in the picture,' added Craig. 'If I hear anything iffy, I'll tell you, and vice versa?'

Dex stuck out his hand. 'Deal.'

As Craig got up to walk away, Dex added, 'Stay safe, mate. I'm not getting good vibes about all this.'

Craig paused mid-stride. 'Yeah, you too, Dex. I feel the same. Watch your back.'

CHAPTER TWO

Jackman's mother led a new pony out of its stable for him to see. If ever there was a soft touch when it came to rescuing animals, Harriet Jackman was it.

'Okay, Mother, what's the story this time?' Jackman asked patiently.

Harriet busied herself patting and stroking her newest acquisition. 'You'd have done the same in my position, darling. And there's plenty of room here now I've cut back on the livery. This beautiful creature was just barely existing in a tiny muddy field at the back of that old farmhouse out on the road to Amberley Fen. Same old story — daughters grow up, move away from home, leaving mother and father with their animals. And in this case, the father, poor man, developed some debilitating illness.' She shook her head. 'Its owner was so relieved that I was prepared to take it on, she almost cried. She didn't even ask much money for it.'

Jackman looked at the pony. It was in dire need of some TLC, but at least it hadn't been ill-treated or starved. He'd seen his mother bring home far worse cases. 'She's a nice little cob, Mum. How old? Ten? Eleven?'

'Something like that, and she's got the sweetest nature. Her name is Fortune.'

Jackman laughed. 'Now that's appropriate! If ever there was a fortunate animal, I'm looking at it.' He ran a professional eye over the mare, summing up her attributes and assessing her potential flaws. 'What does my nephew think of our Fortune then?'

'Ryan is quite taken with her. He's already worked out a feeding regimen and exercise programme — but listen to this.' Harriet gave him an amused smile. 'It's not just Ryan who likes this little girl — your Miles is totally besotted!'

'Really?' Now this was a surprise. Ryan was very similar to the way Jackman had been as a boy — a good rider from a very early age, who had a natural empathy with horses. Miles, Ryan's younger brother, was quite different. He too loved horses but was happiest just being around them, grooming them and, sometimes, making drawings of them. 'You mean as in to paint her?'

'No, I don't,' Harriet said, 'although we do already have several sketches of her up on the stable wall. No, Miles wants to ride her. He says they have a connection, and that he wants to take care of her.' She gave a little shrug. 'And I have to admit, she responds better to Miles than anyone else. I think the boy has a new best friend in Fortune.'

Harriet having handed the pony over to one of the stable hands, mother and son strolled back to the house.

All at once, Jackman felt something akin to relief wash over him. This was the first 'normal' conversation he had had with his mother that hadn't been saturated with his grief. His mother had been a rock over the last few months. They had always been very close, and he understood that she didn't just feel sorrow at Laura's untimely death, but rather the deep pain of seeing her son in such anguish. Today, something had changed, and he was glad. His mother's stables was the one place he could feel something like life begin to emerge. The stables had been his sanctuary, long before Laura came into his life, so it wasn't haunted by her ghost. Laura hadn't shared his passion for horses, so the stables had always been his own place. He came whenever he could, but until today his visits had been dampened by his sense of his mother's sorrow and pity.

'Are you riding today, darling?' she asked brightly.

'Sadly no, Mum, but I'm off tomorrow, so I'll be back in the morning. I can spend the whole day with you, if you like? I might even bring Sam if he fancies a day out.'

'That's great! I'll do lunch. The boys will be here too as school has broken up, and they'd love to see you. Ryan is talking about going to Burleigh Pony Club Camp next year and I know he wants to talk to you about it. Oh, and your father will be so pleased. I do believe he has a rare day free from all his many projects.'

There had been a time when Jackman would have shrunk from spending time with Lawrence Jackman. He had always felt himself to be a disappointment to his father. However, in the last few years, as his father came to under-stand something about the life he led, they had drawn close. 'I'll look forward to it, Mum. Now I must go. Oh, have you heard the news that a film company is going to be shooting on location in Saltern?'

'Yes. It was in the local paper last week.'

'Well, a friend of mine is the police procedural advisor on it. Marie and I are meeting him for a chat in half an hour.'

'Any big stars involved?' Harriet asked eagerly. 'Is Saltern-le-Fen going to be famous? Is someone finally going show the Fens in a good way?'

'There are one or two whose names I vaguely recognise, but I need to ask Max or Charlie. They're young, they're more likely to know who's who.'

'Well, make sure you report back with all the gossip. Your nephews will be thrilled to hear it.'

He laughed, hugged his mother and made his way over to his car. 'I'll ring you tonight and let you know if Sam's up for a day at the stables, okay?'

'All right, darling,' his mother called back. 'Tell him Lawrence would love the chance of a chat, and there will be no mucking out, I promise.'

Jackman drove out and onto the road that would take him back to Saltern. Sam, his dear friend, who had been Laura's mentor and surrogate father, had moved into the converted mill in Jackman's property at Mill Corner. He had taken Laura's passing badly, though he feigned a stoic acceptance, and Jackman was glad to be able to keep an eye on the elderly psychologist. Besides, Sam was good company, and each helped the other survive the dark days.

Jackman drove away, forcing himself to concentrate on this meeting with Marie and Frank Rosen.

In his day, Frank had been a remarkable detective. He had perfected the art of making himself completely unreadable. Thinking of him, Jackman gave an involuntary smile. That gift of Frank's had been extremely useful in the past, especially when they needed a criminal to cough to something. Older than Jackman, he would have worked until he dropped if he'd been able, but he contracted a lung condition that had forced him to retire, which had been a great loss to their division. Jackman wondered if Frank had changed since he stopped working.

They were meeting away from the station, in a small café attached to a garden centre on the edge of town, since they didn't want to be seen. If Marie's old mate, Douglas Marshall, really was in serious trouble, Jackman thought it better that no one should know of their discussion. On the phone to Frank he had given him a very brief outline of what Marshall had confided to Marie. As expected, this had sparked Frank's interest and he had agreed to meet them as soon as possible.

When he pulled into the car park, he was amused to see a familiar old car sitting next to Marie's gleaming Triumph Tiger, and a familiar old man leaning against the vehicle chatting with Marie. As Jackman walked towards them, the man looked up and grinned. 'I know what you're going to say, Jackman. But if it ain't broke, don't fix it, that's my motto. My nephew is a bloody good mechanic, and this old bird,' he patted the old Triumph Vitesse, 'is still as sweet as a nut, thanks to him.'

Rosen had aged somewhat, his hair was greyer and his face more lined, and he was a little heavier, but no more than that. Jackman thought that, overall, he looked pretty good.

Frank took a breath. 'I'll get this over with straightaway.' He held out his hand to Jackman. 'I'm very sorry for your loss, I truly am. I'll leave it at that, okay?'

Jackman clasped his hand in return. 'Thanks, Frank. Appreciated.' And he did appreciate it. He was grateful for Frank's few simple words, and mostly for the fact that he didn't belabour the point.

They went inside, ordered coffee and took their trays outside to a large patio area. A few of the other tables were occupied, but they found one where they could talk without being overheard.

'So, tell me all about this strange mystery,' said Frank, his eyes bright with interest.

Jackman indicated Marie, who recounted what Douglas Marshall had said and his feeling of being under threat.

Frank gave a low whistle. 'But he has no idea what's going on? That's weird. You nearly always get an inkling, don't you? I mean, every crime is flagged up by its own kind of behaviour.'

'Dougie said something like that himself,' agreed Marie. 'And he was an astute copper. It baffled him, which only convinced him all the more that whatever they were up to was deadly serious. He was really scared, so whatever this mystery crime is, it must be worth harming someone to protect it.'

'Which makes this escapade of yours potentially very dangerous,' Jackman added. 'Are you okay with that?'

Frank gave him a withering look. 'What do you think?'

Jackman grinned. 'Just asking.'

'Well, forget it. Think about it, I'm in the perfect position to get to the bottom of it, aren't I?' He glanced about him. 'I've already left a few hints here and there — in low places of course — that I've taken this consultancy because I'm hard up, plus I'm a little bit star-struck, excited about working on a film set. If anybody decides to make a few discreet enquiries about me, it will filter back and I'll register as being no trouble.'

'You really are up for it then?' Jackman asked.

'One hundred percent, mate. Can't wait. My meds are working a treat now, I get no more attacks of breathlessness. Okay, I couldn't do a sprint start or undertake anything too physical, but I see myself as your eyes and ears, your undercover agent on the ground.'

'Perfect,' purred Marie. 'That's exactly what we want. And because you had already been recruited, it can't look as though you've been planted. It's as good as it gets.'

'Unless they suspect that Marshall told someone before he did a runner,' added Jackman, frowning. 'So, Frank, before you start poking about, assess the situation very carefully.'

'When Douglas met me, he made absolutely sure he wasn't followed,' said Marie. 'He believes they think he's too terrified to open his mouth.'

Rosen raised his cup. 'Don't worry. Once a copper always a copper. I'll be careful.' He winked at Marie. 'I'll leave the risk-taking to you guys, since you still have warrant cards and are sworn to protect life and property.' He set down his cup. 'So, what's the plan of action?'

'Marshall gave Marie four names,' Jackman said. 'Nothing definite, but he had reservations about them for some reason. You might start with them. If you find anything worth reporting, use this.' He took a small phone from his pocket. 'It's got our numbers in it. Make sure people see you use your own phone, and keep this one under wraps. We have no idea how organised these people are.'

Frank took the burner phone and slipped it into his pocket. 'I'm going to assume the worst, that we find something big, so I'll tread very warily indeed. If it turns out to be a something and a nothing, then you can nip it in the bud and the cameras can roll. However, as we know, criminals only put the frighteners on people if they've something to protect.'

'Just watch your back, Frank,' Jackman said gravely. 'You're on your own on that set, and you're completely in the dark about what might be going on. One sniff of something bad, call it in and we'll be there — but you know the score.'

'Jackman, you're beginning to sound like my old granny,' Frank exclaimed. 'I may be retired, but I'm not in my dotage yet.'

Jackman was forced to laugh. 'Sorry, I just hate having to deal with complete unknowns. Hell, it could be nothing at all.' He glanced at Marie. 'But who am I kidding? I'm hardly going to doubt what your old friend told you, and as I can't see him as the neurotic type, we must assume it's real. And bad.'

Frank grinned broadly. 'You know what? I'm looking forward to this immensely. Life's been a tad too humdrum of late, and this is just what I need to lift my spirits and tax the old grey cells. Plus, I get to work on the filming of a TV drama. As my young niece would say, how cool is that?'

They chatted for a while longer, until Jackman glanced at his watch. 'We need to get back. Ring us, won't you, Frank, the moment you get a start date?'

His old friend got to his feet. 'I'll contact you the moment I hear, and meanwhile, I'll keep my ear firmly to the ground.'

'Just do it very discreetly,' warned Jackman. 'And we'll pass on any information that comes our way.'

They walked back to the car park, and Frank drove away.

'He's right you know, Jackman, that engine sounds like the purr of a contented cat,' commented Marie. 'I'd hate to trade in something as special as that for some modern job that looks just like all the others. I know I should think of a greener future, but I do love old cars and bikes — especially Triumphs.'

Jackman was only half listening. He was still wondering what kind of crime could be lurking beneath the facade of this seemingly respectable film unit. And why would Dougie the Dreamer have no idea what was going on, other than a few vague indications of people acting secretively?

'Earth calling, Jackman.' Marie looked at him, smiling. 'Am I boring you?'

'Sorry, Marie. I'm still mulling over Frank's comment about picking up on behaviours associated with particular crimes. It is odd that Dougie couldn't pin-point anything, isn't it?'

'Especially when you consider the way he was frightened off,' Marie said. 'Something has to be going down, or there would be no need for threats. It leads me to wonder if they thought he knew more than he did to come down so hard on him.'

'I wondered that.' Jackman paused. 'Or, do you think that maybe he *does* know more but is too scared to tell us?'

'Nah. That doesn't sound like Dougie at all. He took a big risk talking to me in the first place, so why not tell me everything?' She pulled on her crash helmet and climbed onto her gleaming Tiger. 'I must get back to base, boss — Robbie is waiting for me to join him in interviewing that woman who thinks her neighbours are using their house to receive stolen goods.' She gave a grimace. 'See you there.'

Jackman watched her skilfully manoeuvre the big bike out of the car park and speed away. For a moment he envied her. He would have liked to have jumped on a powerful bike himself and head for freedom, leaving his present life with all its heartache and anguish behind.

He shook his head. Stupid. Even if he did run away, he'd be taking all his baggage with him, so what was the point? Best to do what he was doing, surround himself with family, and immerse himself in work.

He unlocked his car and climbed in, trying not to look at the empty passenger seat beside him. Last week he had found a pair of Laura's sunglasses in his glove compartment. It had reduced him to tears. How poignant were the possessions that remained after their owner had departed forever! How did they exert such power?

With a sigh, Jackman started the engine. Back to work, before he became even more maudlin.

CHAPTER THREE

Six Weeks Later

Hazel Palgrave stared at the screen, let out a low whistle, and turned to where John sat, making some adjustments to one of the most complicated cameras she had ever seen.

'Jesus, this research work is something else! My predecessor was meticulous. Did she have OCD by any chance?'

'Yep.' John said. 'But her fussiness did make life easier for me, and it meant few, if any, mistakes were made.'

Hazel took a deep breath. 'Hard act to follow then. Still, I have talents of my own, as you will discover in the fullness of time.'

John gave a small grunt that seemed to say 'we'll see about that'. Fair enough. He had no reason to trust her yet, but it wouldn't take long for him to see how utterly dedicated to this cause she was, and the skills she could bring to it.

'Think you'll be able to take it on?' John asked, placing the camera carefully on the table.

'Oh yes, I've read the whole dossier now. I understand how it's all collated and dealt with. I suggest that to start with, I continue in the same format, so as not to confuse you. But I can already see a few strategic changes we might implement.'

She pushed her chair back and looked John full in the face. 'This work has been going on for many years, hasn't it?'

He nodded. 'I've been working for Alistair Ashcroft, or Stephen, as he wants us to call him, since he was incarcerated and so had Janet, your predecessor. Stephen already had a plethora of files, and it was our job to confirm and update all the information they contained.'

'And it's now ongoing, isn't it?' she asked, though she already knew the answer.

'Absolutely. After all, life doesn't stop, does it? Well,' he gave a dry chuckle, 'it does for some people, of course, as you will have noticed from the files, but generally we watch and prepare new reports. I do the legwork, you do the phone calls and IT searches.'

'And then I collect and combine them, report back to Stephen, and receive new orders. I'm fully aware of my role, John.' She gazed steadily at him. 'Look, I know you don't trust me yet, and why should you? But you will see. There's no one more dedicated or more driven than me, and I'll prove that as time goes on.'

The two of them were very different people. Hazel herself was on a mission. She had a goal, and she believed John to be a mercenary, plain and simple. There was probably not much that John would not undertake, if the price was right.

John's stare bored into her. Then he shrugged and gave her a half smile. 'As long as you do your side of the work, Hazel, keep us out of trouble, and at the end of the day I get my wages, I reckon you and I will tick along just fine.'

It was as she had thought, he was nothing but a mercenary. Which was fine with her. She wasn't sure that having two zealots on the project would be a good thing. She gave him a broad grin. 'Well, that's good. Now, if you've finished tinkering with that camera, I've got today's task for you. Hope you like horses.'

John took the memo with the name and address on it and nodded. 'Good, it's local. I'll be off then.' He picked up the precious camera. 'See you at lunch time.'

Hazel turned back to her screen and was at once so engrossed in the file that she didn't even hear the front door close.

* * *

Thoughtfully, John made his way to his car. Reluctant as he was to admit it, Hazel fascinated him. She was totally different to Janet, with whom he had worked so well. However, he had never found Janet attractive. Hazel, on the other hand, was beautiful, which might not be a good thing where the job was concerned. Still, he trusted Stephen to have made the right decision in reopening the old investigation with a new controller at the helm. He got into the car, marvelling at Stephen's sudden change of plan after having shut it all down following Janet's demise. Whatever the reason, John had been delighted to be contacted and reactivated. And why wouldn't he? He'd never in his life earned such good money.

And he was worth every penny. John was the best. He had a sharp mind and he knew it. Plus, he was an excellent photographer with an uncanny ability to blend into his surroundings. Above all, he had no feelings to muddy the waters. He did what was asked of him, did it well, and got paid accordingly. No emotions clouded John's judgement; he was a consummate professional. And Stephen knew it.

John headed out of town, his thoughts on his sudden resurrection. He had known there would be a Phase Two at some point, but had believed that he and Janet had provided Stephen with everything he needed for whatever end game he had in mind. This was apparently not the case. Somehow, all the files John believed to have been deleted had miraculously reappeared, and he was being given new orders. Apparently, Stephen was far from finished with whatever had been brewing in that unfathomable mind of his.

John pondered Alistair Ashcroft's reason for his insistence on being known as Stephen. He and Janet had used the name for so long that they hardly recalled any other, and it seemed that Hazel Palgrave had received the same instructions. John had noticed that even some of the prison warders called him Stephen. Not that it really mattered. So long as Stephen paid his wages, he'd call him Auntie Gertie if that's what he wanted.

John enjoyed his occasional visits to Stephen. During his time in the force, he had often taken the police meat wagon to deliver prisoners to maximum security jails. It had all been in a day's work. He wondered how Hazel felt about the body searches, the heavy doors that clanged shut behind you, locking you in along with all those psychotics and murderers. He had a good idea that she'd endure anything for Stephen. Women who idolised killers were a strange breed indeed. Why were so many women attracted to convicted murderers, men responsible for the most horrific crimes? What, he wondered, was Hazel's story?

Ah well, time would tell.

* * *

Jackman was surprised to see Sam Page walking into the CID room. He had seen Sam that morning, but there had been no mention of his calling into the station.

'I'm so sorry, Jackman, I hope this isn't a bad time. Do you have a few minutes?'

Jackman didn't like Sam's anxious expression. 'Sure, come on into the office. Want a coffee? I was just about to grab one myself.' He waved to Tim Jacobs, his office manager, and asked him to bring them drinks.

Inside the office, Jackman pulled the door to. 'Is something wrong, Sam? You look stressed.'

Sam sank into a chair. 'Not wrong exactly. It's something Laura and I were following up before . . . well . . .'

'It's all right, my friend.' Jackman smiled understandingly. 'Just tell me what's worrying you. This is going to happen a lot until we start to accept what happened to Laura, but we must talk about her and the things that concerned her, no matter how painful they might be.'

Sam looked up at him. 'This is painful on more than one level, I'm afraid.'

They were interrupted by a knock on the door and the arrival of the drinks. When the door had closed again, Jackman said, 'Right. From the beginning?'

Sam sat back and closed his eyes. 'It's about Alistair Ashcroft.'

Jackman swallowed.

'Laura confided to me that Ashcroft had always haunted her. Even incarcerated, she believed he still presented a threat, even if it was only psychological. She said she felt his shadow over her, and it was preventing her from moving forward freely. I admitted to feeling the same, and I still do, but that's not the point. So, for our own peace of mind, I promised to keep tabs on him through an old friend of mine who happens to be a retired prison governor.'

Jackman pushed one of the coffee beakers towards Sam with a sinking heart. Ashcroft again. 'Go on.'

'My friend rang just after you left for work. Ashcroft was selected to be taken from HMP Gartree to a new experimental unit within a Cat B, high-security prison in Cambridgeshire. It's very much like the PIPE unit that he was trying to get into in Gartree.'

'PIPE unit? Remind me what that is, Sam.'

'Psychologically Informed Planned Environment. If you remember, they were originally designed to implement a new technique for the management of offenders with personality disorder. Its purpose is to develop a deeper interaction between specially trained staff and offenders, focusing on relationships, both one to one and in group discussion and reflection.' Sam pulled a face. 'It's not an easy process for the inmate to undertake. It involves deep psychological exploration, often leading them to confront some of their demons and the situations that brought about their incarceration. But if you are tough enough, the benefits are many, and life in these units is less restricted than that in the main blocks.'

Jackman shook his head in horror and dismay. 'But, Sam, that kind of place would be a dream for Alistair Ashcroft! He'll be in his element, twisting both staff and fellow offenders around his little finger. Who on earth gave a man with his history a place in a programme like that?'

'It appears that he earned it, Jackman. He's been the model prisoner, apparently. I imagine he's convinced one or two officials that he's seen the error of his ways and is truly repentant.' Sam rolled his eyes. 'As if!'

This came like a sucker punch to Jackman. Ashcroft would never be released, it was true — he was serving a whole life tariff. Nevertheless, it made him dangerous once again. 'That man belongs in isolation. My God, Sam, has no one bothered to read up on his crimes? How can he be allowed to form relationships with anyone?'

'I know. I know,' breathed Sam. 'I've made that abundantly clear to whoever will listen to me but, sadly, in the light of a series of incidents that brought the prison reformers out in force, there has been a major move in favour of rehabilitation and a reorganisation of the entire prison structure. Thanks to this I'm told that Ashcroft met all the criteria for participation in the newly formed unit.'

Jackman sipped on his coffee. *I'm sure he did*, he thought bitterly. *In no time at all the bastard will be their star pupil.*

'Jackman, you do know that nothing he does will ever get him a reprieve?' Sam said. 'I just thought you should know about his new status and the fact that he's been moved from Gartree.' He looked at Jackman. 'And I also know what you are thinking. Sure, Ashcroft now poses a clear and present danger, but he always did, even before his transfer. We just have to acknowledge his uncanny ability to make people believe in him.'

Jackman nodded. 'I understand the thinking behind those units — to give those formerly considered beyond rehabilitation a chance to obtain an education, acquire new skills and receive support, and in general I applaud that, but it's not for someone like Ashcroft. That man surrendered all his rights when he tortured and murdered so many — and injured someone as precious as you!'

'Oh, I wholeheartedly agree with you, believe me,' said Sam. 'I was assured that everyone involved is fully aware of the atrocious acts he committed. Despite this, because of his conduct and the results of his assessment, he was considered eligible.'

How that man must be feeling, thought Jackman sourly. *He must be laughing his socks off.* 'What's more, Sam,' he continued, 'this will just feed his psychosis. He'll believe in his omnipotence more than ever. Dammit, he's pulling the strings even from inside a high-security prison.'

Sam nodded. The truth was, Alistair Ashcroft was a megalomaniac, convinced of his own superiority. And they couldn't escape the fact that he was a master manipulator. Jackman felt sick when he recalled some of the things this evil man had made people do. 'I just hope they watch him like a hawk. And never believe a sodding word he says.'

'I'm told their clinical lead is a most experienced psychologist. If I can, I'll try to get a private word with him. My friend is sending me his details.' Sam smiled, wearily. 'Luckily, I'm still well respected in those circles, and since I have personal experience of Ashcroft, I can't see him saying no.'

'He'd be an idiot if he did,' grunted Jackman. 'If it were me, I'd bite your hand off for your knowledge.'

'Well, it's the best I can do, Jackman.' Sam hesitated. 'I hope I've done the right thing in coming here, I just felt you should know at once. Now I'm wondering if I've upset you.'

'Oh Sam, of course not. You did exactly the right thing. Sorry for sounding off like that. He just did so much damage to people I love that his name is a red rag to a bull. Hell, just the thought of him sends my blood pressure up. But no, I'm glad you came.' He sighed. 'I'm just sad to hear that he haunted my darling Laura right to the end. I wish she'd told me.'

'She didn't want to worry you,' Sam said kindly. 'Laura thought you'd moved on from Ashcroft after his sentencing. She also felt she was over-reacting. People in our profession see so much mental carnage that we sometimes keep digging when we ought to let go. Anyway, we always said we'd tell you if there was anything concrete to worry us.'

'At least Ashcroft had absolutely nothing to do with what happened to Laura. It means I'm not obsessed with him as I would have been if that were the case.' Jackman looked hard at Sam. 'I can even get some measure of satisfaction in that my girl got the better of him. She is one trophy he can never claim.'

'I understand that.' Sam stood up. 'Right, I'd best be going. Thank you for the coffee, and I'll see you tonight.'

'Oh, by the way, Hetty Maynard said she'd cook us one of her chicken curries, so if you're up for it, I'll call in at the supermarket on the way home and pick up some naans and papadums.' What would they have done without his lovely old cleaning lady? Jackman wondered. Since Laura's death neither he nor Sam had felt the inclination to cook, so they would probably have starved — or doubled their weight on junk food.

'Yes, please,' said Sam. 'Sounds perfect.'

'Then I'll see you later, and take care, okay?'

After Sam had gone, Jackman tried to push aside his worries about Alistair Ashcroft. The TV series was due to begin filming today, and he'd heard from Frank Rosen that after spending some time with the crew in their preparations, he reckoned Dougie the Dreamer had been right. He sensed a definite undercurrent, and he'd be keeping a particularly close eye on the names Dougie had provided.

Jackman and Marie had agreed not to try and guess what was going down. Dougie had been adamant that it wasn't anything obvious like drug dealing, so what could it be? He re-read the message from Frank.

Their first location was to be the Old Oaks Rectory, in Amberly Fen. The place was up for sale and the owners had moved out, so the film company were renting it and using its extensive grounds as a base camp.

Amberley Fen. Jackman smiled sadly. This was where his brother and his young family had lived until his sister-in-law's death, following which James had sold Rainham Lodge and he, Miles and Ryan had gone to live with Harriet and Lawrence. There had recently been another serious crime in that area, and Jackman wondered if the location manager had picked Amberly Fen because of its sinister reputation. Whatever, Jackman knew the place very well, including the Old Oaks Rectory, which was always a bonus in an investigation.

Now there was little more they could do other than wait for an update from Frank. With this in mind, Jackman decided to gather the team and get them to tidy up all the smaller investigations that were running. Then, if the shit hit the fan, they'd be ready.

He strode out into the CID room feeling increasingly anxious. He didn't have a shred of proof but the feeling in his gut that something was about to break, and he knew well never to ignore his gut. Now he had to try and explain it to the team.

'Okay, troops, gather round. Uncle Jackman has a little story to tell you. Now, if you're sitting comfortably . . . Once upon a time in the Fens, a film was being shot . . .'

CHAPTER FOUR

Marie was enjoying a day off. For once she had even managed to completely switch off from work. After cleaning her beloved motorcycle and putting it back in the garage, she showered and pulled on clean jeans, a white T-shirt and a light grey hooded sweatshirt, growing more excited with every moment that passed. Ralph was due to arrive at any moment, to take her for a second viewing of a property in a small village just north of Saltern-le-Fen. Situated on the Fenchester Road, it would make it easier for Ralph to get to work, while not inconveniencing Marie. Of the twenty or thirty places they had viewed in the past month, this was the one that had really caught their eye.

Ralph's home in Fenchester had already sold and they had the money in the bank. Meanwhile, they were living in Marie's house while they searched for a proper home. The house they liked was called Peelers End, which made them both laugh. Discovering that it used to be the old village police house was even more amazing. If they both felt certain about it on this, their second visit, they planned to put in an offer there and then.

She and Ralph had been seeing each other for a while now, and it had become clear to both of them that despite their demanding jobs — which they loved — they wanted to stay together permanently. Laura Archer's death had put a temporary hold on their house hunting, since Marie didn't feel she could be happy and excited about her own love life when Jackman had lost everything. Ralph had understood how she felt, which made her love him all the more.

Now, after several months had passed, they felt able to move forward again. She had hesitated to tell Jackman but when she did, he had said he was thrilled for her, and wished them all the luck in the world. But even as he said it, she had seen the sadness in his eyes. She had been through a similar bereavement herself, but somehow in Jackman's case it seemed so much worse. Maybe women coped with emotional trauma differently, or maybe time had mellowed the memory of her own anguish, she didn't know.

She heard Ralph's car drawing up outside, and, fifteen minutes later, they were parking outside Peelers End.

They sat in the car for a few moments, looking up at the house. Ralph squeezed her hand. 'Okay, Evans. Remember, we need to be practical and level-headed, and look for the downsides. It does look totally charming, but—'

'Shut up, Enderby. We'll know how we feel the moment we set foot back in that house. Trust your gut feeling.' She kissed his cheek. 'Come on! I can't wait a minute longer.'

Peelers End was a stone house, dating from the late 1800s or early 1900s, and what you might call a 'character house'. Upstairs there were three bedrooms, two with ensuite shower rooms, as well as a massive bathroom, with a clawfoot bath. Downstairs, a fairly sizable double aspect lounge, a separate dining room and big kitchen, all with open fireplaces. Most interesting was that the prison cells had been retained, complete with heavy doors and giant locks and bolts. These were accessed from the kitchen, through a large metal-barred door and along a wide corridor. The three cells had been cleverly renovated, keeping the old stone floors and all the original fittings, but now one was used as a utility, another as a storage room, while the third, leading out to the back garden, was a garden store.

The young estate agent who was showing them around admitted it might not be for everyone. 'After all,' he said, 'it's got a bit of a, er, history, and it was in use as a police station and sergeant's house up until the late fifties.'

Marie loved it, but she knew enough not to say so. She listened while Ralph asked all the sensible questions — about council tax bands, utilities, and the rest. As far as she was concerned, all that remained to see was the garage, she was itching to know if her Tiger would be safe and happy there.

'The house sits on just under an acre of ground,' the estate agent intoned, 'with outbuildings and a garden divided into different sections, a very nice patio, and some well-kept beds and borders, plus some more natural areas of grass and shrubs and trees.'

Marie liked the sound of that, but wondered if its upkeep would be too much for them, considering their demanding jobs.

'An older local man comes in every week to cut the grass and keep it all in check. I do know that he's quite anxious to keep his job . . .' The estate agent looked at her hopefully. 'He has a disabled wife and they only live a few hundred yards down the road, so he pops back to keep an eye on her. They aren't very well-off and this place helps to keep food on the table.'

Better and better, thought Marie, and made some appropriately conciliatory noises. As far as she was concerned the search was over. She glanced at Ralph, trying to read his thoughts. Was he as excited as her? He was now discussing structural surveys, and it was hard to tell what he was thinking.

'I'll leave you both to have a walk around on your own,' said the agent. 'I'll be in the lounge when you've seen all you need.'

They did a complete tour of the interior again, before going outside.

'You have a very strange look in your eyes, Marie Evans. Has the place put a spell on you?' Ralph looked at her in mock horror.

She adopted a faraway look. 'Yep. Totally besotted.'

'I thought as much. No need to point out a few possible pitfalls then?'

'Did you say something?' she said innocently.

'Ah, right.' Ralph pulled a face. 'Could be on a loser here, Enderby, so maybe it would be sensible to leave this train of thought for the time being?'

Marie laughed. 'Okay, yes, I do love this place, but it must be right for both of us, not just me. So, what are your pitfalls?'

'None that I can think of.' He grinned back. 'Just winding you up. I love it too, especially the thought of some old boy cutting the grass for us! I might want to take up gardening later in life, but not just yet. There's much more exciting stuff to do before I throw myself into mulching lawns and discussing the merits of various weedkillers.'

'You're sure? You really do love it?' Marie demanded. 'You're not just saying it for my sake?'

'No way. If we are going to start a new life together, we must both be happy with it. I reckon Peelers End fits the bill on all counts.' He beamed at her. 'It's funny, you know, but it feels like this place has been waiting for us. Who better to assume custody of an historical old police house than two serving coppers?'

Marie hugged him.

'So, let's go and talk details with our tactful estate agent, shall we?' Ralph smiled. 'And don't appear too enthusiastic, I'm going to try for a cheeky offer first, and see what happens.'

As they walked back inside, Marie added, 'Oh, and ask what he meant about a "bit of a history".'

After a few minutes' discussion, the estate agent suggested they accompany him back to his office in Saltern to negotiate a deal. As the young man was locking up, Ralph said, 'What was that old history you mentioned earlier? Something sensational, was it?'

'Well, I suppose you could say it was very sensational at the time.' He jiggled the keys, hesitating. 'Of course, it was a long time ago. Um, well, back in the fifties, the sergeant who was living here went crazy, er, lost his mind, and he killed a man in the cells. The Corley Eaudyke Police House, as it was then called, became the site of a bloody murder.'

Looking utterly downcast he waited for their response, obviously assuming the sale was off. He could not have expected what followed.

After a few moments' silence, they burst into guffaws of laughter. Ralph spluttered, 'Sorry. I know it's not funny, but . . .'

'No, not funny at all,' Marie added, giggling helplessly.

The young estate agent's look of utter bewilderment only made it worse.

'Talk about taking your work home with you!' gasped Ralph. 'We do apologise. Better get back to your shop and discuss an offer. Shall we go?'

They were still laughing as they got back in the car.

'This is too weird for words, isn't it?' he spluttered. 'Remember declaring that no way would we live in a house where a murder had taken place? We both said that buildings seem to hold memories and all that. And now here we are, about to buy one.'

'Well, there's no sinister atmosphere in Peelers End. I just love it.' Marie beamed at him. 'Time to eat our words, I think, and chuck those old ideas in the bin.'

'You're so right. This place really is made for us, isn't it?' chuckled Ralph. 'Two murder squad detectives. Where better?'

Marie smiled happily. 'And we might even get a good deal because of it. He said so himself: a house where a murder has taken place isn't for everyone. I bet they'll jump at a fair offer, don't you? Looks like win-win to me!'

'My thoughts precisely.'

Less than an hour later their offer had been accepted and the wheels were in motion. Peelers End was about to welcome its new owners. Outside the shop, they embraced.

'New beginnings!' breathed Ralph happily.

And then Marie's phone rang. 'Oh, bugger! It's work.'

'Par for the course,' said Ralph with a sigh. 'It could just as well have been me.'

'Show me committed,' Marie said into the phone. 'ETA thirty minutes.' She ended the call. 'Sorry, Ralph, we have a body. Can you get me home fast? I'll go in from there.'

Ralph was already hurrying towards his car. 'At least they gave us time to buy our dream home. I guess we must be grateful for small mercies.'

Marie climbed into the car next to him, saying, 'I really love you, Ralph Enderby.'

'I know. Now let's get you back, Sergeant. We can talk carpets and curtains later.'

* * *

Jackman stared down at the body lying on the floor of the police dinghy. For some reason he found it particularly uncomfortable to look at. He'd seen enough dead bodies to usually feel quite detached. He would examine the corpse closely, looking for the slightest hint that there might be something amiss. But today he couldn't summon up the same clinical attitude, and he wasn't sure why.

The man, who had probably been in his late twenties or early thirties, was naked. His skin was dappled with mud from the river, and long strands of weed clung to his hair, his arms and his legs.

Jackman overheard one of the Marine police officers — called in to extricate the man — make a joke about it being a poor choice of venue for skinny dipping. About to reprimand the officer, he stopped himself. It was how people coped, he knew that. So why was he so edgy?

The sight of Professor Rory Wilkinson approaching him, accompanied by Marie, cheered Jackman up considerably. He wondered what the Home Office pathologist would come out with on this occasion. Rory was renowned for his distinctive mix of camp and black humour, and he was also the best pathologist a detective could ever wish to work with.

34

'Dear hearts and gentle people, what have you got for me today?' He smiled benignly at Jackman, then looked down into the boat. 'Oh my! I haven't seen one of those in a while.'

Trying not to smile, Marie said gravely, 'Condolences, Rory. I feel your pain.'

Rory puffed out his cheeks, 'Oh, please! I've seen an erection, any number of them as a matter of fact, but not recently on a cadaver.'

'Well, it's a first for me,' said Marie.

'Ditto,' said Jackman. 'And I have a feeling we are about to get one of your incredibly informative tutorials on the subject. However, at this moment we need answers of a different kind, somewhat more serious ones, I'm afraid.'

'Mmm.' Rory stared at the dead man. 'Well, initially I need to get him out of that dinghy.' He looked up. 'Aha! Here come my trusty cohorts, Spike and Cardiff, who can instruct those good officers — the ones in those very fetching waders — to assist in its removal to terra firma.'

A few minutes later the man, in an open black body bag, was laid carefully on a protective sheet covering the concrete quay, and Rory, clad in a disposable coverall, booties, mask and gloves, made his initial appraisal.

Jackman and Marie stood watching in silence. It was not unusual for a body to be either retrieved or washed up from the local rivers. In recent years there had been a steep rise in violent knife crime, usually attributed to drugs or rival organised gangs. There were many reasons for this, one being the exodus of Eastern European field workers, who were replaced by workers from even further east and south, not all of whom got on. Bootleg alcohol and drugs fuelled some terrible attacks, and the resulting bodies were nearly always dumped in the river.

'Not what I was expecting, dear hearts.' Rory, kneeling beside the dead man, looked up at them. 'And you, lucky souls, are about to benefit from both my considered opinion regarding this man's demise, and that illuminating tutorial you mentioned.'

Jackman knew it was useless to object. Things would get done much more quickly if he just shut up and listened.

'This handsome Adonis did not drown. Neither did he suffer a brutal attack. He was strangled, asphyxiated, and very quickly too. Hence the post-mortem priapism, a death erection, often referred to as "angel lust".' He paused for effect.

'Okay, Prof,' said Marie. 'Tell us why.'

'I just knew you'd be fascinated. Let me explain. It can happen when death is either very sudden, or extremely violent. It often occurs during an execution, mainly by hanging. It's attributed to pressure on the cerebellum created by the noose "exciting" the nerves. Among other suppositions, it is thought that a sudden massive spinal cord stimulus generates an erectile response. It's rare, but it does occur, as you can see.' He stood up. 'And apart from telling you that he hadn't been in the water long, that's it for now — back to the mortuary where I will delve deeper.'

'He's in very good condition, isn't he?' murmured Jackman, almost to himself.

'He *was*,' corrected Rory. 'He obviously took care of himself. But as I say, more to come. I'll be in touch as soon as, so bye bye for now, children, the master has work to do.'

Marie looked at Jackman. 'I do believe that's our cue to leave.'

'Agreed. Exit stage right,' said Jackman. Taking one last look at their 'Adonis', they returned to their vehicles. Jackman took her arm. 'Look, Marie, it's your day off, so now you've seen what we are dealing with, you get away while I go back and set up an action plan.'

'Thanks, Jackman, but I'll just call by the station first and see if anything connected to this has been reported. It's clear to me that this isn't one of the gang-related deaths that have plagued the area recently, and it puzzles me.'

It puzzled Jackman too. 'I hope I'm wrong, but I've a sneaky feeling that this could be the precursor to something bad. There's absolutely nothing about that body that indicates a simple solution.'

'There isn't, is there?' Marie grimaced. 'Just one hell of a lot of questions. Like, was he stripped to make it hard to identify him? Or to make him feel vulnerable? Did he happen to be naked when he was killed — taking a shower, sleeping, or, er, on the job even?'

Jackman smiled. At times like this, Marie's wonderful Welsh accent always came to the fore. 'Any of those is a possibility. You never know, there might be other, even stranger reasons as well. One thing's for sure, this case isn't going to be straightforward.'

'Then we'd better buckle down and sort it. I'll see you back at the station.' Marie climbed onto her motorcycle. 'Last one back buys the coffees.'

'You're in a very good mood, considering we pulled you in from a day off to stare at a dead body,' called out Jackman.

'I am indeed, but I'll fill you in later. You are *never* going to believe what Ralph and I just bought.'

'Well, what is it?'

'Don't worry, I'll tell you. And I can hardly wait to show it to you.' As she roared past his vehicle, she called out, 'And don't forget those coffees!'

Alone again, without Marie and Rory's company to buoy him up, Jackman's discomfort returned. Maybe it was just a phase, a stage one passed through following a death. But why did he feel so edgy?

* * *

Dex was heading towards the catering truck for a much-needed coffee when Lance called out to him.

'Get Craig, will you? There's a couple of changes for the next scene that we need to go over. My van in five.'

Lance threw him a meaningful look, not lost on Dex. *Next scene, my arse*, he thought. *This is extra-curricular business.* He hurried off to find his colleague.

A few minutes later, he and Craig were sitting inside Lance's mobile home, the doors and windows closed so as not to be overheard. Lance looked unusually sombre. He was not exactly a barrel of laughs at the best of times, but he was at least usually full of energy. Not today.

'I'm sorry to tell you both but tonight's little caper will be our last. I'm pulling the plug on the whole thing. I know you depend on the extra cash, but there it is. Sorry, but it's over, *finito*. It was good while it lasted, wasn't it?'

Dex could have cheered. He had been planning on doing a runner after *Fen Division Five* was sewn up, though it wouldn't have looked when other work had already been contracted. Now he had been handed a get out of jail free card, and he wouldn't even have to lose his job.

He stole a glance at Craig, who couldn't disguise his relief.

'Er, is it anything to do with the new police consultant guy?' Dex asked.

Lance snorted. 'That old fart! No way. He's star-struck, as much of a concern as a bloody girl guide. No, mate, it's logistics. I've hit a problem with our receiver across the water. It's too risky to start looking for new personnel at this stage so, as I said, tonight goes ahead and then it's curtains.' He looked each of them in the eye. 'I don't need to tell you to keep your mouths shut about our, er, "other business," do I? Because if you say one word, you'll be in deep shit, right up to your eyebrows.'

'We're hardly likely to talk, are we? We aren't fools, Lance, and I, for one, have no wish to get on the wrong side of the law,' muttered Craig.

'And I'm sodding well saying nothing,' added Dex.

'Well, keep it that way, all right?' Lance gave them a rare smile. 'There'll be a bit of a bonus for you both after this evening, by way of a thank you. So. Usual place, same time, and then we move on with our lives. Any questions?'

Craig shook his head. 'No, Lance. As you said, it was good while it lasted, and I appreciate it.'

'And you, Dex?' asked Lance. 'No hard feelings? I know you really needed the extra cash.'

'Tonight's work will see me okay again, Lance. Like Craig, I'm grateful for the extra work you put our way.' He hoped he sounded sincere.

'I'll tell the others later when they've finished for the afternoon, but don't discuss it with them, or with each other either. Walls have ears. And thanks. You both did a great job.'

They stood up and left. Outside, Dex had to stop himself from punching the air and dancing.

'Result!' he whispered to Craig.

'Yeah. Although . . .' Craig fell silent.

'What's the matter? This is the best we could have hoped for, isn't it? Now we are out of it, and with Lance's blessing.'

'Didn't that little speech of Lance's seem a bit odd to you, Dex?'

'No. Why? Should it?'

'I think he's ditching us because he doesn't trust us. A pound to a penny says he isn't folding at all.' Craig bit his lip. 'The others will go on working for him, you'll see. And I'm wondering why. You and I might not have been high up in the gang but we did play an important part.'

Dex shook his head. 'You've got it wrong, mate. I think he really has hit a problem and he's hedging his bets. No point in risking everything if you know there's a weak link in the chain. Sure, he'll regroup at some point, because it's a bloody lucrative business. But he can do it without me. I'm glad to be free of it all. After tonight, that's it for me. I'm drawing a line under the whole thing. Take my advice, pal, and do the same.' He gave Craig a friendly nudge. 'Come on. We're being let off the hook. Enjoy!'

Craig shrugged. 'I guess so, but . . .'

Dex raised his hand. 'Let it go. Here, I'll buy you a cuppa. We'll do a good job tonight, then we'll take the money and run, what d'you say?'

Craig sighed. 'All right.'

Dex refused to listen to any more of Craig's doubts. After he'd been paid, he would throw himself into his proper job and forget this ever happened. He'd also do his damndest to stop the fucking gambling. It was the gee-gees, that was the trouble. It was because of them that he'd crossed the line from 'honest Joe' to criminal.

Somehow he had to break the cycle.

* * *

Flooded with mixed emotions, Craig went back to work. Dex was right in one sense: their escape had been made easy and risk-free. Yet he couldn't rid himself of the feeling that they had just been cut out of something big. And that something might have set him and his Joannie up for a better future. He loved his wife to pieces but, hell, she had such expensive tastes! She seemed to think that because he worked in film she should live a celebrity lifestyle and, man, was he struggling to keep up! When he talked to her about cutting back, she just laughed it off, and then she chided him for not providing for her needs. He would have given her the world but the truth of it was, Joannie was bankrupting them. Sure, he had wanted out, terrified to even think what kind of game Lance and his mates might be running, but he was even more terrified of losing Joannie. So he made a decision. He would go back and talk to Lance — on his own this time.

He found Lance poring over the next day's schedule.

'Sorry, Lance, it's about those scene changes. Can I have another word?'

Without a word, Lance stood up and made for his van, Craig hurrying after him. Inside, Lance said, 'Was there something I didn't make clear, Craig? Only, time is money.'

'Look, I'm good at what I do, Lance, you know that. You can use me, I'm sure of it. You're not really pulling the plug, are you? You've found a better, more lucrative game, and I want in.'

'I have no idea what you are talking about. Look, Craig, when I told you to move on, I meant what I said. There's no "better game," and I made it clear that the one we're running folds tonight, so drop it.'

Now what? Maybe Dex had been right. 'I . . . I'm sorry, I just thought . . .'

'Well, you thought wrong.' Lance's cold eyes pierced his. 'There is nothing else going on. I've got serious problems in Holland, that's all. I need to quit while we're still ahead. One day I might sort things and get the team back together but, sorry, kid, tonight really is the finale.' He smiled, though not with his eyes. 'You be there and I'll see that your bonus is worth having.'

Craig mumbled an apology, said he'd be there and that he'd do a good job.

Lance clapped him on the shoulder.

Craig walked back to his unit, sensing those cold eyes following him.

CHAPTER FIVE

Having found no clue as to the mystery man from the river, Marie headed home again. She was riding away from Saltern when her phone bleeped with a message — Marie's motorcycle helmet was equipped with a Bluetooth headset that connected wirelessly to her phone. She could only smile when she listened to the message: "There are evil forces at work here! I was just thinking about preparing dinner for you when I got a call from base. And, snap! We also have a body on our patch. So see you as and when. Love you, and sorry about dinner."

And this was to be their life together.

But instead of doubts, Marie had thoughts of the lonely years she had spent following the death of Bill, and she smiled. She could hack a few missed dinners, she had a partner who understood how important her work was to her, and felt the same about his. A rare thing indeed.

Marie travelled the familiar route home, her mind full of plans for Peelers End and their life there together. She was happier than she had been in years, although she didn't forget Jackman. She also thought of the beautiful young man from the river — Adonis. Rory's name for him had been apt. Such a beautiful murder victim, who could possibly want to end the life of one so perfect? A jealous rival? Maybe he had been caught *in flagrante* with someone's wife or girlfriend. That would answer why he had been naked.

Marie shook her head at herself. She and her partner had just purchased the house of their dreams and here she was with her mind full of her job. Old habits die hard, she told herself. Work had been everything to her for so many years she was hardly going to change in five minutes, was she?

What's more, she thought, pulling into her drive, *I'm not even going to consider changing. Jackman needs his right-hand woman to be firing on all cylinders, he needs my support now more than ever. New man and new home notwithstanding, I will be there for him.*

* * *

Alistair Ashcroft had spent the morning engaged in a long conversation with the prison chaplain about redemption.

The chaplain, Patrick Galway, was part of a multi-faith team that took care of the spiritual and emotional well-being of the prisoners and assisted with some aspects of their rehabilitation. On meeting him, Ashcroft had dismissed Galway as a pushover, but he soon discovered that this gently spoken man was a greater challenge than he had at first appeared.

Having spent a few hours talking with him, Ashcroft realised that he would need to adopt a different strategy to the one he had used with previous chaplains. Softly spoken Patrick seemed to be all compassion and benevolence, but the mild Irish lilt concealed a steely, tough, inquiring mind. Galway was shrewd, fiercely intelligent and a deep thinker, not a man to be fooled so easily.

Ashcroft had come to relish their conversations. He didn't often come up against a mind as quick as his own. Ashcroft meant to manipulate them all, staff and fellow-inmates, into believing that he, Alistair Ashcroft — or Stephen as he preferred to be called — was a special case. His aim was to make everyone involved, including the clinical lead, believe that 'Stephen' deserved special treatment. Afforded the utmost freedom, he could then make amends for the terrible things he had done. Each had been treated to a heart-rending performance in which Ashcroft played the role of a man consumed with remorse, who was desperately trying to come to terms with the atrocities he had committed.

And how he revelled in it. It gave him immense satisfaction to see his 'audience' taken in. Psychologists and counsellors with years of experience would gradually come to see this most wicked of murderers as a repentant sinner, a victim almost, who, all because of them, had seen the error of his ways. It gave him a feeling of mastery, almost as if he might rise out of his wheelchair, stride over to them and make them cower.

'What do you miss most, Stephen?' asked Patrick.

'Being able to sit in a church,' Ashcroft said truthfully, 'especially when it is empty, and drink in the silence and quieten my mind. Or going out to the marshes at night, to howl at the moon and no one hears. I miss those places where I can be truly alone.'

Ashcroft failed to mention that prison, too, suited him very well. He revelled in the rage, the seething emotions of the other inmates, and the solitude of his room, which in this unit was soundproofed against the constant row. Like a child in a sweetshop, he was left on his own to feed on any number of damaged minds and wrecked lives.

'So, how do you cope with knowing that you will never see those marshes again?'

'No one can rob me of my memories, Patrick. I can shut my eyes and smell the salty air. I can feel the light touch of diaphanous sea-mist on my skin. With my eyes closed I see my lonely places. It's enough.'

There was a silence. That often happened with Patrick. It seemed to Ashcroft as if he were sifting and assimilating every word.

'Is that really enough?' he asked softly.

'It is,' said Ashcroft. 'When you have no possible alternative, you accept what you do have and embrace it. It saves one a lot of torment.'

And, oh, he did embrace it, more than anyone could conceive, certainly more than the man of God seated opposite him.

Who would believe him if he told them that this unit he was confined to, within a high-security prison, was his haven. He couldn't have found a better place from which to command his empire. Anything he wanted was available at a price, peopled as it was by men and women fuelled by greed or the desire for self-preservation. Foreseeing his eventual incarceration, he had set up an intricate system for the management of his wealth. The one man he trusted enough to take care of his financial affairs was paid a fortune for his loyal service. Thus, Ashcroft was able to mastermind his various schemes, both in and outside the thick, impenetrable walls of his jail. No one knew just how powerful this supposedly helpless man was, or what he was capable of.

Something brought him up short. In his hubris, he had forgotten the two exceptions, men who would never underestimate the power of Alistair Ashcroft.

These two men were Rowan Jackman and Sam Page. He hadn't added a third — Marie Evans, whose vicious kick at his already shattered knees had caused him such excruciating pain. Marie's was a case of an eye for an eye, because he had kicked just as viciously, at her already broken bones as she lay injured on a desolate fen lane. Touché, Marie Evans.

'You look miles away,' Patrick whispered. 'Back in one of your lonely places?'

'You might say that.' And he smiled benignly at Patrick Galway.

After a while, the priest stood up. 'You can always contact me, Stephen. Just tell anyone here that you want to speak to me and I'll come as soon as I can. It's been good talking to you today.'

Ashcroft smiled as the door closed behind him. He had seen tell-tale signs today that he was making headway with the enigmatic priest. He would need to tread carefully but he had infinite patience and time on his hands. He would win Patrick Galway over. Just like all the others.

* * *

45

As the shadows of evening crept across the fen, Dex got himself ready for a final night of unofficial work. He put the things he required into his car and checked his watch. He knew exactly where he was going and that it would only take fifteen minutes to get there, but he felt unexpectedly jittery. As far as he was concerned, the moment tonight was over, he'd be master of his own future again. He wondered what Craig would do. He wasn't a close friend exactly, but they worked well together, and he didn't like to see him caught in the horns of a dilemma like this. Dex knew all about Craig's wife's extravagance, and that Craig was terrified to lose her, but they were living way above their means.

Dex grunted to himself. Marriage was supposed to be about love and consideration for your partner, not about giving them grief. Joannie was a looker all right, but he wouldn't have touched her with a bargepole. He could almost see the pound signs flashing up in her eyes, and she had a laugh like a cash register ringing. Talk about love being blind. After all, Craig was a pretty good-looking bloke, he looked after himself, and many of the women on set considered him really fit. But there it was — poor bloke was bankrupting himself for love of a mercenary woman. No matter how much their special bonus turned out to be, it wouldn't last long in Craig's wallet. Poor sod.

As he watched the minutes tick by until it was time to leave, he considered his own position. The money he made tonight would clear his debts. They weren't huge, thank God — yet. Whatever happened, from tomorrow on, he must kick the habit. He'd been on the brink once before, and he knew that a small debt could so easily escalate into a major problem. After all, he was young, he had a life. There was a woman he wanted to see a lot more of, but there was no way he could contemplate starting a serious relationship until he was able to walk past a betting shop and not go in. It had cost him one girl already.

He also knew that he was in danger of falling into a life of crime. So long as this last job went off smoothly and he got

46

paid straightaway, he would remain clean as far as the police were concerned. And that would be that. New beginnings for Dexter Thompson!

He glanced at his watch, got into his car and turned on the ignition. Dex shivered. All he wanted was to get this over with.

* * *

But Dexter Thompson was being watched. Frank Rosen had been a police officer for long enough to master the perfect technique for covert observation, and he was still very good at it.

Thompson was one of the names on his list. Thanks to DS Marie Evans, Frank knew all about him. A single man aged thirty-nine, he lived alone and had a reputation as a hard worker. He was employed by the film company as a lighting technician and programmer and was said to be good at his job. He had come into the film industry via work on live events. He had never been in trouble with the police, not even for minor offences. All well and good, except that Thompson was a gambler, which would make him susceptible to offers of work that involved extra cash.

This put Thompson at the top of Frank's list of people to watch. He checked the time. If Thompson took roughly as long as he had a few nights ago, he would be back in around two and a half hours.

Frank hurried across to where he had parked his car and climbed in. If things followed the same pattern as the last few weeks, another car would soon be heading off in the same direction as Thompson's. Frank had been careful to park away from the exit so Craig Turner's headlights wouldn't pick him out.

His job did not oblige him to live on site, so no one would think it odd if he were seen driving away. Still, he had taken the precaution of mentioning meeting up with an old mate for a drink to give himself additional cover.

It was five minutes before he saw Craig hurry into the car park. It seemed the bloke was always late.

Craig Turner, a thirty-five-year-old man, was also on his list, and another individual with a squeaky-clean record. With a well-paid career as a CGI — computer generated imagery — animator, Craig's weak point was his wife. Behind his back, Craig's mates called her Joan Collins, as she aspired to a similar lifestyle. So Craig, too, was someone in need of a generous cash booster.

But what were they doing to make that extra cash?

Frank Rosen followed Craig out into the road. He drove for almost ten minutes before he began to get an inkling of where Craig was heading, and it puzzled him. The only place that lay in that particular direction was the village of Spelsby. Beyond that was open farmland, then marsh, and finally the tidal river. Frank could think of only one destination his two marks might be heading for — the Schooner's Mate.

The Schooner, as everyone called it, was a straggling, semi-modern hotel. Not pretty, and not something you saw too many of in the Fens. As Frank watched Craig pull into the car park, he began to wonder if this could be a red herring. They had function rooms here, and the management was known to offer private suites to men who liked to play poker for money. It wasn't illegal, so long as the public were not allowed in and no charge was levied for playing. So, was that it? Dex was a gambler after all, and maybe his mate Craig was desperate enough to try his luck on a big win.

Frank slowed right down and then pulled into the big car park, coasting quietly into a space some distance from Craig. Dex's car was already there, so there was no doubt that this was their destination. He turned off the engine and heaved a sigh. It looked as though he'd been wrong about them heading off for some big illegal heist, they were just joining a poker game.

He grunted and sat back, gloomily watching Craig unload several large, heavy-looking cases from his boot.

Hang on. Suitcases? You didn't need luggage to play a few hands of poker. He recalled seeing Dex also packing various items into his car. This was no card game. The problem was, how to discover what they were up to? He certainly didn't want anyone seeing him here. He considered ringing Jackman but changed his mind. It could still be something quite harmless. He had no proof at all that anything illegal was going on, just a strong gut feeling, and that wasn't enough to warrant sending in the cavalry.

He was stymied. He knew he couldn't follow them inside, and he daren't wait for them to finish whatever they were doing. If they got the slightest hint that he was following them, it would ruin everything. No, he'd just have to give up for tonight and report what he'd seen to Jackman. He'd suggest they put a couple of undercover detectives inside the Schooner to keep an eye open for Craig and Dex, and their heavy cases. They might also check what went on there, other than the gambling.

And what the hell was in those cases?

* * *

Dex felt almost euphoric as he packed up his things. As he had hoped, they had carried it off like clockwork. For once, even Lance looked pleased. He even smiled.

Lance called out, 'Two minutes, Dex,' and winked. 'Come and find me, okay?'

Sounded like it was 'splash the cash' time. 'Sure, Lance,' Dex said.

Lance lowered his voice. 'And on your own, all right?'

Dex looked around and saw Craig talking to another man. They usually got paid together, but maybe the amounts were different and Lance didn't want any arguments.

Mentioning that he was just going down to his car, Dex took one of his bags and left it by the door to the small room that Lance had just entered.

Inside, Lance told him to shut the door. 'Thanks for everything, mate. Sorry the party is over, but it's safer this way.'

All Dex wanted was his money and away from that place. 'It's fine, Lance. Like you said, it was good while it lasted. Now, as far as I'm concerned, it never happened.'

'Good man.' Lance proffered an envelope, it looked nice and fat. 'Don't mention what's in this to anyone, especially Craig, get what I'm saying? You did a good job and I appreciate it. Go back to the day job, and who knows, one day you might hear from me again but don't count on it.' He stuck out a hand. 'Now bugger off.'

Dex pushed the envelope deep into his pocket and hurried back to where he had left his bag. There was nothing he wanted more than to be back in his little mobile home, counting his money and savouring a very large whisky.

As he carted away the last of his things, he saw Craig going into the same room, an expectant expression on his face. Silently, Dex wished him luck. If only he had been a fly on the wall, for then he would have heard Lance say, 'Craig, old buddy, I've been thinking about what you said earlier, and on reflection, maybe I can use you after all. We'll talk tomorrow, all right?'

CHAPTER SIX

Marie pushed her phone back into her pocket with a frown. Though Dougie the Dreamer had refused to say where he was going, he had given her that mobile number. Emergencies only, he had said, but she was worried about him. The more she recalled how terrified he had been, the more anxious she became.

'You look a tad unsettled, my friend,' said a voice, breaking her train of thought.

She looked up. It was Jackman, standing in his office doorway. 'It's Dougie, boss. I've been trying to get hold of him for three days now but he's not responding. I've tried the new number and his old one, and I'm worried something's happened to him.'

Jackman beckoned to her and she joined him in his office.

'Sadly, there's not much we can do since we have no idea where he went. It's not even a running case so we can't use the official channels to find him,' Jackman said. 'I do understand your concern but I can't see them chasing all over the country after him when he doesn't pose a threat. I mean, what does he know? Nothing that would incriminate anyone. Anyway, if it's as serious as he suspected, they'll have much bigger fish to fry.' His phone buzzed. 'Hey, it's Frank calling on the burner phone, let's see what he has to say.'

'Listen,' Frank's voice rang out on speakerphone, 'I've got something for you, Jackman, and I'm pretty sure it's going to lead us to what they're up to.'

Marie smiled. It seemed Frank was enjoying his new role as undercover agent. Then she pictured Dougie's troubled face and was immediately afraid for Frank. They were very different men, however. Unlike Dougie, Frank was careful. He had planned ahead, passing himself off as some retired old plod, happy with his lot and delighted to be rubbing shoulders with a film crew and actors from the TV. Jackman had assured her that Frank was experienced in this kind of job and would make sure to maintain his cover.

Meanwhile, Jackman was asking Frank for details.

'I expect you know the Schooner's Mate at Spelsby. Both Turner and Thompson went there last night, and they took what looked like luggage with them, heavy suitcases and carrying cases. I wasn't able to see what was in them, unfortunately. I watched them unload and go in but couldn't hang around in case I was seen. I did watch them arrive back at the site though. They still had the cases and other paraphernalia with them. From the way they handled them they were just as heavy as when they arrived so they couldn't have left anything at the hotel.'

'Great stuff. Well done, Frank,' said Jackman, with a smile at Marie. 'I'm guessing your idea is to let us know when they go there again, so we can get a couple of plainclothes officers there to watch what they do.'

'That was my immediate thought,' said Frank. 'Trouble is, it takes only around a quarter of an hour to get there from the site, so you wouldn't have a lot of time to get to the hotel ahead of them. They don't have a regular schedule for these night-time excursions either.'

'In that case I'll send Robbie Melton and another female detective to have a few drinks in the hotel bar to see if they can glean anything about what the place is used for,' said Jackman.

'It's well-known for the gambling that goes on there, but no other activity — nothing that we know of anyhow.'

Marie tried to recall anything that she'd heard about that rather unattractive hotel. It looked seedy enough to be a destination for illicit sexual assignations but that was all.

Jackman asked Frank how everything was going otherwise. Did he suspect that anyone might be suspicious of him?

Frank laughed. 'Oh, it's going just fine, Jackman. Everyone thinks of me as this old windbag who is being paid — rather well — to tell them how policing works, and is thoroughly enjoying his fifteen minutes of fame. I'm being careful though, doesn't pay to get too complacent. Anyway, must go now, I've got work to do. I'll be sure to update you as and when.'

Jackman thanked him and ended the call. He sat for a while in silence.

'So Dougie was right,' said Marie. 'Something is going on.'

'And now we have a venue for whatever it is. The problem is, will Ruth Crooke sanction a budget for something as tenuous as the hunch of a retired copper?' He chuckled. 'I'm going to look a bit of a prat, aren't I, requesting funds to look into a crime when we have no proof that there even is one, and throw detectives at it on the off-chance that we are right. Meanwhile, we have a real case of murder in our Adonis of the River. I can't say I hold out much hope.'

'Just ask her nicely,' Marie said. 'We have the Adonis case in hand, and we can't do more on that until we get the results from forensics. We already have uniforms out on the streets making enquiries, so now is your best chance. Go on, go and beard the lioness in her den. After all, you are our Ruthie's favourite detective.' It was true. Superintendent Ruth Crooke actually seemed to like Jackman. He held a special place in her affections, although she would never have admitted it. 'Put on your best charming smile, then we can start delving into the Schooner's unofficial side-lines.' Marie's smile faded. 'And, boss, can I run a trace on Dougie's phone? I've got these really bad vibes about him.'

Jackman thought for a moment. 'Yeah, I guess so. You sort that while I go and polish my grovelling skills. Wish me luck.'

* * *

Hazel Palgrave had obviously got in early again, for when John arrived, exactly on time as usual, she seemed to have been working for hours. Doesn't the woman have a home to go to, he wondered.

John told himself to get a grip. He was spending far too long wondering about Ms Palgrave these days, and it was neither professional, nor appropriate. He was usually in charge of his own feelings — what there were of them — and this new sensation was foreign to him. Part of him wished that Stephen had chosen someone else for the job . . . *But on the other hand* . . . He pushed the thought aside.

'Morning, John,' she said without lifting her eyes from her screen. 'Kettle's boiled if you want to make yourself a drink. Oh, and we had a message from Stephen. He is very pleased with what we've achieved so far, and you have a new instruction.' This time she looked up. 'You are going to need an overnight bag for this. In three days' time you will be taking a trip. Your assignment is to assess how well a particular job has been carried out, and if any part of it is less than perfect, you are to rectify it. Details to follow.'

John shrugged. He didn't mind what he did as long as he got paid. 'Destination?'

'Not yet confirmed.' Her eyes went back to the screen.

Doesn't that woman think of anything but work? John had hoped that one day she'd ask him how he was, ask something, *anything*, personal, that she thought of him as a human being and not some tool.

He went to the tiny kitchen and made himself a coffee. Working out of Janet's home had been much more pleasant than this dreary rented flatlet over a shop. It was safer than operating from a domestic address — the landlord was in

Stephen's pay — but it discouraged its two occupants from engaging in casual chat, which, normally, he would have welcomed, except that his fellow occupant was Hazel Palgrave.

Stirring his usual one spoonful of sugar into his mug, John wondered about techniques that blocked obsessive thoughts. He had never been so distracted by another person, and it was beginning to worry him. In order to do his job properly, John needed to be as single-minded as he always had been, capable of concentrating on the task at hand, no matter what distractions arose. Stephen had hired him for just this quality and paid him well for it. If he wanted it to continue, he could not afford to lose his edge.

He took a deep breath and returned to the office. 'So. Today's schedule, please? I need to keep moving.'

* * *

Hazel listened to the door close behind him and frowned. She was a perceptive woman and had observed that John was attracted to her. This might not have been much of a problem except that she now read confusion in his eyes. Well, no way must he be allowed to jeopardise the operation. He was no good to them as anything less than one hundred percent committed to it. She knew his history and what he had done. It was very dark. She would have expected such a man to be devoid of emotion, so how should she proceed?

She would have to allocate some time to the problem, and decide how to deal with it. She couldn't take the issue to Stephen; it was up to her to resolve. Somehow, she must turn this unforeseen development to her advantage — and that of Stephen. Stephen came first.

* * *

Marie gnawed anxiously on the inside of her cheek. The last of the traces had just come back. Dougie's two phones had been out of use for days, the last time one was used was to call his office at the Police Federation from Greenborough. Since then, both had been switched off — or possibly the batteries were flat — and were untraceable.

Marie stared into the distance, going back over their last conversation. Had he given her any clue as to where he might go? Had he let anything slip? No, on both counts. She tried to think of any place he might have spoken about in the past — a place he loved, somewhere he like to visit. She drew a blank. Her only hope was that Dougie had been frightened enough to completely disappear and would remain underground until he heard that his mystery crime had been solved, and the people responsible locked up. It *was* possible. He had said that was what he intended to do, and she hoped that he had.

Her phone rang, bringing her back to earth.

'Is that that wonderful Welshwoman, Marie? I do hope so. I wouldn't bother you, but our dear boy is out of his office and I have news to impart.'

'Yes, Rory, I'm all ears.'

'Well, I'll spare you the details but what a pleasure it was to deal with such a fine young man, that Adonis you so kindly presented to me. Don't get me wrong, now, I am simply referring to the fact that few of the cadavers you put my way are actually spotlessly clean. And thereby hangs a tale—'

Marie shook her head and smiled. 'Any chance of an actual report, Rory? Or is the story essential to it?'

A loud harrumph issued down the line. 'Don't spoil this, please! You know how much I enjoy our little chats. As I was saying, our dead young man was indeed spotlessly clean, and since he wasn't in the river for long, we found that his body had been generously rubbed with oil — a quite expensive one, I might add.'

Marie's smile turned to a frown. 'What kind of oil?'

'As it happens, I can give you a definite answer to that. It's a "shimmer" body oil, I have been told, which produces an attractive, sun-kissed, summer glow to the skin. I've isolated jojoba seed oil, olive fruit oil and safflower, and I can even supply the maker's name. Check it out immediately, my little

56

Welsh sleuth. It produces a most sultry effect — not that I would know from personal experience of course — along with the captivating fragrances of white florals and sandalwood. Oh my! I'm tempted to rush out and buy, aren't you?'

'Er, probably not,' grunted Marie, stifling a giggle.

He tutted. 'Spoilsport. Anyway, this leads one to the question of whether he applied this himself, or did someone anoint him post-mortem? And I'm afraid that is going to be your main line of enquiry, because all our other findings were unremarkable. We found a very fit, well-nourished male, of around twenty-five to thirty. Superb muscle tone, excellent teeth but with no identifiable work done on them, no scars, healed fractures or body art, and no underlying diseases or malformation of the internal organs. In short, dear heart, apart from the fact that he was strangled with a ligature, a thin cord, which we are tracing as I speak, he was a perfect specimen.'

Marie groaned. 'Oh, great. So, apart from some poncy oil, we have absolutely nothing to go on. Thanks, Rory.'

'Sorry, but in a way it does speak volumes. You are not looking at some low-life, and you might do well to search out someone with a goodly amount of cash to spend on his diet and his physical appearance, for I'd say that was very important to him. For his career perhaps?'

Marie considered that point, 'I see. As in maybe a fashion model?'

'Now you are thinking along the right lines, in which case I will leave you to contemplate my words of wisdom. *Ciao* for now, dear heart!'

He's right, she thought. *Maybe our Adonis has a lot to tell us after all . . .*

Before she could consider this any further, she saw Jackman returning from Ruth Crooke's office, so she stood up and followed him into his own.

'Whew! That was not easy,' he exclaimed, smiling in triumph.

'But you charmed her, didn't you?' She beamed at him. 'That's a relief. Shall I call Robbie in?'

'Why not?' said Jackman, 'but not until you've organised us some coffee. I need a shot of something revitalising after my harrowing experience. Pity the vending machine doesn't dispense whisky.'

Marie grinned at him. 'That bad, eh?'

'Let's just say our Ruth was not in the best frame of mind. Hell, Marie, we'd better come up with something or she'll flay me alive.'

'We will, never fear,' she said. 'Now I'll go and get those drinks.'

A few minutes later, the three of them were seated in Jackman's office.

'You already know the background, Rob,' said Jackman. 'But we have just been told that there's something going on at the Schooner's Mate hotel out at Spelsby. Trouble is, we have no idea what.' He recounted what Frank Rosen had told him. 'So, I want you and a female officer to go there as if you're out for a quiet, intimate drink. Maybe you can be an adulterous couple or something a bit shady like that. Maybe make a few trips, as if you were having a clandestine liaison. See if you can spot any sign of something iffy taking place. Ears to the ground, eyes open, and see what you can pick up.'

Robbie looked delighted. He had always loved undercover work, and was good at assuming disguises. 'If there's something dodgy at the Schooner, and it certainly wouldn't surprise me, I'll sniff it out, boss.'

'That's what I'm relying on you to do,' said Jackman. 'Start tonight, if that's okay? And I'll try to charm some money out of petty cash. Drinks at hotels cost a fortune.'

Robbie laughed. 'My dream job! An evening out making advances to some gorgeous woman, and the Fenland Constabulary picks up the tab! Life doesn't get any better than that!'

'Don't get too carried away, sunshine,' warned Marie. 'Most likely the budget will only stand one round of drinks and a packet of crisps between you, *if* you're lucky.' All three of them smiled.

'Maybe I should have a word with uniform, see if they've had any dealings with the Schooner recently,' Robbie said. 'We all know it's used for gambling, but maybe they suspect other activities as well.'

'Do it now,' said Jackman. 'That place has never been fingered for even the slightest misdemeanour, but I wouldn't mind betting that it's a cover for some kind of illegal activity.'

'Can I just suggest that you take DC Lynne Foreman?' said Marie. 'Other than Cat Cullen in Greenborough, I reckon she's the best. Lynne's brilliant at undercover work and really knows how to change her appearance.'

'Good idea. Try and commandeer her from DI Jenny Deane's team for a while,' Jackman said.

'If Lynne's not free, I could always use my girlfriend, Ella. She'd definitely be up for it,' Robbie said.

Marie smiled. 'That's true. She's no stranger to police work either.'

Ella Jarvis was the forensic photographer in Rory's team, and a good friend of theirs. She and Robbie had been together for quite a while now.

'Thinking about it, maybe Ella would be the best choice,' said Jackman. 'I'll never forget all the help she gave me and the family after my sister-in-law's death. She was a positive terrier at getting to the truth.' He looked at Robbie. 'And you two have such a good rapport, I think it might make the subterfuge more convincing. Give her a ring, Robbie.'

After Robbie had left, Marie told Jackman about Rory's call.

His initial reaction was to be as frustrated as her, then he came round to her way of thinking.

'Rory was adamant that our dead man had eaten a healthy diet and must have spent a lot of time and money on his physical appearance and physique.' Marie took out her notebook. 'I thought I'd make a list of the names of local and national modelling agencies, then get Gary, and maybe Robbie, to start ringing round. Maybe someone on their books who answers his description has missed an appointment, or become suddenly unavailable without warning.'

'Yes, and I suggest that if anyone has a model who fits the bill, we show them the post-mortem photographs of our Adonis. It could secure an ID for us if they are prepared to look at a picture of a dead man.' He thought for a moment. 'I know this is a long shot, but if you have no luck there, try agencies who supply Kissogram performers.'

Marie tried, and failed, to stifle a grin, 'You think he might have been a male stripper?'

'Why not? They exist. Body beautiful and all that.' Jackman shrugged. 'Could be the reason he was covered in expensive oil. What did you call it, "shimmer" body oil? Sounds a bit suggestive to me — you know, "attract the ladies with a glowing sexy body."'

Marie giggled. 'Why didn't I think of that? You could well have hit the nail on the head there, boss. I reckon I'll prioritise that over the modelling agencies.'

'Well, it's a starting point, isn't it? Until we know who he is we have no idea of where to look for his killer. Go and talk to Gary and Robbie, and try to find a real name for poor Adonis.'

Marie made to leave, then stopped. 'I've just had a thought. You don't think Frank Rosen would try to go it alone at that film set, do you? After all, he did tail two of the crew out to that hotel. That was risky.'

Jackman exhaled, 'And what would you have done in that situation?'

'Er, I'd have tailed them.'

'Exactly. He's still a copper at heart, Marie, and I think it was a calculated risk. After all, he didn't stay and risk being seen, and he didn't try to enter the hotel. He just secured us a location. I hope . . .' He stopped and pulled a face, 'I hope he won't do anything more dangerous than that. Too much poking around could get him noticed.'

She opened the door. 'Remind him again when you next speak, boss. I'm shit-scared about what might have happened to Dougie, and I don't want to start worrying about Frank as well.'

CHAPTER SEVEN

If any of DC Robbie Melton's mates had spotted him that evening, he would have been the talk of the mess room. Fancy our Robbie playing away like that, they would have said. And with a right tarty woman too!

They would never have recognised Ella, who looked completely transformed. Robbie already looked unremarkable, though a few small changes to his style of clothing and his hair made him, too, look faintly sleazy.

They sat in the corner of the lounge bar nursing their overpriced drinks. They had come by taxi as opposed to their own private cars, which also allowed them to have a few drinks. They planned to make several visits, this first one being to set the scene and make themselves known to the bar staff. The story was that Robbie was married, Ella was the 'other woman', and the Schooner was a discreet place to meet without anyone recognising them.

'Blimey, this whisky is a bit rough!' Robbie stared into his glass.

'That's because you don't like whisky,' Ella murmured.

'I know. I picked it because it suits my image. Now I wish I'd had wine, like you.'

'Don't worry, the wine's not much better,' Ella said, pulling a face. She leaned forward and took his hand in hers. 'Keep up the act, darling.'

'It's no act, kiddo. I love you. Even though I'm not sure who I'm saying it to right now.'

Ella smiled warmly at him. 'Despite the shitty drinks, I'm enjoying this. I used to love amateur dramatics when I was younger.' She gazed around. 'First impressions?'

'Busier than I expected.' Robbie looked out across the lounge, which was vast and impersonal. 'Most people here seem to know the staff, so I'd guess they come here regularly.' He sniffed. 'But why? It's way off the beaten track, not on a major route to anywhere, and it certainly hasn't got any Olde Worlde charm, or even character.'

'Yes, they obviously come here for a reason.' Ella glanced across at a group of men who kept looking expectantly at a rather petite, dark-haired girl in the hotel uniform.

'*They* are poker players,' whispered Robbie. 'They're waiting for their function room to be free.'

As he spoke, the girl beckoned to them. As one, they all stood up and followed her to a wide staircase leading to an upper floor.

'Ah,' Robbie breathed, 'Well, what d'you know. I do believe we've just had a bit of good fortune. See that girl behind the bar, the one with cropped white-blonde hair?'

Ella nodded. 'You know her?'

'Not exactly, but I know her father, Les Smithson.' He smiled. 'A while back I did that man a favour, which he'll no doubt remember if I jog his memory. Maybe his daughter has told him something tasty about her place of employment.'

'She won't recognise you, will she?' Ella asked anxiously.

'Not dressed like this, that's for sure. But she wouldn't anyway. I only saw her once, and that was over a year ago. She was having a blazing row with her mother at the time. I very much doubt she had any interest in the random bloke her dad was talking to.'

'Good stuff. A line of enquiry on day one. Result! Jackman will be pleased.'

Robbie noticed a waiter heading their way and leaned towards Ella, as if he was saying something suggestive.

'Can I get you more drinks, sir?'

'I'll have a beer this time, thank you.' Robbie turned to Ella, 'What about you, sweetheart?'

She placed her hand over the top of her glass. 'No more for me just yet, my angel. Can't have you getting me drunk, can we?' She winked at him and licked her lips.

As the waiter moved off, Robbie stood up and followed him, telling Ella to stay put.

'Excuse me, waiter. Can I ask you something?' He looked around, as if not wishing to be overheard. 'Er, bit embarrassing, but is it possible to take a room here, like just for the evening? We'd like somewhere private where we can talk.'

'Of course, sir.' The waiter smiled politely, though his eyes were mocking. 'The manager is on duty this evening. Speak to him. I do know that the charge is the same as for one night bed and breakfast, no matter how long you stay in the room. Laundry and cleaning, you understand.'

'Thanks, I appreciate it. We can't stay tonight, but this place was recommended by a friend, so we're just having a look for now.' He glanced around. 'It seems perfect to me. Discreet, I assume?'

'Oh yes, sir. Absolutely.'

Robbie glanced at the waiter's name badge. 'Thank you, Darren, that's good to know.' He tucked a ten-pound note into the lad's pocket. 'We'll see you again.'

The waiter's eyes sparkled. 'Ask for me, sir, and I'll make sure you have a nice quiet room.'

'Is it always this busy?' Robbie asked, looking around at the full tables.

'Yes, sir. We have a lot of game players in, and, er, businessmen, who take the bigger rooms for their meetings and conferences and so on.'

Robbie beamed at him. 'Good for business, then.'

'Oh yes, sir. Now if you'll excuse me, I'll get you that beer.'

Robbie returned to Ella, made a show of kissing her and told her what he had learned.

'Meetings and conferences, eh? Why out here and not in town?' Ella said. 'And while you were gone, I noticed that not everyone waits to be called to their rooms like those poker players. Some people come in through that side door over there.' She indicated a door leading in from the car park. 'And they all hurry straight up what I presume to be a back staircase.'

'Mmm. I can't wait to have a word with Les Smithson,' muttered Robbie. 'I have a suspicion this dive of a hotel is the epicentre for a whole lot of interesting goings-on. You still up for a couple of return visits, Ells?'

'Try and stop me! This place reeks of illicit activities, and now you've really whetted my appetite to discover what they are.'

Robbie knew what a terrier she was. SOCOs are always curious and very observant and Ella was no different. She was just the right person to have by his side. With her painstaking attention to detail, Ella Jarvis would miss nothing.

* * *

John decided to get everything ready for his trip right now, just in case it was brought forward. It had happened before, and he didn't like to do things in a hurry, so he packed a small overnight bag and assembled everything he might possibly need for the task, checking his list of items with military precision. Stephen's operatives were generally pretty thorough, but there had been occasions when an assignment had been left uncompleted. It wasn't his favourite part of the job but, given what he was paid, he wasn't about to complain.

John wondered about his future. The problem with earning such good money is that you find you can't do with less. Before he began working for Stephen, he had aspired to nothing more than a comfortable middle-class life. Now, there were any number of things he wanted. He wanted a fishing lodge in somewhere remote and beautiful — in, say, Wales. He saw himself striding out across a mountain range, Labrador at his heels. He wanted to travel. He wanted to embark on a cruise, heading to somewhere exotic. He wanted . . . John dragged himself back to the present. Thanks to Stephen, the things he wanted might actually come to pass.

He looked at the printout Hazel Palgrave had given him and noted the destination. What on earth could Stephen want doing in Dungeness? The place was even listed as Britain's only desert. The massive shingle beach, the largest in Europe, was littered with the skeletons of ancient fishing boats, derelict huts and the occasional bleak chalet. John was no bird watcher, so the place filled him with distaste. Dungeness seemed to offer nothing but a nuclear power station and two lighthouses, the only form of transport a miniature passenger railway connecting it with Romney, Hythe and Dymchurch.

John scratched the back of his neck in puzzlement. All he had to go on was a contact, in the form of someone called Bryan. On his arrival in New Romney, he was to ring a mobile number and then this Bryan would bring him his instructions. No matter, whatever it was, he would cope with it as always.

John yawned, wondering vaguely what awaited him in Kent. He glanced at his watch. Time for sleep.

Brushing his teeth, his thoughts returned to Hazel. He had never met anyone so single-mindedly dedicated to a cause. Stephen had really picked a zealot there.

John climbed into bed and closed his eyes, but the image of Hazel Palgrave remained in his mind, shining through the dark.

* * *

As Dex finally walked back to his old motorhome, having just finished shooting some night scenes up on the sea-bank, he saw Craig hurrying towards him.

'All right, mate?' Dex called out.

His friend lifted a hand. 'Yeah, apart from being totally knackered. Bloody long day, wasn't it? Don't need too many like that.' Craig clapped him on the shoulder. 'Better get back. My Joannie will think I've run off with the make-up artist! See you, Dex.'

Dex watched Craig stride away. His friend seemed energised somehow, and Dex wondered why. He didn't believe that it was simply because they were no longer involved with Lance. There was something else going on.

Well, Dex wasn't about to ask. It was none of his business.

Dex was still elated at being let off so easily. His life of crime was at an end. Today, he had found the courage to delete all the betting apps on his phone. It wasn't much, but it was the first step on a long, tough journey.

As he pulled his keys from his jacket pocket to unlock his vehicle, a folded sheet of paper fell out. He picked it up and went inside to read it:

I was right! Don't mention this whatever you do, but I'm in! I really need the money. If you ever find yourself in the same position again, talk to me and I'll see if I can get you in too. Now forget this, and get rid of this note. Your friend.

Dex groaned. Craig had been handed the perfect opportunity to keep himself safe, and he'd just thrown it away. Who knew what he could be getting himself into, the fool.

He screwed up the paper in disgust, tossed it into the bin and sat down. He stared at the bin for a few seconds then went over and retrieved it. Without knowing why, he smoothed out the creases and pushed it into the side pocket of a rucksack in which he kept a few personal bits and pieces. He stood for a while, hesitating, and then thought of the promise he'd made to himself.

'You're on your own this time, mate. I'm never going to put myself in that position again.' Nevertheless, he feared for his friend. He had seen the look of utter ruthlessness that sometimes crossed Lance Newport's face.

'I can't help you, Craig, mate, I can't. I'm going to need every ounce of energy I possess to stop gambling and getting into debt. I have to save myself.'

* * *

It was after three in the morning and Jackman lay awake. Ever since Laura's death, he had been sleeping badly. He still lay on 'his' side of the bed, Laura's empty pillow beside him, the cover unchanged. Occasionally he sniffed it, searching for the slightest hint of his lost love's scent.

He had refused to seek out a counsellor, and Sam's own grief precluded him from assuming that role, until, finally, he acquiesced to Marie and Ruth's pleas and sought out Julia Tennant, the new force psychologist. Unbeknownst to his friends, his real reason for agreeing to talk to her was to accustom himself to working with this woman who was not Laura.

Despite himself, he began to open up to her and tell her how he felt. Little by little, he began to use her as a sounding board as he went through the stages of grief — denial, anger, bargaining — though he hadn't yet worked through them all. Some things were a little easier now, but still, his insomnia did not improve.

With a sigh, Jackman closed his eyes and prayed for just a little sleep before dawn stained the Fenland sky.

CHAPTER EIGHT

Two days later, John received the go-ahead to embark on his journey. It was a nightmare. On three separate occasions, roadworks forced him to deviate from his route, and the traffic around London made him appreciate driving in the Fens.

When at last he arrived in New Romney, he needed something to relax his mind before confronting his task. What he needed was a full English breakfast and mug of builder's tea. During his time as a police officer, he had eaten enough fast food to last him a lifetime, so he sought out a nice little café and ordered a large home-cooked breakfast.

As his stomach filled, he began to relax. New Romney appeared to be a nice market town, and its proximity to the Romney marshes made him feel at home. A leaflet for tourists he had found in the café called it one of the original Cinque Ports, yet the sea was at least a mile away. While the East Coast was being eaten away by the North Sea, Kent seemed to be acquiring more land.

Breakfast over, he made his call. In ten minutes' time, he was told, in a secluded memorial garden down a quiet street opposite the church of St Nicholas, Bryan would be waiting.

John paid his bill and asked the café assistant where he might find the Burma Star Memorial Garden. Out in the chilly sunshine, he strode forward, eager to begin his assignment.

Bryan turned out to be a nondescript sort of man, who greeted him briskly before saying in a low voice, 'There was a directive regarding a termination of employment.'

John knew exactly what that meant. 'One of Stephen's operatives?'

'Maybe. We believe so, but it is unconfirmed as yet. All I was told was that he was a risk to one of the organisation's branches, and termination was requested.'

'Was it successful?' asked John.

A beat. 'Affirmative.'

Noting Bryan's hesitation, John asked, 'So why am I here?'

'Have you ever been to Dungeness?'

John stiffened. He disliked being answered with another question. 'No, and I repeat, why am I here?'

'First, you have to understand about the place,' Bryan said. 'It's unlike anywhere else in the country. It's incredibly bleak, but the people who live there love it that way, even their homes, most of which are little more than shacks. Right now, there's a storm brewing down there.'

John wondered what this could possibly have to do with him. 'Storm?'

'It's a place of special natural significance and is governed by more preservation orders and regulations than anywhere else in the country. Residents can't even put up a simple fence without breaking some law or other, which means that weekend visitors trample with impunity through their gardens and peer in their windows. As more and more people flock to take a look at the "English desert", the residents' idyll is turning into a nightmare.' John's impatience was beginning to show, so Bryan held up his hand. 'Bear with me, John. I had to give you the background. Anyway, here's where we come in. The residents are a tight-knit community, and watch for any incomers who are disrespectful of the location. They call these people the "DFLs" or, "down from London."'

'Continue,' said John, who was beginning to see where this was going.

'Our mark was no DFL. If he had been, our job would have been easy. He knows the place well. His uncle had lived there for years, since the seventies I believe, and our man had often visited him.' Bryan began to shift uncomfortably on the wooden seat. 'The residents thought nothing of his presence here.'

'But they *were* interested in the person sent to deal with the situation?'

'It's not that, although if our operative had been seen — which I very much doubt — he certainly would have aroused suspicion. The worry is that our mark might have spoken to someone before he was dealt with.' Bryan shrugged. 'It's not a certainty, but I suspect he confided in an old man who had been one of his uncle's friends.'

'Where is the uncle?' asked John.

'Died last year. He left his shack of a home to his nephew, so it was the perfect place for him to hide out in.'

'And the old man you mentioned? You have a name? An address?' John now knew what he had to do.

'Colin Lucas,' Bryan said. 'He lives about a quarter of a mile further down the beach towards the lighthouse. He calls his bungalow, which is actually more like a black-painted shed, "Periwinkle." He's a widower, and a real loner.'

'Is there a reason why you haven't rectified the matter yourself?' John's tone was business-like.

'I can't be seen to be involved in the mark's death. I have fingers in too many official and unofficial pies in that neck of the woods, and we daren't muddy the waters. I know Colin Lucas too, so it needs to be an outsider.' Bryan gave him a look that said, 'Over to you, mate.'

'Okay. Details, please, but first, two questions. One, did the termination go smoothly?'

Bryan nodded. 'Textbook.'

'Where is the body?'

'Disposed of, permanently. He'll be fish food by now. That part went without a single hitch.' Bryan drew an envelope from his pocket and passed it to him. 'These are the details.'

John took the envelope and opened it. Inside was a brief rundown on the man who had believed he had found a safe haven there, in that strange, desolate place. He skimmed through it quickly and nodded. 'I will sort out your problem. If you hear nothing more from me, you can consider the case closed.' He stood up. 'And you won't hear. I don't make mistakes.'

Back in his car, he rang Hazel Palgrave. 'I need some additional information before I can draw a line beneath this job.' He rattled off what he required.

'Give me twenty minutes.' She hung up.

There were times when John appreciated a mind as focussed as his own. This was no time to engage in small talk, and Hazel understood that.

Exactly nineteen minutes later, his phone rang and he was provided with all the details he required.

'What's your ETA back at base?' she asked.

'Midday tomorrow, barring any holdups.'

'Understood. Good luck.'

The phone went dead.

John started his car. He needed to pay a visit to the last English desert.

* * *

At the same time as John was setting out on the drive to Kent, Bernadette Wilkins, as she did every single morning, mug of tea in her hand, stepped outside and stared across the lake. The season was changing, and there was a chilly nip to the early morning air. It had been a strange summer — blistering hot days followed by torrential rain that threatened to flood the parched ground. Now, like the flick of a switch, autumn was descending.

On her first morning in her new home, she had stood as she was standing now, and promised herself never to let a day go by without taking a few minutes each morning to show her appreciation of the idyllic place it was her fortune to be living in.

The water looked cold today. The tall reeds had lost their plumes and rose in spikes at the water's edge, while the trees that skirted the lake on two sides were dappled gold and russet brown.

Winter was approaching. Although here in this place every season had its own beauty, and winter could be spectacular, Bernadette was a spring person. Her heart swelled along with the buds which, this far from traffic and urban pollution, remained fresh and bright all season. And after spring would come the warmth of summer.

Bernadette resigned herself to the long trek through winter, sighed and turned away from the lake, then turned back again. Having, with the help of her neighbours, recently cleared the lake of rubbish tossed in by tourists and weekend visitors, her first reaction was anger. What was that floating in the reed bed on the far bank? More garbage? Had something happened to one of the white egrets that populated the lake?

Bernadette went indoors and snatched her binoculars from the windowsill. She adjusted the focus, but still couldn't make out the object clearly. It was too big to be an egret, thank goodness. Ah well, nothing for it but to go and take a look. She grabbed her coat and set off down the lane, growing angrier by the minute. People didn't understand the damage they did to the environment when they dumped their rubbish in the water like this. Any number of wild birds and animals made their home at this lake and could be killed by the pollutants from old oil cans and other harmful wastes.

She stepped off the lane and into the trees that surrounded the lake on two sides. She seemed to recall the object bumping along by the reeds beneath that tall willow just over there . . . Pushing her way through the undergrowth, she got closer to the water. Yes, she could make out something there, but it was still obscured by the reeds.

Still furious, she made her way to the very edge of the small reed bed — and stood stock still. Was that really what she thought it was?

It was. A man, and he was naked.

Bernadette ran home, stumbling and in tears, where she dialled 999.

* * *

For two days after Jackman received Frank's call, Robbie and Ella continued to visit the Schooner and conduct their supposed illicit affair. Smoothed with a few surreptitious 'tips', Robbie's relationship with Darren became ever more amicable, though Darren hadn't yet provided any information worth knowing.

Now Robbie was in Jackman's office, giving him and the sarge a report on progress.

'I managed to get a word with Les Smithson, sir. His daughter works at the Schooner. He said he'd initially been dead chuffed that she'd found a steady job, even if it did mean long and sometimes very late hours. Then she started mentioning that the management seemed to be engaged in more than just selling drinks and renting out rooms. Now he's not sure that she should even be working there.'

Jackman frowned. 'More? Like what? Did she mention anything specific?'

'She was cagey, sir, but I'm certain she knows more than she's let on to her dad. Anyway, he said he'd do a bit of digging for me. He worked in a hotel once himself and according to him, nothing happens without the staff knowing, and they love to gossip. He and his daughter are pretty close, so he reckons he'll get something out of her. Even if there's no proof, it'll give Ella and me something to look out for, won't it, sir?'

Rob was getting well into their covert mission. 'Les promised he wouldn't mention us at all. He said he's a nosey bugger at the best of times, so his daughter won't wonder why he's so interested in the place. Meanwhile, we'll keep up our visits. We're going again tomorrow. I've spun Darren a line about her husband being away for a week on business, while my wife thinks I'm working in Yorkshire for a fortnight. Of course, that could go tits up if Ella gets a call out. She's told Professor Wilkinson what we are up to, and he's going to try not to call her out in the evenings unless it's urgent.'

'Good work, Robbie. At least now we know that something definitely is going on there. So keep it up — if you don't mind, that is?'

Robbie grinned. 'It's not exactly an arduous task, sir!'

Marie laughed. 'You're probably getting to see more of Ella than you normally do!'

'You can say that again, especially now she won't have to do evening shouts. A few bevvies with my girl more than once a week — it's a real treat.' He became serious. 'Now we have been going for a while, no one is taking much notice of us and we can keep our ears and eyes open. We're certain the place is being used for something big, we just don't know what.

'Push your Mr Smithson. Inside info is worth a lot. See what the daughter comes up with and report back immediately,' Jackman said.

Robbie stood up. 'Will do, boss.'

'Hang on a minute, Robbie,' said Jackman. 'Marie was just about to update me on Adonis.'

'For what it's worth,' grumbled Marie. 'As you know, we were checking the modelling agencies. Gary has been through all of them, and no one has reported a man of Adonis's description missing. Gary looked at modelling, photographic and escort agencies of all types. He also contacted some fashion houses, and companies that cast actors for adverts — Adonis would've been perfect for one of those sexy men's fragrance ads.' She shrugged. 'So we're right back where we started, with no idea who that young man is. It's really bugging us.'

74

'Sounds like he's not from round here,' said Robbie. 'He might not even be British.'

'We checked his DNA and fingerprints with the Police National Computer database, just in case he'd been in trouble in the past, but we had no joy. We've alerted all forces and gave them a post-mortem photograph. Hell, it's like he dropped out of the sky, and—'

Jackman's desk phone began to ring.

He listened with a set expression. 'Where exactly? Fine, We'll attend, Sergeant. ETA twenty minutes. Please see that it's cordoned off and a log set up at once. No one in, no one out, until I get there.'

Jackman set the receiver down none too carefully and reached for his jacket and car keys. 'We have another one. Marie, with me, please. Robbie, you stay here — we might need liaison, so keep your line free, okay? Sounds very similar to Adonis.'

* * *

'I don't think I've heard of Lake Evelyn,' Marie said.

'Few people have,' Jackman said, staring at the road ahead. 'It's one of those old salt pans that filled with water over the years. It's about a mile outside my village of Cartoft behind a V-shape formed by two lanes and sheltered by trees, so you hardly notice it from the road. There are a couple of nice bungalows close to the edge, with small wooden jetties. It was stocked with fish ages back, and I think the owners have private fishing rights. Pretty spot, kind of peaceful.' He accelerated to pass a slow-moving farm vehicle. 'It was one of the residents that found the body, and she's understandably very shaken. Luckily, PCs Stacey Smith and Jay Acharya are with her.'

'So she's in good hands then,' Marie said. Young Jay Acharya was one of the most caring and considerate bobbies she had ever had the privilege to meet. Teamed with the streetwise and experienced Stacey Smith, they were the go-to crew when empathy and thoughtfulness were required.

They drove on in silence. Marie glanced at Jackman. One of them needed to say the word. She cleared her throat. 'Do you think we have a serial killer here?'

Jackman kept his eyes on the road. 'Let's hold judgement on that until we see what has occurred.' He grimaced. 'But I'm telling you, if we do, I'm giving up the job and moving into a hermitage somewhere way off the map!'

'Make it one with a flat for me!' She laughed, humourlessly. 'I've had my fill of evil people.' She was only partly joking.

Jackman, who had heard her sigh, glanced her way. 'Come on, Marie,' he said, gently, 'you know we both love the job. We are bloody good at it, too. Just think, what would the good people of Saltern-le-Fen do without Jackman and Evans?'

Marie grinned. 'Madame Arcati strikes again! And you're right, as always. Adonis the Second, here we come!'

'That's my Marie. Let's get to it!'

By the time they arrived, two officers had waded into the lake and extricated the body from where it had lodged in the reeds. This new Adonis now lay on a tarpaulin in a grass-covered clearing beneath the trees.

They stood and looked at the naked man in silence.

'Well, there's one glaring difference, isn't there, boss?' she said in a low voice.

'Isn't there just?'

For this Adonis had not been strangled, he had had his throat cut. 'Are you as puzzled as me?' Marie added.

Jackman nodded. 'Well, I don't know about you, but I think we badly need the services of a certain pathologist.'

Marie pulled her phone from her pocket and made the call. 'ETA thirty minutes,' she told Jackman. 'He's coming in person, and he said to tell you that he's more than intrigued.'

'He's not alone there.' Jackman frowned, then he turned away from the pathetic figure on the groundsheet. 'Let's go and talk to the woman who found him, the neighbours too.'

Stacey had already called on the Johnsons, who lived in the neighbouring bungalow, and asked them if they would come over to comfort Bernadette Wilkins. When Marie and Jackman arrived, they were all gathered in Bernadette's lounge holding steaming mugs of tea. Bernadette herself had both hands round a small tumbler of what Marie guessed to be brandy. Jay Acharya told her he had suggested that something stronger than tea might help with the shock.

As they all said, the far side of the lake was accessed from a turnoff from the main road into Cartoft Village, so no one had seen or heard any vehicle pass that way.

'I'm a light sleeper,' offered Kerry Johnson. 'If anyone had driven past this side of the lake, I'd have woken up. It's very quiet here, and other than farm vehicles, you hardly ever hear a car.'

'I do know that there was nothing in the lake at ten thirty,' added her husband, Dave. 'I took the dog all the way round for his last walk before bed. I had a powerful torch with me and I always check for wildlife. It was quiet as the grave — oh dear. Sorry.'

No one spoke for a moment or two, then Jackman asked, 'Have any of you seen any strangers around here recently, anyone who looks as if they might be checking the place out?'

The three of them shook their heads. 'We get the occasional walker,' Kerry said, 'but not recently.'

'They usually stop and say what a lovely place it is to live,' Bernadette added shakily. 'And it was, until this happened. Now I'm not sure if I want to stay here anymore.' She began to cry.

Kerry Johnson sat down beside her and put an arm around her shoulders. 'There, there, Bernie. It's just the shock. It'll pass, love. These police officers will catch whoever did this and then we'll all get back to normal again.'

Marie wondered if Bernadette ever would. Something like this often tarnished a place forever.

She recalled her and Ralph's reaction to hearing of the murder that had taken place at Peelers End, and what a joke they thought it was. That, however, had happened a long time before they ever set eyes on the place. This had happened last night.

Jackman beckoned to her and they went outside. They walked out onto the landing stage and looked across the lake, to where a cordon had already been set up.

His gaze on the fluttering tape, Jackman said, 'One strangled and one with his throat cut, but other than that, we have two white males, possibly of similar age and exceptionally good-looking. Both were stripped, or were already naked, and both were left in water. It has to be the same killer, Marie.'

'Absolutely, and here comes the man who will confirm it for us. That green car belongs in a museum.'

They walked back around the lake and met Rory at the cordon.

'We have to stop meeting like this!' Rory said. 'Now, is it really true that you have come up with yet another beautiful body? You really are spoiling me, you know.' He began pulling on his protective suit and overshoes, while Jackman and Marie remained behind the cordon awaiting his verdict.

When he returned after a few minutes, Rory's expression was grave, and very angry. 'Wicked bloody waste! He's no more than his mid-twenties, to all intents and purposes another fit and healthy young man. What's going on here, Jackman? Why would anyone want to kill these two Adonises?'

'So far, Rory, we have no idea whatsoever. But even if the manner of death is different, it's the same killer, isn't it?'

Rory nodded. 'I'd say so — off the record, of course. There are far too many similarities, aren't there? Still, I'll do the PM as quickly as possible for you. Though killers don't often change the way they kill. They have one modus operandi, which they have perfected and are comfortable with. It becomes their trademark. I can't see whoever it is sitting at the breakfast table thinking, "Mmm, what's it to be today? Strangling? Or maybe a nice stabbing? Where's a coin? I'll toss for it."'

He was right. Unless there were extenuating circumstances, killers followed a pattern. 'Looks like we need to wait for your forensic reports then, Rory,' Marie said. 'Because we can't even find an ID for our original Adonis. It's like he never existed.' She looked fleetingly at the shape on the ground. 'And I get the feeling that it's going to be just the same with number two.'

'I'll do all I can to assist, dear lady,' said Rory, 'and as expediently as is humanly possible. To that end, I'll push on and get our second lovely young man back to the morgue. If he has secrets, I shall coax them out of him, never fear. Now, I bid you adieu!' With a little bow, Rory was gone.

Marie and Jackman walked back to Bernadette's bungalow.

'I'll ring Robbie and update him,' said Jackman. 'Maybe Mrs Wilkins could do with a victim support officer.'

'Okay, boss. That poor woman is a wreck. Her perfect little lake-side world has just been turned upside down, and it's shaken her to the core.'

Marie glanced back across the still waters of the lake. This really was a most beautiful place to live. Had death forever ruined it for Bernadette?

CHAPTER NINE

From the images on Google and Bryan's portrayal of 'Britain's only desert', John had an idea of what to expect, but the reality took him by surprise.

As he tramped along the pathway leading to Colin Lucas's black-painted bungalow, he wondered why anyone would want to make this desolate spot their home.

Luckily, Colin was in his garden — for want of a better description of the scrubby, gravelly area surrounding Periwinkle. John had a good idea that had the old man been indoors, he would have stayed there and refused to answer the door.

'Colin Lucas? I'm DS Murray from the Metropolitan Police. Sorry to bother you, sir, but could I have a word?' He held out an authentic-looking warrant card.

The old man squinted at him, his craggy, weather-beaten face annoyed and suspicious. 'Out here is private enough, ain't it? I don't see too many people earwigging, do you? Whadyerwant anyway?'

John smiled. 'Well, Colin, I'm in the middle of a serious investigation and I need your help.'

The old man spat on the ground. 'You want *my* help? How'm I supposed to help the Met?'

John lowered his voice and glanced around. 'To be honest, I shouldn't really be here at all, but it concerns an old mate of mine. He's in a lot of bother, and I want to help him. He spoke a lot about his uncle, who left him his place, here on this beach . . . He talked about you too. Fact is, Colin, he's gone missing, and I'm shit-scared something's happened to him. Look, can we just go inside for a bit? And do me a favour — if you have a kettle, can you please put it on? It's a bloody long drive from the Smoke and I'm gasping for a cuppa.'

Colin Lucas narrowed his eyes, and without a word turned his back on John and shuffled towards his half-open door.

John followed him inside.

Still silent, the old man made the tea, strong with milk and no sugar.

Colin shoved the mug of tea across the wooden kitchen table and lowered his creaking joints onto a chair. 'What sort of trouble?'

John took the only other chair and stared across the table at Colin. 'I wish I bloody knew, but he's got himself mixed up with a very bad bunch of people.' He eased his chair a little closer and dropped his voice, as if afraid of being overheard. 'See, he did a runner. He rang me, sounding terrified, and said he was going to take off for a bit, but he'd keep me posted.' He heaved a sigh, 'I never heard no more.' He sipped the hot tea and winced. 'Then I remembered him telling me about this place. And here I am. Trouble is, he's not here, his little place is empty. Then I thought of you. I guess you're my last hope.'

Colin rubbed at his knee and muttered to himself. He blew on his tea and took a loud slurp, staring at John over the rim of his mug. 'He was here. I saw him two days ago.'

'When did he leave?'

Colin shrugged. 'Yesterday, I suppose. He never said goodbye nor nothing. I've always liked the lad, we got on, him and me, like I got on with his uncle.'

John saw the hurt in the old man's rheumy eyes. 'Did he say anything when you saw him, like if he was in trouble?'

'Nah, but I could tell. He's gone off, you say?'

'Place is empty, Colin.' John shook his head. 'Silly bugger! He should have known I would have helped him, whatever shit he'd got himself in.'

The old man grunted. 'Ah, prob'ly nothing serious.'

Sorry, old-timer, it's about as serious as it gets. 'I guess. But tell me, did he have any other mates here he might have talked to?'

'No. Sure his uncle and me were close, but you don't come here to socialise, you come here to be alone. We support each other but other than that, we keep to ourselves.'

John sat back in the creaky wooden chair. This man was no threat. He knew nothing at all. Now John had to make a decision. He never left loose ends. When he tidied up other people's mess, he did it thoroughly. He put his hand into his pocket and touched the knife. But when he withdrew the hand again, it was empty.

He stood up. 'It was good to meet you, and thanks for the tea. You got a phone, have you? I could ring you if I hear anything.' John knew very well that there was no telegraph pole near this cottage. He couldn't see Colin Lucas with a mobile either.

'No. No phone. If the lad needs me, he knows where I am.'

John left. *Well, old man, you have no idea how close you just came to joining your only friend.*

Smiling grimly, he walked back along the track, away from the nuclear power station towards the beach. Passing a line of fishermen, he greeted them and asked how the fishing was here. He was beginning to understand why this desolate shoreline could attract a certain type of person. A person like Colin Lucas. He touched the blade inside his pocket and assured himself that he wasn't going soft. If Colin had given him any hint of concern, he would have used it. He would.

He returned to his car and climbed in.

* * *

With every day that passed, Frank Rosen grew more certain that there was something here he was missing. There had been no further trips to the seedy hotel, but nevertheless, an undercurrent remained. Furthermore, he had sensed a change in relations between Craig and Dex. It seemed that Dex was doing all he could to avoid his friend. A falling out of thieves? Or something more personal? Craig did have a rather attractive wife after all.

Frank's job no longer took up much of his time. All he had to do these days was advise actors on how the police dealt with criminals, as in handcuffing someone, or reading them their rights.

He had phoned Jackman who had told him that the Schooner was being watched, in the form of two detectives, working undercover. The thought of them, out there on the job, made Frank nostalgic for his days on the force. And he wished he had been able to get a look at what was in those suitcases.

Right now, he was off to the catering area. Lining up for a pizza, the man behind him struck up a conversation. 'Enjoying your first time on set?'

The man who had just spoken, Andrew Shaw, was one of the four names on Dougie Marshall's list. 'Yeah, I'm really enjoying it. It's a real eye-opener. I had no idea so many people were involved in filming for TV.'

'Few people do,' said Andrew. 'Unless they have watched the list of credits roll after the programme is over.'

Andrew was the key grip, responsible for the support systems for lights and cameras. Frank had seen him organising a crew to set up a lighting rig and get the cameras mounted on their cranes or dollies. It was an important job which involved liaising with the director, the producers, directors of photography and location scouts.

Frank wondered why he was on that list. He had a very good job indeed, so what would make him want to jeopardise it for something that could land him in jail? 'I was surprised at how much tech you use. I suppose it shouldn't these days,

83

but the special effects and backgrounds you guys produce is amazing!'

Andrew shrugged but looked pleased. 'It's the way forward, and it means no one gets hurt doing the stunts.'

Frank grinned. 'Bet the stunt men are a bit pissed off though.'

'Oh, we still use them,' said Andrew. 'We just combine them with digital images and effects.'

Frank had seen some of the actors working in front of the green screens and couldn't imagine acting in what was essentially a vacuum — no scenery, no props. He'd been told that CGI, computer-generated imaging, was extremely cost-effective — going on location often required permits, extra crew, and terrain that was often difficult of access. With computers, the actors could work against a backdrop of anywhere in the world.

'So, how long were you in the police force?' asked Andrew suddenly.

'Not nearly as long as I would have liked, as it turned out. Just sixteen years then I got retired out on ill health grounds.'

'Miss it, do you?' Andrew said.

'At first, every day,' Frank admitted. 'But not now. I'm enjoying doing all the things I missed out on while I was working.'

'Still, you must have a lot of contacts in the police. You're well in the know, aren't you? You've obviously kept up with changing procedures. Does the local constabulary help you out if you need it?'

Andrew sounded very interested in him. Far too interested as a matter of fact. 'No, I don't have a lot of contacts anymore. I've lost touch with the people I worked with, and I don't know the local lot at all. I use the internet to follow the changes in policing. Tell you what, I wouldn't like to be a copper these days, what with all the red tape and things they're not allowed to do. All that human rights crap means that everything is stacked in favour of the villains. Good luck to 'em is what I say. I'm well out of it.'

Andrew nodded. 'The pizzas here are bloody good, aren't they?'

Frank was relieved to have been let off the hook, he hadn't been fooled by Andrew's casual grilling. Hopefully, he'd just convinced him that their police consultant was no threat whatsoever.

Frank was just considering whether to get himself another slice of pizza when Dex Thompson approached.

'I need to talk to you,' he hissed, 'but not here. Car park at the Golden Dragon in twenty minutes. It's half a mile along the Saltern road.'

Frank knew it. It was a Chinese restaurant and takeaway, sitting, like some American highway motel, in the empty countryside.

'Okay,' he said, but Dex was already hurrying away.

Frank watched him go through narrowed eyes. Dex had never approached him before, other than a polite hello. It could be a trap, coming so soon after Andrew Shaw's questioning of him, but he didn't think so. Dex had seemed more nervous than anything, and if he had been planning to do Frank harm, he would not have chosen a restaurant car park to do it in.

Shelving the idea of more pizza, Frank made his way to his car. No one would miss him if he disappeared for a while.

Dex was waiting for him when he arrived at the Golden Dragon. Immediately, he beckoned to Frank to join him in his car. 'I don't have long. I think something has happened to a friend of mine. He's disappeared, and, well, you see, he's mixed up in something bad.' The words tumbled out. 'I can't go to the police, because . . . because . . .'

'Because whatever this bad thing is, you are involved too?'

Dex nodded. 'Yeah. I'm shot of it now but I can't afford to get into trouble with the police, I just can't.'

A friend. Frank thought for a moment. He hadn't seen Craig around today. Come to think of it, he hadn't been on set the day before either, not since the early morning. 'You mean Craig?'

Dex blinked. 'You know?'

'No, I just noticed he wasn't working today. Why do you think something's happened to him, Dex? And why are you telling me?'

Dex swallowed. 'I'm telling you because I think I can trust you. I reckon you ain't the star-struck old codger you make yourself out to be. I've seen the look in your eyes sometimes. You see more than you let on.'

Maybe I'm getting too old for this, Frank thought. *I'm clearly losing my edge, if this lad can see through me.* He made no comment. 'And Craig?'

Dex settled lower in his seat. 'Me and him, along with a couple of the other crew, were doing some, er, private work. Don't get me wrong, it's nothing too heavy, but it pays. Anyway, Craig reckons there is more going on than we were told, something big, and he wanted in. I'd had enough, and so I bailed out when I got the chance. So did Craig, but he missed the money, so he asked if he could come back in. As far as I know, he was told to sling his hook, then later they changed their minds and said he could.'

'What kind of "something big" are we talking about?' Frank asked.

'I have no sodding idea! I just know that Craig promised to ring me after he'd been given his instructions, but he didn't. And he never turned up for work this morning.'

'What does his wife say?' Frank asked.

'Joannie is visiting her mother, so she doesn't know.'

'Surely Craig would have rung her?'

'I don't know. Normally he would, but if he was doing a difficult shoot, he often left calling her till he'd finished. Signal's crap here anyway, so I doubt she was bothered.' Dex gave a little groan. 'I really didn't want to get involved, I've problems of my own. But I'm scared for him. He's so sodding bloody naïve!'

Frank thought fast. 'Look, can you at least tell me what this private work you were doing was?'

Before he could answer, Dex's phone rang.

Dex listened, and then almost threw him out of the car. 'Got to get back! My boss man is screaming for me. I'll talk to you again, but please help me! Help Craig. I don't know what to do.'

Frank was left standing alone in the car park watching the gravel fly up from Dex's wheels.

He climbed into his own car and sat for a moment, scratching his chin. This was the first evidence that there really was something illegal going on, but what?

* * *

'Skin-Sateen Deluxe.'

'Pardon?' Jackman stared at his phone.

'Apollo. Skin-Sateen Deluxe.'

'Rory, what the—?'

'Really, Jackman. Do try to keep up. I'm talking about body oil of course. Our latest resident here in the mortuary also has body oil on his skin, and to avoid confusing him with our original guest, I've chosen to call him Apollo, after the Greek god of the sun, and music, etc, etc. — Apollo. See? It's quite simple.'

'I see. So, was it the same oil?'

'No, no, quite different. Nevertheless, like Adonis, he was either anointed with it or had used it prior to his death, thereby providing a link for you, dear boy.'

So they were both smeared with oil. Didn't do much to help them identify them.

'The two men are very different in appearance. Adonis was tanned and muscular, with light brown hair. He was five foot eleven inches tall, and from his athletic appearance, clearly worked out regularly. Apollo, on the other hand, has light blond hair cut short at the sides and full on top, and very pale skin. He is also fit, but not like a body-builder. I would call him the aesthetic type, like one of those moody men's fashion models.' Rory sighed. 'No more of these gorgeous young men, please, dear Jackman. My heart weeps at the loss of such beauty.'

'Believe me, Rory,' said Jackman, 'I'd be most happy to oblige you. If only we could discover who they are and why they were killed. I can't think what's going on.'

'I'm still waiting on the toxicology results, which might possibly shine a light on some of it for you — drugs for a start. All I can tell you is that they were both taken by surprise, from behind, and death was sudden. It looks to me as if they were concentrating on something, someone crept up behind them, strangled Adonis and cut Apollo's throat. There are no other injuries, certainly no defensive ones.'

'Then there's the question of why they were disposed of in shallow water,' mused Jackman. 'There are any number of remote spots they could have been left in so the tide would carry them away.'

'I can only imagine that the killer, or killers, weren't particularly worried about the bodies being found, believing that any residual evidence left on them would be washed away by the water.'

'And does it?' asked Jackman.

'Depends on the type of water and the length of time they were immersed. In this case, they weren't in the water for nearly long enough to destroy all evidence.' He gave a little laugh. 'In fact, although water does cause DNA to be degraded, we have recovered exploitable DNA profiles after three months' submersion in five metres of river water. But then, of course, we are geniuses!'

Jackman chuckled. 'No doubt about it. So, we'll hang on for those tox reports, and thank you for the update.'

'The moment I have any news, you'll be hearing my dulcet tones again, dear boy, but for now, it's *au revoir* from this genius!'

No sooner had Rory rung off than Jackman heard the burner phone ring. He pulled open his desk drawer and answered. 'Frank?'

'Well, I'm one step forward, Jackman, but it's a work in progress. I'm just giving you an update on how things stand.'

Jackman listened carefully and his eyes lit up. 'So, this guy really knows something, even if it's not the big picture — excuse the pun.'

'Oh yes, and I swear that if he hadn't been called back into work, he'd have spilled the beans about what went on at the Schooner.' Frank sounded hyped up. 'I'll pin him down as soon as I can, and let you know at once. He's worried sick about his friend, by the way.'

'Listen, if this is serious, your new informant could be in danger,' Jackman said. 'He might have left the organisation, but what if they think he knows too much? He could go missing just like his mate.'

Frank grunted. 'That occurred to me too. Especially as he obviously knows who is involved, and possibly who is running the operation. I'll try my best to keep him in sight — as far as it's possible on something as frenetic as a film set. If I think he's in jeopardy, I'll pressgang him out of there. Wish me luck.'

Jackman didn't like the way this was going. 'Don't take this too far, will you, Frank? There's not enough evidence to charge in there just yet. This Craig guy could have just been occupied with something — even this illicit job he's supposed to be doing — and you'll find him back on set when you return. Or he might be playing away while the wife is with her mother. Who knows? Dex could be overreacting. Just remember, if things get any darker, you back out, got it? No messing, just up and away on your toes.'

'I don't have a death wish, Jackman. Don't worry, I'll do just that. I'll be in touch.'

Jackman went out into the CID room and looked around. Robbie was talking animatedly on the phone. When he saw Jackman, he ended the call. 'Got a lead, sir!'

'So have I,' said Jackman. 'You first. What have you got?'

'Les Smithson's daughter, sir. She's agreed to talk to us. She thinks she knows what's going on at the hotel.' Robbie looked excited. 'Les said he's convinced her that she should tell us, or she could find herself in trouble too. She's a good kid and would never have gone to work there if she'd known it was being used for illicit activities.'

'Then get yourself over there and talk to her. Take one of the others with you. Where's Max? Charlie?'

'They are tying up loose ends, boss, like you told them to. Apparently, they've hit a couple of hitches and are trying to sort them.' Robbie looked around. 'Gary's available, I'll grab him. Oh, what's your lead, sir?'

'Frank Rosen has been approached by someone who is prepared to blow the whistle on the illegal activities at the film set. It's looking a bit worrisome over there. I get the feeling it won't be long before we are paying an official visit.'

Robbie raised his eyebrows. 'Sounds promising. Anyway, we'll get over to Les Smithson's place before young Melissa gets cold feet and clams up.'

He yelled for Gary, leaving Jackman with the certainty that the ball was starting to roll. He wondered where it would finish up, and what it would gather as it gained momentum.

CHAPTER TEN

It had taken Sam Page some time to arrange a meeting with
Theo Carmichael, the clinical lead of Alistair Ashcroft's special prison unit.

He had gone to visit Theo at his home, and they were
now in Theo's study. 'Sorry to bring you here, Sam,' Theo
said. 'I would have loved you to see the unit — though I
imagine you might not have wanted to.'

'On the contrary,' said Sam. 'I'd have been very interested to see it, though it's true I wouldn't have wanted to
bump into one particular resident.'

Sam had expected Theodore Carmichael to be a man
much like him. He had read a number of his papers, which
indicated a man of wide experience. Thus he was surprised
to find the man sitting opposite him, in a matching wing-
backed chair, to be nothing like the stooped, grey-haired
figure of his imagination. For a start, he looked more like
an athlete than an erudite psychologist, despite the glasses.
He was around forty, shaven-headed and suntanned, with a
neatly trimmed beard and moustache. Sam imagined that he
spent his free time either hill-walking or sailing.

Carmichael smiled, displaying slightly uneven teeth.
'Have you come to warn me of the dangers of allowing a

devious manipulator, a killer with a talent for persuading others to do his will, the freedom a unit like ours allows?'

'Well, yes, in a nutshell,' Sam replied, trying to keep his voice even. 'You see, I have personal experience of Ashcroft. I am one of the few people who have been on the receiving end of his attentions and lived to tell the tale. That's why I considered it my duty to make you aware of the extent of his powers.' Sam's expression was almost pleading. 'I do not exaggerate when I say that I fear for every person who comes into contact with Ashcroft, staff or inmates. He is capable of persuading the strongest person to believe what he says and act accordingly. He is truly the most dangerous man you will ever meet.'

Theo returned Sam's intent gaze. 'I know. That's the very reason why he's here.'

Sam's astonishment must have registered in his expression, because Theo laughed out loud. 'Sorry, Sam. But in any case, I'm very glad you have come to see me.' He settled back in his chair. 'I've wanted to contact you for a while now, but when I heard you'd retired, and about the sad death of Dr Laura Archer, I put it off. The truth is, I'd very much value your help.' Theo paused. 'How about a cup of something? I'll get my housekeeper to make us a pot of coffee, or maybe you'd prefer tea? Then I'll explain.'

'Tea for me, please,' said Sam, glad of some refreshment.

Theo went out for a moment or two. On his return, he settled back in his chair and said, 'While we wait for our tea, suppose you give me your idea of the purpose of our special unit.'

Sam mentioned its similarity to the PIPE units in other maximum-security prisons, reiterating his opinion that it was not an appropriate environment for Alistair Ashcroft.

'Yes, that's the way most people see it. Whereas in reality, that's far from the truth.'

A middle-aged woman with a broad face and twinkling eyes whisked into the study, set down a tray on the table between them and promptly retreated, closing the door behind her.

Sam accepted his cup gratefully. 'I'm intrigued, Theo. If it's not a PIPE unit, what exactly do you do there?'

Theo smiled. 'The unit — which we call the Aegis Unit by the way — is my brainchild. I specialise in psychological manipulators — people who like to control others.'

'I thought your field was cognitive psychology?' commented Sam. 'I read a brilliant paper of yours on perception.'

Theo inclined his head. 'Thank you. Praise indeed, coming from you, Professor Page. Yes, it is, but my true passion is the controlling personality, the way of thinking of people like Alistair Ashcroft.' He looked straight at Sam. 'I built Aegis with the sole purpose of studying him. He did not "earn" his place there, he was brought. I had him transferred here to Cambridge, then simply allowed him to believe that his good conduct merited inclusion in a special unit designed to accommodate disabled prisoners. Aegis is about nothing but Ashcroft. The staff, who are carefully vetted, are all immune to his powers of persuasion. Every person who comes in contact with him, even for a few moments, is debriefed afterwards, and all, from counsellors to cleaners, are evaluated weekly by myself. Even the other "inmates", for want of a better term, are present only to give the appearance of an authentic PIPE unit and are very, very carefully selected. It's as you say, Sam, he's the most dangerous of manipulators, and I want to study him in order to better understand the minds of people such as he. It's one field that has received little attention so far, and I want to open a door on it and let some light in.'

Sam was completely taken aback but couldn't suppress a smile at the thought of Ashcroft being manipulated in his turn. But then, was he? Sam's fear of Ashcroft was such that he doubted Ashcroft had been fooled at all. The question remained — who was manipulating whom?

'I know what you're thinking, Sam.'

Did he? Could this erudite and well-respected academic possibly comprehend the enormity of what he was taking on?

'Before coming here and setting up Aegis, I was a clinical psychologist at Broadmoor,' Theo said, as if reading Sam's thoughts. 'So, you see, I am not without experience.'

Broadmoor was one of the three major high-security psychiatric hospitals in the country. Along with Rampton and Ashworth, it housed some of the most violent and disturbed men and women in the country.

Sam set down his cup. 'Theo, I have no doubt of your expertise, or your competence, but knowing what Ashcroft is capable of, can you really trust every single member of your staff not to fall prey to his wiles?'

Theo finished his own tea. 'This project was a long time in the making, Sam. We began training the staff at once. Everyone knows what he's capable of, and the atrocities he has committed. Some of them are wired. I, or my second in command, can hear any conversation as it takes place. Five of them — four men and one woman — have been coached to respond to him in such a way as to lead him to believe that they're falling under his spell.' He smiled at Sam. 'And it's working. We are beginning to discern a pattern in his approach to people and the way he communicates with them. Already, he's teaching us so much.'

Sam was still wary. 'Forgive me, Theo, if I seem stubborn. I'm still convinced that no one who comes into contact with him can remain unaffected by him.'

'But that's part of it, Sam, they *are* affected by him. So we study *them* and record what he said and how he acted to make them feel as they do. If anyone exhibits the least sign of distress or confusion, they are removed from duty for a while and counselled.' He looked directly into Sam's eyes. 'Their safety is paramount, I assure you.'

Despite Theo Carmichael's reassurances, Sam privately wondered how Ashcroft would respond if he became aware of the true purpose of the Aegis Unit. He seemed to recall that Aegis meant protection — a shield, or support. He suddenly felt very alone now there was no Laura to share his thoughts with. Alone and old, and wanting nothing more than to go home.

'I really don't think I can help you,' he said slowly. 'I admire your courage and your good intentions, Theo, but the subject of your Aegis Unit caused me more than mere physical harm. I'm not strong enough to bear a return of that nightmare into my life. I wish you well, and I can only advise you to exercise the greatest caution.'

Looking a little downcast, Theo said, 'It's me who should be apologising, throwing this at you without warning. It was thoughtless of me. I suppose I hoped it would be cathartic for you too, sharing your story.'

Sam shook his head sadly. 'Actually, it's been good for me. I don't think I realised just how badly the whole thing affected me. Now I know I'm just not ready to deal with that man again.' He stood up. 'Having said that, I'd still appreciate the occasional update, if you have the time.'

Theo accompanied him to the door. 'Of course, Sam, and if at a later date you feel stronger, maybe you'd be able to fill in some blanks for me?'

'Of course, but just not now.'

Still turning the visit over in his mind, Sam drove back slowly. The fact was he had not had the slightest idea that Ashcroft's re-emergence into his life would prove so traumatic. More than that, he could feel all the progress he had made following the death of Laura slipping away.

As he joined the A1M, he began to think of Jackman. Seeing him like this would do his friend no good whatsoever. He'd be home in just over an hour, traffic allowing, so he'd damned well better use the time to get a bloody grip. He turned on the radio and found a channel playing hits from the seventies. He tapped his finger on the wheel for a while, listening, until Gordon Lightfoot launched into, "If You Could Read My Mind."

Quickly, he turned the radio off.

* * *

At the end of the working day, John reported in to Hazel. As usual she was seated at the computer, typing furiously, but for once, she turned and smiled at him. 'Successful day?'

'Er, yes, I'd say so.' Somewhat taken aback, he handed her an SD card. 'I got everything you requested, and more. I'll type up my report tonight and email it over immediately.'

'Tomorrow would be fine, John. Why don't you relax tonight? You've been working non-stop for a week now. Grab a little down time.'

Now he was well confused. 'Nah, I'll get it done while it's all fresh in my head. I don't want to forget anything.'

'You forget nothing, John. You are fastidious with your reports, and your photography is second to none. I can see why Stephen rates you so highly.' She gave him another smile before turning back to her screen. 'By the way, I've just had a memo from Christos.'

Christos was Stephen's right-hand man, his link with the accountant and his business organiser on the outside. You never questioned what Christos said.

'He tells us that there are only three more files to update and we have a week to complete them in. Stephen will then hold a video meeting with us and we'll get our instructions for the implementation of Phase Two. Christos says we will be busier than we've ever been, but we will receive a commensurate remuneration.'

John smiled. That cruise was starting to look even more like a possibility. 'I'll be ready.'

'Me too,' Hazel breathed.

* * *

At first, Melissa was reluctant to talk to Robbie. He, too, had hesitated to meet her face to face. No doubt she would recognise him as the bloke from the Schooner who was two-timing his wife. He wouldn't be blowing his cover, Les Smithson had assured him. Melissa would keep her mouth shut.

Robbie was on the verge of throwing in the towel when Les turned on his daughter.

'Come on, Mel! This is serious, my girl. I've had enough of pussyfooting around you. You must help these people, and I want to know as well. If something bad is happening at that hotel, I don't want you within a mile of the place! If need be, I'll support you until you find another job, so just tell them everything you damned well know, and be sharp about it.'

Mel looked like she'd been slapped. Her dad obviously never spoke to her that way. 'I really don't know that much, honest. It's probably not even important.'

'Good lass!' Gary said kindly. 'You tell us what you can, and we'll decide whether it's important or not. Go ahead, starting from when you got an idea that something was going on.'

Melissa sighed. 'All right. It was months ago, I suppose. I mean, we all know about the gambling. That's what keeps the hotel going, along with the conferences and private meetings, but this was something else. Raymond Glazier, the owner, has got an eye for anything that makes a profit.' She shifted in her chair. 'There's these rooms, you see, that we're not allowed to go near. He has a couple of staff who just work in that part of the hotel, and they don't mix with the rest of us.'

'Have you ever been in them, Mel?' asked Robbie.

'Just once. Two of us, my friend Amy and me, thought we'd go and see what all the secrecy was about, you know, like a dare. We knew no one had been down that way all evening, so we pinched a pass key and sneaked in.' She bit her lip. 'They're just big posh bedrooms, nothing weird about them, except that they're much smarter than the ones in the rest of the hotel, and the beds are super-kings.' She grinned sheepishly. 'We were really disappointed. We were sure we'd find something dead shifty going on in there.'

Robbie wondered where this was going.

'Anyway, a few evenings later, we were filling up the mini-bars in the vacant rooms, ready for the next guests, when we saw a stream of people heading down the corridor towards those big rooms we looked in.' She looked from Gary to Robbie. 'They had a whole lot of stuff with them too — cases, bags and those tripod things like the one Dad has for his telescope.'

'It's an Astro-scope — I sky watch,' added Les.

Camera equipment! And it was heading into a lavish room with a super-king-size bed! Robbie glanced at Gary, who gave him a nod. So that's what the film crew were up to in their spare time — pornography. Robbie remembered having seen memos from DI Jenny Deane, whose team were handling a vice case. They suspected that hardcore Dutch videos were being made in the UK, then shipped to Holland for distribution. Up until now, they hadn't been making much headway. Robbie couldn't wait to tell her about this.

'That's not all,' continued Melissa. 'One of the rooms we were stocking the bar in backed onto one of those posh rooms. We put some glasses to the wall and listened to what was going on, and . . .' She trailed off, staring down at her feet.

'It's all right, lass,' said Gary gently. 'You just tell us what you heard. We won't be shocked, don't worry.'

'Well . . .' Mel faltered. 'To start with, there was a lot of chatter, you know, like people giving orders and that. Someone was talking about the lighting, I think, and someone said something like, "more revealing bra." Then it went very quiet, and we thought they must have left the room. We were just going to get back to work, but then . . .'

'It's okay, Mel,' her father said softly. 'Just tell them.'

'There were like groans and little screams, and then we realised what we were listening to. They were . . . well, you know. At it. So, we left, and that was that.'

Robbie smiled at her. 'You've been really helpful, Melissa. If you stay away from that area from now on, and if you see me at the hotel, don't let on that you know me, then neither you nor your friend will be in any trouble.' He turned to Les. 'She won't come to any harm working there, since most of the hotel's business is legal, or thereabouts. The worst that can happen is that if we make an arrest, she gets interviewed along with all the rest of the staff. It's up to you both.'

Melissa looked anxiously at her father. 'I like working there, Dad. I've got some good friends and the money isn't bad. I'd like to stay on, at least for a bit longer.'

'Personally, I think it's a good idea,' added Gary. 'If she suddenly decides to leave, well . . .'

'I agree, keep things as they are.' said Robbie, 'but if you do notice anything particularly suspicious, ring us, okay?'

Reluctantly, Les agreed to let her stay. 'Look out for her when you're there, won't you, DC Melton?'

'You can be sure of that.'

Back in the car, Gary put his foot down. 'The boss'll still be at the station. I wonder what his reaction will be when he hears what we have to say.'

'He'll be dead chuffed, and if Frank's little songbird tells him who is behind it — bingo! We'll have a full house in the custody suite, and then the boss will be able to throw everything we have at the Adonis killings.'

CHAPTER ELEVEN

In the hope that the gaffer had believed his story about an urgent errand, Dex buckled down and put in several hours' hard graft. Now they were winding up for the evening, and all his anxiety about Craig's safety came crowding back into his mind.

As he was on his way to the catering area, a stranger approached him. Despite the number of people surrounding them, Dex glanced around involuntarily, looking for a means of escape.

'You Dex?' the man asked.

He nodded.

The man lowered his voice to a whisper. 'Check your texts. There's one from Craig. It'll explain everything.'

With a hasty squeeze of Dex's shoulder, the man proceeded in the direction of Craig's mobile home.

Dex pulled his phone from his pocket and read:

Dex, mate! Sorry about this, but I've got to get out, right now. I've bit off more than I can chew. Thank God Joannie is with her mum, so I can pick her up and we can be gone by morning. This shit is serious all right. That bloke who spoke to you is an old mate. He'll be collecting my caravan for me.

I told him to show himself to you so you didn't think it was being nicked. Don't mention this to anyone! Especially don't blab about the other work we did at the Schooner, and never say who we were working for. Keep your head down and your mouth shut and you'll be okay. I'll miss you, mate, but don't try to find me, ever. Good luck.

Dex read it again, then, food forgotten, he walked slowly over to where Craig's caravan was parked. As Craig had said, the man was making it ready for the road.

He watched from a distance, wondering what the hell he should do. He'd already said far too much to that old retired copper. Dex took a deep breath and hurried off to look for Frank Rosen. He needed to defuse the situation he'd caused, and fast.

He asked around and was told Frank had been seen heading for the car park. Dex sprinted across, only to see the car heading for the exit. He threw himself in front of it.

Frank jammed on the brakes. 'Dex! What are you doing? I could have killed you!'

Dex ran around the car and, panting, got into the passenger seat.

'Hang on,' Frank said. 'I'm just moving to a spot closer to the exit.'

'Forget parking. Just drive. Take me somewhere we can talk in private.'

Without a word, Frank drove away, off the main road and along a winding lane between the fields, towards a wood.

'There's a place up here where we can get a decent cuppa and a bacon sarnie, and almost nobody knows about it.'

A few moments later they were parking in front of a big wooden chalet on the edge of the wood. A rough timber sign over the door read, 'Woody's Place.'

'It belongs to a friend of a friend of mine,' Frank continued, 'and for the time being, it's my home. There's a cluster of log cabins further into the wood, and I've rented one while I'm working for the film company. They're pretty basic, but

Woody will do all-day breakfasts, and he serves hot drinks and such-like right up to ten at night.'

Frank led the way inside, greeting the man behind the serving counter with a friendly smile. 'Two large teas and two of your bacon butties, please, Woody.'

Woody gave them a broad smile. 'Coming right up, Frank. I got some lovely fresh rashers just crying out to be eaten.'

They sat at a distance from the counter and waited for their tea. As soon as it arrived, Frank said, 'What's happened, son? Why are you so scared?'

Frank's fatherly tone made Dex feel like crying, just like a little boy. He had approached Frank with the idea of simply telling him that it had all been a mistake, Craig had been moved to another location and hadn't had time to get in touch. Now, under Frank's curious gaze, he realised the enormity of the situation. He was in real danger. What if Lance and the others suspected that Craig had told him what his new job entailed? Would they let him just walk away?

'Come on, son. You are talking to the one person who can help you. Just give it to me straight.'

So he did. Once he started talking, the relief at being able to unburden himself took him over. He told the old copper everything, even showed him Craig's text. He retained just enough sense not to mention names.

While Frank was reading the text, their food arrived, and they waited until Woody had finished serving.

'I had a call just before you tried to commit hara-kiri in front of my car, telling me what was going on at the Schooner. Now,' he tapped at Dex's phone, 'normally, I'd advise you to do what your mate Craig has done, and get away smartish. You're right, this thing stinks, and to be honest, I think you probably are in some danger. However, I'm going to put another suggestion to you.'

Dex put down his sandwich, listening.

'Do you have a lot of precious things in your motorhome?'

Dex shrugged. 'Not really. I don't bring much on location with me, just my laptop, some paperwork, clothes and that. Why?'

'The sudden disappearance of Craig's big motorhome is going to make waves. If you then slope off . . . well. Get the picture? You really do not need that kind of attention. So. Know what I think? I think I should take you back to the site, we collect whatever you can't do without, and you come back here with me. No one knows I'm here; they believe I lodge in the town You'll be safe while we work out what to do.' Frank put his cup down and looked Dex in the eye. 'My suggestion is that you cut your losses and turn police informant.'

Dex started. 'I can't possibly do that!' He returned Frank's gaze. 'This is a stitch up, isn't it? Are you working with the police? Is that it?'

Frank shook his head. 'Relax, lad. I just think you could save yourself a lot of grief if you go voluntarily to the police. They'll appreciate your help. A deal can still be made, even in this day and age. Some detectives still use their discretion.' He leaned forward. 'I'm not sure you realise how serious things are, lad.'

But Dex realised all right. Only too well.

'I'll tell you another thing, Dexter. I'm pretty sure Craig didn't write that text — or if he did, he was forced to. That guy who drove off in Craig's motorhome was one of the villains, and all that garbage about running away with Joannie is a crock of shit. Craig's in big trouble, Dex. Stick around here much longer and you'll be in it too — if you aren't already.'

Dex looked down at his half-eaten sandwich, suddenly nauseated. How the hell had he got himself into such a mess? Here he was, about to make a brand-new start, and this had happened. What was there left for him? One thing remained, his decision to live his life on the right side of the law. 'Will you help me? If I talk to the police, will you be there with me?'

'Of course, I will, lad. More than that, I'll make sure you get to see the fairest and most humane policeman on the force.'

103

Again, his words brought tears to Dex's eyes. 'I never meant to get into all this trouble. I've never done anything illegal before. I just had these terrible debts and I didn't know what else to do.'

'Well, my friend Jackman will see you right. He'll see you're not some career criminal, but just an ordinary guy who's got himself in a bit too deep.' He smiled. 'As I do, Dex. Do the right thing, yeah?'

Dex took a deep breath. 'Okay. I'm ready. Take me to this friend of yours and let's see what he has to say. What have I got to lose?'

* * *

That evening, Jackman returned home buoyed up by the imminent resolution of the film crew case. But on seeing the dejected expression on Sam's face, his good mood evaporated.

They sat down to one of Hetty Maynard's restorative beef stews, and Sam spoke of his reaction to his conversation with Theo Carmichael, which had left him in such distress.

'I'm so very sorry, Jackman. I feel I've let you down,' he said. 'I expected more of myself, and I never imagined that I'd feel so . . . so weak. Theo believes he is totally in control of his prize guineapig and that his staff are too, but what do they really know of Ashcroft?'

Jackman shook his head. 'I agree, Sam. They are playing a dangerous game if they think they can fool Ashcroft for long — if indeed they are fooling him at all. Can you imagine his satisfaction at having an entire unit, along with its staff, devoted solely to him? It doesn't bear thinking about. Sam, don't beat yourself up over this. You're not weak. Think of what you went through at that evil man's hands, followed by the loss of Laura. Anyone would feel the same.'

Sam conceded that it had been a lot to take on board. He had gone to see Theo in the belief that he'd be asked his advice on the establishment of something like a PIPE unit. He'd been ready to give Theo a few pointers about

Ashcroft, warn him of how dangerous the man could be and hear how he was doing. Instead, he had been told that this new unit had been established with the sole aim of carrying out research into how Ashcroft's brain worked. Doing a case study was one thing, but pouring so much effort and money into one individual was unprecedented.

Sam laid down his fork. 'You know what. I think Ashcroft has fully adapted to a life in prison. I don't think he sees it as a place of incarceration at all. It's his castle, his stronghold, and a safe place in which to practise his evil stratagems. I think he bloody loves it in there.'

'I think you're right,' Jackman said after a pause. 'And think of the fun he'll have, playing with top-rate counsellors and therapists who hang on his every word. He'll be in seventh heaven.'

They sat for a while in silence, pondering this unit and how it could have come into being. Then Jackman's mobile rang.

Frank Rosen.

'Listen up, old mate,' came the man's voice, 'I've taken it upon myself to get my informant out tonight. You know where I'm staying, don't you? Can you be there in, say, three-quarters of an hour?'

Jackman didn't hesitate. 'I'll be there. Do you need any help?'

'No time, we've needed to act fast. He's grabbing a few personal things as I speak, and then we'll be off.'

'Are you sure no one else knows where you are staying?'

'I've led everyone to believe that I'm lodging in town. Now, listen. This guy — his name is Dexter Thompson, by the way — knows a lot. Not everything, but plenty to be getting on with. More than enough to put him in danger. Gotta go. See you soon.'

Sam smiled, having heard the conversation. 'Things really are slotting into place for you, aren't they?'

Jackman shrugged. He felt uneasy. 'I don't like the idea of Frank playing Lone Ranger out there on his own. He was a damned good copper, but he could be up against an organised criminal gang. It's certainly up to more than producing a few blue movies.' He looked at Sam. 'Come with me. It's not far and I'd value your opinion on this Dexter fella. You up for it?'

Jackman's first thought had been to ring Marie. Then he remembered that she had a life now, outside the force, and wouldn't always be available at the drop of a hat. It hurt, but he was happy for her. He knew, too, that if he really needed her, she would be there. It was up to him to loosen the ties that bound them.

Suddenly, Jackman had never felt so lonely.

* * *

Side by side on the sofa, Marie and Ralph gazed around her lounge. 'Not much longer before we're arranging the furniture in our new home.' She nudged Ralph. 'I can hardly wait.'

'You don't think you'll miss this place?'

'Nope.' She smiled. 'It's a step forward. Like my mum said, treat every new situation as an adventure.'

'Well, it's that all right,' Ralph said. 'And I certainly won't miss my house. You know, I've never thought of it as home, it's never been more than somewhere to eat and sleep and store my belongings.'

Marie, on the other hand, had an attachment to this little house. She and Bill had made a home here, and it held all her memories of their time together. But she couldn't live in the past. 'It's going to be fun sorting out two lots of furniture and belongings.'

'I've a feeling that most of mine will be sent to the charity shop.' Ralph chuckled. 'It's hardly worth a place on the *Antiques Roadshow*.'

'We may have to buy some new things — things that belong to the both of us.'

Having spent so long as independent, career-driven coppers, they found themselves facing a new way of life. Just

106

to think of an 'us' after all these years made Maria tingle with anticipation. Yet she couldn't quite abandon herself to the thrill. She could never quite forget Jackman's sadness. It hung like a dark cloud at the back of her mind, casting a shadow over her bliss.

After a while, inevitably, their conversation returned to the job.

'So, your mysterious body wasn't a police matter at all then,' Marie said. 'Unlike ours.'

'Accidental death. Very sad but nothing suspicious. We were stood down very quickly.'

'Well, *we* have another beautiful young man, dead in the water, so to speak.' Marie grimaced. 'Neither of them has been identified, and I have a feeling that for once, the forensics won't be any help.' She told him about the body oil on both bodies. 'God, Ralph, I hope we're not looking at a serial killer.'

'Peculiar,' he mused. 'Maybe they were stripped to prevent anyone identifying them, and the oil is just a red herring?'

'Who knows?' Marie said. 'We've checked every modelling agency in the book. We've even resorted to Kissogram, the escort agencies and actors for adverts. Nothing.'

'What if they are regular guys who take care of their bodies? If I was you, I'd hit the gym clubs,' suggested Ralph. 'They have plenty of clients obsessed with their looks and physique.'

She nodded thoughtfully. 'You could be right. Perhaps they were just body conscious. That looks like someone's job for tomorrow. Thank you, Ralph. I'll enjoy checking out all those rippling muscles.'

'I knew I should have kept my mouth shut.'

Marie laughed and gave him a kiss. 'Don't worry. I'll send Kevin Stoner. He'll leap at the chance.'

Laughing happily, the two of them prepared for bed.

CHAPTER TWELVE

Theo Carmichael was busy on his laptop. Every so often he would stop to think, gazing up at the painting that hung above his desk. It was a gift from his father, the man who had inspired him to take up psychology.

Heavily influenced by Hieronymus Bosch, the painting depicted a human head, the open cranium a scene of horror and depravity. The head, with its expression of anguish, had been set against the background of a beautiful sunlit landscape, a peaceful idyll where birds soared in the blue sky, above green fields and a stream whose rippled surface sparkled like a jewel. To Theo's mind the painting was a metaphor for his profession. With skilled and careful treatment, the demons crowding the damaged mind are released and the sufferer restored to a place of peace and beauty.

Theo was well aware that Ashcroft was beyond rehabilitation, but he believed in studying him, they might be able to help others in the future. He had to understand what made Ashcroft different so different from other insecure, abused little boys, leading him along a path to arch manipulator and ruthless killer.

He looked again at today's reports, especially the one from Patrick Galway. Apart from Dr Casey Naylor, Theo's right-hand woman, Patrick was his greatest hope. Theo seemed to sense that Ashcroft harboured a secret respect for the prison chaplain.

According to his memo, Patrick had sensed a shift in Ashcroft's attitude towards him, a sort of changing up in the gears of their engagement:

> *His responses to questions are more calculated, as if he is giving them a great deal of thought. He seems to be wanting me to believe that I am succeeding in coaxing more out of him than I am. He is feeding me with small titbits, flashes of insight into the real Ashcroft. What I can't understand is whether he is being sincere. Can he really want me to see him not just as a killer, but as a human being, capable of feeling joy, anger, pain? I could be wrong, but I think he might consider me a challenge worthy of his efforts. I'll be sending you a full report tomorrow. I'll be in early, by the way, and would be glad to know your thoughts.*

Theo made a note to see Galway as soon as he arrived the following morning. It was getting late, and tomorrow he intended to take some time out to walk in the Peak District. He needed to breathe fresh air, stride alongside a rushing river, climb to where he could see for miles in every direction. Theo understood the danger of living too long with damaged minds. You needed perspective, to look upon the world from a height and remind yourself that the world could be a beautiful place.

He glanced up at the painting again, and its backdrop of clear sky and green fields. Unless he escaped from time to time, he could never hope to remain one step ahead of Alistair Ashcroft.

* * *

Not too far away, Alistair Ashcroft lay on his bed and sighed contentedly. Both here and in the world out there, matters were proceeding just as he wanted. He was in control.

His thoughts wandered to Hazel and John. He had made a good choice in those two. Apart from Christos, they were his most valued operators. It was rare to find that amount of dedication combined with such cold-blooded focus. He smiled to himself. Ashcroft was no fool, he knew it was the money that drove John. As long as the money was available, John was his. As for Hazel . . . poor Hazel. She would do anything he asked of her, with or without pay, simply out of love for him.

People were so simple to deal with. All you had to do was find what drove them and use it to your advantage.

This brought him to thoughts of a fellow inmate. Jeremy Shaler was serving a life sentence for murdering his brother. There was no doubt about Shaler's guilt, he freely admitted to doing it. However, unlike the other prisoners, Shaler didn't boast about it, nor did he try to justify his act. He wasn't aggressive and neither did he show any remorse. He seemed cold, detached, and Ashcroft found this interesting. He wondered why Shaler had been given a place in this special unit. He must have expressed a wish to work with the rehabilitation team, which entailed deep and extensive psychoanalysis. How had Shaler coped with it? Could Shaler be playing the staff as he was?

He took his nightly painkillers and waited for them to kick in. Maybe he should get to know Shaler better. It would be easy to engage him in conversation during the 'socially creative' sessions that amused him so much. 'Enrichment activities.' Jesus.

He yawned. Anyway, Shaler would have to wait. He had much bigger fish to fry. He closed his eyes and gave himself up to his plans for Phase Two — and the chaos it would unleash.

* * *

Jackman and Sam had started to get anxious. They stood at the door to the log cabin, which was in darkness, and wondered what had happened to Frank. Just as Jackman was fearing the worst, Sam touched his arm.

'Look! Headlights, coming in through the gates.'

A few moments later, Frank's old Triumph Vitesse drew up next to Jackman's 4x4. Two men jumped out.

'Let's get inside,' Frank said in an urgent whisper. 'There's not many people here, but I don't want to risk this lad being spotted.' He unlocked the door and pushed Dexter in through it.

Jackman looked around. It was certainly no palace. It had a slightly musty smell to it, like damp wood, and it reminded Jackman of an old caravan one of his mother's visiting horse trainers used to live in.

'Sorry, folks,' Frank said, 'it's not the Ritz, but it's also not well known, so it's the perfect place for Dexter to lie low in until we decide what to do.' The young man had seated himself on the tatty couch, hunched forward, his arms around himself as if to ward off the cold.

'It's okay, Dex,' said Frank kindly. 'This is the man I told you about, my friend, DI Jackman. You can trust him.'

'And this is Professor Sam Page,' added Jackman to Dex. 'Now, can you tell us what's happened.'

'*After* I get him a drink,' said Frank firmly, retrieving a half bottle of whisky from one of the cupboards. 'I'm not offering it around, as you guys are driving and I don't touch the stuff.' He chuckled. 'I've been washing my mouth with it to give the impression that I like a tipple. Makes me look more "authentic", if you know what I mean.'

'And it works,' muttered Dex, looking up. 'Everyone reckons you're a right old duffer. I never fell for it though.'

Frank passed him a small glass of Scotch. Dex took a gulp, winced, and shut his eyes. 'This is one fucking awful mess.'

'You can say that again,' Frank said. 'But Jackman will help you.'

'I reckon it's too late to help Craig though.'

Frank sat at the other end of the couch, while Sam and Jackman took the two armchairs. 'We don't know that,

Dexter,' Frank said, reassuringly. 'Just talk to Jackman, and he'll do his best to find your friend.'

Dex took a deep breath. 'All right. I'm a gambler, you see. That's what brought me to this. I had debts and I needed money.'

Jackman wondered how many times he'd heard someone say that. He knew just what the next line would be: *So I got offered a job, cash in hand, no questions asked.* The slippery slope into crime.

'Then one of the crew asked if I might like to take on a private job. Good money, he said, if I did what I was told and kept my mouth shut.' He shrugged. 'It seemed like the answer to a prayer. Plus, I was told that if I was good at it, there'd be more work if I wanted it.' He looked up at Jackman. 'I'd never stepped out of line before, DI Jackman, and there didn't seem much harm in what I was doing.'

'Which was?' asked Jackman, even though he knew the answer.

'Filming blue movies. Clever stuff though — artistic, not just your seedy porn. Most of it was shot at a hotel, a place where if you pay the right money, they don't ask questions.'

'Yeah, the Schooner's Mate,' added Frank.

'Can you tell us what you mean by "clever stuff," Dexter?' asked Sam. 'Forgive a simple-minded old man, but I would have thought it was pretty straightforward — sexually explicit activities of, er, various kinds?'

'Well, you see, we used CGI to enhance it. We placed the couple in all sorts of fabulous settings. Not only that, we changed a few things, "enhanced" them, if you catch my drift. The results in terms of cinematography were extraordinarily good. I might say we took blue movies to another level.'

Jackman desperately wanted to ask Dexter for names but he held back. Dexter was still nervous, and he didn't want to push him.

'Well,' Dexter continued, 'I tried to look at it that way, but really I was sickened. How could I have let myself stoop so low? Sounds daft but I felt like I'd sold my soul to the devil, just to pay off my sodding debts.' His leg jiggled, and one foot tapped an agitated tattoo on the wooden floor.

Jackman glanced at Sam, who said, 'Keep calm, lad, you're out of it now. Tell you what, when everything's all sorted out, maybe I can help you with kicking the gambling habit? I'm a psychologist and retired, and I'd like to help.'

Dexter gave Sam a nervous smile. 'I think I can do it myself. I'm so scared about what's going on and what has happened to my friend that I don't think I'll ever go near a bookie again. But thank you. I appreciate your kindness, and if I start to backslide . . .?'

'I'll give you my number. Now, give us the rest of your story.'

Dexter finished the last of the whisky and gathered himself. 'We did maybe six sessions. I reckoned that when I'd done number six, I'd have cleared my debts, so I planned to take off. I told Craig I wanted out, and he said he'd do the same. Then he got the idea that something bigger and far more lucrative was in the offing, but we were being cut out of it. His wife is a big spender, you see. She was draining him and he needed cash badly. We were told there was some problem in Holland — they sent the films there for distribution — and the whole thing was closing down.' Dex looked from Sam to Jackman. 'It was just what I wanted. It meant I could get out without having to do a runner. Craig started on about it being a cover-up, and that they just wanted him and me out while they got on with the bigger stuff.'

'Have you any idea what this "bigger stuff" is?' asked Jackman.

'Oh God! Not a clue. Could be drugs, or maybe, well . . .' Dex grimaced. 'I don't know, but I wondered whether immigrants — women — were being groomed and used in less classy films than the ones we were making.'

Jackman nodded. That was a distinct possibility. These days you could find a market for anything.

'Anyway, bloody stupid Craig must have told the others what he thought, because he slipped me this note.' Dexter reached into a pocket of his rucksack and took out a crumpled piece of paper.

Jackman read it, and frowned. 'So, this is proof that something else was going on?'

'Yeah. And now he's missing.' Dexter started to nibble furiously at a thumb nail, and still his foot tapped non-stop on the floor.

'Show Jackman the text message you received, purportedly from Craig,' Frank said.

Dex found the message and handed the phone to Jackman. 'Frank thinks it wasn't Craig that wrote it, or if it was, they forced him to send it.'

Jackman read the message. Frank was probably right, but there was no way of knowing for certain. 'Do you know where Joannie is, Dex?'

He shook his head. 'Craig said Joannie was happy to be in this area filming, because her mum lives somewhere near Chapel St Leonards, which isn't too far away, but that's all I know. I don't even know her surname, I'm afraid.'

'Doesn't matter. If we have Craig's full name, we can check his wife's maiden name.' He looked straight at Dex. 'Now, I'm sorry but I have to ask this. I need the names of everyone involved in that illegal filming.'

Dex dropped the glass and started to shiver uncontrollably.

For a brief moment no one moved or spoke, then Sam said, 'It's shock. Quick, get something to wrap round him.'

Frank ran into the bedroom and snatched a blanket from his bed. He wrapped it around Dex and held him tightly. 'It's okay, lad, take it easy.'

When the shaking didn't stop, Jackman said to Frank in a low voice, 'You said he'd had a bit of a scare before you left. What was it?'

Frank nodded at the terrified man, obviously reluctant to speak in front of him. Jackman indicated for Sam to sit with Dex, while he and Frank went outside.

'Well, when we got back, we saw some people hanging around by Dex's caravan. We had to wait ages for them to go.

Finally, Dex went inside and got some things together, while I kept watch outside and rang you. Just as we were leaving, I saw this under one of his windscreen wipers.' He pulled a folded piece of paper from his trouser pocket. 'Don't worry, I used gloves. I still keep them on me. Old habits and all that.'

Jackman took a nitrile glove from his own pocket and opened the note:

> *You were paid to keep your mouth shut. Big mistake to open it. So watch your back, Dexter, you're next.*

Before Jackman could comment, they heard Sam calling them urgently. They hurried back inside and found that Dex was struggling to breathe.

'Panic attack,' said Sam. 'Have you got a paper bag anywhere, Frank? It doesn't work for everyone but breathing into one can control hyperventilation.'

While Frank hunted for a bag, Sam spoke quietly to Dex, telling him not to be afraid, it would pass quickly.

As no paper bag came to hand, Sam continued to calm him. It took about ten minutes for Dex's breathing to slow to something approaching normal, but it was clear there would be no more questions tonight.

Jackman took Frank aside. 'I'm making this official now, Frank, which means I want you out of there. Heaven knows what's going on, but whatever it is, it's far too dangerous for you to remain.'

'No, Jackman. Think about it. If you go in all guns blazing, without names or any shred of evidence, they'll shut down the operation, and that will be that. I'm certain no one saw me with Dex, up to now we've done nothing but greet each other in passing. You heard him: they think I'm an old duffer, good at clapping on the handcuffs and quoting the rule book, and revelling in being part of a film set. Leave me there, Jackman. You need me to feed you information. By all means check on Joannie and Craig but don't pull me out, or you'll cut off your only source.'

If only Marie had been here. One tiny nod from her would have reassured him that he was doing the right thing. Jackman told himself to get a grip. He was big and ugly enough to make his own bloody decisions. He sighed. 'Okay, Frank. This is against my better judgement, but you may stay. Only until I have those names, mind. Then we hit them hard. Now, let's see how this poor guy is getting on in there.'

Sam looked worried. He drew Jackman aside. 'I suspect there's something deeper going on here, Jackman. Possibly he already has existing anxiety issues and this situation has pushed him too far. His reaction is way over the top. I'm going to suggest we take him back with us to Mill Corner. He can stay in my guest bedroom where I can keep a close eye on him. If we ask him any more questions now, I can see him clamming up completely. If he's with me, I can monitor him and judge when it's safe to push for those names again. That okay?'

Jackman agreed. If Frank went back on set the next day, Dex would be alone here, he'd most likely take off and they'd never see him again. Not only would they not get those valuable names but Dex could also be in serious danger, and clearly a night in the custody suite would do him no good at all.

He put Sam's suggestion to Frank, who readily agreed. 'I can't lock the poor sod in when I go off tomorrow morning, so if you're okay with it, it sounds like the best solution.'

Soon, the three of them were speeding towards Cartoft Village. With every mile they covered, Jackman grew ever more convinced that he had made a mistake in leaving Frank on the set. But Dex, at least, was safe. He was their golden goose — if they could just calm him down enough to cough up those bloody names!

CHAPTER THIRTEEN

Lance was convinced that his side of the operation was about as watertight as it could possibly be. He'd been in this game for almost a decade now without being caught. There had been a few close shaves over the years, but he had always managed to get himself and the others out in time. He was beginning to wonder at the depravity of the human race. Not that he cared, people might sink as low as they liked as far as he was concerned. According to his mother, he was lacking some vital part of his make-up. She'd never said what it was, but Lance knew all right. A lack of compassion had proved to be most useful in his line of business.

He was in a well-paid job in the film industry when he learned about the law of supply and demand. It came to him like a revelation. If supply increases and demand stays the same, prices will fall. If supply remains constant and demand decreases, prices will fall. If supply decreases and demand stays the same, prices will rise. Finally, if supply remains constant and demand increases, prices will rise.

Lance began to search out a commodity in very short supply but for which there was a big demand. Sent to Holland on location, he found that very thing. It was fast making him a rich man.

He had started small, with just two carefully chosen helpers. He hadn't expected much from it, but to his surprise, good old demand was high. His commodity was not easy to come by, and he made far more money than he had anticipated. His distributor kept asking for more and more, so Lance decided to expand his operation. He continued in this vein until, on a further trip to Holland, he was approached by a representative of an underground organisation operating in the UK and Holland. In their second meeting this representative had offered him what he referred to as 'a rare opportunity for the right sort of man'.

Lance had proven himself to be the right sort of man time and time again. Twelve months down the line, he was approached — this time in England — with the suggestion of a slightly different kind of undertaking. Lance accepted without demur, thus securing his future. He decided to give himself two further years, after which he would retire. Subsequently, demand escalated, providing him with more money than he had ever in his wildest dreams imagined making. So he extended his time frame. Who wouldn't? He had become an integral part of a very profitable scheme that used his undisputed professional talent, and that one little gap in his genetic make-up, to supply a unique commodity, one that the niche market was willing to pay a great deal of money to acquire.

Mulling this over, Lance swirled the brandy in the balloon glass he was holding and came to a decision. This latest operation would be the last. There had been too many close calls recently, and he had been forced to make alterations to his schedule once too often. He had always prided himself on his careful selection of trustworthy assistants, but for the first time ever, he had made two errors of judgement. Twice in the last six months he'd had to call in the specialised clean-up team that the organisation sometimes employed. This was unacceptable as far as he was concerned. The larger organisation that he was part of would soon be casting a critical eye.

As always when he was on location, he had checked into a hotel. He set down his glass and began to make himself ready to leave his room on this, his final job, which, barring unforeseen complications, would be completed the following night. It was a carefully orchestrated affair, to be carried out in combination with two other sections of the larger group. On completion, the normal practice was to lay low for a month and wait for their pay, before embarking on another job. But there would be no other job for him. The moment his money landed in his account, he'd be off. He had already worked out his escape plan — two phone calls and a fast car, and Lance Newport would be history.

He locked his door and hurried out to the car park. The venue was about a twenty-minute drive away, and not easy to find. He had chosen it for that very reason. Foxdown Lodge, as it was called, was a large rambling country house with numerous outbuildings. The owners were away at their Spanish villa, so Lance's bogus film company had rented it out for the purpose of shooting some interior footage for a supposed episode of a well-known sit-com.

He arrived to find two vehicles already there, and he could see headlights weaving their way through the fen lanes below. Lance smiled to himself. This, his final shoot, involved satisfying several very specific requests that the client had made. Just what Lance would have wished for his final production.

* * *

Craig had never felt so nervous. He had taken the job in the belief that he would be called upon to do as he had on previous occasions — get a call, put the stuff in the car and drive to the venue. Instead, he had been told to pack an overnight bag and his laptop, and someone would come to collect him. At the appointed time, a stony-faced man had picked him up and driven him to a small house in a nearby village, where he was told to wait. It might happen that night, or it might not.

Lance had duly contacted him but the setup at the venue made him feel no easier. The crew gathered in front

of Foxdown Lodge — the old house they were to film in —
were all strangers to him. He was given no shooting schedule
and would be using equipment that wasn't his own.

Craig shifted from foot to foot as he waited for instructions. Since he knew none of this new crew, he couldn't ask
what they were to film. It seemed that everyone else knew the
score, and he didn't like to show his ignorance. Craig looked
across at the truck full of equipment and a car with what
were obviously the actors sitting inside. He also noticed two
4x4s with blacked-out windows parked a little further away.

Finally, Lance approached him, looking anxious. 'Sorry
for the delay, Craig, my boy. There's been a hitch. We can't
afford not to continue the shoot — we're on a deadline — so
I don't know quite what to do.'

Craig was taken aback. He had never seen Lance anything but completely in control. Seeing his desperately needed
money slip out of his grasp, he said, 'Can I help at all?'

'Nah. Well, there is something you could do but — no,
it's too much to ask. Fucking actors. Think they can just
decide not to turn up when everything's ready to roll. Well,
he's lost a fortune, that's all I can say. And he's not even one
of the main characters.'

'What is his role?' Craig asked slowly.

'He's not one of the main performers, but he's essential
to the story.' He looked at Craig. 'It's all right, I'm not going
to ask you to strip off and get stuck in — don't think your
Joannie would be too happy with that, Craig, lad.'

Craig swallowed hard. Just what kind of money did this
actor get? 'What does this guy actually do?'

'You saying you'd really do it? I mean, you know what
these movies are about, you've filmed enough of them.' Lance
took a step back. 'You're quite a fit bloke, aren't you? I'd never
really noticed before. Got any nasty scars or other blemishes?'

'No, and I look after myself.' Jesus, was he really going
to do this?

'What about Joannie?'

'She won't know, will she?'

'Well, you'll be wearing a mask anyway.' Lance beamed at him. 'And have you seen the women we've got tonight? Mwah.' He blew a kiss. 'You know, Craig, I had my doubts about you. To be honest, I almost cut you out, but, shit, I'm glad I didn't. I owe you one, mate!' He turned away. 'Guys! Show's back on the road!'

* * *

Sam settled Dex in his spare room, and he and Jackman sat with him for a while. The panic attack had been real — Sam had seen enough faked ones to know the difference. Dexter was terrified for his life. Even though he knew almost nothing about the illegal operation he had been part of, he still believed it to be very, very dangerous. As had Dougie the Dreamer. That man had run for his life on nothing but a hunch.

Dex was looking exhausted, so they left him and went into Sam's living room.

'Will you be okay?' asked Jackman. 'He's still very disturbed, isn't he?'

'He knows he's safe, so I'm thinking he will sleep. I'm a light sleeper these days, Jackman. If he gets up, I'll hear him, and if I'm concerned, I'll ring you.'

Jackman yawned. 'Maybe we should get some shuteye. I have to be up at the crack of dawn, it's going to be a long day tomorrow what with these two murders.'

Sam commiserated, 'And this is the last thing you need. Anyway, I'll do my best to get him to open up over breakfast. I know how important those names are to you and, hopefully, by tomorrow he will have recovered enough to talk.'

'I really appreciate your help, Sam. This thing with the film shoot is beginning to bug me.'

After Jackman had left, Sam locked the door and pocketed the key. *Don't want to lose him, do we, not now we have him.*

121

CHAPTER FOURTEEN

John arrived at their miserable headquarters at just before seven thirty. Still, Hazel had beaten him to it. There was already an empty mug beside her work station, in her tray a pile of printouts that had not been there the night before.

'I got your report, John,' she said brightly. 'Excellent, as ever. Everything's been dealt with, and we've already received today's instruction.'

For once she turned around to look at him. 'You okay? You looked tired last night.'

He smiled. 'I'm fine, thank you. Raring to go, as always.'

She stared hard at him. 'Don't burn out, John.'

Was she concerned for him? Or was it fear that he might jeopardise the operation. 'I assure you that's not going to happen.'

She gave a little shrug. 'You shoulder some pretty heavy responsibilities, which doesn't go unnoticed. Just take care and look after yourself as well as getting the job done. Okay?'

For once in his life, he found himself stuck for words.

'Go and grab a drink and I'll explain what we have lined up for today. I'm afraid your first job is another assessment of an ongoing situation in another section. It's local this time, so you won't have to go trekking off across the country.' She turned back to her screen. 'I'll print it off for you.'

He made his drink and brought it into the office. 'Today's assignment won't interfere with what remains from Phase One, will it?'

'It shouldn't. You are only required to talk to one of the operatives on the ground, assess what he has to tell you and maybe take a look around. You won't have to take any action, John. Your opinion will suffice, and if necessary, it will be dealt with accordingly. Couple of hours at the most.' Hazel handed him a sheet of paper. 'Contact's name, and time and place of meeting.' She glanced at her watch. 'One hour's time. Just long enough to have your tea and take a quick look at the rest of the day's agenda, and then off.'

The hour having elapsed, John walked to his car, deep in thought. He just could not understand that woman. Prior to yesterday he could have had a serial number rather than a name for all Hazel seemed to care, yet today she had been all solicitousness.

He shook his head, climbed into his car and headed for the address he had been given. No good mulling over Hazel Palgrave. He had a job to do.

* * *

When Sam went in to see how his guest was doing, he was disappointed and surprised to see Dex sitting on the edge of the bed staring blankly at his phone. The bed looked just as it had when they'd made it up, unruffled, the cover smooth. Dex didn't look up, even when Sam asked him if he'd had any sleep.

Had Dex sat there all night, in this strange, dissociated state? When they had left him yesterday evening, he had at least been talking. Now he seemed worse. It looked to Sam as though he was going to have to draw upon his considerable therapeutic prowess if Jackman was to get those precious names.

'I'm going to get us some breakfast, young man. You have a shower, then come to the dining room and we'll have some breakfast.' He smiled encouragingly. 'Come on, Dex, you're perfectly safe, and you need to eat, or you'll be no good to anyone, least of all your friend Craig.'

There was a brief flicker of recognition at the mention of Craig, but it was very brief.

'I'll call you when it's ready. You get showered, eh?'

In the kitchen, Sam rang Jackman at work and apologised for interrupting. 'It's going to take considerably longer than I hoped, I'm afraid. Our friend is not in a good state at all this morning.'

'Be honest, Sam, is this an act? Something to get us off his back?'

'He's in a sort of fugue state, Jackman. It's genuine all right. They're usually triggered by a trauma or some highly stressful event, and if his life was threatened and his friend is missing, that would have done it. Hopefully, it'll pass quickly but I must warn you, they can go on for some time. I'm going to do a bit of work with him, and if I get a breakthrough, I'll text you.'

'I'd be grateful if you could,' said Jackman. 'I don't want to leave Frank on that film set a moment longer than I have to. I need something concrete to take to the higher-ups, then we can move in and get him out of there.'

'Then I'll try to feed my reluctant guest and see what I can do.'

Making breakfast, Sam heard the shower run. He smiled in relief. Fugue states could sometimes dissipate quickly.

He was toasting the bread and musing over the increasing use of porn when he became aware that the water was still running. Had Dex gone? Oh, why had he unlocked the door when he got up?

He hurried upstairs. He found the bedroom empty. The shower cubicle was not.

Fully clothed, Dexter sat cross-legged under the spray, still staring intently at his drenched mobile phone, which he held gripped tightly in both hands. Water cascaded over his motionless figure.

'Oh my God,' murmured Sam. This young man was badly in need of professional help. Sam turned the water off, but Dex gave no sign of having noticed.

Sam found several big bath towels and wrapped them around him. Dex was now shivering uncontrollably. For once in his life, Sam didn't know what to do. Then he remembered that Hetty Maynard's husband, Len, had arrived just as he was getting breakfast. Len was old but he was strong, which was exactly what Sam needed right now.

Leaving Dex where he was, Sam hurried down the stairs and went to find Len, who was busy in the garden.

It took a while, but they finally got Dex to his feet, removed his clothes and did their best to dry him off. They then ushered him down to the kitchen and sat him on a chair, wrapped in a large fleece blanket. Sam made some tea and put it down in front of Dexter.

'I need to make a phone call, Len,' said Sam anxiously. 'Would you watch him for a few moments and make sure he doesn't try to drink that tea until it's a bit cooler? I don't want him adding to his problems by scalding himself.'

'You go ahead, Prof. He's safe with me, poor lad.'

Sam hurried into the lounge and grabbed his phone. With Laura gone, the only person he could call on was his ex-wife, Julia Tennant.

'I need your help.'

'Where are you?'

'At home, at Mill Corner.'

'I'm on my way.'

* * *

Theodore Carmichael stared at the video report on his iPad. 'What do you think, Casey?'

Dr Casey Naylor, Theo's second in command, pursed her lips. 'To be honest, I have a few reservations about Thomas. I'd

125

rest him for a few days if I were you, get him away from Aegis. A short break and I'm sure he'll be back firing on all cylinders. He's a good man, I'm just a little concerned that he's been the focus of all Ashford's attention for a couple of days now. We don't want him planting any insidious thoughts in Thomas's mind, do we?'

Theo nodded. 'Okay. I'll debrief him and give him three days back in the main block. That should get his head sorted, there's no time to think over there. Especially at the moment, they are missing a number of the staff due to some bug that's doing the rounds. Thomas will be kept so busy he'll forget all about Alistair Ashcroft.'

Casey smiled. 'There's no other issue at present, is there?'

Theo shook his head. 'All the reports are positive. You should read the chaplain's. It's most interesting. I'll send them when we've done our rounds.' He stood up. 'Ready?'

Casey stood up. 'As I'll ever be. Let's go and see what our very own Svengali has been up to lately.'

Theo was extremely happy with his choice of deputy at the unit. Casey Naylor had shown herself impervious to Ashcroft's charisma. She saw through every attempt at pretence, and she also picked up on anything troubling one of the staff. It was their customary routine to walk around the unit each morning and have a few moments with everyone. Generally, they did it together but on occasion, one of them did this alone. Few among those they spoke to aired any grievances. Given the considerable privileges it afforded them, and the comparative comfort of Aegis, no one was keen to return to the main prison block.

'The only one who seemed slightly off-kilter when I spoke to him last night was Jeremy Shaler.'

'Ah, our little cuckoo in the nest,' murmured Theo. 'The one unknown quantity.'

'If it weren't for Ashcroft, Jeremy Shaler would be my main focus of study,' said Casey. 'Although,' she glanced at Theo, 'I sometimes wonder why he came to be here. He doesn't fit the pattern of the rest of the supporting cast in the Alistair Ashcroft Show.'

'We needed one or two complex cases, or Ashcroft would have seen what we were up to. Hence Shaler and Fleming.' Fleming was a nasty, weasel-like character who had admitted to killing three women, but hinted at more. Theo didn't believe that for a second. Fleming was boasting; he revelled in the status being known as a murderer gave him. He liked to see himself as a big, dangerous man, whereas in actuality, he was weak and insecure. He had taken his victims' rejection of him so badly that he had battered the three women to death. He was overjoyed at being given a place at Aegis — it gave him all the attention he craved. He was unaware that he was soon to lose it, having been deemed unsuitable for treatment.

They stopped at the door to Shaler's room. It was open to reveal Shaler lying on his bed, legs crossed, hands behind his head, gazing at them.

'Can we come in, Jeremy?' asked Theo.

'Why not? It's your unit.'

'There's a new session we'd like you to attend, if you would. Headed up by Casey, it starts tomorrow.'

'Oh? And which part of my mind are you probing this time, Doctor?'

Casey smiled at him. 'Not your mind exactly, it's your brain we want to look at. The anterior insular cortex? Or how about the right supramarginal gyrus?'

'Sounds riveting.'

'So, can we count you in?' asked Theo.

'If you tell me what all that crap means, I'll consider it. But what's to investigate? I killed a man. He's dead, I'm paying the price. Guilty as charged. End of story.'

'That statement is the reason why I want you to come along,' Casey said.

Shaler sighed. 'Okay, so what does my ant . . . gyro thing tell you, Doc?'

'That part of the brain is responsible for empathy,' Casey said.

'Oh, that again. My lack of remorse. That it, Doc?'

'Yep. So will you attend?'

'If you want to waste your time, I'm all yours, and so is my super gyro.' He sat up. 'Can I go and get breakfast now, please?'

Theo stepped aside. 'Be my guest.'

Jeremy Shaler grunted. 'That what I am then? Your *guest* in Aegis?' He brushed past them out of his room.

Theo watched him go, a thoughtful expression on his face.

'And so, on to our next "guest",' said Casey. 'Mr Ashcroft — or Stephen rather.'

From the moment he had been incarcerated, Ashcroft had referred to himself as Stephen. After conducting some research into Ashcroft's background, Theo discovered why. As a child he had been bundled into a special boarding school under the name of his dead brother — Richard Stephen Ashcroft. Later in his life, he had assumed the persona of a man he called Stefan Ashcroft. He didn't want to be the troubled and abused child, Alistair, so he became someone else. Stephen was powerful and in control; he hadn't been humiliated and abused. Stephen was free of all that emotional baggage.

They walked along a wide corridor to the room at the end.

'Ah, good morning! It's our revered clinical lead and the talented — and beautiful — Dr Casey Naylor! Do come in.'

'Cheery as ever this morning, Stephen?'

'And why should I not be? Every day I give thanks for my good fortune at being accorded a place in your unit, and every day I try a bit harder to justify my presence here.' He smiled. 'Sincerely, I do truly appreciate it.'

And he did sound sincere. Well, why wouldn't he be? Even the comfort it afforded him was reason enough to be grateful. Theo cleared his throat. 'We've come to tell you about a new programme we're launching. It will involve one-to-one discussion, followed by a session with the four other participants in the group. The main focus is to look into the capacity for empathy, and whether it can be learned.'

Ashcroft looked suitably impressed. 'Fascinating. If you think it would be of benefit, then of course, I'd love to participate.'

I bet you would, thought Theo. *There might even be a few new people whose minds you can tinker with.*

'Excellent,' said Casey. 'We start tomorrow. I'll put you down for ten a.m. Oh, and we may be joined by the chaplain at some point.'

Theo caught the glint in Ashcroft's eye when Galway was mentioned.

'The more the merrier, I'm sure,' said Ashcroft evenly. 'May I ask who else is participating?'

'Only you and Jeremy Shaler so far, we have still to select the other two. Maybe Ronnie Little will be one of them, if he agrees.'

'Shaler's a good choice,' said Ashcroft. 'And if I might be so bold, why not young Paul Bell? If anyone needed to learn empathy, it's him — considering what he did.'

Ashcroft was right. Bell was convicted for having brutally killed two of his so-called best mates — in a row over football. His defence had been simply that they deserved it. Upon being asked if he could go back in time and undo what he'd done, he had asserted with no hesitation that he'd do it all again. What Ashcroft didn't know was that Bell had been suffering from a mental illness that had only been diagnosed after his arrival in prison. It had since been successfully medicated. He was genuinely repentant, and with Theo's help, his case was to be reviewed, and the young man had a good chance of being released. Bell was a plant, and had earned himself considerable Brownie points by means of some clever acting, which had enabled him to infiltrate the prisoner community and report back to Theo.

'He's worth consideration, yes,' said Theo dismissively. 'Now, anything worrying you, Stephen? Any anxieties?

Any change in your day-to-day routine you'd like to see implemented?'

'I have no complaints,' said Ashcroft. 'I have all I need, thank you.'

'Then I'll see you at ten tomorrow, Stephen, and thank you.' Casey and Theo left the room.

Dealing with Ashcroft was a double-edged sword. Despite Theo's intense interest — or perhaps because of it — Theo always left his company with a sense of relief.

* * *

Ashcroft stared after them. It was somewhat of an irritation having to entertain the terrible twins — and before breakfast too! But it was rather fun, all the same. Still, he had more important business to attend to at the moment. Phase Two was only days away. He'd waited a long time for this, and had spent a fortune on setting it up. That he had enough funds to finance the operation was entirely down to his accountant and Christos. Between them, using some of his family money, they had invested in a variety of illegal businesses which had all paid off handsomely.

He glanced at his wrist watch and saw he had half an hour before cleaner Louis Smythe would be coming in, so he needed to be back in his cell within thirty minutes. Dear Louis had something for him.

Ashcroft manoeuvred his wheelchair through the wide doorway and headed for the dining area, where he ate a healthy breakfast. Thus refreshed, he returned to his room, eased himself out of the wheelchair and onto his bed, and lay down to wait.

''Allo, Mr Stephen.' Louis stood in the doorway with his little trolley of cleaning equipment. 'Oh, you're restin'. Want me to come back later?'

'No, no, come in. Just resting the legs. I had a bad night and I'm waiting for this morning's painkillers to kick in. You get on, Louis, I'll not be disturbed.'

'Okay, Mr Stephen, if you're sure?' Louis brought his trolley through the doorway and got down to work.

Ashcroft watched him with interest. He was surprisingly fast and thorough. In the other prisons Ashcroft had been detained in, the cells were only cleaned when the prisoners were out. Here, the disabled were given leeway to remain, for which Ashcroft was grateful. 'Everything okay with you, Louis?'

'Couldn't be better, Mr S, thank you.' He looked at Ashcroft. 'Mind if I just move your chair in order to do the floor? I'll put it back after.'

'Go ahead.'

Unless you had the sharpest eyes, or you knew what was going on, you would never suspect what Louis managed to do in the process of moving the wheelchair. Ashcroft never ceased to be amazed at his sleight of hand.

Cleaning operation over, Louis wheeled the chair back by the bed and applied the brake. 'Don't use your sink for a bit, Mr S. I'll pop in before I go and give it a rinse. I put some bleach round the plughole.'

Ashcroft nodded. 'No problem. See you in a while. Oh, and push the door to, would you? I'll try to grab half an hour's shuteye before you come back.'

Louis left. Ashcroft checked his watch again. With any luck, he'd have twenty minutes. He reached beneath the seat of the wheelchair, removed the mobile phone and pushed it beneath his bedcover. He was allowed to phone from the unit payphone, but some calls demanded absolute privacy. He would not, for example, use the payphone to call the person he was speaking to now.

'Everything in place, Christos?'

Some ten minutes later, Ashcroft ended the call and put the phone back where he had found it. He wouldn't dare keep it, as even in this unit, room searches were still a regular occurrence.

All was ready. A very big smile spread across his face. Not long now. Hardly any time at all before it all kicked off and Saltern-le-Fen police station erupted in chaos.

CHAPTER FIFTEEN

Craig woke up in a strange bed, in a room he didn't recognise. Then he remembered — the place he'd stayed in from which he'd been taken to the old house they'd been filming in. Filming. Jesus, what had he done? His cheeks flamed with shame and embarrassment.

Joannie must never find out, that was for sure. Joannie! Oh fuck. She'd be wondering where he was. What if she called the police?

He leaped from the bed and rummaged through his jacket pockets for his phone. It was gone. *Think, man.* When had he had it last? He could have sworn it was in his pocket last night. He'd been going to chance a swift call to Dex, though he had been expressly forbidden from mentioning the film to anyone, so he'd chickened out. Oh shit, had he dropped it when he took his clothes off last night?

A sharp rap on the door made him gasp. He had forgotten that a couple of the others were also staying in this house. He opened the door and Lance marched in. 'Well, well, Craig, lad! Aren't you the dark horse? You put in a brilliant performance.'

'Er . . . thanks. Look, I can't find my phone, Lance.'

'I've got it, remember? We put them all in the car before we started filming. Can't be too careful. People always forget to turn them off and no way will I have one ringing on set.'

'Oh . . . yeah.' He had no recollection of handing over his phone, but he supposed he must have done. 'It's just that I need to ring Joannie. I never leave it this long without contacting her, and I'm afraid she might go looking for me and stir up trouble.'

Lance gave him a puzzled smile. 'I reckon your performance last night has addled your brain, old son — not that I'm surprised. I told you yesterday, I'd sorted Joannie myself. You gave me the number and I rang and explained you were on a three-day shoot out in the marshes and there was no signal. She was fine with it, and in any case, she can't leave her mum just yet. Surely you remember now?'

'I . . .' He didn't.

Lance held up a hand. 'Okay, Craig. I'll come clean with you. We put a drop of something in your water bottle last night. It's a performance enhancer the professionals use, and it can make you a bit fuzzy the next day. Shouldn't have done it without telling you, but, hell, did it *work*.'

At least he wasn't losing his mind . . . but Craig still felt he'd been played.

'Anyway, old mate, listen, I've got a suggestion to put to you.' He leaned closer. 'Last night's footage is in the can. We've got that house for two more days, so . . .' He looked at Craig hopefully. 'D'you think you could do one more night?'

Craig's eyes widened. 'What? The same sort of stuff?'

'Kind of. Just in a different setting, and maybe a bit edgier. No rich bitch seducing you this time, it's a tad more feral, if you get my meaning.' Lance winked. 'And you get a bigger cut. In fact, if you nail this one, we might be able to double it. How's that grab you?'

Craig thought about it. Double what he had picked up for yesterday was more than he could earn in a year . . . For a few hours of excitement. And he *had* been excited. Then he became embarrassed again. Sex with Joannie was okay, but after ten or so years of marriage, it no longer produced the same thrill. Last night, he had lost all his inhibitions, he had been free. No ties, no money worries, the act was nothing but pure pleasure. And Lance was offering him the chance to do it again, with a promise of big bucks when it was done.

'Feral, you said?'

'Bondage, lad. Good old-fashioned bondage. We shoot it in the stables. Gives it that dark atmosphere. We might even let you loose with some CGI on it after, make it even more sinister. No champagne and king-size beds this time, Craig — you'll be rolling in the hay, literally! Oh, and we have a new performer — a real pro, expert in all that equipment. So, what d'you say?'

'I dunno. I've never been into all that sadomasochism stuff, Lance. What if I mess it up?'

Lance nudged him. 'Come on, mate! We aren't giving you the starring role. You're the warm-up act — getting it on with the lady of the manor before the chains come out. The heavy stuff gets left to the experts. Tell you what, I'll let you have the script, and you can see what you think.'

All that money for a supporting role? 'Okay, Lance. If you think I'll be up to it, count me in.'

'That's my boy! So, you chill out here today, conserve your strength like. There's food in the fridge, but the guys'll bring a proper meal in later. We'll head off out at the same time as we did last night. Now, I must get back to base and make like normal on the *Fen Division Five* set. You just relax and dream about that cash. See you later!'

It didn't dawn on Craig until later that he still didn't have his phone.

* * *

Marie had been in early too but hadn't had a chance to catch up with Jackman, who had been on the phone for almost an hour, then in and out of Ruth Crooke's office. So, Marie had buckled down to her paperwork, and by ten in the morning was way ahead. Funny, she was so happy about buying Peelers End and starting a new life with Ralph that she'd wondered if her work might suffer. As it was, she brought renewed energy to it. Two things worried her, however. One was her failure to contact Dougie. The other was Jackman. He wasn't calling on her as he usually did, instead he was dealing with issues on his own. She knew why he was doing this, but she didn't want to be left out this way. Just because she finally had a life outside policing didn't mean she was no longer interested in it.

Having finished her office work, she headed towards the vending machine, intending to take Jackman a coffee and give him a proper 'Welsh' dressing down.

'Oh dear,' said Jackman when he saw her. 'I've seen that look before, and it doesn't bode well.'

Marie placed his coffee in front of him and closed the door. 'Time we had a talk, boss. And it's me doing the talking. You just listen.'

It was hard not to laugh at her fierce expression.

'Right. Now I know you mean it for the best, and don't think I don't appreciate it. We've worked together and been friends for years, but—'

'Marie, any chance of getting to the point?'

She opened her mouth and they both started to laugh.

'Damn it! I had prepared one of my most profound lectures. Oh well. In a nutshell then, I'm still your sergeant, no matter what else is going on in my life. You do *not* exclude me from call outs, no matter what the hour, just because you think you'll be intruding in my cosy little love-life. Ralph's a policeman too, you know. Chances are he'll be chasing some drug dealer down an alley somewhere and I'll be home alone. I'm still here for you, Jackman,' she said firmly, 'one hundred percent, as I always have been. So there. Lecture over.'

For a moment Jackman didn't speak. A number of different emotions flitted across his face. 'Thank you, Marie,' he said softly. 'I've got to admit, ever since losing Laura, I've been all over the place. I get these ideas, like if I don't let you go, I'll jeopardise your happiness in your new life. And I don't discuss them with anyone, so I never find out if I'm right or not.'

Heart-broken as she was at the knowledge of what he was going through, Marie decided that nevertheless he needed some tough love. 'Well, I'm telling you now, that's all a load of bollocks. Next time you get an idea like that, you run it past me immediately, all right? I'll set you straight.'

Jackman lowered his head, then raised it again and laughed. 'Received and understood, DS Evans. Business as usual?'

'As usual. Just as it's always been. Now, how about these murders?'

Over rapidly cooling coffee, they discussed the latest reports on the Adonis and Apollo killings.

'The forensics are scant to say the least,' said Jackman. 'And some results have been held up because of a glitch at the lab. Rory says he'll deal with them as soon as they come in.' He sat back in his captain's chair. 'D'you know, these are two of the most baffling deaths I can recall having to deal with since I don't know when. For a start, men's dead bodies are rarely recovered naked. Neither man has any distinguishing marks, they're not street people, nor do they resemble anyone we're looking for. And no one has come forward to report someone of their description missing. It's like they don't exist.'

'As soon as I've had my coffee, I'm off out with Kevin Stoner. We're going to hit the local gyms and fitness clubs. Rory has made their post-mortem photographs look quite beautiful — unlike some I've seen.' Marie pulled a face. 'I'm not holding out much hope, but we have to start somewhere.'

'Yes, that's a smart move, Marie. We do know that they were both in excellent condition. You don't get that without working on your body.' He sifted through some papers, then pushed them roughly away. 'Hell, Marie, I really don't like Frank being out at that film set, and I'm scared shitless about this freaked-out man in Sam's spare room. He swears he's suffering from a fugue state, but I'm worried he's faking it, rather than give us the names we need, and that could put Frank in danger.'

'Can't you pull rank and get him out?'

Jackman shook his head. 'Not a civilian. Plus he's adamant that his presence there is our best chance of finding out what's going on. I guess he's right when he says that if he disappears so suddenly after the other two have done a runner, the gang will get cold feet, close up shop and we'll never know what they were up to.'

Marie thought about it for a while. 'If I were you, I'd bring this Dex character in for questioning. If he's really disturbed, we can call in Julia Tennant, and if he's shamming, well, we take it from there. I don't like the thought of him being alone with Sam, boss. Sam's a bloody good psychologist but he's no spring chicken, is he? His guest could easily decide to leg it.'

Jackman shook his head. 'I knew I should have called you out last night. What a plank I've been! Yes, I'll—'

His mobile rang. 'Talk of the devil. It's Sam.'

As Marie waited, tense, Jackman's anxious, set face relaxed. It wasn't a long call. 'Your idea is coming to fruition in a roundabout kind of way. Julia's there with Sam. She's assessing Dex now, with a view to either getting him brought here or taken to hospital.'

'Oh good! I feel happier about that. Oh, and don't fret too much about Frank. He's no fool. He'll call in the cavalry if he needs to, I'm sure he will.' Marie finished her coffee and stood up. 'Right. I'm off to check out a few fit males. Will you ring me when you've heard from Sam?'

'I will. I won't leave you out this time. Would you send one of the others to see me on your way out? I want someone to find out where a woman called Joannie Turner is and get a check done on her husband, Craig. It appears that he's also missing.'

'I think Gary's free, boss. I'll send him in.'

'Good luck at the fitness clubs, Marie, and keep me posted.'

Marie gave him a thumbs-up. Thank goodness she'd had that talk with him. Hopefully now they could get back to normal. She and Ralph would survive a few disturbed nights — they always had, after all. She smiled to herself. Living in a police house. How good was that!

* * *

Sam had always been struck by Julia's beauty. Seeing her today, many decades and a divorce later, he still was.

They were sitting in what would forever be known as Laura's consulting room, on the ground floor of the mill. Now it was Sam's, but everything in it was just as it had been when Laura occupied it.

Dex was asleep upstairs, Julia having given him a mild sedative. Sam told her what had happened, and what he'd learned of Dex and the mess he had got himself into.

'He was threatened, you say,' said Julia, sinking back into the cushions on 'Laura's' sofa.

'A threatening note was left under the windscreen wiper of his camper,' Sam said. 'After the disappearance of his friend Craig, the warning terrified him.' He went on to describe the panic attack in Frank's log cabin.

Julia frowned. 'Bit of an over-reaction, wouldn't you say? I mean, anyone would be scared in such a situation, but people usually only fall apart like that when they've gone through some devastating trauma.'

'That's what I thought, Julia. But it's real all right. That panic attack was no act. And seeing him crouching in that shower . . . it sent shivers down my spine.'

'Don't get me wrong,' Julia said. 'I'm not saying he's faking it. It's just so completely out of proportion. Which of course makes me very interested to find out more of his history.' Her eyes lit up. 'I'm glad you brought him to my attention, Sam. I'd really like to take him on.'

'I rather hoped you would,' said Sam. 'I'm not at my best right now, and it's too much for me to cope with.'

'Utter rubbish, Sam Page! You are not getting away with it that lightly. You're going to help me on this one, or I shan't take him on at all.'

Sam rolled his eyes. 'You haven't lost your old spark, have you? Well, if you put it like that . . . I suppose I have no choice.'

'That's right, you don't. So, how do we proceed? Since he's part of an official investigation, I suggest the first thing you do is contact DI Jackman and ask him to provide us with as comprehensive a background check as possible. I have a good idea that something from his past has risen to the surface — most likely triggered by that death threat. What do you reckon?'

'I totally agree. So . . . no time like the present.' Sam picked up his phone and made the request to Jackman.

Call over, he said, 'Sorted. Jackman is going to get someone working on it immediately. Now, what do we do with our Dex when he wakes up?'

'Listen, Sam. It's what we do, listen and talk. Then we'll decide how to help him.'

* * *

John felt oddly unsettled. It was almost lunchtime and he'd already completed the task Christos had given him — trouble-shooting a possible problem in a venture Stephen was associated with. It seemed a rather strange kind of thing for Stephen to be involved in, not that John knew much about Stephen's interests, nor did he really want to. He was aware, however, that from the confines of his prison cell, Stephen had somehow managed to create a network of illegal ventures, all of which were highly profitable.

Tasks like this were all well and good, but John's main concern was bringing Phase Two to completion, on time and without a hitch. He returned to base where, to his amazement, Hazel made him a drink.

'Okay,' she began. 'What's the matter?'

John stared at her. 'I'm not exactly sure.'

'Talk to me.'

He frowned. 'The local set-up that I've just assessed. The one Christos added. I was just about to round this extra job off but, well, something is bothering me—'

'And you don't know what it is yet,' Hazel finished.

'There was . . . something that didn't register while I was there, but now . . . I think I have to go back.'

'So do I,' said Hazel at once. 'I trust your judgement completely, John. You cannot put your name to a report when you have reservations.'

'At least it's not bloody Dungeness,' he muttered.

'If it makes you feel better, I've managed to complete one of the outstanding files from here, so you only have one more to bring up to date before we are ready to receive a new instruction.' Hazel seemed as keen as he was to move on to Phase Two. 'Grab something to eat, John, and go back and discover what is bothering you.'

He shook his head. 'I'll eat later, Hazel. I should get back. Something is wrong in that film unit. I just need to find what it is.'

CHAPTER SIXTEEN

Rory tore off his mask and stepped away from yet another completed post-mortem. At least this departed soul was simply a medical mystery — which he had, of course, solved. Unlike the more complicated mystery of his two beautiful Greek gods. By now, they were haunting his days and worming their way into his dreams. He had never before been presented with such exquisite and healthy-looking young men to practice his skills on.

He cleaned up and went into his office. He had sent out a nation-wide request for any other pathologists with a similar case to contact him. He sat at his desk and went through his in-box. There was a new message from a colleague in the West Country:

Dear Professor Wilkinson,

This isn't recent, but I can report having had three similar incidents within two months in the early part of last year. There is one essential difference, however. My bodies — all recovered from water like yours — were female. However, each had traces of body oil on their skin. As with your cases, all the women were young, fit and healthy and, without exception, unusually beautiful. Each woman

*was killed using a different method — a strangulation, a
stabbing and, oddly enough, a drowning, although she had
drowned in fresh water — bath water to be precise — and
not in the sea, where she was found washed up on a beach.
I can send you the full autopsy reports and my findings if
it will be of help. It should be noted that none of them was
ever identified, and the cases remain open.*

> *Yours sincerely,*
> *Professor Dennis Copperthwaite*

'At last!' Rory muttered. 'Someone to discuss Adonis
and Apollo with.' He quickly typed a reply, saying that he
would be more than grateful for his esteemed colleague's
findings. To his satisfaction, these landed in his inbox in fifteen minutes. Rory immediately got down to studying them.

After an hour of close reading, he was on the phone to
Jackman.

'This is not the first time beautiful young people have
been murdered and left in water. I'm going to suggest that
you make a call to your counterparts down in Cornwall, my
dear boy. Last year they had three bodies that — apart from
being women — replicate those of Adonis and Apollo. Now,
like my good self, you have someone to compare notes with.
You can thank me profusely and shower me with accolades
at a later date. *Ciao, mio amico!*'

He hung up and started to go through the Cornish
post-mortem reports for the second time.

* * *

At the very moment when Rory was absorbed in his reports,
Frank Rosen was trying to make sense of a text message he'd
received. It had come from an unknown number and not on
the burner phone.

> *Get away from that film location as quickly as possible! It's
> a very dangerous place!*

For a moment he wondered if Jackman had sent it, but dismissed the thought at once. For the first time since he'd taken on this job, Frank felt uneasy. Perhaps he had wandered into something that was beyond his capacity to deal with. He told himself he'd enjoyed the experience but maybe it was time to bow out. After all, he didn't really need the money. At least Jackman would be relieved to hear of his decision. And right now, he would be too.

Frank didn't delete the message. He wanted to keep it, so that if he had second thoughts, he could take note of the warning and act on it. The sender of that message had got one thing right, it was a dangerous place, and it was becoming more so with every passing hour.

* * *

Dispiritedly, for they held out little hope of success, Marie and Kevin opened the door to the third fitness club on their list.

The Fen Fitness Hub was more upmarket than those they had seen so far. The equipment was new and gleaming, the clientele obviously rich enough to spare no expense on the care of their bodies.

The young man who greeted them had startlingly good looks. Marie noticed that he addressed himself to Kevin, practically ignoring her. Fighting back a smile, she tried to catch his eyes, and explained the reason for their visit. She showed him the photographs of the two dead men, which he stared at without flinching, but he said he couldn't help them.

'I suggest you go to the studio, and ask for Leo,' he said to Kevin. 'He's a personal trainer who works in a number of other gyms besides this one. If anyone can help you, it's Leo.'

They thanked him and started off in the direction he had indicated. Marie nudged Kevin. 'You made a big hit there, boyo.'

'Nice to know I've still got it in me — even if I am spoken for.' He chuckled. 'I can't wait to tell Alan where we've been today. He's always winding me up with descriptions of the gorgeous bodies he gets to x-ray.'

'Well, I'm sure he has his share of gross ones as well.'

They arrived at the studio just as a class was leaving, and a woman in vivid pink yoga pants pointed out Leo to them.

When they showed him the photographs, Leo stared for some time at the second one. His face went white.

'Oh my God, that's Edward!'

'Is there somewhere more private where we could talk?' asked Marie quickly. Leo looked like he would either pass out or burst into tears.

They followed him into a small office with just two chairs, an empty desk and a weighing machine. He perched on the edge of the desk and pointed to the chairs.

Kevin and Marie sat down. Marie showed him the picture again, that of the second man to die, who been in the lake in Cartoft. "So, you recognise this man? Was he a friend, or someone you know from here?'

Leo made an attempt to pull himself together. 'Not from here. He used to go to a smaller place in Greenborough. I used to work on his muscle tone. I wondered why he wasn't coming anymore.' He sniffed. 'Now I know why.'

'Do you have his details?' asked Kevin.

'No, but I can get them for you. His name is Edward Keating. He said he worked in entertainment.'

Ah, another field we haven't checked out, thought Marie. 'We'd be very grateful for any information you can give us about him. I must tell you that this is a murder enquiry, so we'd like it as soon as possible.'

Leo slid off the edge of the desk. 'Just a second.'

A few moments later he returned carrying a gym bag. He removed his mobile from the front pocket and made a call to a colleague in Greenborough.

'Yes, that's right, Edward, or "Eddie" Keating. He was one of my personal training clients. His last appointment was around a month ago, I think. Thank you, Beth, can you email me those details, please?' He ended the call and looked at them. 'Five minutes and she'll have them to me. He lives, er, lived, in a village over Holbeach way. She has all his contact details — not that they'll be much good now, I suppose.'

'They're very useful to us, believe me,' said Marie. 'And we appreciate you identifying him for us. Disappointing that the other guy didn't move in the same circles.'

'Can I see that picture again?' asked Leo, then he grimaced. 'I can't believe I just asked to see a picture of a dead man.'

Marie handed it to him. 'Maybe he just came once or twice? He was one very fit man.'

Leo looked at it for a long while. 'I don't know him, but . . . maybe I recognise him from somewhere, though not here, but . . . could it have been on the telly? I don't know, maybe I'm wrong.'

Marie didn't think he was. Those little glimmers of recognition often proved to be right. 'If it comes to you, could you ring me?' She handed him her card.

So, one of their two victims had an identity. This was more than they'd hoped for. Two more gyms to hit, then back to base. First, though, Marie needed to tell Jackman. It felt good to be passing on positive news for once.

* * *

John's contact had been taken unawares by his unexpected return to the Old Oaks Rectory film set. 'I thought you were happy with everything,' he said, looking rattled.

'Maybe I am,' replied John noncommittally. 'Can we go through the place again, retrace our steps, and as far as you can, tell me what you said first time around.'

'Look, I'm going to be needed soon, pal, and I've got nothing to add to what I said last time.'

'Humour me, would you? There's a lot at stake, as I'm sure you realise, so just walk me through, like you did before.'

The man shrugged. 'Well, as I said, it's a perfect place to film in — it's uninhabited at present, and big enough to accommodate the lot of us.' They walked through a big gate into the

145

grounds. 'Well, you've got the arable fields on one side, and the marsh on the other, which means we're able to shoot what appears to be multiple locations, but which are actually all in this one place. The river is only five minutes away if we need a bit of atmosphere and, since it's empty, we can do the interior shots here too. Oh yeah, and we've set up one of the outbuildings as the DI's office, so we can even shoot some of the police station footage here as well. Saves on the budget.'

The contact droned on, leading John along the route they had taken earlier. Soon they were walking through the catering area, where groups of people huddled around camping tables. No one took any notice of them.

John's eyes were everywhere. What had he heard, or was it something he'd seen?

His contact was growing increasingly restless. 'Look, it'll draw attention to us if I'm late for this afternoon's shoot. I need to go. I suggest you do the same. I don't want security getting hold of you and asking questions. Come on, mate, I'll walk you back to your car.'

John certainly couldn't afford security poking their noses in, so he was obliged to acquiesce. Maybe his instincts had finally let him down.

They had almost reached car park by the old chapel when it came to him. He understood exactly what had been bothering him, and it almost took his breath away.

Three men and two women were deep in conversation, apparently discussing some actors standing a short distance from them.

'Who is that man in the green wax jacket?' John asked.

His contact squinted. 'Oh, that's the police consultant, advises on police procedure. Frank something or other. You don't have to worry about him. Old codger's starstruck, can't get over actually hobnobbing with actors he's seen on TV.'

'He's not been any trouble then, he's not a cause for concern?' John said casually.

'Not him. It was the last one who smelled a rat, but as you'll know from the reports, he was frightened off. This one hasn't set off any alarm bells at all. Like I said, just a boring old fart.' The man stopped walking. 'Anyway, I've *really* got to go now.'

John waved him away, then remained standing by his car, trying to decide what to do. After a while, he got in but didn't start the engine. He knew exactly who the man in the wax jacket was — Frank Rosen. Of all people! The memories chased each other around in his head.

He had to act, but how to do it without blowing the whole sleazy operation sky high? God. Why did this have to happen at such a crucial time? Phase Two was far more important than this tinpot scheme.

He called Hazel and told her that his gut feeling had been correct. There was no time to allocate the job to anyone else, and he would deal with it personally.

'Take great care, John. I know you are aware of it, but our work here is far more important.'

He said he understood, and that he'd ring her as soon as he had it all sorted.

He considered his options for a few moments. According to his source, the 'other shoot' at the different location would be completed by midnight tonight, so whatever he decided to do, he had to wait until that was done. If things went wrong, the whole place would be crawling with police. Stephen would not be happy.

John cursed the fact that he had been put in this position. Nonetheless, he was probably the best person to sort it out. He checked his watch. It was approaching half past three, and he had been told that filming would stop at five. So, not too long to wait, and by early evening, if all went well, the crisis would have been averted.

John got himself into a position where he could see the entrance to the car park clearly and settled down to wait. Only then did he allow himself to summon all those memories that the sight of Frank Rosen had stirred up.

* * *

Julia and Sam had spent the early part of the afternoon trying to find a psychiatric unit that would take Dex in for observation. They agreed that there had to be some underlying issue that had caused him to react as he did. He was certainly not fit to be taken into police custody for questioning. Jackman had managed to provide a fairly detailed picture of his life and circumstances, but little on his medical history. His team were working on that now.

'It used to be so simple finding a bed,' muttered Julia. 'These days they're like gold dust. The hospitals are full, and even some of the private clinics are stretched to capacity. I'm relying on Oatlands Hall, but there's no guarantee they'll have anything.'

'At least he's safe here for the time being,' said Sam, 'but we can't actually do anything to help him without knowing the root cause of his breakdown.' He looked intently at Julia. 'If you had been there when he and Frank arrived at the log cabin, you'd have thought his reaction to what had happened was perfectly natural. He was quite understandably afraid to name the people involved, considering that they had threatened his life, and he knew full well that the previous police consultant had been driven away under extreme pressure. Then the panic attack hit him. After that, he went downhill fast, until the shower episode, which was when I knew I needed your help. I did wonder if he might be on some strong medication that he had forgotten to take?'

'Maybe, but I'm now wondering . . . Could it have been the panic attack itself that brought it on?' mused Julia. 'What if he's experienced them in the past, perhaps many years ago, because of some other fear? Then the shock of going through the attack triggered a deep-seated memory and it all flared up again?'

Sam nodded slowly. 'That would fit in both with what I witnessed and the downward spiral that followed. Yes, I think you are right, but we are still left with the mystery of his past.'

'And until we know what that is, or we find a bed in a place of safety, I'm not leaving you here alone with him, Sam,' said Julia firmly. 'I've cancelled all my appointments and there isn't anything urgent I have to deal with. So, as you seem to have forgotten about lunch — unless that mug of tea and the digestive biscuit could be construed as such — let's order a take-away, shall we? It might be only four o'clock, but I'm starving!'

'I'm sorry,' Sam apologised. 'I should have thought.'

'Yes, you should. People do deliver to this tiny hamlet, I suppose?'

Sam nodded. 'Yes, all the usual suspects.'

'Remember our early years, when we were studying and dreaming of brilliant futures. What did we eat then? Can you remember?' She smiled.

'Pizza! With extra cheese and no pineapple.'

She wagged a finger at him. 'You forgot the black olives.'

'But not the tin of anchovies you kept in the kitchen cupboard that we added to those black olives.'

'I'll let you into a secret . . . I still do.' She laughed. 'Now, before I expire, get on that phone!'

Oatlands Hall called back at five. They could take Dex, but only for a three-day assessment. Julia agreed. Hopefully, once he was in the system, she would be able to use her influence to make sure he stayed there.

Following a nostalgic meal with the woman he had never stopped loving, the time had come to move his unfortunate guest to a proper facility. Sam went to prepare Dex for the journey. Julia said she would drive if he would sit in the back with their charge. Sam hoped Dex would be compliant. If he fought against them . . .

As it was, he needn't have worried. Dex, still under the influence of Julia's sedative, managed to dress himself in fresh clothes supplied by Sam and walked out to the car like a man in a dream. Within an hour, he was checked into the psychiatric hospital, where Julia gave them all the information they had and promised to ring as soon as a medical history became available.

They drove back to Mill Corner, not speaking, their thoughts with the sad young man they had left in the hospital.

Sometimes the career he had chosen weighed heavily on Sam's heart. After all these years it still pained him to see a bright, intelligent young man reduced to a husk.

Her familiar voice interrupted his gloomy thoughts. 'Cheer up, Page, you old fool! He's safe now. When we can tell them more about his background, our colleagues at Oatlands will get him back on the level again. He's obviously done it before — he must have if he can hold down a demanding job — so he'll do it again. Then your friend Jackman might get those names. He was lucky you were around. Now you'll be able to sleep tonight without worrying about the stranger in your spare room.'

That was Julia for you, sensible and always right.

CHAPTER SEVENTEEN

'Got something, Sarge!'

Marie hurried over to Gary's desk.

'I found Dex's former GP. He was quite decent about it but said patient confidentiality meant he couldn't hand over any information to me. He's happy to talk to his current doctor, though. I've got his details here.' He held out a piece of paper.

'Great stuff, Gary. Jackman will be pleased.' She took the memo from Gary and went off to find the boss. Okay it wasn't much, but it was another step forward and, boy, could they do with some of those.

On her way to Jackman's office, her mobile rang. It was an unknown number and she almost didn't respond.

'Detective Sergeant Evans?' said a voice. 'It's Leo, from the gym.'

'Oh, hi, Leo. Have you got something for us?'

'Well, I, er, I know where I'd seen that man before. It was in a movie. An, er, adult one.'

Marie blinked a few times. 'You mean porn?'

He cleared his throat. 'Well, er, yes.'

Thank goodness he'd had the courage to ring her. It must have been embarrassing for him, poor bloke.

'Was it a kind of mainstream porn film, or more hard-core, Leo?' Marie's mind went to the clandestine movies being made in the Schooner's Mate. Could there be a connection? She waited, imagining the phone glowing as his mortification increased.

'Um, hardcore, Sergeant. One of my brother Callum's friends is a lorry driver and he brings them back from Holland.'

'Look, Leo, do you think you could get hold of that movie for me? No one need know it came from you. I just need to make sure it really is our dead guy, and find out a bit more about where the movie was made. This could be a major step forward for us.'

Leo sounded doubtful. 'I'll try, Sergeant, but it wasn't mine, I watched it at a mate's place. People don't hang onto them. They fetch good money on the street.'

'Well, if you can't get it from him, ring me and I'll see if we can persuade him.'

'All right, Sergeant. I'll be in touch.'

Marie burst into Jackman's office, and told him about Leo's call, and her theory that the film he had seen could be connected to Dougie's disappearance.

Jackman received her outpouring in silence. 'All right, Marie. Let's take a step back and go over what we actually know. It started with Dougie's suspicion that there was some sort of wrongdoing behind the scenes in a film he was working on.'

'And now Dougie is missing. And . . . and Frank Rosen, his successor, agrees with Dougie's assessment, and has come up with proof that some of the film crew are making blue movies on the side.' Marie drew in a breath. 'At the Schooner's Mate, and this has been corroborated by one of the hotel staff. We have one deeply affected member of that renegade film crew in the care of our new force psychologist, although at present, he is in no state to identify the others.

'Enter two murdered young men, one of whom is now identified and the other is alleged to be a porn actor . . . Could all that really be coincidence?'

'They could be connected, I agree,' said Jackman, 'but it would be a huge mistake to assume anything on the basis of what you've just described. We have a lot of work to do before we can link them — if indeed there is a link. We only have this Leo's vague notion that he might have seen Adonis in a dirty movie. We need to see that film for ourselves, and if he did work for this particular crew, which is by no means certain, why would they get rid of him? Not that many actors are willing to do porn.'

Marie sighed loudly. 'I understand all that, and I've got no answers, but still, I'm convinced Adonis and Apollo are connected to that film unit.'

'Then we'd better prove it.' Jackman stood up. 'We'll throw it at the team before they go home. But first, I'd better go and put Ruth Crooke in the picture. We need to work these two investigations in tandem in case they do slot together at some point. To get this case moving, we have to have two things — a copy of that film and,' he narrowed his eyes, 'Dex Thompson to find his marbles and give us some bloody names!'

* * *

At last John saw Frank Rosen walk into the car park. He jumped out of his car and hurried over to him.

'Frank, my old mate! I thought it was you. How are you doing? More to the point, *what* are you doing in this place?'

After only a split second's hesitation, Frank said, 'Talk about a blast from the past! Me? I've been doing a bit of consultancy since I retired. That's why I'm here, I'm on a job. But how about you? You went right off the radar after that rotten time you had. In fact, most of us believed that you'd, well, I hate to say it, mate, but everything pointed to you topping yourself.'

'Well, it was a close call. I went downhill for a while, pretty well hit rock bottom. Then I got my act together and did a spell with a private bodyguard company and

I'm now back on track. I'm in insurance now, dead boring really. Keeping an eye on health and safety and making sure everything is in accordance with the terms of our contracts. A far cry from policing, but there you go.' Oh, the lies came so easily. 'Hey, have you got time for a swift drink somewhere? Or just a coffee maybe? It'd be good to catch up, and I'm off again tomorrow. Heading up north somewhere.'

'Sure. I know somewhere not too far away that does good coffee. You want to follow me?'

'Great. Lead on.'

The car park Frank had led him to was the perfect spot, quiet and situated on the edge of a wooded area. John got out of his car and followed Frank into a café that looked like a cross between a Swiss log cabin and an American diner.

John didn't do fond memories, yet gazing on his former colleague, he couldn't help feeling a sneaking nostalgia. As they talked, he ruminated on how far he had travelled since those days, and how much darker the road was now.

He brought himself back to the present, and what was fast becoming a jolly old boys' reunion. This was not why he was here.

'So, a film set consultancy? How did you manage to land that?'

Frank shrugged, 'Their agency rang me. They were looking for a retired detective who knew the area, and I thought, why not? Turns out to be rather exciting, as a matter of fact.'

All keen interest, John coaxed more information out of him, looking for the slightest indication that Frank Rosen had smelled a rat. For Frank Rosen had been good. He had been an exceptional detective with a well-earned reputation for getting to the heart of a case.

In his turn, John spun a complicated yarn about all the things he'd done since leaving the force. Frank listened. How true, he said, that no longer carrying a warrant card made you feel vulnerable suddenly.

John looked around. The place was now empty and there seemed little else to say.

'I'd better make a move, mate. Got an early start tomorrow.' John cleared his throat. 'One last thing. I'll never forget what you did for me, Frank, and I mean that sincerely. There's not a day goes by when I don't give thanks for your actions.'

Frank waved this away. 'Anyone would have done the same. Forget it, mate. Just have a good life, hey?'

They walked back to their cars, John still undecided. Did Frank suspect, or did he not?

Then there was the matter of the debt he owed him. Frank had taken down an armed drug dealer who had been about finish off the already injured John. He owed Frank his life.

'You take care, my old friend.' He stepped forward and gave Frank a warm hug. 'It's been bloody good to see you again.'

Then he slid the long sharp blade of his knife through Frank's jacket and deep between his ribs.

* * *

Long past the time when they should be heading for home, all the team were still in the CID room. The meeting was over, but no one seemed to be in any hurry to leave. It was as if they needed to talk through what they now knew and suspected to be going on.

Marie's phone rang, and silence fell. Everyone waited on tenterhooks until she ended the call. Then, 'He's coming in! He's got the film for us. Oh hell, someone stop me from hugging him when he arrives!'

Jackman grinned. 'Well, it looks like it's going to be blue-movie night at the nick. That'll be interesting.'

'I'd offer to dive out and get some popcorn, boss, but somehow I don't think it's appropriate,' chortled Max.

Jackman pulled a face. 'I'd like to say that we only have to decide whether it's our Adonis or not and then we can go home, but . . . I'm thinking that at least two of us will need to watch the whole thing, just in case we see anything, or anyone, that might be connected to our investigation.'

The chorus of giggles that followed his words was interrupted by the unexpected entrance of Rory Wilkinson.

'Hey, Prof! You are lucky to catch us still here,' said Marie. 'What can we do for you?'

But Rory was not his usual effervescent self. 'Well, my lovely friends, I've been talking to my colleagues in Cornwall, surfing some rather grim websites and thinking some very dark thoughts. So dark that I needed to share them, and who better than this auspicious assembly? I only banked on one or two of you, but this is perfect.'

'You've arrived just in time to possibly see your Adonis when he was alive, and doing what he apparently did for a living,' Jackman said. 'So, if you care to join us for this evening's feature film?'

As he spoke, a civilian approached Marie. 'There's a gentleman in reception asking for you, Sergeant Evans.'

She went out, returning a few minutes later with a DVD case in her hand and a smile on her face. 'I refrained from hugging him, you'll be pleased to hear, but it was an effort.' She handed Jackman the film. 'Will you be projectionist, or shall I?'

Jackman took it. He turned to the others. 'Look, if any of you don't want to watch this, it's fine, you don't have to. It's going to be bloody embarrassing.'

Max laughed. 'Oh, get on with it, guv! We didn't come down with the last shower, did we? We've all worked vice cases.'

The film rolled on, accompanied by the odd ribald comment.

Rory, surprisingly perhaps, had been silent. Suddenly, he cried out, 'Hold it, Jackman! That's him! That's Adonis.'

'Yes, it is,' echoed Marie, nodding. 'That's him all right.'

Jackman, too, recognised their young victim, and was deeply saddened by the terrible waste of it. That a young man of such perfect beauty had been driven to do this kind of work in the first place was bad enough, but to then be murdered was heart-rending.

They watched for a while longer, but it soon became clear that Adonis wasn't going to appear again. Jackman stopped the film.

'We know what he did for a living,' murmured Robbie Melton, 'but we are no closer to knowing who he was.'

'I'm not so sure.' Jackman took the disc from the machine. 'DI Jenny Deane's team handled that massive vice investigation earlier in the year, the one where women were being brought into the country for prostitution. Well, you might recall that it also landed a big haul of pornography. They engaged a special forensic unit to work on the discs, to discover where and how they were produced. I'm going to get her to pass this to them. They might be able to trace it to its source.'

'And another thing,' Marie interjected. 'Suppose we let Dex see it — if he's recovered enough, that is. He was part of the crew who were shooting it, so he might recognise some of the actors.'

Jackman wasn't sure they could wait for Dex to recover. From what Sam had told him, he was in a bad way. '*If* he's recovered. We need to move on this.'

'If I might just throw the proverbial spanner into the works.' Rory sounded uncharacteristically sombre. I have mentioned my counterpart in the West Country, haven't I? Well, he and I have come to a similar conclusion. Should we be correct, I would recommend that you get your man away from that film company, and move in and close it down.'

'What?' Jackman cried. 'Without evidence?'

Rory merely looked at him.

* * *

Last night's stage fright was nothing to Craig's current state of anxiety. Suppose he forgot his lines, few and simple as they were? He was to play the head groom of a stable belonging to a rich family, on his usual late evening round of the horses when he finds one of the stable-hands and the wife of the landowner having sex in an empty stall. According to the script, he throws the lad out and is then seduced in his turn. The husband discovers them and gives Craig's character a beating. There is a tussle, Craig is to limp away, apparently injured, after which the really hardcore action takes place.

Despite his nerves, Craig couldn't help casting a professional eye over the setting. He already had a few ideas about how he might enhance the look of the place, make it more dramatic and sinister.

'All ready, Craig, lad?'

Lance's sudden appearance made him jump. 'As I'll ever be.'

'We've a different crew tonight, but don't let that put you off. These guys are specialists, and we can't afford to be doing unlimited takes. So we aim to do it in one, okay? We can edit it afterwards if we need to.' Lance looked around. 'As soon as I get the thumbs up from lighting, we are ready to roll. Make-up and wardrobe all right, are they?'

Craig almost smiled. Under the tweed jacket and jodhpurs he had nothing on.

'I'm very grateful for this, Craig,' said Lance seriously, 'and for last night. This is all new to you, and you did bloody well. It'll be reflected in your money. Our buyer is a generous man — if we come up with the right movie.' He glanced around. 'All set to roll. Are you ready?'

Craig nodded.

'Take your position outside the stable and wait for your call. Break a leg, lad.'

Craig tried to think of the money he'd be getting. Imagine being able to give Joannie everything she asked for!

'Quiet on set! Everyone ready? Okay, roll the sound! Action!'

Craig strode into the barn.

* * *

158

But the scene didn't unfold according to the script. In the skilled hands of the dominatrix, Craig had forgotten the cameras, forgotten where he was, he had even forgotten who he was. According to the script, the husband was to enter, discover him with his wife, and give him a beating. So Craig wasn't surprised when with rough hands, someone took hold of him and dragged him away from the actress. He was pushed to the ground and kicked, hard, on the ribs. Craig gasped in pain and shock. This wasn't how it was supposed to play out. He became dimly aware of two strange men in dark clothes and full-face masks. Who the hell were they? They hadn't been in the script.

Something was horribly wrong. He was supposed to walk away at this point, his scene over. Instead, he was pulled to his feet, his hands were wrenched behind his back, and he heard a metallic click. He had been handcuffed. A blow to his cheek sent him reeling, and his mouth filled with blood. Why hadn't they told him this was going to happen? He cried out to Lance, begging him to cut the cameras and stop them hurting him.

Now he was being dragged towards the door, the concrete flooring lacerating his naked body. His last memory was of Dex, begging him to get out while he could. Why hadn't he listened?

CHAPTER EIGHTEEN

Jackman waited for Rory to explain his reasons for urging him to act so precipitately.

'Please bear in mind that this is not just my hypothesis, my colleague in Cornwall has come to the same conclusion. We don't believe that these deaths are the work of a serial killer, but at the same time we are certain they are connected.'

Rory continued, speaking without a trace of his usual flippancy. 'We believe that whoever caused these young men's deaths did so for extortionate sums of money.' His gaze bored into Jackman. 'No doubt you've heard of snuff movies.'

Someone gasped.

'They're usually considered to be one of those urban myths. The notion of someone being murdered on camera originated in the late seventies, and to this day still has a place in the popular imagination. My colleague and I are convinced that our dead young people probably began as porn stars but ended up being used by someone callous and evil enough to make an urban myth real.'

Rory's words were followed by a long silence.

It was broken by Marie's phone ringing. "Hello, DS Evans. My name is DC Bellows from Kent Police and I'm calling in response to your enquiry regarding a missing man called Douglas Marshall."

Fearfully, Marie told him to go ahead.

'We've had an unidentified male washed up on the beach at Dymchurch,' he said, 'on the South Coast. There was no identification on him, but he does fit the description you circulated. We'll be sending the forensic photographs and we'd be glad to hear what you think.'

Marie asked him to send them immediately and she'd ring him back with her response.

Jackman threw her a worried glance. If this dead man did turn out to be Dougie the Dreamer, and he had been murdered, then it lent credence to Rory's horror story. And anyone who got an inkling that snuff movies were being made would be in mortal danger.

Frank Rosen! Hell, he had to get him out, and fast. He pulled his phone from his pocket and rang his friend on the burner. There was no answer. When it rang out, he called Frank's own mobile, with the same result.

Marie's printer whirred into life. She snatched up the pages, scrutinising the photos on them, and her face fell.

'It's Dougie,' she whispered. 'He's almost unrecognisable from having been in the water but it's him, I'm sure of it.'

'And Frank isn't answering either of his phones,' Jackman added quietly.

They stared at each other.

'I suggest,' said Rory, 'that you do as I advised and get out to that film set.'

'I'll run up and see if Ruth Crooke is still here,' Jackman said. 'Marie, contact Kent Police. The rest of you, get ready to move out, and, Robbie, ring down and ask the sergeant for a couple of units of uniforms to go with us. As soon as I'm back, we'll be off.'

* * *

John felt unaccountably tired. He rested awhile on his couch, telling himself it was due to the physical exertion of hauling Frank Rosen to that drainage ditch in the middle of nowhere.

Dismissing the thought that his present state was caused by the emotions his unexpected encounter with this figure from his past had brought forth, he went over every move he had made that day. He found nothing to connect him to Frank's death. Besides, John didn't exist. With the assistance of Stephen, he had erased all trace of his former identity.

It had surprised him to find that Stephen was involved in the porn movie business. It didn't fit with the idea John had of him. Most of his business concerned illicit finance, money laundering in particular had funded the soon to be implemented Phase Two.

Ah, Phase Two. Tomorrow he would submit his latest report, and the fun would begin. When it was completed to Stephen's satisfaction, he would be able to retire, a rich man.

Pity about Hazel. For when Phase Two was over, he would never see her again. He just hoped the job would not end as the last one had. Janet had been expendable. It was unfortunate, but it was what he had been contracted to do, and he had honoured the agreement. Hazel wasn't another Janet, however. Hazel was unique.

With that thought in his mind, John drifted off to sleep.

* * *

That evening, Alistair Ashcroft sat in the meeting area and waited for his visitor. He had seen the chaplain earlier in the day but only briefly, and had asked him if he'd be able to spare him a few minutes before lockdown. He had sensed a certain resistance in Patrick during their last meeting and was anxious to overcome it. He always enjoyed the challenge of pitting his wits against a mind such as the chaplain's.

He had deliberately requested a meeting at the end of the working day. The chaplain was a very busy man and would be tired — and therefore at his most vulnerable.

And Patrick Galway did look tired, exhausted even. Good. Ashcroft mentally rubbed his hands together.

'I won't keep you long, Patrick,' he said. 'You look all in. You should have said, we could easily have met another time.'

'I'm fine, Stephen. I always have time for you. Is there something bothering you?'

'Well, I do have something on my mind, though it's not remorse, Patrick. I'm incapable of that.'

Patrick Galway listened without interrupting. He was good at that.

'What worries me is the fact that I am differently wired to others. If I can't experience certain emotions because of some physical damage to my brain, where does this leave me in terms of redemption? Do you think I'll be judged according to the same criteria as a man whose brain is perfectly whole? And if so, is that fair?'

Patrick considered this for a few moments. 'Do you believe in God's redemption, Stephen? Is it important to you to save your soul?'

'I'm thinking hypothetically. I guess you could say I'm hedging my bets. If God does exist, what then? Does this supposed all-powerful being judge all souls equally, whether they are sound or defective?'

'It would be my thought that God can see into your heart, and therein would lie the truth. You would be judged fairly and impartially, as will all souls, and in terms of you as an individual.' Patrick smiled at him. 'It's good to know you feel the need to cover all bases. It will give God a fighting chance to reach you.'

'And save my soul?'

'That's down to the Almighty, Stephen.'

'And you? Would you save me, Patrick?'

The chaplain looked deep into his eyes. 'I do not command the wisdom or the righteousness of the Lord, and I cannot look into your heart. That is a power God alone possesses.'

Ashcroft had noticed the glint of amusement in the chaplain's eyes. 'Nicely avoided, Patrick. Now, I think you should go, I've taken up too much of your time already. I'm grateful for the time you spend with me, and I'm truly sorry

163

I cannot tell you that I feel sorry for what I've done. It's just not in me, I'm afraid.'

'Thank you for your honesty, Stephen. It's a step in the right direction. I'll see you soon.'

Ashcroft watched him leave. He'd had his fun, now to more serious matters, such as ensuring that everything was in place for tomorrow. The moment he heard from Hazel, he'd be bringing down his own little Armageddon on a small section of humanity.

Redemption. What a joke!

* * *

Foxdown Lodge had been made ready for when the owners returned from Spain. Lance did a final tour of the house and its outbuildings while, out in the drive, the vehicles were loaded and ready to depart.

As he was leaving the oldest barn — the one his specialised team had had the most work to clean — his phone vibrated in his pocket. The man who'd sent the message was someone he'd never met, one of the Dutch organiser's top agents. It was short and to the point:

> *Evacuate all relevant personnel from film unit. Assignment terminated. Deliver tonight's production using emergency channels. Repeat, evacuate.*

Shit.

Of course, he was prepared for this. He had had his bail-out plan in place from the start. It was just that he hadn't expected to have to implement it right now. Everything had gone so smoothly at his end, it had to be a problem somewhere else along the line.

Lance hurried out to the waiting vehicles and issued the order.

'We've been stood down. This is finished. Complete the sanitising operation and disappear. Your money will be paid in the usual way, and a termination bonus added. We know how to contact you if we need you in future. Thank you for your cooperation.'

After the last vehicle had driven away, Lance made two short calls, took one last look at the old house and hurried to his car. From here, he would drive to a certain garage where he would pick up a new vehicle. By the end of the week, the little Chevy, now a different colour and with a different set of plates, would be on sale in a second-hand car mart in another part of the country. It had served its purpose and would now disappear. Just like Lance.

CHAPTER NINETEEN

The team, along with a hastily assembled group of uniformed officers, were in the car park of the station, awaiting orders.

'Change of plan,' said Jackman crisply. 'Marie and I will go straight to Frank Rosen's cabin, while everyone else will go to Old Oaks Rectory at Amberley Fen. You will be accompanied by Superintendent Ruth Crooke as OIC, and DC Robbie Melton will be co-ordinating. Okay with that, Robbie?'

'Yes, boss. What are our orders?'

'Seal off the site. No one in and no one out. Superintendent Crooke will explain to whoever is in charge of the place that we are investigating an alleged serious crime. If Frank Rosen is still there, put him under immediate protection and get him back here as fast as you can. We have two more crews being mobilised and they are already on their way. They will await your arrival before going in, so you will have enough officers to cope. Keep in radio contact at all times, understand?'

He saw Ruth come out of the back door and hurry towards them. 'Time to go,' he said, 'and be careful. We have no idea which of them is involved in this, but they are very dangerous men. Watch each other's backs.' He turned to Ruth, who nodded.

'Go!'

He and Marie raced to his vehicle and, in moments, were heading towards Frank's cabin in the woods.

As they pulled into the car park, Jackman was relieved to see the old Vitesse parked up near the café.

'We'll try Woody's Place first,' he said to Marie. 'He could be having his supper there.'

A couple of people were seated at the tables but there was no sign of Frank. 'Anyone see Frank in here this evening?' Jackman called out.

'Yes, he was in earlier, with an old friend.' Woody pointed to a table near the back of the café. 'Sat there and had a couple of coffees, then they left. Must have been a couple of hours ago, I suppose. Isn't he in his cabin?'

Jackman didn't answer. He didn't like the sound of this 'old friend'.

'What did this friend look like?' he demanded.

Woody looked blank. 'Well, I didn't really notice. He was just an ordinary bloke. Didn't make an impression on me at all, I'm afraid.'

Marie touched his arm. 'Come on. We need to check the cabin.'

'This doesn't bode well, Marie.'

'You can say that again.'

They picked up speed and ran down the path towards Frank's little log cabin.

It was in darkness, the door was locked and the place looked empty. Without a word, Jackman put his shoulder to the door. The lock gave way easily.

The cabin had the slightly musty smell he had noticed before. Jackman switched on the light and stared around. No one here.

Marie peered into the bedroom. 'He's not here.'

'But his car is, so where the hell is he? And who is this "old friend"? He hasn't got any friends here, he told us that, and why bring someone to his hideout?'

'Come on,' said Marie, moving towards the door. 'We need to check that old car.'

Back at the car park, they approached the Triumph cautiously. The lights outside the café were no help. Frank's car was parked in a deep pool of shadow. Jackman took a torch from his pocket and shone it through the windows. It was as empty as the cabin.

'Boss.' Marie's voice was unsteady. 'Look.' She was pointing to the ground, quite close to the driver's door.

Jackman shone the torch at the place she was indicating. Blood. They were too late to save Frank Rosen.

* * *

While Jackman radioed in with their finding and requested a team of uniforms to contain a possible crime scene, Marie went back into the café.

Taking Woody aside, she whispered, 'We suspect something has happened to Frank. We had to break his door down, I'm afraid, but we'll make good the damage.'

Doors could be fixed, Woody said, but Frank was a very nice man.

'Are you sure there's nothing you can tell us about the man who came in here with Frank, Woody?'

'I don't know what to tell you,' Woody said. 'He was one of those men you just don't notice — average height, average build, nondescript clothes.' He pursed his lips. 'Um, dark trousers, brown jacket. His hair was brown too.' He shrugged, 'Just ordinary.'

'Do you have CCTV?' Marie asked, knowing what the answer would be.

Woody looked even more miserable. ''Fraid not. We've never had any trouble here, and, well, there's not much cash in the till, we don't have that many customers.'

'Okay. So, can you tell me anything about their behaviour towards each other? Was it friendly? Animated? Did they argue?'

'They didn't argue, far from it. They were definitely old friends. I caught a few snippets here and there, and gathered they had worked together years ago. They laughed a lot, like they were going over old times.'

Another copper then. Marie was puzzled. 'And they left together?'

Woody nodded. 'They did. I heard one car drive off about ten minutes after they went out. I saw that Frank's was still here, where he always parks it at night, so I guess that was the friend leaving.'

But was he alone, or was Frank with him? She needed to talk to Jackman.

* * *

The film company's second assistant director, who was still on site, was outraged at the incursion but he was no match for Ruth Crooke. Even when he told her they'd lose a fortune if they failed to keep to their tight schedule, his words were water off a duck's back. When Ruth demanded a full list of everyone working on the project, the man's face fell even further.

'Have you any idea how many staff and actors are involved in a production like this?' he exclaimed in horror.

'No,' said Ruth, 'but you are going to tell me, and I'm going to interview each and every one of them. Meanwhile, I want everyone still on set gathered in the catering area. With immediate effect, no one leaves this location, and I want all of those connected to this project who are out on location brought back here, and if they are indisposed, to remain available to be interviewed as soon as I have officers available. No exceptions.'

While a runner was sent to contact the production manager, with whom the buck stopped, and get them to return to the rectory forthwith, Ruth stood, tapping her foot and praying that Jackman had been right. Because if he wasn't, Ruth would be in a whole lot of trouble — career-changing trouble. She had obtained a warrant, and was now winging its way across the fens, brought by motorcycle courier. It would be some help, but even so, this was one of the biggest risks she had ever taken.

As people streamed in from all over the site, Ruth received a call from Jackman.

'Ruth! Frank's gone missing, and there is blood next to his car. He was last seen with a man purporting to be an old friend. I've requested forensics, but I shan't wait for them. As soon as we have a uniformed presence out here, we'll be heading your way.'

'I could do with you here, Rowan, and that's a fact. But I'm not sure what to make of what you say about Frank Rosen, especially in the light of what you've told me about Douglas Marshall. It's all adding up to you being right about this whole set-up.'

'I *know* we are right, Ruth,' said Jackman. 'It's an illegal film unit, hiding inside a genuine one. We just have to pick out the rotten apples from the barrel.'

'Well, I've ordered them all to gather, so get back here and we'll see what we can find.'

Ruth joined Robbie and the rest of Jackman's team, who were taking the details of the staff members who had presented themselves.

'The producer and the production co-ordinator are on their way here, ma'am, ETA ten minutes. They have the names we want,' Robbie told her. 'There's a few people who appear to be missing, so we are paying particular attention to them.' He frowned. 'This is a massive undertaking, ma'am. Some of the crew have motorhomes and caravans on site, some are locals, and others get digs or hotel rooms close by. We were lucky because they were filming some evening shots just before we got here, so we've managed to catch a lot of them before they left.'

'What's the overall feeling about this, Robbie?' asked Ruth. 'Do they seem nervous, on edge?'

'Quite the opposite. Everyone seems excited, and dead inquisitive. By the way, we are going to need a command centre if we are to ring all the personnel who are not on site. Could you arrange something, ma'am?'

Ruth had two choices. She could commandeer the film company's production office, or bring in the Fenland Constabulary mobile command centre from Greenborough. She decided to wait and speak to the producer before she decided which course to take. The mobile unit had all the basic communications equipment on board, and being independently powered, was probably the most efficient, but her budget was groaning already, and it would take a while to get the unit over from Greenborough.

She was distracted by Gary Pritchard, who was hurrying up to them. 'I've got a name that has set off warning bells, ma'am. One of the crew phoned him to get him to come in but his phone is out of service. Apparently, he always stays in a hotel, even though he has a motorhome on site. His colleague just rang the hotel, and was told he'd checked out earlier this evening.'

'Name?' asked Ruth.

'Lance Newport, he's the sound mixer,' said Gary, checking his notes. 'He was on set this afternoon, and his motorhome is still here, but he also brings a little Chevy Spark, which is what he left in earlier. When I asked about him, his colleague mentioned that he had seemed unusually pre-occupied of late. I don't know if this is relevant but apparently, although he's very competent, he's not a friendly kind of guy, and not particularly well-liked.'

'You think he's done a runner, Gary?'

'I'm certain he has, and his colleague thought so too.'

'Then chase up licencing, and access the APNR system. See if that vehicle has been picked up on number plate recognition cameras, then get a call out to apprehend the driver.'

Gary hurried off, already talking into his phone, and Ruth turned to Robbie. 'The moment that producer arrives, get everything you can on Lance Newport from him. Ask him about Craig Turner and Dexter Thompson as well. We've gleaned quite a bit from the official police channels, but I want to know what kind of people they are, and what the others think about them. Thompson, I know, is in psychiatric care, but who knows, he could be a bloody good actor.'

Robbie turned towards the car park. 'I'm on it. They should be here any minute, so I'll go and meet them.'

Left alone for a few moments, Ruth began to worry about Frank Rosen. She didn't know him personally but from what others, including Rowan Jackman, had said about him he was a good man.

* * *

The residents of Amberley Fen had got used to seeing the headlights of vehicles racing to and from the Old Oaks Rectory over the last few weeks, but the flashing blue lights were something new. But then it was a police drama they were filming, so it was probably related to that. They settled back down on their couches and continued to watch TV.

Tonight, as she and Jackman drove at speed along the dangerous fen lanes, Marie thought the brightly illuminated location site looked like a spaceship that had just landed on a deserted planet.

Then she thought of Dougie the Dreamer, and the full weight of his death descended on her. He had come to her in the hope that they might prevent some terrible occurrence, and she had failed him. Even if they succeeded in stopping it now, it was too late for Dougie. For Frank too, possibly. The pool of blood beside his car had been significant, it wasn't just a few splashes. If he were dead, and she believed that he was, it would be very hard on Jackman. He was already berating himself for not insisting that Frank get away from the shoot.

It was difficult to find anywhere to park. Even outside in the lane, vehicles stood nose to tail. Jackman inched into a space between two trucks and they hurried inside to find Ruth. Inside, they came upon a scene of utter chaos. Crowds of people were milling around, among them uniformed officers waving sheets of paper and calling out orders that nobody seemed to respond to.

'Bloody hell!' exclaimed Marie. 'What a circus.'
'More like the county fair,' muttered Jackman. 'Look, there's Robbie. He'll tell us where things stand.'

Robbie looked flustered and excited. 'There's loads of people still unaccounted for, boss, most of them irrelevant apart from five crew members we are keen to track down. One of them is a bloke called Lance Newport, who could possibly be key to what we think is going on.'

Marie touched Jackman's arm. 'Is it too late to ring Sam and see if there is any news of Dex? If we could reassure him that we already know about Lance and that he wouldn't be dropping anyone in it, he might at least confirm our suspicions.'

Jackman looked at his watch. 'Sam won't mind. I'll give him a call.' He put the phone on loudspeaker.

Sam told them he was on his way to Oatlands Hall. They had called to say that Dex seemed to be coming out of the fugue state but was agitated, insisting that he must speak to Sam urgently.

Glancing at Marie, Jackman said, 'Sam, we need Dex to answer one important question. If you can't get anything else out of him, can you at least ask him if a man called Lance Newport had anything to do with the porn movies and whatever else was going on?'

'Lance Newport. Got it,' repeated Sam. 'Okay, we're almost there, Jackman. I'll ring you as soon as I get it out of him.'

Marie smiled. 'Sounds hopeful.'

'But he's just one man,' said Jackman grimly. 'Who knows how many others are involved.'

'And Dex might tell us who they are, so let's hang onto that, huh?' It was unlike him to be so negative, Marie thought. Then she told herself to make allowances for his mood. Already dealing with his bereavement, Jackman had then learned that an old friend of his had probably met with his end. It was almost too much to deal with.

They proceeded to the catering area, where, in contrast to the chaos beyond, all was quiet and orderly. The tables were being used for interviewing, and a dozen or more officers were busy recording people's details. Gary moved among them, asking questions and taking notes.

'I see the catering firms are doing a good trade,' Marie remarked, seeing a queue at a massive white van selling sandwiches, paninis and hot snacks. Her stomach rumbled.

Gary caught sight of her and waved. Marie went over to him. 'Anything new come to light, Gary?'

He shook his head. 'We are still looking at the same five suspects, the prime one being that Lance feller. I chatted with one of the sound trainees that he supervises, a really nice girl called Sophie. She told me quite a lot about him. Now, sound trainees have to have good hearing, since they often have to isolate a particular noise from among others. Sophie overheard quite a few things Lance said in various whispered conversations. I've asked her to talk to you and the boss when you're ready.'

'Good. I'll just grab Jackman and you can point her out to us.' She gazed around the sea of faces. 'Where's the super?'

'She's with the producer, telling him what's been going on under cover of his shoot. According to Robbie, he's incandescent with rage.'

'I don't blame him,' said Marie. 'You know what, Gary? When we arrived I thought there were rather a lot of uniformed officers I didn't recognise, then it dawned on me that these were actors. It is a police drama, isn't it?'

'It had me confused too at first. They all look so authentic. Frank's doing a damned good job.'

Marie winced. They hadn't had time to tell everyone yet. 'Frank's missing, Gary.'

'Oh no! I assumed he'd just gone off home. What happened?'

She told him. 'Robbie knows, but maybe you could update Max and Charlie for me? Now I'd better find Jackman so we can talk to your Sophie.'

'That's her over there.' He pointed to a young woman with a long, light brown ponytail, wearing cargo pants and a sweatshirt with a logo on it. She was seated on her own, on a low wall that surrounded the garden. 'I'll fetch her over.'

CHAPTER TWENTY

Ashcroft sat up in bed and looked with interest at the figure in the doorway. It was rather late in the day for anyone to come visiting.

'I can only think that this is something very important,' he said quietly.

Without answering, the stranger walked in and handed Ashcroft a piece of paper with a few words written on it.

Alistair took it, switched on the light and read what it said. He handed the note back and whispered, 'Contact Christos. Phase Two to be activated immediately.'

The man turned and left. He hadn't uttered a single word.

Ashcroft lay back and took a few deep breaths. It was hard not to get excited after so long, after so much careful planning. As soon as he learned of the furore out at the site of the filming, he knew that the time was right. There would be no sleep for Alistair Ashcroft that night.

* * *

Hazel Palgrave was a light sleeper, when she slept at all, so she answered her mobile at once.

She had known the call would come soon, but it was still a shock to hear that it was happening now.

She was out of bed and into her clothes in moments and was soon speeding towards the office. On arrival, she filled the kettle and switched it on. She and John could have a cup of coffee while they waited for the call.

Hazel had been through the procedure a hundred times, but still her heart beat fast. A lot was down to her and she didn't want to show herself wanting. She closed her eyes and muttered a prayer. It was not to a deity, but to someone very special. 'I have to get this right . . . for you.' The emotion in her voice made the words even more powerful. 'I have to.'

John arrived moments later. She could sense his tension as soon as he walked in the door. Good. It meant the outcome was important to him too.

She checked through everything one last time. Every file was in place, every piece of information to hand. John's final piece of investigative work had been cancelled, deemed no longer necessary at this late hour.

They waited, their eyes fixed on her screen.

* * *

Sam and Julia arrived to find Dex much calmer. His doctor had received his medical history from the GP who had treated him when he was younger. 'It answers a lot of our questions,' said the doctor. 'As you thought, something triggered a memory of a past trauma. We think his mind couldn't cope with it, hence his retreat into a fugue state. Luckily, it was short-lived.'

'But you will keep him for the full assessment?' asked Julia warily.

'Yes. I'd like to make sure he's on an even keel again before we discharge him. Don't worry, Dr Tennant, we'll take very good care of him. Now, I'll take you to his room.'

They found Dexter sitting in a chair by the window. He even managed a wan smile when they entered and stammered an apology for the trouble he'd caused. 'The doc told me I'd worried you badly, though I can't remember what I did to upset you. I'm sorry, especially as you were trying to help me.'

Sam and Julia waved his apology away. 'You wanted to see us,' said Sam. 'So, how can we help you?'

Dex let out a breath. 'It's me who needs to help you, and your detective friend. Listen,' he leaned forward, and his voice fell to a whisper, 'I believe my friend Craig is dead. I did try to stop him, but I obviously didn't do enough. Now, well, the least I can do for him is put the police onto the people who're behind the blue movies.' He pulled a sheet of paper from his pocket. 'I've written their names down, and the parts they played. I'm sorry, I don't know what their other game was. If I did, I'd tell you. I hope you believe me.'

'Of course we do,' said Julia. 'You are being a great help.'

'I should have told you earlier, but . . .' He started to shiver.

'No need to explain, Dex,' Sam said. 'You've told us now, and if it helps, Jackman already knows about one of them. And I promise you, none of this will come back on you. So you can push all this aside and concentrate on getting well again.'

'Tell your detective not to trust Lance Newport. I believe he is very dangerous, and if Craig is dead, Lance will be behind it.'

Sam pocketed the paper. 'Let's leave it there, Dex. You've done your part. We'll keep in touch with the doctor here, and we'll see you when you are discharged. We'll help you all we can.'

As they closed the door, they heard Dex sobbing.

While Julia went and spoke to the nurse in charge of Dex, Sam rang Jackman.

'Lance Newport, sound mixer. Andrew Shaw, key grip. Rick Grace, stills photographer and Ben White, video assistant operator. Along with Craig Turner and Dexter Thompson, these were the main crew on the porn films. Dex said a few others helped out, but they weren't from his film company and he had no idea where they came from. Lance is your main man, Jackman. As well as the porn films, he would have been the boss man on whatever other unscrupulous scheme they had on the go. He's the one you need to find.'

'And unfortunately, it's him who has disappeared,' growled Jackman. 'But thank you for this, Sam, it's what we were waiting for. You've really come up trumps.'

'Dex is the one who came up trumps,' Sam said. 'That took a lot of doing. Oh, and that really is all he knows, so we'll back off now and let him rest, and hopefully he'll start to recover.'

'I've taken that on board, never fear. Now I need to get out an all-points bulletin on Lance Newport, so thank you again, Sam, and thank Julia for me. See you when I see you.'

Driving them back to Cartoft Village, Julia glanced at Sam and patted his knee. 'Don't worry about Dex, I'll look out for him. And if he needs specialist care, he'll get it.'

'I always said you were a psychic rather than a psychologist, my dear.' Sam chuckled. 'As it happens, I was just thinking about that young man, and worrying about his future.'

'I thought as much. And by the way, the nurse showed me the GP's letter. It turns out that Dex's father was a gambler too. He lost everything and could see no way out, so he killed himself. It was young Dexter, then only nine, who found him in the bath with his wrists slashed. That's when the panic attacks started.'

'So it was the panic attack itself that triggered the fugue.'

'Mmm, and I'm thinking I can help him myself. I've had good results with eye movement desensitisation and reprocessing, and I think he'd be a good subject for that.' She nodded to herself. 'Yes, that's what I'll do. As soon as he's been assessed, I'll speak to his doctor and see if I can take over his treatment.'

Sam smiled in satisfaction. *Lucky young man. If anyone can get him through this, it's this woman I'm sitting next to.*

* * *

Energised by Sam's call with the list of names, Jackman hurried off to look for Marie. He met her in the company of a young woman.

'Boss, this is Sophie Clark. She's been working with Lance Newport, and has some information for us.'

'Excellent! Because I've just received a list of the names we wanted, Mr Lance Newport being number one.' He smiled at Sophie. 'Maybe we should find somewhere we can talk. It's like Trafalgar Square here.'

On their way to the main house, Jackman received a WhatsApp message. He gasped, stopping mid-stride.

The message read, 'Is this boy safe?' Attached to it was an image — a photo of his nephew, Miles.

He looked at Marie and saw that she too was staring at her phone, a look of horrified disbelief on her face.

Jackman took her phone from her shaking hand. Marie's message read, 'Is this man safe?' An image of Ralph Enderby had been attached. He showed her his.

'What is this?' she hissed.

Suddenly, he remembered Sophie. 'Er, bit of a hitch, Sophie. Do you mind hanging on for a while?'

'Sure. I'll go and get something to eat and wait for you there.'

She had barely left them when Robbie, Gary and Kevin all came hurrying towards them, holding out their mobile phones.

'What? You too? Let me see,' Jackman said.

Gary's read, 'Is this woman safe?" and showed a picture of his partner, Gilly. Robbie's had the same message, along with an image of Ella Jarvis. The picture in Kevin's was Alan, his partner.

It was therefore no surprise to see a white-faced Charlie Button running their way. His phone had a photo of his mother. Max followed, a picture of his wife, Rosie, on his screen.

It was obvious that they were being targeted but by whom? How? Why? He needed to find Ruth Crooke. 'Stay here, Marie, and you lot too. I've got to tell the super about this.'

'Can I ring Ella?' asked Robbie nervously.

'And I'd like to check on my Gilly,' added Gary.

'Yes, yes, all of you, you must check on your loved ones. But don't panic them, whatever you do.' As he sprinted off towards the rectory, Jackman called his mother.

'Thank God!' she exclaimed. 'I've just had a horrible message, asking if you are safe, with a photo of you attached. What's going on, Rowan?'

If only he knew! 'I'm fine, Mum, busy working. Are you all okay there?'

'You had one too, didn't you? That's why you're asking. Are we in danger, son?

'I don't think so, Mum. I think this is some nasty scam. I'll get the tech guys on it straightaway, but take care, yes? Just to be on the safe side. Stick together and keep the boys close.'

'Not again, Rowan! When is all this going to stop? We can't go through something like that again.'

Jackman's heart went out to her. 'I'm sure this is nothing but scare-mongering, Mum. And I will personally hang those responsible out to dry! I'll call you back when it's all cleared up. All right, Cap'n?'

His mother sighed. 'All right, son. Just take care, and ring me when you can.'

When Jackman caught up with Ruth, he found her staring at her phone.

'You as well?'

'A picture of my niece—'

'And a text saying: *Is this girl safe?* He held up his own phone. 'We've all had one.'

'What in hell's name does this mean?'

A few possible answers were starting to trickle into his brain, as yet too incoherent to express. 'Let's assume that someone really does want to mess up this investigation — and really mess it up. Or a certain person is buying himself time to get away.'

'Maybe they do have a commodity that is valuable enough to warrant protecting,' mused Ruth, calmer now. 'I guess the people here who do the digital imagery could manage a sophisticated hack like this?'

But Jackman felt uneasy. It went deeper than this, surely? He shook himself. He didn't have the time for speculation. Finding Lance Newport had to come first.

'Is there a private room we can use, Ruth? We have a lass who apparently knows quite a bit about Lance Newport. We have to get that man before he tries to leave the country, which no doubt is his intention.'

'I've arranged for us to use the production office, Rowan. Get your team and I'll take you there. I'll sit in too.'

Jackman hurried back to the others. Soon, they were all following Ruth to the office she had commandeered.

They settled themselves down, every face creased with anxiety.

Jackman needed to allay their fears before the investigation did indeed fall apart. He held up his phone. 'We have to see this as a deliberate attempt to cause panic among us, and to derail the investigation. I cannot believe that every single one of our nearest and dearest could be in danger. It's not possible to accomplish. We have to stay focussed, no matter how difficult that seems.'

Marie raised her hand. 'Sir, I was about to contact Orac and ask her about it when she rang me.'

Jackman raised his eyebrows.

'She had one of the messages too.'

Everyone looked at Marie. Orac, their computer analyst and resident genius, was a loner. She had no friends, only colleagues. So whose was the face in her message?

'I know what you're thinking,' said Marie, with a sigh. 'She was sent a picture of me. I'm the closest thing she has to a friend.'

Her words sent another question searing through Jackman's brain. Who could possibly know that? He decided to move on quickly. 'So, did she tell you how it was done?'

'Oh, apparently it's quite possible if you know what you're doing. There are lots of ways of mass text messaging, although not quite so easy to add different images. She suspects a clever system using a timer and several different methods simultaneously. Anyway, Orac is on the case.'

Somewhat relieved, Jackman said, 'Guys, listen. I know how you feel — I'm worried too. But we *have* to focus on Lance Newport. That man cannot be allowed to get away. Think about what we suspect him of doing. He lures attractive young men and women into the porn industry, then sets them up to be killed — slaughtered on screen! It's almost beyond belief, but it seems like he's making the urban myth of the snuff movie a reality.'

'Can we be sure of that, Rowan?' asked Ruth.

'From the reports provided by Rory and his colleague in Cornwall there appears to be little doubt as to what was going on, Super. All five bodies had body oil on them, and had been involved in sexual activity prior to their deaths. The single common denominator is Lance Newport, the man who has taken off, and who I suggest is behind the murder of Douglas Marshall *and* the disappearance of Frank Rosen.'

'Then you'll need all the help you can get, won't you?' Ruth gritted her teeth. 'I'm sticking my neck out here, Rowan, but as I've already committed us to shutting down a major film unit, I might as well carry on. Tell me what you need and I'll get it if I can.'

Greatly relieved, Jackman also felt huge affection for the woman who implicitly trusted his instincts, despite the consequences if he were wrong.

'I'd like as many officers as possible out here talking to people. I'd like Lance's face plastered over all national media platforms. I want the whole country looking for him.'

'Okay. I'll leave you to talk to your young woman while I go and organise a message to go out. The production manager will be able to give us a recent photo, I'm sure.' Ruth left the room.

'Right, Gary,' Jackman said. 'Would you go and fetch young Sophie? I want everyone to hear what she has to say.'

CHAPTER TWENTY-ONE

Orac glared angrily at the screen. 'Well, you cheeky bastard.' Whoever had sent the messages had bounced them halfway round the world. It would take months to trace them and time wasn't on their side.

Marie had said they suspected the sender to be deliberately derailing their current investigation, but that made no sense. No case, however serious, warranted someone going to such lengths. It reminded Orac of an international spy ring she had once been part of taking down. That, or some adolescent genius holed up, pale and red-eyed, in a stinking bedroom, surrounded by pizza boxes and empty Red Bull cans.

Orac flexed her fingers. It was time to get down to some serious work.

* * *

It took Sam a while to ring Jackman after he received the strange message on his mobile. He would have called him sooner had not Julia rung to tell him about hers. It had a picture of Sam attached to it, his had a photo of her. After a lengthy discussion, they decided that, late as it was, Jackman should be told.

The call did nothing to reassure him.

'How many people have had similar messages, do you think?' Julia asked.

'It's hard to tell, since their loved ones have also been targeted. Naturally, Jackman is worried sick, but he can't afford to let up on the hunt for the missing film-maker, who is responsible for several deaths.' Sam sighed. 'I wish you were here, Julia.'

'Would you like me to come over?'

If only she would! 'Oh no,' he said, 'not at three in the morning. But could you come and have breakfast with me tomorrow morning? I have something in my head, this crazy notion, and I'd like your opinion.'

'Crazy, eh? Okay, I'll be there for breakfast.'

After the call, Sam lay in bed, thinking about the messages. Jackman had blamed the runaway film-maker, but Sam knew it was far deeper and more dangerous than that. Was his friend making a mistake in putting all his efforts into the one person? One thing was clear. Whoever had sent those messages had spent an enormous amount of time gathering information on each member of the team, and their loved ones, and was now using this to spread panic and chaos.

Hence the idea. With growing horror, Sam was coming to realise that the only person he knew with the time and patience to undertake such a task was Alistair Ashcroft. No. It wasn't possible. For a start, Ashcroft hadn't been at the Aegis Unit long enough to bring something of this scale to fruition. It would have taken months, years possibly. But who else could it be?

* * *

The overheard conversations Sophie told them about only served to reinforce Jackman's suspicions about Lance. Jackman retired his team with an order to get some sleep and come in the following day whenever they were ready. There would be no one watching the clock to see what time they turned up. They could do little more in the hunt for Lance; it was now in the hands of traffic cops and the border

184

agencies — customs officials and airport staff — and, when the message went out, the general public.

Jackman drove home to Mill Corner utterly spent. Further examination of the situation was out of the question. All he was capable of was pouring himself a brandy and taking to his bed.

Jackman let himself in, hung up his jacket, threw his keys onto the hall table and went into the kitchen. It smelled like home. He poured himself the promised drink and took it to his bedroom, where he flung off his clothes and sank into bed and a dreamless sleep.

* * *

Early the following morning, Sam heard someone tapping at his door.

'Just checking you are all right, my friend,' said Jackman, when he opened it.

In the harsh early morning light, Sam thought that Jackman looked haggard. What a weight of responsibility he carried, so soon after his bereavement. The lives of his whole team, their families and friends, rested on his shoulders.

'I'm fine, Jackman,' he lied. He didn't tell Jackman of his idea about who might be responsible for those messages. In the cold light of day, it seemed less reasonable. After all, his hatred of Ashcroft might well have clouded his judgement. He needed Julia's opinion of his theory before he shared it with anyone else.

'I've had a thought, Sam,' Jackman said. 'Why don't you and Julia come to the station at around ten this morning? I'm calling a meeting to go over what we know. It would be helpful if you could listen in and give us your thoughts.'

'Julia will be here early, we'll have breakfast and join you at the station. I'm sure she'll agree. She's cancelled her appointments until she's sure Dex is making good headway, then, if he agrees, she's taking over his ongoing therapy.'

'Great. Then I'll see you both later.'

* * *

Neither Hazel nor John had been home, nor had they taken a break since the early hours of the morning. At six o'clock, nowhere else being open, John had been forced to break his rule about not eating fast food and had gone out and collected a takeaway.

The hamburger brought back memories of being with Frank Rosen on obo, swapping stories and noting the comings and goings of the felon they had been sent to observe. Poor old Frank. Such a shame he'd got involved with that film crew, and what bad luck that Stephen had sent his best man to check on them.

He glanced surreptitiously across at Hazel. She had not left the computer, not even to go to the toilet, for four hours. Her eyes remained fixed on the screen even while she ate her burger.

Finally, she pushed her chair back and rubbed her aching neck.

He had an urge to lay his hand on it and ease the stiffness. Instead, he offered to make her a coffee.

She accepted and sat back, her legs stretched out in front of her. 'I really hate that word "textbook." Ugh. But it really was, wasn't it? What a night!'

'I bet you can't wait to pass that on to Stephen,' he said.

'He already knows. Christos patched in earlier, and by now, Stephen will be fully aware of what our night's work achieved.' Hazel looked at him with what he hoped was affection. 'You did well, John. Now get some rest.' She pointed to the flat's only bedroom. 'You need to be fresh for the rest of the day's tasks. I've ordered lunch to be delivered at half past one, so you can sleep until then.'

'What about you?' he asked. 'You've been on the go even longer than me.'

She smiled. 'I have one more job to do, in around an hour's time, then this will do nicely for me.' She patted her office chair. 'It's also a recliner. I don't want to miss anything.'

'That's dedication for you,' he said.

'What else?' Hazel flung back immediately, and her eyes shone with fervour.

'Absolutely.' John cleared his throat. 'Don't let me over-sleep, I have a lot of work to do later. Hope you get some rest.'

He went into the small bedroom, closed the door and stretched out on the single bed. They had a bloody good working partnership, but he wondered how it would end. He hoped that when the time came, they would be able to part without the use of a sharp blade.

* * *

Hazel waited until John had closed the door, then turned back to her screen. Rather than the special job she had mentioned, Hazel wanted to know more about that last trouble-shooting job John had undertaken. Why had he not done as requested and handed the problem to Stephen's operatives to deal with? And why had he not mentioned that he knew one of the people involved? As she worked, her eyes became hard and flinty. This was not good, not good at all.

* * *

'Well, I'm impressed! But breakfast always was your forte, wasn't it?' Julia sat back in the kitchen chair and patted her stomach. 'That was lovely, thank you.'

'We aim to please,' said Sam with a little bow. 'Now, coffee, and we'll get down to our deliberations.'

They took their coffees into the lounge and Sam began. 'Last night, I tried to work out how long it would have taken to set up a scheme like yesterday's and target all those people simultaneously with texts and images. You'd have to learn enough about people to trace their "significant others," find their mobile numbers, source their photographs . . .' He threw up his hands. 'It could take years!'

'Someone has been watching all of us,' added Julia darkly. 'And I, for one, deeply resent that.'

'Don't we all?' muttered Sam. 'But the thing is, although it happened just as the police moved in on the film company and the ringleader absconded, I'm sure it's not connected to that at all. Jackman had barely started on the investigation; it wouldn't have been possible to orchestrate something on this scale in such a short period of time.'

'You're right,' Julia said. 'We can only assume that whoever is behind it took advantage of the police moving in on the rectory.'

'And that brings us to the question of why. What is it all for?'

Julia frowned. 'Well, there are six possible reasons. Hate, love, jealousy, retribution, money, and revenge. I reckon it's revenge. What say you?'

Sam remained quiet.

Julia glanced at him. 'Oh, I see. Who would want revenge so badly that they would spend years in order to gain it? You're thinking of Ashcroft, aren't you?'

'Who else?' Sam leaned forward. 'Can you think of anyone other than Ashcroft with the skill and patience to pull it off? Because I can't.'

'And Jackman was responsible for his downfall and incarceration,' mused Julia. 'Tell me more about him, Sam. I need to know how he could possibly have done it from within a high-security prison.'

'Ashcroft had a lot of money, Julia, and I mean a lot! He escaped Jackman and Marie's first attempt to arrest him and remained free for years. He had a lot of time to set things up while he recovered from the injuries he had sustained. I believe that was when he started to plan his revenge.'

'And his money, if carefully handled by some trusted financial manager, would buy him whatever he needed to carry out his plan,' Julia added.

'We both know how things work in prison, don't we? The other inmates hold him in high regard. Add to that his exceptionally high IQ and his ability to control people . . . Need I say more?'

'You make a very good case for the prosecution, dear Sam,' Julia said. 'And I'm assuming you will close your case with a speech about the ill-advised decision to move this man into a unit such as Aegis?'

'A lamentable mistake, and one that has provided him with the perfect situation from which to launch his attack.'

Julia narrowed her eyes. 'Tell me about this Theodore Carmichael. Why didn't he see how dangerous Ashcroft is? Why establish this unique unit entirely for him?'

Sam exhaled. 'I believe he is sincere in wanting to study the brain of a killer like Ashcroft so as to prevent others from going the same way. But scientific reports and even face-to-face encounters aren't enough when you're dealing with an Ashcroft. Theo never personally witnessed what Ashcroft did to his victims.' He sighed. 'I mean, you can empathise with someone who tells you they had a terrible nightmare, but it's only when you experience one yourself that you truly understand how terrifying they can be.'

'Then I think it's time I met this colleague of yours. With luck I can sweet-talk him into giving me a guided tour of Aegis, including an introduction to the genius murderer who is its *raison d'être*.'

Sam knew his Julia. It would be no use objecting, even if he'd wanted to, which he didn't. 'I think it's an excellent idea. I'll ring him after Jackman's meeting.'

'Good. Then that's settled.' Julia rested her gaze on him 'And Sam . . . I can't help noticing how apathetic you've been lately. Well, that has to go. Don't think I'm underestimating the suffering you're undergoing because I'm not, my heart breaks for you. But you have to think of your friend. Jackman needs you firing on all cylinders if he's to get through this mess. Is that clear?'

Like he had a choice! He smiled somewhat sheepishly. 'Clear as day.'

Julia glanced at her watch. 'Well, we'd better get going then, and see how we can help.'

CHAPTER TWENTY-TWO

Marie entered the CID room to find a team engaged in their work like never before. It affected every one of them personally and they approached it with none of their usual cheerful determination.

For her part, she was incensed at the invasion of her privacy the messages implied. Her biggest worry, however, was Jackman. How much could he take before he was crushed by the weight of it all? She would have dearly loved to get her hands on whoever had thrown this last load of shit at them.

Was she the only one who suspected that this had nothing to do with the Adonis/Apollo murders, or the blue movie maker? She had her own suspicions as to who was behind it but had voiced them to no one, especially Jackman.

When she saw Sam and Julia walk in, she decided that if there was anyone to go to with her fears, it was them.

'Everyone here?' Jackman's voice rang out across the room.

'Gary's on his way up, sir,' someone called out from the back of the room. 'He had to speak to uniform about something.'

A few moments later, Gary hustled in, apologised and took a seat.

'We will begin with the investigation into Lance Newport and his disappearance. We'll come on to the, er, other matter later.'

They discussed what they knew about the people illicitly making porn, and Lance Newport in particular.

'We have nothing on him at all, sir,' said Charlie Button. 'He's no record, no past misdemeanours. He's a skilled technician and his previous employers all agreed that he was smart and skilled at his job. He's worked all over the world, though mainly here and in Europe. Other than that — zilch.' Charlie raised a finger. 'Though I did hit on something a bit odd. I asked Orac to get into his bank account and, although his wages have been paid in, he's made no other transactions for almost a year. So Orac thinks he has another account, in a different name.'

Jackman thanked him. 'Very likely he has a pseudonym, and his other bank accounts are in that name. He had to have somewhere to stash the cash he earned from the work he did on the side.' He glanced at his notebook. 'I think the statement from the young sound trainee, Sophie Clark, should be considered as a major indicator that he is definitely the ringleader, and it confirms what Dexter Thompson said. Sophie said she wondered why there were so many poker games of an evening, always with the same players. Now Dexter has told us that they used the games to discuss the next porn film they'd be shooting. And it should be noted that the other names Dex sent us — Andrew Shaw, Rick Grace and Ben White — cannot be accounted for as of an hour ago.'

'I think it's safe to assume that the rest of the production team — crew, staff and actors — are all innocent and none of them were involved. The producers and directors were horrified to learn that something like this was going on under their watch. I've spoken with Superintendent Ruth Crooke and we are hoping to have Lance Newport's motorhome collected from the rectory later today and taken to the pound. Forensics will take it apart if they have to. After that, we see no reason to hold up the shoot any longer. It's not our intention to lose them money or disrupt their work more than we have already.' He looked around. 'Robbie? Any news on Craig Turner, or his wife, Joannie?'

Robbie stood up. 'No sighting of Craig at all but the wife has been located at her mother's place in Mablethorpe. Uniform have been to see her, and she was distraught to learn he is missing. She did receive a message from a "mate" of his, who we suspect was Lance Newport, who told her that Craig was filming in an area of the marsh that doesn't get a signal. A traffic camera sighted his Winnebago being removed from the area, but then it dropped off the radar and we've no idea where it went. We suspect it's probably been concealed somewhere. The wife is desperate to get it back because there's a lot of her belongings in it. The local division have provided a liaison officer to talk to her, and they'll be in touch if they get any further information from her.' Robbie sat down.

Jackman thanked him. 'We've circulated photos of the four men wanted in connection with the making of the illegal videos, plus the murder of Edward Keating and another unknown male. They've gone out to all forces, the ports, and the air terminals, but much as we want to talk to these men, it's Lance Newport we really want in handcuffs.'

Marie noticed that Jackman seemed hesitant about launching a discussion of the messages. She was just wondering how to bring it up tactfully when she received a message. She looked at her phone and saw a picture of her mother, along with a text:

Rather a long way away to keep an eye on her? Such a pity.

Her rage now at boiling point, she swore loudly. Then she looked around. Jackman, Robbie, Gary, Charlie and Sam were all staring incredulously at their phones.

'Who is it this time?' she demanded of Jackman.

'My mother, with Ryan,' he said quietly. 'And a caption saying, *Is there safety in numbers? I wonder.*'

Charlie's was a photo of his youngest sister. Robbie had a picture of his old crewmate and friend, Stella North, and

Max was staring at a photo of his twins, Jessica and Tim. Kevin's message showed his father, the diocesan bishop.

'Happy bloody Families,' said Max through gritted teeth. 'I'm telling you, if I get my hands on the bastard who's playing this game, I'll fucking kill him!'

No one disagreed.

'DI Jackman!' A civilian appeared and thrust a memo at him. 'From the desk sergeant, sir. He knew you were in a meeting, but he thought you needed to see this.'

Marie saw his face fall as he read it. She moved quickly to his side and took the memo from his hand:

Body found in drainage ditch by dog walker. It's on the out-skirts of Randall's Hurn, nearest landmark an area of hard-standing and a disused farm oil tank. Victim, an older man, matches your description of the missing police consultant from the film unit. Fatal stab wound to heart. Will you attend?

After a long moment, Jackman said to the waiting civilian, 'Tell the sergeant we'll take this one. Radio full details to us, please. We are on our way.' He turned to Sam. 'Can you and Julia wait until we get back?'

Sam glanced at Julia, who nodded. 'We'll be here. We have some work to do and things to discuss.'

Jackman was already getting his keys from his pocket. 'Then feel free to use my office.'

There was little doubt in the minds of either Jackman or Marie. This was Frank Rosen. They barely spoke on the drive to Randall's Hurn, which took them just under half an hour. By the time they got there the body was lying on flattened reeds on the bank above the water-filled ditch.

Side by side, they stood and gazed down at Jackman's old friend.

Marie remembered how keen Frank had been to get to the bottom of the mystery. She saw him patting the bonnet of his precious old car and it was all she could do to stop the tears from rolling down her cheeks. It shouldn't have happened to this good man. Neither should Dougie the Dreamer be cold and dead and lying in a morgue.

Her anger mounting, she glanced at Jackman's lost expression. This one was going to be down to Marie Evans to take on, and take it on she would.

She made the relevant phone calls, organised the crime scene and liaised with uniform and forensics, all in double-quick time. 'Want me to drive?' she asked Jackman when she'd finished.

'No, it's fine.' He pulled his keys from his pocket and made for the car.

It wasn't, but Marie knew not to argue. They set off, but before they had travelled more than a few hundred metres, Jackman pulled over and switched off the engine.

'It's him, isn't it? Ashcroft. I don't know how, but he's behind this, isn't he?'

Marie nodded slowly. At last, he was facing up to it. 'Yes, it's him.'

The face he turned towards her was contorted with pain. 'Marie, I can't let my family go through yet more pain. He nearly destroyed us once before, and then there was that awful attack during the Solace House case. And now this.' He showed her his phone with the picture of Harriet hugging Ryan, both grinning broadly. The tears coursed down his cheeks.

Marie leaned over and put her arms around him.

After a while, he pulled away. 'How can we stop that monster, Marie? I feel like David going up against Goliath with no weapon in his hand.'

'You're not alone, Jackman. I'm right here beside you, and that improves the odds somewhat, doesn't it?'

'You have a new life ahead of you, Marie. You have Ralph to consider now.'

'Did you not hear what I said the last time you went on like this? Ralph Enderby is one of us, Jackman. He thinks like we do, and he'll back us up to the hilt. Yes, things have changed — now you do not have one David by your side, you have *two*. Got it? If it really is Ashcroft who's behind this, we'll shut him down, and we'll have him removed from that sodding Aegis Unit to somewhere more appropriate. Remember what happened to Robert Maudsley.'

She knew Jackman would be familiar with the fate of one of Britain's longest serving prisoners, a man so dangerous he was kept in a special underground 'glass' cell at Wakefield Prison.

'Ashcroft might believe he's untouchable because he's already in for life, but we can see to it that he's put in a far less comfortable place than he is now, banged up in solitary for twenty-three hours a day, with no one to brainwash. See how he likes that. We can do it, Jackman.' She sat beside him, fists clenched, willing him to take up the fight again. When he didn't speak, she upped the ante. 'Come on, Jackman! Your team needs you. You might not have noticed, but they've turned into a bunch of zombies! You could rent them to that film producer for extras in *The Night of the Living Dead*! Do what you do best, and light a fire under them!' She turned and gave him an exasperated smile, 'Do you really want to sit here and listen to me ranting on? Because I can, you know!'

Jackman glanced at her fierce expression, then gave a short bark of laughter. 'You're right, Marie Evans, as bloody always. And as I can't stand another lecture, I'd better ignite that flame thrower.'

Marie buckled her seat belt, exhausted but relieved that she had some of the old Jackman back.

He went to start the car, then stopped. 'I'm so sorry, Marie, it was just looking at that ditch, and seeing Frank, it brought it all back; the horror of seeing Laura's car and knowing she was dead. I miss her so much.'

'I know you do,' Marie spoke softly. 'But please, don't ever apologise to me for being human.' She sighed, then took a deep breath. 'But right now we have some serious work to do, don't we?'

He turned on the ignition and pulled away. 'We do. And regarding our nemesis, that glass cell is looking like a very good idea right now. I reckon we should organise a change of residence for Mr Ashcroft, what do you say?'

* * *

As they did every morning, Casey Naylor and Theo Carmichael were reviewing the current state of play at the unit. 'He's not his usual self this morning,' Casey said. 'He seems hyped up about something.'

'I haven't seen him yet,' Theo said. 'I had a bit of staff reshuffling to do so I'm rather behind.'

'I'd be grateful if you'd give me an opinion, Theo. I don't like being in the dark, especially regarding Stephen.'

'If it worries you, it worries me too. I'll go there now. Want to come?' he asked.

'No, I'd rather you saw him on your own. I wouldn't want my presence to affect your observations.'

As soon as Theo left the office, Casey began to read through that morning's reports.

She loved working in Aegis. She believed wholeheartedly in Theo's mission to discover a means of detecting early indicators of psychosis in order to prevent those affected from committing the heinous crimes of an Ashcroft. The pity of it was that she couldn't stand the person at the centre of the entire Aegis Unit — Ashcroft himself.

He seemed to look down on her expertise as a psychologist, as if she were some pretty young thing who wasn't worthy of his attention. Oddly enough, his dismissive attitude gave her something of an advantage. Since he took little notice of her, she was often able to catch glimpses of the real man behind the facade, and she didn't like what she saw.

On the other hand, there was Jeremy Shaler. Shaler didn't disregard her qualities as a professional. Unlike Ashcroft, he seemed to take her quite seriously. Casey worried about him — you couldn't worry about Ashcroft. Underneath the air of nonchalance she sensed a desolation in Jeremy He seemed truly alone, inhabiting his own private world, having given up all hope of the real one. He had once said that in taking the life of another human being, he had forfeited his own right to humanity. He had resigned himself to a life in prison and had given up all hope of any other.

Again, not like Ashcroft. He hadn't given himself up to anything. She pondered his strange behaviour of that morning. She had never before seen him other than in complete control of himself, whereas today he seemed to be in the grip of an almost uncontrollable excitement. Maybe he held her in such scant regard that he couldn't be bothered to hide anything from her. Well, hopefully Theo's impression of the way he was acting would answer that last question for her.

She didn't have to wait long. Soon, Theo was flopping down in his chair, a puzzled expression on his face.

'You were right, Casey. He was definitely agitated. Yet nothing has happened to cause him to be this way, so what's going on?

Casey told him of Ashcroft's attitude to her. 'I hadn't been aware of it but he probably keeps it from me.' He shook his head. 'Whatever, he'll have to be monitored very closely from now on. I'll send out a directive for all staff to be on their guard, and I'd like the CCTV footage of him checked more often.'

Casey felt gratified that Theo took her opinion so seriously. Casey felt rightly proud of what they had together achieved at Aegis. Having Ashcroft thrown out of the place would be the end of Theo's experiment and all the work they'd done here, but he'd go on to some other exciting project, and she'd be done with Ashcroft.

CHAPTER TWENTY-THREE

By the time they were back at the police station, Jackman had recovered. His breakdown upon seeing his old friend dead had acted like a catharsis upon him and he was galvanised into action.

Even as they marched through the foyer, he was giving directives. 'First, we talk to our two psychologists and get their opinions on our belief, and then we'll take it to the team.' He glanced at Marie. 'How's that sound, Robin?'

'Music to my ears, Batman!'

Jackman had his hands on the reins once more.

Sam and Julia were deep in discussion, neither, he noted with amusement, having taken advantage of his captain's chair.

Sam looked up at him from his visitor's chair with some trepidation. So Jackman decided to put his mind at rest. 'It was Frank Rosen. I'm sincerely sorry about his death but it's forced me to come to some conclusions. Marie agrees with me and we'd like you both to tell us if you think we're on the right track.' He looked at Sam. 'Sorry, old friend, this might be tough for you after what you went through at his hands, but we both believe that Alistair Ashcroft is behind those messages. He's trying to cause chaos among the team just when we have a serious case running.'

Sam and Julia exchanged a swift glance. It was Julia who spoke. 'Well, you may be interested to know, DI Jackman, that I have an appointment at the Aegis Unit in two and a half hours.'

Jackman looked at Sam. 'You all right about this?'

'Let's just say that Julia has, er, thrown down the gauntlet, so I have no choice in the matter. Nonetheless, I completely agree that this nightmare has to be stopped, and as soon as possible and no matter what it takes.'

Jackman squeezed Sam's shoulder affectionately. 'Good man! So, let's take it to the team and see how they react.'

Sam held up his hand. 'Before we do, I noticed that although I've received a second message and image, Julia hasn't. I went and asked the others and no one other than you, Robbie, Max, Charlie and Kevin have received a second one either.'

'That says a lot, doesn't it?' said Jackman thoughtfully. 'We always were Ashcroft's prime targets. Looks like we still are.'

'But not for long,' growled Marie.

'I'll get away now,' said Julia. 'Sam, I'll ring you as soon as I'm through at the unit and am on my way home.'

'Go directly to Mill Corner, Julia,' said Jackman. 'Have dinner with Sam and me, and you can stay over if it's late. We'll need to debrief you on your findings.'

'I hope I don't disappoint.' She raised an eyebrow. 'But yes, I'll accept the offer of a meal, thank you. I'll see you later.'

As soon as the door closed behind her, Jackman glanced at Marie, who nodded. Time to set the team on a new path, and what could turn out to be a bumpy ride.

* * *

PCs Stacey Smith and Jay Acharya were patiently listening to a very protracted story from one of the older residents of a small hamlet called Sedgley Fen.

'Came through here like they were on a racetrack, they did. Big black cars.' Tiny Lottie Baker looked up at them, affronted. 'Nearly killed my neighbour's cat and all. Then, ten minutes later, back they come, even faster, I swear! Where they'd been I've no idea! There ain't no more houses down that way, just Cairn's Farm, and that's an empty wreck since old man Cairn passed on — oh, and the pit, of course.'

'Pit?' asked Jay, who wasn't familiar with this part of the fen.

'You know, one of them old places they used to pan for salt in the olden days. Now it's just a big pond, all overgrown too, now there's none of the Cairns left to look after it.'

Stacey shivered. They were only there to return a missing dog, found running scared on the A17, to its owner in Sedgley Fen, but the owner's sister, Lottie, had taken the opportunity to launch into her story about those dangerous drivers. Initially, Stacey had been itching to get away, now she was all ears.

'Do you really mean only ten minutes, Lottie? Are you sure that was all the time it took to drive past, then come back?' she asked.

'If that!' Lottie exclaimed. 'One lot of ads had just finished in my favourite true crime programme on telly, and they were back long before the next lot came on. Too many ads, ain't there? Ruin the programmes.'

'So, what time would that have been?' asked Jay patiently.

'Twenty past eleven,' stated Lottie. 'Checked the clock I did.'

Stacey threw Jay a look.

Jay nodded. This didn't look good. Promising Lottie that they would look into it, they hurried outside.

'After what we found in Lake Evelyn, I think we'd better make a detour on our way back to base, don't you?' Stacey said. 'Unless they were dumping something in that wreck of a farmhouse, the only other place to go is the pit.'

'We'd better get up there before we lose the light,' said Jay. 'Luckily I put wellies in the boot before we set out.'

'Are you psychic, Acharya?' demanded Stacey.

'No, just practical. Two bodies previously found in water, and knowing our track record, if there was going to be a third, we'd be the mugs that'd find it.' He grinned at her and they climbed into their vehicle.

It was a strange spot. Gates, fences, barns, and the old farmhouse itself, everything was either in disrepair or already falling to bits. The house was boarded up and there were heavy chains looped across the entrances and the doors to the house.

'No one's been in there anyway,' murmured Jay.

'Which adds to the fact that our big dark cars were looking for the pit.' Stacey was starting to feel apprehensive. 'And why would you want to visit a water-filled pit late at night?'

'I suspect a spot of night fishing is out of the equation?'

'About as much a midnight dip, I'd think,' muttered Stacey.

The pit sat on the Cairn's land, a short distance along a weed-covered drive that led into the farm itself. Jay eased the police car down the track and pulled up on a small area of hard-standing not far from the water. They got out and looked around.

'Over here,' Jay called to her. 'Someone has been this way very recently. Look, drag marks through here, and the long grass has been flattened.'

'And the marks are heading straight towards the water.' Stacey wanted to call it in, but she knew they needed more than that. 'Okay, partner, let's take a look.'

The body lay half in and half out of the weed-covered pond. Like the others, it was naked.

'It's like sodding Groundhog Day,' muttered Jay.

'Trust you to be right about the wellies.' Stacey sighed. 'We *are* the mugs finding the third victim, aren't we?'

They stood for a while, unwilling to make the move. There was no doubt that the man was dead. If Lottie Baker's report was correct, he'd been here for maybe twenty hours, and, as he was face down in the brackish water, he couldn't possibly have survived. Nevertheless, they had to check.

'I'll go,' said Jay quietly. 'It doesn't need two of us.'

Normally, Stacey would have demurred, but this time she just nodded. Jay inched his way into the reedy sludge at the edge of the pond to where the body lay, lapped by the rippling water. He pressed the neck, feeling for a pulse. Nothing. Jay looked back at Stacey.

'He's ice cold, no sign of life. Time to call it in.' He stepped back. 'I'd better retreat before I bugger up the scene, but I get the feeling this poor guy didn't fare as well as the other two.'

Stacey started forward to take a look but Jay blocked her way.

'Leave it to forensics, Stace.'

She backed off. 'I'll ring the sarge and tell Marie to warn DI Jackman.'

'Good idea. Although you could break the rules and ring Marie before the sarge. Jackman and his team could do with a heads up on this one, what with all the pressure they're under.'

Stacey nodded. She too felt for Jackman and his beleaguered team, so she did as Jay had suggested.

'I'm just about to ring this in officially, Marie, but I thought you and Jackman should know. We've got another Adonis.'

* * *

'That was PC Stacey Smith,' Marie announced to the team. 'They've found a body in water, and she thinks it's another Adonis.'

There was a low groan from around the room. Charlie Button said flatly, 'Well, that's that then.'

Everyone looked at him in mild surprise.

Charlie shrugged. 'Stands to reason, doesn't it? If what the boss says is right — about them making snuff movies — they've made another one and dumped the body. End of. And if they've sodded off, that should be the last one we'll ever have to deal with.'

Jackman smiled faintly. 'A little on the blunt side, Charlie, but you have a point. Lance disappeared last night,

202

possibly *after* he'd completed another illicit film. But that still means a death to investigate.' Just then, his phone rang. 'And this, no doubt, will be the official version of what Stacey's just told Marie.'

Marie felt somewhat relieved. What Charlie had said did make sense. If the shits who had been producing these movies had gone, that should mean there would be no more deaths connected to them.

Jackman put his phone back in his pocket. 'Okay, guys. I'll update the super and get everything moving from this end, while you, Marie, take one of the team and get out to the scene. Report back as soon as you have anything to tell me. Forensics have already been notified.'

Marie nodded. 'Will do, boss. Where is it?'

'Sedgley Fen,' he said. 'Unremarkable tiny village, about six miles outside Saltern. The body is in an old salt pan turned pond, much like Lake Evelyn but much more overgrown. It's in the grounds of Cairn's Farm, which is deserted, awaiting probable demolition.'

'Unremarkable, that is, until the blue lights and sirens headed their way,' muttered Marie. 'But I know roughly where it is.' She turned to her colleague. 'Robbie? Fancy an evening trip to a stagnant pond?'

'One with a body in it? Why, of course!' He raised his eyebrows. 'My favourite kind of evening venue, although must say I preferred the Schooner with Ella and the free drinks.'

Marie left, Robbie trotting at her heels.

They were back on track at last, she thought. Jackman was once again injecting new energy into their flagging team. They would get this dealt with, then throw their all into stopping Ashcroft and bringing an end to his bloody threats.

As she ran across the car park to the waiting vehicle, one sentence played on a loop in her head: "This will be the last time Ashcroft gets to mess with us."

It had to be, for until Ashcroft was stopped, none of the good things in her life could flourish, not her future with Ralph, or Peelers End, or exciting times policing with

Jackman. And after all the shit she'd been through, she was damned well going to have it!

* * *

'Well! To say I'm impressed would be an understatement. I congratulate you, Theo.' Julia had also seen a number of improvements that might be made at the Aegis Unit, but she was nothing if not diplomatic — especially when she wanted something.

'Praise indeed, coming from you.' Theo Carmichael looked suitably gratified. 'I can still hardly believe you are here and that I've had a chance to meet you at last. When I was at university, your work had the greatest influence on my choice of career.'

Julia brushed his words aside. She hadn't come here to hear praise. She returned to the subject of Aegis.

'I suppose your biggest concern must be your staff,' she said thoughtfully. 'How do you ensure they don't succumb to the manipulations of Ashcroft?'

'We have given very serious thought to the staffing of the unit,' Theo said. 'Before we take them on they have to undergo extremely rigorous vetting, and I can vouch for every one of them.'

Such a sweeping statement, thought Julia sceptically. *I'm willing to bet there are some whose backgrounds your precious vetting hasn't unearthed.*

Their professional lives and conduct were one thing but what of someone whose mother had dementia, or an adolescent son or daughter with a drug habit? How deep could one go into the personal lives of such a large staff contingent?

They walked on through the unit, their path inexorably leading to Ashcroft, the man who had so damaged her beloved Sam. Theo seemed certain that Ashcroft would be most willing to receive a visit from her. He welcomed any attention, especially if it came from someone in authority.

On the way here, Julia had wondered how best to approach this meeting, deciding in the end to let her response to Ashcroft be her guide. At this stage in her life she was certain of her ability to resist his wiles.

Even so, when she finally reached his room she felt a slight tremor of apprehension. After all, this was the man who had nearly killed Sam. But more than that was the thought that if Alistair Ashcroft had organised the sending of those messages and photographs, he would know exactly who she was, and the reason for her visit.

The door stood ajar. Julia tapped on it and politely asked if she might prevail on a little of Stephen's time.

'Come in, come in! I've been expecting you,' said a voice from within.

Her heart beating rapidly, Julia stepped inside.

CHAPTER TWENTY-FOUR

The rapidly descending sun sent long shadows across the scene. Alone for a moment or two, Stacey cast her eyes around her gloomy surroundings. Set apart from the activity around the pond — vehicles, police officers, halogen lights and swarms of officers — the brooding hulk of the deserted old farm appeared to be watching them. Even the sight of Marie arriving did nothing to lighten her mood.

Jay appeared, stood beside her and put his arm around her shoulders.

'It's all right, Stace,' he said, his gaze following hers to Cairn's Farm. 'I feel it too. This place would get to anyone. It's no wonder they want to pull it down. So, just to cheer you up, as soon as we're through here, I'm going to buy you a bucket of your favourite KFC.'

She was forced to smile. 'Hot wings?'

'Hot wings. As many as you can eat.' Jay looked askance at her. 'I think.'

'It's all right, I promise not to break your bank. I might even go Dutch.'

Good old Jay. She hoped the powers that be never saw fit to split them up. Crewmates like Jay were rarer than hen's teeth. 'Well, I suppose we'd better go and see if we can help,' she continued.

'Log's already set up and the body's just been retrieved.' He swallowed. 'I was right. It wasn't pretty.'

'I expect I've seen worse, mate,' Stacey said, patting his arm. 'Okay, here we go.'

As they moved away, Jay suddenly muttered angrily: 'Evil bastard. If this is the work of that Lance character, someone better collar him smartish. He has no right to freedom. No right all.'

Jay was a peaceful man usually, but he hated injustice. They all did, only Jay seemed to feel it more. Perhaps it was his faith or his vegetarian diet. Or perhaps he was just a good guy. Whatever it was, Stacey wished she could be more like him, instead of the hard-nosed, suspicious woman she felt she had become.

A nudge in her side interrupted her reverie.

'The pathologist has just arrived, Stace. And look at his face!'

Stacey saw the familiar figure of Rory Wilkinson stomping towards the crime scene. 'I see what you mean,' she replied. 'And he hasn't even seen the victim yet.' She glanced at Jay. 'Maybe you're right about this place getting to you.'

'More like he's pissed off at having to dissect all these good-looking young men,' muttered Jay. 'Imagine seeing nothing but death, morning, noon and night.'

'Uh, he's a pathologist, Jay. He conducts post-mortems. It's what he does.' She giggled. 'You are a wally, aren't you?'

'It has been said, mainly by you,' said Jay, giving her a baleful look. 'Whatever his job, he's still a human soul, and if what I've heard about him is true, he's a very caring person.'

'Right as always, Acharya. Don't you get fed up with being perfect?'

Jay smiled innocently. 'Come on, let's get this over with before KFC run out of chicken.'

* * *

Marie walked beside a curiously quiet Rory Wilkinson to where the third victim lay. She had already seen the body being lifted from the water and had had time to assimilate it. Rory hadn't, and he was visibly shocked. Marie was perturbed to see him so affected. The one thing that made these awful occurrences bearable was his black humour. Without that, she felt somehow vulnerable.

'Same killer, I believe,' she said quietly. 'But a very different method of killing. It fits in with your idea about the snuff movies, Rory.'

But Rory didn't seem to be listening. 'Body oil. Even after having been left in the water, I can see traces on his back. What have they done to you, dear boy?'

Marie glanced at him. *Surely, Rory couldn't be crying?*

'Forgive me,' he said, his eyes still on the body. 'I know I'm not being the Rory you know and love, dear Marie, but this case is personal.' He lowered his voice. 'My darling David's nephew disappeared two years ago. He was the spitting image of our second victim, Apollo. Ever since then, I've been expecting — no, dreading — that he'd turn up as a guest in my mortuary and I'd have to break it to David. Young Jack was obsessed with his looks and health, and it's my belief that he'd been lured into male prostitution. I did a bit of ferreting into the people he was mixing with — behind David's back, of course — and I didn't like what I found. Then he just vanished. David loved Jack dearly and he was devastated.'

'Oh, Rory, I'm so sorry. You should have got Spike to handle this one for you, rather than go through it all again.'

'I had to see for myself, and no, it's not Jack, but it's someone else's son or nephew, isn't it? And it breaks my heart.' He straightened his shoulders. 'So, I'd better do something to help rather than standing here like a wet lettuce.' He turned to her. 'Thank you for listening. Now you can forget what I said and we'll get on with our jobs. Right?'

She nodded. 'Right, Professor. So, what have we got? Your initial thoughts, please?'

'Immediate impression is that we have a white male, possibly late twenties, early thirties. Prior to whatever happened to him, I'd say he was fit and healthy. He has sustained multiple injuries, and until I am able to get him to the mortuary and clean him up, I cannot tell you more about what caused such severe damage. Other than that, yes, same killer, I'm sure — *killers* rather, because I think more than one attacker was involved. His injuries will tell us everything, once we can examine him forensically.' He looked again at the body. 'Needless to say, this will be a priority.'

She touched his arm. 'Thank you, and when this is over, if I can help in your search for Jack in any way, just ask, won't you?'

He blew her a kiss. 'I might take you up on that, Marie. Now I have work to do, and another dead soul to try to put back together again, so off you go! The Maestro is once again in control. Night, night, DS Marie Evans.'

* * *

Julia Tennant was finally face to face with the notorious Alistair Ashcroft.

At his suggestion, their conversation took place in the communal area, where tea or coffee was available. Most of the other inmates were in a group therapy session, so they were alone. Ashcroft sat for several minutes, saying nothing — summing her up, she assumed. It felt like the opening moments of a boxing fight, when the contestants gauged each other's weaknesses. Julia wondered what Ashcroft saw. For her part, she saw a man in a wheelchair, affable and seemingly pleased to see her. Yet his presence was utterly overwhelming.

At last, he began to speak, not taking his eyes from hers. 'So. The eminent Julia Tennant herself. Did dear Theo ask for the heavy guns to be brought in?'

'No, Theo did not request the "heavy guns", as you describe me. I came here of my own volition.'

'Oh really? And I suppose your precious ex-husband had nothing to do with it either. Fancy giving up love for your careers. How short-sighted! No doubt he'll be pacing the floor waiting for your esteemed professional opinion.' He laughed, sardonically. 'Well, you'll get nothing from me. You've had a wasted journey.' He spun his chair around and moved away.

'Thank you for your time, *Alistair*,' she called after him, deliberately using the name he hated. 'But in fact it hasn't been wasted. I have met you, and you are exactly as I suspected. Goodbye.'

She stood and made her way back to Theo Carmichael's office, where she closed the door behind her.

'Are you all right?' asked Theo anxiously. 'He didn't frighten you, did he?'

She answered his question with another. 'Do you have any idea what you're up against?'

'He's a challenge, certainly. We have to take every precaution in our dealings with him, but he is just such a fascinating case study. That's what Aegis is for, Julia, to study him, find out what has made him what he is, but also to keep others safe from his devious schemes.'

Well, he had failed, thought Julia, but she wasn't about to tell him so. She merely said, 'I have to get back, Theo, and thank you for letting me see Aegis. It is a credit to you, but I can't help wishing you had chosen a different murderer for your case study. And, please, do look again at your staff. I fear there may be a weak link somewhere.'

Poor Theo. He had established Aegis with the best of intentions but he had made a serious error in his choice of subject to study. Ashcroft was no phenomenon to be held passive under a microscope but a monster with a will of his own.

* * *

Sam welcomed Julia like the proverbial prodigal. 'Jackman said to go over to the house the moment you get back. Dinner is ready, and we've both been climbing the walls worrying about you. Are you all right? Was it terribly draining? I mean, the moment you left I regretted ever—'

'Sam Page!' she exclaimed. 'That's enough. You're worse than a mother hen. I'm fine. Now, if you could just let me get my coat off and freshen up a bit, we'll go and see Jackman. I'm so hungry I could eat a horse.'

Sam sighed. She was back safely, and clearly unfazed by her meeting.

Ten minutes later, they were sitting in the kitchen of Mill Corner before a delicious repast, courtesy of the redoubtable Hetty Maynard.

They ate in silence for a while, until Jackman was unable to wait any longer. 'Okay, crunch time, Julia. What do you think?'

'Oh my! Where to start?' She gave a deep sigh. 'Well, Theo has done an excellent job in establishing that special unit, and I applaud his good intentions. We do need to know more about the psychopathic brain, but he should not have chosen Ashcroft to study. I believe it was either naïve or ill-advised of Theo Carmichael to attempt to contain so powerful a man.' She drew in a breath. 'I only spent a few minutes in his company but it was enough for me to understand why Sam objected to our meeting.'

'Little doubt about his power,' muttered Jackman, stabbing his fork into a new potato. 'And I speak from personal experience.'

'Luckily, there are few like him. I suppose, like me, Theo read up on his background, and his heart went out to the maligned and damaged little boy. But he should have read further and considered the effect of what he was exposed to, and the path those things sent him down, culminating in the twisted and malevolent Stephen of today.'

'I'm relieved to hear you say that,' Sam said, taking another forkful of cauliflower cheese. 'But what do you think about his possible involvement in the threatening messages?'

'Oh, it's him, without a doubt. It didn't take us long to size each other up, and when the gloves came off, it was crystal clear. He even mentioned our marriage, Sam.'

Jackman exhaled. 'So there we have it. I'm both relieved and overwhelmed to hear your verdict, Julia, for it means we have a huge task ahead of us in trying to prove it.'

'Find me one piece of solid evidence, Jackman, and I'll personally see to it that Aegis is shut down.' Julia looked hard at him. 'As I said, Theo Carmichael is a good man, and I'm sure that if I can prove that his precious Stephen has been using his privileged status in the unit to manipulate and cause harm, he will listen to reason and have him transferred to solitary confinement in the high-security block.'

'Well, it's good to have you on our side,' Jackman said. 'I'm going to need all the help I can get in persuading the authorities to accept what we're telling them. They won't like to hear that their precious flagship enterprise has been compromised by one of their own carefully chosen prisoners. I'm a long way from that yet, but I'll be asking for your help when I get there, Julia.' He sipped from his glass of wine, 'But my main objective is to find that sick bunch of perverts who have murdered three young men. There was news of a possible sighting of one of them just before I left tonight, so we are putting everything into tracking them down. As soon as I can be sure that they'll be causing no more deaths, we'll use every minute of our time to put a stop to Alistair Ashcroft.'

'And we'll help you all we can,' added Sam, with a glance at Julia.

By way of reply, she raised her glass. 'Oh, we will. Here's to the end of a reign of terror.'

* * *

John returned to the flat at around midnight to give Hazel his report, after which they were both free to catch up on their sleep. His task for today had been rescheduled, as yet another damned clear-up job had been thrown at him. Even Hazel had been annoyed at the disruption.

As soon as he entered, Hazel turned from her computer and looked up at him. 'Everything go well?'

'Mission completed, as they say.' He spoke cheerily enough, though it had been an unpleasant experience, even for him. Still, it took him one step closer to kissing the whole enterprise goodbye and sailing off into the sunset.

It didn't take long for Hazel to record his comments in a memo for Christos, after which they both relaxed.

'Am I back on schedule tomorrow?' he asked.

'Yes. First thing, at around eight a.m., you tackle the job that was shelved from today. As soon as that's dealt with, Christos will give us the next step in Phase Two.' She yawned. 'Let's get away, quick, before you get asked to sort out somebody else's shit.'

'Let's just hope that tonight's assignment will see an end to that particular balls-up of an operation. Talk about falling at the last hurdle.' John gave a dry laugh. 'I imagine Stephen won't be too pleased with the operatives working that little side-line of his. If I were him, I'd leave that particular caper to others and stick to the things he's so good at.'

Glancing at him with a look of disapproval, Hazel said, 'I thought Stephen would be above that kind of thing but he's far too intelligent to have undertaken it without some object in mind. He'll have had his reasons, even if only as a money-spinner to fund some of his more important projects. Or possibly it's part of something else altogether.' She yawned again. 'But anyway, it's not our affair. Besides, you, my friend, will be reaping a hefty bonus for what you did tonight, so it's not all bad.'

Yes, he thought, *there were benefits to such grim work.*

Hazel stood up. 'Time to go and catch up on some sleep. I'll see you tomorrow. I'll be in at seven to prepare your rota . . . And John. Get rid of that jacket, it smells of petrol.'

Did she have to use that headmistressy tone with him? 'Sorry, I should have noticed. Of course, I'll ditch it. Must have had a splash back. Occupational hazard. See you in the morning.'

CHAPTER TWENTY-FIVE

Jackman hadn't been in the station ten minutes before he was bombarded with a hail of reports.

Marie looked at him quizzically. 'I'm beginning to wonder if I had enough Weetabix for breakfast. Is all that paperwork actionable?'

'Most of it certainly needs following up,' he said, his eyes on the printouts. 'But this one, now this *is* interesting.' He handed her the sheet of paper.

'Oh my! Could we really be that lucky?' Then she made a face. 'Probably not the best way to put it, given what it is.'

'Forget it. This is our first job for the day. As soon as the team are all in and we've briefed them, we'll head over to the Greenborough marina. Hopefully, the victim will be with Rory by the time we get there and he can tell us just how lucky we are.'

'Shall I grab us a swift coffee? We probably won't get the chance to have another one for hours.'

As Marie went out of the office, Jackman re-read the report.

Police had attended a vehicle fire in a little-used overspill car park attached to the marina. The car, a dark blue Toyota, had been badly damaged, but wasn't completely burned out thanks to the swift reaction of a couple of men working a late night shift on their boat, who had rushed to the scene with fire extinguishers. The driver, however, had been declared dead at the scene. The paramedics who attended reported that it didn't appear to be an accident and that, although badly burned, the male victim had been stabbed before the fire had been started. The local fire chief had also taken a look at the vehicle and confirmed that the car had been deliberately set alight, with the driver still inside. What interested Jackman was the mention of a particularly unusual wristwatch the victim had been wearing. Maybe Marie was right, and they had been lucky enough to have found Lance Newport.

On top of that, an anonymous caller had reported seeing one of the four wanted men, Rick Grace, the stills photographer, getting on the last train to London from Peterborough. Following a call to the Met he had been apprehended as he got off the train at Kings Cross station. He was now in custody, and according to the officer in charge, singing as loud as a male voice choir!

Marie returned, coffees in hand. 'Only Charlie Button to come, and then the team are all here.' She set down the drinks. 'Is this shitty investigation reaching a turning point, boss?'

'I sincerely hope so, Marie. Because when it's over, we have the most important case of our professional lives to deal with.'

'And as soon as I see it stamped "*Case Closed*", I'm going to throw the biggest party ever!'

'Can I hold you to that?' he asked.

'I'll go one better. It won't be just a party, it will be a wedding reception. How's that for an incentive to lock fucking Ashcroft up in an underground cell until he rots!'

Jackman's face lit up. 'Really?'

'Yes, really.' She grinned. 'You can start practising your best man speech right now. Still, first things first. Let's sew up this bloody murder investigation. I can feel Dougie and Frank breathing down my neck and telling me to get my sodding finger out.'

215

'Then bring that coffee with you and let's start getting some organisation into the day.' Jackman had just been given the best incentive imaginable. Marie, more than anyone, really deserved to be happy.

'DI Jackman!' called a voice. 'Sorry to interrupt, sir.' Tim Jacobs entered the office carrying a plastic evidence bag. 'Uniform found this on a second sweep of the area where Frank Rosen was discovered. It's definitely his phone, and it's on its way to forensics, but the duty sergeant thought you might like to take an unofficial peek at the last text message he received.'

Now what? Jackman read the message. Then he read it again. He blinked.

'Come on! What does it say?' asked Marie.

'Someone was warning Frank off, telling him to get out fast. Who would do that?'

'Orac is the best person to ask, boss,' said Marie. 'If anyone can trace the sender, it's her. Shall I run down there now and ask her to make it a priority?'

'No, I need you here. I'll get you, Tim, to take it.' He put the phone back in the bag. 'But that is weird. Someone was looking out for him.'

'Pity he didn't take their advice,' said Marie.

'Maybe he never had the chance,' said Jackman grimly. 'That message came quite late in the day, only an hour before he left the rectory.' He moved to the door. 'Come on, Marie. I'll give this to Tim; you get the others together. We've no time to waste on guessing games, we should look at the solid evidence. A burnt-out car, complete with driver, and a felon with verbal diarrhoea.'

'I can hardly wait.'

* * *

With the team now in the picture, Marie was pulling on her jacket, eager to get things moving, when her mobile rang.

'Sorry if you're busy, Marie,' said her mother's voice, 'but the oddest thing just happened, and I thought you should know.'

Marie was gripped with sudden apprehension. Rhiannon was a down-to-earth, sensible woman. She wouldn't be calling for nothing. 'What, Mum? Tell me.'

'This child just knocked on my door and handed me a sealed envelope. Inside was a photo of you and Ralph and written on the back were the words, *Treasure them, because life can be short.*'

Marie's throat went dry. He was at it again. *Fucking Ashcroft!*

'The child said he'd been handed it by a woman who told him that she was looking for me but didn't know where I lived, and the message was very important. When he said he knew me, she gave the boy five pounds to deliver it for her.'

Trying hard to keep her voice even, Marie said, 'Don't worry, Mum, it's that bloody trickster again, trying to put the frighteners on everyone. We are all fine and we're doing all we can to stop him. Meanwhile, can you slip that envelope into a clean plastic freezer bag and keep it safe, just in case there's any trace evidence on it. We'll try and get the local bobbies out to collect it from you. Now, you just hang on in there, and I'll keep you updated.'

'Then I won't hold you up, but, darling, be careful, won't you? And tell your lovely Ralph to do the same. I'll be thinking of both of you.'

'Thanks, Mum. Now, go and rescue stray dogs, run that food bank, or whatever was on your agenda for today. The village will grind to a halt without you!'

When she arrived at Jackman's office, he informed her of a change of plan. 'The trip to the marina is cancelled. We are now heading for Rory's Retreat. The body is already with him, and the car's on its way to the lab.'

'Good. But I've got something to tell you before we go.' She gave him her mother's story about the message.

'Sod it! Sod it!' growled Jackman. 'We desperately need to be hitting back but without proof, no way can we get the bastard out of that unit! Come on, let's go and see Rory. Once we know for sure that it's Lance Newport on that slab, we can focus our attention on where it's most needed.'

Marie hastened after him out of the door. DCs Kevin Stoner and Charlie Button were already driving to the Met's headquarters in London to interview Rick Grace, and then escort him back to Saltern-le-Fen. So, all that remained was for Rory to identify the body.

On the drive to the morgue, the car phone rang for Jackman. It was Harriet Jackman, who'd been delivered a message with an uncanny resemblance to Rhiannon's: 'A man called into the stables this morning at around eight o'clock, saying he was looking for a young Labrador who had bolted. The man was carrying a lead and looked really worried, so I believed him. Now I've just gone into the tack room where he found me earlier, and there was an envelope on the floor with my name on it. It had a photograph inside . . .'

'Yes?' Jackman asked.

There was a pause, then Harriet said, 'I'm sorry, son, but it was a picture of Laura's headstone.'

Marie set her jaw, silently consigning Ashcroft to all the fires of hell.

Sounding perfectly calm, Jackman reassured his mother. 'It's all right, Mum. It's just Ashcroft and more of his games. But tell me about this man. Did you recognise him? Could you describe him?'

'Oh dear. I've been hoping you wouldn't ask. The trouble is, he was just so, well, ordinary. So unremarkable that I doubt I'd recognise him again. He appeared to be in his early forties, his brown hair had flecks of grey in it. I couldn't begin to describe what he was wearing, except that it was darkish.'

'Okay, Mum. And was there a message?'

Harriet sighed. '"*Life is short. What happened to one, can happen to another.*" But don't you go fretting about us now, Rowan. Your father and I have got the family covered.'

After telling his mother to keep the envelope safe, Jackman ended the call. 'It was only to be expected, Marie. And there's nothing we can do about it until we are free of this other case.'

Marie was pleased and relieved to see how calmly he'd taken this latest setback. As he'd said, there was nothing they could do about it until they heard Rory's verdict.

Rory, too, was in a lighter mood. He ushered them into his office, where Spike was ready with real coffee and a box of Danish pastries.

'I don't get too many visitors, so I thought we should make an occasion of it,' Rory said. 'I can't understand *why* people don't seem to like coming here . . . Anyway, dig in. Spike's sitting in because I have a lot to tell you, since we have two different dead men, and we'd rather explain than show them to you, considering the condition they're both in.'

Seeing Spike's grim expression, Marie was perfectly happy with a verbal account. She took a bite of her pastry and steeled herself.

'I'm going to start with our third Adonis. I haven't given him a name, since I believe we know exactly who he is. I'll get you to confirm this in a while.'

Rory placed a post-mortem photo on the desk in front of them. The young man extracted from the salt pan had been cleaned up and his facial injuries tended to.

Marie gasped. 'That's the man we've been looking for, Dex's friend, Craig!'

'No wonder you only recognise him now, cherub. From the state of him when they pulled him out, his own mother wouldn't have known him.' He grimaced. 'The full details will be in my report, but you should know that this victim was the most damaged of the three. He sustained multiple injuries and, to put it bluntly, he was tortured to death.'

Spike's angry voice filled the ensuing silence. 'All for someone's gratification. What wouldn't I'd do to them if I ever got my hands on them.'

'I'd do the same to those animals that actually filmed it,' added Jackman.

'Well, methinks someone felt the same way as you,' Rory said. 'Because that last cadaver is most definitely Lance Newport, the man you believe to have directed those nightmare films.'

'Are you absolutely sure?' Marie said.

'Without a doubt, dear heart. DNA gathered from personal items left in his motorhome matches perfectly with his. I will have it double-checked, but if you add a signature wristwatch, engraved with his name, and a deformed bone in his elbow from an old fracture, the man in the burnt-out car can be no other than Lance Newport.'

'And how did he die?' asked Jackman.

'A single stab wound that penetrated the ribs and punctured his lung incapacitated him, then he was secured into the driver's seat and barbequed.' He exhaled. 'I might have been a bit more sympathetic towards him if dear Spike and I had not just counted the wounds on young Craig's body. When we reached thirty, we somehow lost all compassion for Mr Newport.'

Marie's thoughts inevitably turned to the visit they would soon be making to Craig Turner's wife, Joannie. How on earth would they explain what had happened to him when they themselves were still trying to assimilate it?

'Correct me if I'm wrong,' Jackman said, 'but your findings would indicate that Craig — one of the original makers of those porn films — was himself the victim of a snuff movie directed by Lance Newport.'

'Which ties in with what Dex told us about Craig wanting to be part of the bigger operation,' said Marie.

'And it would appear that dear Lance was perfectly happy to give him the starring role,' said Rory. 'Ten to one, poor Craig thought he was just going to do a bit of naughty filming and didn't have a clue what was planned for him.'

'I reckon,' added Spike, 'that those bastards were delighted that a good-looking bloke like Craig offered himself up for a role. It would have been the perfect way to get him off their backs.'

Marie thought that was probably all true but wondered what had happened to make them all run for the hills. Someone had known it was getting too dangerous and pulled the plug on the whole operation. She just wished she knew who that had been.

'There's one other thing you might like to consider, my lovely friends,' said Rory. 'Whoever killed Lance also killed your friend. The same knife was used on both men. It's a bit of a conundrum, isn't it? You have one killer who terminated a man posing a threat to the operation who then went on to murder the organiser himself.'

Marie knew why Jackman looked so uneasy. Instead of being free to move on to Ashcroft, they now had yet another killer to hunt. With a quick glance at her, he said, 'If someone is tidying up, there could be more deaths — like Andrew Shaw and Ben White. We have Rick Grace in custody, so he's safe, but the others might not be.'

'And since we have no idea where they are, we can't protect them,' she added. 'We'll probably only know if they turn up stabbed in a ditch.'

'Part of me is sorry that Lance is dead,' said Jackman. 'I'm pretty sure he was the only one who knew who is behind these death movies. Now we know how deeply he was involved, we can start to dig backwards into his life and his comings and goings, and hopefully that could lead us to his associates but, hell, that could take years.'

And my wedding will get pushed back until I'm drawing my sodding pension, thought Marie. *If Ashcroft lets us live that long.*

'We need to get all this back to Superintendent Crooke, Rory,' Jackman said. 'We have a more pressing concern at present, and it's more important than someone topping bad guys. Our opponent is planning an out and out attack on the team, and that has to be my priority.'

'Hear, hear!' said Rory. 'And I guess you mean the sender of these.' He showed them a picture of his husband, David. The caption read, *Until death us do part.* Rory snorted disdainfully. 'Shows all he knows! We didn't have that line in our wedding vows, we wrote our own, so there!'

'You never said you'd got one too!' Marie exclaimed.

'I heard about everyone getting them, and then we got busy with our young Greek gods, so it slipped my mind. Even so, I'd be very grateful if you could stop him.'

'That's the plan, Rory.' It gladdened Marie's heart to hear the resolve in Jackman's tone.

They took their leave of Rory and Spike and in no time at all, Jackman had his foot down and they were hurtling back to the station.

* * *

Ruth Crooke looked long and hard at him. 'Okay, Rowan, I'm seeing the bigger picture now, and I'll do my best to free you up — but for a limited period of time only. I'll give you and your team one week to pin enough on Ashcroft to prove — irrevocably mind you — that he is still a clear and present danger to society. Can you do that?'

'Seven days.' He thought about it. 'Yes, we can do it, so long as we have all the backup and support we need.'

In response, Ruth picked up her phone. 'DI Deane, can you come to my office immediately, please?'

Almost instantly, so it seemed to Jackman, Jenny was sitting next to him.

'What's your workload looking like at the moment, please?' Ruth asked.

'Tying up the drugs case, ma'am. Our main inquiry has ground to a halt due to lack of evidence.'

'In that case, I'm going to ask you to take over Jackman's current investigation for at least a week. It's big, Jenny. I'll let him give you the full picture in a minute, but it revolves around the making of snuff movies. To date we have three murders — young men, presumably the victims of said movies — one murdered ex-detective, and the incinerated body of the man we believe to have directed these films.'

'Bloody hell, ma'am. Talk about slinging a girl in at the deep end!'

'So, you'll do it?'

Jenny smiled uncertainly. 'Of course. I'm just a tad surprised, that's all. But I'll get over it.'

Jackman had always liked Jenny Deane, now he loved her. 'I really appreciate it.'

'So you should! You'll treat me to a slap-up meal if I do a good job for you then?'

'Deal!'

'Sort out the rules of engagement later, officers!' snapped Ruth.

'Of course,' they said in unison.

'Don't let me down, Rowan. This has been hanging over our heads for far too long, so just put an end to it, once and for all.'

Jackman closed the door behind them and they went out into the corridor.

'Now what the chuffin' hell was that all about?'

Jackman made a face. 'Let's go to my office. I've got rather a lot to tell you.'

CHAPTER TWENTY-SIX

Ashcroft eyed the chaplain, trying to decide if he had the heart for another discussion. He had been feeling unsettled ever since that bitch had come marching in with her superior air and her look of invincibility. Her visit, brief though it was, had taken the edge off his pride at the flawless execution of his plans.

Dismissing these thoughts, he turned his attention back to Galway. There was something different about him this morning, a slight ruffling of the calm waters of his exterior. Could it be Jeremy Shaler, whom Galway had visited before coming to him?

'Why don't you tell me what you'd like to discuss today, Stephen?' said Galway affably. 'It always seems to be me who sets the agenda. Is there anything I can help you with? Any other subject you'd like us to consider?'

All Ashcroft wanted was for the man to go away, but it was important not to give the slightest indication of the true state of his feelings. So he said, 'How do you cope with men who bring down the shutters on you, Patrick? Do you sometimes have to accept that there is no way in? Or do you continue to dig away regardless?'

Galway pondered the question, as he always did. 'I'm here to offer a listening ear. If it's asked for, I'll provide an opinion, or perhaps a suggestion. If I believe someone is struggling but cannot open up, I continue to try to assist. If they remain closed off, all I can do is be available in case they change their mind.'

Ashcroft shifted in his chair and flexed his painful legs. 'I know what your remit is, Patrick. What I want to know is, does it trouble you? Do you lose sleep over those locked doors? Does it hurt your pride, or make you feel a failure?' He intensified his stare. 'It interests me to know how you —Patrick the man, not Patrick the priest — feel when somebody shuts you out.'

'There is no distinction between man and priest, Stephen. I am both at the same time. So I feel only compassion for this lost soul, and I remain determined not to give up, for there may come a moment when I can help. Nevertheless, as they say, you can't win 'em all. If one day you said you no longer wanted to see me, then I'd respect your wish and leave you alone.'

If only, thought Ashcroft, and said, 'I value the time you take with me. It's refreshing to talk to someone intelligent for once.'

Soon after this exchange, Patrick stood up. 'I'll leave you now, Stephen and, as always, if you need me, you only have to tell someone and I'll be with you as soon as I can. But I must say, you seem pretty sorted at the moment.' He winked. 'See you tomorrow.'

Alone once more, Ashcroft pondered their conversation. What they had said was irrelevant, it was Patrick's body language that interested him. He came to the conclusion that Patrick had behaved towards him exactly as he always did, so it must have been Shaler who had disturbed him. He usually looked in on Shaler before visiting him. Ashcroft determined to spend more time with his fellow inmate — someone who definitely had his doors locked and his drawbridge up. He was a challenge, and Stephen liked challenges. He liked them a lot.

* * *

Casey Naylor looked up at the chaplain expectantly when he walked in. 'So, Patrick? What did you think?'

'You're right, Casey, there's something going on in that head of his, though I didn't sense excitement. It was more like anger.' He flopped into a chair. 'He was rattled about something, but it was hard to discern. If you hadn't alerted me, I think I'd probably have missed it.'

'Do you think he suspected that you were watching him more closely today?' she asked.

Patrick shook his head. 'I don't think so, but who can know with Stephen? Let's hope that if he did, he assumed it was something unconnected to him.'

Theo raised his head from his jotter. 'Julia Tennant, the eminent psychologist who came here yesterday, is very concerned about the freedom being at Aegis is granting him. She admired the concept, but she wasn't sure about the choice of Stephen as our subject of study. She also questioned our staff selection procedures, which I admit smarted a bit, since I've put so much effort into getting the right people here.' He shrugged. 'However, I don't think this should cause us to change anything about the way we are working. What do you think, Casey? Patrick?'

'I agree with you,' said Patrick. 'After all, what harm can he actually do?' He is still incarcerated. His calls are monitored, and he has CCTV cameras recording his movements. His visitors are carefully vetted and, anyway, they are all basically officials, plus the two or three people who contact him by letter — letters which are read. Other than these people, he seems to have no friends.'

'Exactly,' said Theo. 'I still believe he is no more of a danger here than he would be anywhere else. In fact, he's probably got far less freedom because of the constant scrutiny he's under.'

Casey said nothing. They were right, of course. Stephen was watched like a hawk, and their security system was second to none. There was no way he could escape Aegis. So why did she feel so apprehensive?

'So, are we agreed?' Theo said. 'We continue to keep a close watch on him, and go on as before?'

Casey had no alternative to put forward, so she nodded. Yet her feeling of unrest prevailed.

* * *

Marie wondered if Jackman's office door was ever going to open. He and DI Jenny Deane had been ensconced in there for over two hours. From his swift thumbs-up, Marie had gathered that he had got some sort of concession out of Ruth but she wasn't sure what. Meanwhile, she and the team were heads down trying to collate all the information that had come in over the last twenty-four hours. Rob and Charlie had rung her in a state of high excitement. In order to make things as easy on himself as possible, Rick Grace had agreed to give evidence in court. The three men were now on their way back to the Fens.

Marie wasn't quite so delighted. She had a feeling that Rick knew only what he'd been allowed to know, which probably wasn't much. Even so, if it backed up what Dex had said, it would help when it came to court.

'Sarge? Got a mo'?' Gary asked.

'For you, Gary, all the time in the world. Especially as you have two beakers of coffee in your hands. Take a perch.'

Gary sat down. 'Would you mind if we had a bit of a recap? I know that for once in my life I have other things to care about, not just work and being the best detective that I can be for the best team ever—'

'Stop wittering, Pritchard, and cut to the chase.' She sipped the coffee he'd offered her. 'Just admit it. You're confused.'

'Too bloody right I am. It doesn't make sense!'

'Let's hear it then, what's the problem?'

Gary screwed up his face. 'In a nutshell, we have a film company shooting a new TV drama series. All good stuff. Great actors, excellent crew, and it's going to put the Fens on the map. All well and good. But within this unit of professionals, we have a small group who are making a fair old wedge from shooting blue films in a seedy hotel out at Spelsby.'

'Bang on so far,' encouraged Marie.

'One of this group, Dexter Thompson, has given us the names of all those involved. The main man was a sound mixer called Lance Newport. As far as they knew, all they were being asked to do was produce a few porn films. According to Newport, these were going to a distributor in Holland who handled the marketing for him.' He took a gulp of coffee.

'With you so far,' said Marie. 'But you could add that generally these technicians were just regular guys who, for various personal reasons, badly needed extra cash. They didn't like what they were doing, but the money was good enough to make them close their eyes to how unsavoury it was.'

'Exactly. Then Craig Turner, a CGI animator, and one of the gang making those films on the side, gets the idea that there is more going on than just filming sex. He tells his mate Dex that he wants in. So he goes to see Newport and then tells Dex that he was right, there is another scam going down and he's been signed up. At that point, it all goes tits up — people start disappearing, including, eventually, Craig himself.'

'And from that we can deduce that Craig had been right. Lance was running a second illegal scam, in which a very ruthless crew was filming people being killed on camera.' Marie shuddered. 'Which ties up with what we had believed to be a separate investigation, that of our dead Adonises.'

'And Craig — for reasons we may never know, unless Rick Grace can tell us — became the third victim. Then suddenly, before they even got back to base, the plug was pulled on the whole operation, and, wham, it's all over and the crew disappears into the night.'

Gary sighed. 'That much I get. But here's where it all gets fuzzy. It's the two deaths that have me confused, Sarge. Why them? Frank Rosen, I can vaguely understand, since he was about to spirit Dex away and would no doubt have learned who was involved in the crime. But wouldn't it have been safer to kill Dex? If they'd done that, Frank wouldn't have known any more than he ever did. And why would anyone want to kill the man who organised the whole thing? Why murder Lance?'

Marie thought about it. 'I learned a few things earlier today that might shed some light on it. A lot could be down to timing. Dex had already talked to Frank, probably told him quite a bit, so Frank was already aware of the porn films.' She groaned. 'If only he hadn't gone back to that film set after delivering Dexter to us, then he'd still be alive.' She paused. 'Oh yes, and another thing you don't know yet, Gary, is that someone had warned him to get out. We found the text on his phone. So either he didn't have time to run, or he ignored it.'

'That's an odd one. I wonder who that was?'

'We have no idea,' Marie said. 'Orac is trying to trace the sender for us. As for Lance's killer, Rory has confirmed that the same person murdered both him and Frank. Jackman hasn't had time to put everyone in the picture yet. He'll call a meeting as soon as he's finished with Jenny.'

'He and DI Deane have been talking for ages. Is that a good sign, do you think, Sarge?'

'I certainly hope so. I'm pretty sure she's going to take over for a while, leaving us free to tackle these threatening messages.'

The thought seemed to cheer Gary. His expression cleared. 'Oh, please! My blood boils at the idea of someone threatening my Gilly when she's done nothing other than care for me.'

'We all feel the same, even me. My Ralph may be a strapping copper but I still fear for him.' She frowned. 'But I was telling you about Rory's findings linking those two deaths. The same knife was used, and a similar MO — two stabs between the ribs, one aimed for the heart and the other puncturing a lung. Which means that although Lance Newport was probably dying, he was basically burned alive.'

'Bloody hell! But doesn't that sound a bit, well, professional, you know, like a hit man at work?'

That was precisely what Marie had been thinking. 'I haven't discussed it with Jackman yet, but I do have a theory . . .'

'Yes?'

'It's my belief that the original blue films were Lance's own baby. I reckon he started small and found he was making a lot of money. Maybe someone saw how well he was doing and offered him a chance to make more from making the snuff films. I mean, only organised crime could possibly be behind something like that.'

'Ah, yes, the type of organisation that would use a fixer to clean up any loose ends,' added Gary. 'That would make sense, Marie.'

'It will also make Jenny Deane and her team the best people to take it over. She's the ace when it comes to vice crime. I ran into her earlier and she told me that the snuff film was no urban myth. Someone was producing them to order, but they had no concrete evidence as to who that was. It might even help her sort some of her old cases.'

'It's all so sleazy,' muttered Gary. 'How can a good-looking young man or woman stoop so low as to perform sex acts in front of a camera? How can they live with themselves afterwards?'

'Money, mate. And believe it or not, a lot of them enjoy it, although I suspect they might not feel the same when they're older and look back on what they did. Talk to Jenny one day. After years working on vice, she has stories to tell that would make your hair curl.'

Gary grimaced. 'Maybe I'll give that a miss. Vice was always an area I tried to steer clear of.'

Before Marie could answer, Jackman's door opened, and he and Jenny finally emerged. To say that Jenny looked shell-shocked would be an understatement but Jackman looked rejuvenated. He had done it. They were now free to pursue Ashcroft and get him out of their lives — forever.

CHAPTER TWENTY-SEVEN

While Gary cleared the whiteboard of photographs and memos and packed them up ready to pass on to DI Jenny Deane, the rest of the team dragged up chairs and waited for Jackman to begin.

He perched on the edge of a desk and looked around. The air in the room was electric with excited anticipation.

They were waiting for Kevin and Charlie, who were taking Rick Grace into custody. After a few minutes they entered, closely followed by a rather surprised-looking Stacey Smith and Jay Acharya, who had been allotted to them for the week.

'Room for two more?' Sam Page and Julia Tennant pulled up chairs and sat down. Jackman was pleased to welcome them. Having recently been to Aegis and met Ashcroft, Julia's opinions could be invaluable.

With everyone now assembled, Jackman commenced. 'First, thank you all for the hard work you've put into the Adonis case, and the even weirder goings-on at the film set — two cases we now know to be one. Now I'm going to ask you to do the unexpected and down tools on this investigation. You should pass everything you have to DI Jenny Deane and her detectives. As of now, we are committed to solving another mystery entirely, but before I say more, you should understand that the case we are handing over is in the main, a *fait accompli*.' He looked at Kevin and Charlie. 'Rick Grace is filling the gaps in our knowledge, I believe?'

'Yes, sir,' said Kevin. 'He knows a lot more than Dexter Thompson because he worked on the snuff movies too, although he denies being actively involved and swears he never saw any of the actual deaths. These were always filmed by a group of outsiders. He also swears he thought it was extreme S&M that was being shot, not murder.'

'What he did say, boss,' added Charlie, 'was that Lance Newport was working for a much bigger organisation that Rick thought was based in Holland. DI Deane would do well to pursue that with the Dutch police or Interpol.'

'Not only that,' added Jackman, 'I believe this organ- isation that Charlie just mentioned had been keeping tabs on the TV film company as a whole, and decided it was a risk they weren't prepared to take. They shut Lance down, killed the police advisor, Frank Rosen, and then, to be on the safe side, terminated Newport himself. And just in time, it would seem. He had a boat waiting at the yacht marina. A few minutes more and he would have slipped out of the country under cover of darkness.'

Jackman stood up and walked towards the now empty whiteboard. He picked up a marker pen wrote the name 'Alistair Ashcroft' across the top. 'This is our new case, our chance to get back our lives and those of the people we care most about. We have one aim. To prove that this man,' he tapped the board, 'is still causing mayhem from inside a max- imum-security unit in a Cat B prison. It's a big ask, I know, but I need you to commit everything you have to the task of gathering enough evidence to get him removed from the Aegis Unit and — hopefully — placed in solitary confine- ment for the rest of his term of imprisonment, that is, for life. It's the only way we can be free of him.'

For another hour, they debated how to proceed. Julia Tennant's statement made the most impact. She said she had little doubt in her mind but that Ashcroft remained a

clear and present danger to society. Far from being rehabil-
itated, he remained, and in her opinion always would be, a
controlling monster.

'The problem is this,' Jackman concluded. 'We who have
suffered at his hands already know he is behind the threats to
us and our loved ones. However, the higher officials, the people with the power to act, do not. They need proof. And it is
us who will provide it. Are you with me?'

There was a chorus of affirmations. They were with him
all right, every one of them.

'We only have one week in which to make our case, so
we have to move fast. While you get your files ready to pass
on to Jenny Deane, Marie and I will put together an action
plan. Can you all be back here at five p.m., when I'll explain
how we are to proceed. Tomorrow we begin in earnest.'

Amid the scraping of chairs and the buzz of excited
voices, Jackman beckoned to Marie, along with Sam and
Julia. 'If it's all right with you, we could do with your input.'

'Try and stop us,' said Julia. 'I have a vested interest in
this.'

Sam and Marie looked puzzled, but Jackman knew what
she meant.

In the space of a very brief visit, Julia Tennant had placed
herself firmly in the centre of Ashcroft's crosshairs. Jackman
gave her an understanding nod. 'Point taken, Julia, and if
you have the time during the coming week, we'd appreciate
your help.'

'Believe me, it will be my pleasure. Every minute that
man spends in Aegis is a minute too long. He must be made
safe, no matter what Theo Carmichael and the prison authorities believe.'

Jackman led the way into his office. 'Then let's get
down to work. We have one big advantage in that Ashcroft
believes we are bogged down in the film crew murders case.
He doesn't know we have turned our attention to him. So,
let's not waste a minute. I suggest we start by identifying the
paths we should follow that will lead us back to Ashcroft.'

'Okay, boss, where do we start?' asked Marie.

'He obviously has people on the outside who do his dirty work for him. These must have been recruited a long time ago. We need to look at the people we know of that he used while he was free. They may have either visited him in prison or contacted him by letter or phone calls, especially recently.'

'We need Orac,' stated Marie.

'We do.'

She looked at him, her head tilted to one side. 'Shall I?'

'Go.'

He watched Marie go. His small army was gaining strength. Only one comrade was missing — Laura. She would have been beside him, standing shoulder to shoulder, urging him forward whenever he doubted himself. Now he must fight on alone.

He set his jaw.

'Right, Julia, you've seen the Aegis Unit first hand. Can you make me a list of any aspects you were dubious about? I'm interested in personnel, or practices, rather than the building itself.'

He turned to Sam. 'And you, old friend. I'd like to know more about Theo Carmichael as a man, along with your opinions of him and his project. Can you do that?'

When they both declared themselves able, Jackman said, 'I'll make a desk and a computer available to you. Welcome to the team!'

* * *

Hazel Palgrave took a rare break from the office and went out into the town. She was aware that she'd been driving herself far too hard. She no longer went home to bed — her sleep had been reduced to the occasional nap on the office chair. But she could not stop now. This plan had to succeed. It was her one chance to shine.

Hazel walked into a small square tucked away at the end of a narrow cobbled alley. She sat on the one bench and rested her gaze on a single tree, an ornamental cherry, the only living thing in this arid landscape of brick and paving. It even seemed to thrive, although there was nothing there to nourish it. *Like me*, she thought, *alone in an alien world*.

* * *

At five o'clock sharp, the team were all back in the CID room. This time Jackman outlined their plan of action.

'We'll work in pairs,' said Jackman. 'Now, before we were given the go-ahead, Tim compiled an extensive file on Ashcroft, covering pretty well all we know about his early history, his capture, the trial, and what he could glean about the time he served in prison. You should all familiarise yourselves with it. I warn you, it makes grim reading, and a lot of it will stir up memories of things you'd rather forget. I urge you to read it however, as we must know the man and what makes him tick if we are to find out who his accomplices are. Meanwhile, Julia and Sam are looking into his current circumstances at the Aegis Unit.

'We urgently need to know more about this "ordinary" man, who delivered my mother's letter,' Jackman continued. 'What is his role in Ashcroft's scheme? Stacey and Jay, I'd like you two to make a start on this. Visit the stables. He had to have driven there, so maybe someone saw the car? And talk to my mother. Maybe if someone other than me is asking the questions, it might prompt her to remember some detail she'd forgotten. Oh, and if it hasn't already been collected, pick up the photo and envelope for forensics.'

Jackman next gave Charlie and Max the task of looking into Ashcroft's financial situation, both past and current, especially where his funds were being kept and who was managing them.

'Right,' said Max. 'That's dead important. He must have loads of people running around delivering messages and all that and he'll have to pay them somehow.'

Jackman nodded. 'Find that out, Max. It could be key to all the rest.'

235

Robbie was to work with Gary, looking at each photograph that had been sent to their phones or email addresses and noting when and where they had been taken. Maybe the photographer had been seen or caught on a CCTV camera, Jackman had thought. 'It's a bit of a long shot,' he admitted, 'but worth a try. The recipients might well remember where they were, or what they were wearing.'

Kevin, he had decided, should assist Marie, because although Jackman would be working with her, there would be times when he would have to meet with different members of the team, as well as Ruth. With Kevin's help, Marie could push on with whatever she and Jackman had been doing.

'To keep everything moving as swiftly as possible, I've enlisted the help of two volunteer detectives from the pool who will work nights. If anything needs attention urgently, they can either deal with it, or contact us, meaning we are functioning day and night.'

'And we can get some rest,' said Marie, 'so we can hit the ground running as soon as we get in.'

Before Jackman could continue, DI Jenny Deane appeared.

'Sorry to interrupt, Jackman. I won't keep you long, but you asked me to update you if anything important occurred.'

'That's quick work, Jenny, we've only just handed it over!'

'It's nothing to do with us, I assure you. It's the feelers you put out before you handed over. Well, they've paid dividends. We've got Andrew Shaw on his way in, courtesy of an eagle-eyed traffic cop not far from Birmingham Airport. Shaw's coughed to the porn movies and says he has information about Lance Newport's contacts in Holland. He also has something to tell us about that extra crew Newport used to bring in for his "special" films. He swears that none of the crew from the TV company had anything to do with them. He knows a lot more than that little canary down in the custody suite.' Jenny sounded as if she were already wholeheartedly engaged in the case. 'I'm going to lean on him hard about those Dutch contacts. I want to find the organisation behind this evil trade. I've been looking for these people for over a year, and this is the first proper lead I've had.'

'We knew you were the right person for this job, Jen.' Jackman smiled, relieved that their case was in such capable hands; relieved, too, that he no longer needed to feel guilty at having left it unfinished.

'And finally,' said Jenny, 'he told the officer who interviewed him that Lance had nothing to do with the death of that police advisor, Frank Rosen. He swears that Lance considered Frank to be completely harmless, and he wasn't remotely bothered by his presence on set.' She shrugged. 'More than that I don't know, but we'll keep you in the loop. Now, I'm off to hone my grilling techniques. Ta-ra for now.'

Jackman nodded and thanked her. That confirmed their earlier supposition that Frank had been killed by the clean-up operation conducted by the organisation running the snuff movies. They clearly wanted no weak links left dangling. He shook his head as if to clear it. It was Jenny's worry now, if only for the next week. Meanwhile, he had bigger fish to fry.

* * *

John had been taking a brief nap in the flat's only bedroom. He awoke to hear Hazel moving around in the office which had been silent when he'd drifted off to sleep some thirty minutes ago. He wondered where she'd been, and what she had in store for him this evening. Apparently, Christos had said that, henceforward, John's 'exceptional talents' would be called upon only in the execution of Phase Two. John had sensed a note of sarcasm behind the reference to his talents but the money that had appeared in his bank account that morning had served nicely to smooth any ruffled feathers he might have had.

John sat on the edge of the bed and stared at the door, listening to the noises on the other side of it. Having Hazel so close to him, and yet so distant, was becoming almost too much to bear, especially since she had become more solicitous towards him.

Yet again, he caught himself considering his future. He had had it all worked out: with the job complete and his money squirrelled away, he had only a simple decision to make. Should it be cruise ship or log cabin? Now, however, thoughts of Hazel were muddying the waters. Would she, could she consider joining him on a voyage to the South Seas? And how would Stephen want the end game played out? If Hazel's fate was to be the same as Janet's, could he do it? What if he, John, decided otherwise, what then?

CHAPTER TWENTY-EIGHT

Ella Jarvis checked her watch. She had hoped to get home early today, but a request had come in to attend a crime scene on the outskirts of Saltern. Apparently, the SOCO who was supposed to be on call had phoned in sick, and she was next in line. Ah well, at least it didn't sound too arduous, just a series of break-ins at houses where the owners were away, and several valuable pieces of jewellery had been taken. She guessed it would be a straightforward walk-through, checking for broken windows, footprints, fingerprints and the like. A detective would be meeting her at the scene.

The house where she was to meet the detective was situated along a dark fen lane. As she pulled into the drive, she was relieved to see another car already outside. Hopefully this wouldn't take long.

The lights were on and the front door was open, and a man she took to be the detective called out, 'Door's open. I'm DC Jones, come on in.'

'Are you suited up?' asked Ella.

'Yep. My skipper told me to bring a zoot suit and shoe coverings.'

Ella pulled on her own protective clothing, pushed the door wider with her hip and carried her equipment cases into the hall.

It was a smart looking residence, of average size and with a couple of rather beautiful abstract paintings on the wall.

'I'm in the kitchen, Ella. Looks like he got in through the French doors,' called out DC Jones. 'Want a hand with your cases?'

'No, I'm fine,' said Ella, and walked over to the open kitchen door.

She stepped inside.

Then something dark and rough was pulled over her head. Her equipment cases crashed to the floor. Her hands were pulled behind her back and she was shoved, face down, onto the floor.

'Stay still, and you won't get hurt. Struggle, and you'll find I'm not very nice to know.'

Given her current position, Ella had little option but to do as she was told, though she wasn't the sort to give in easily. Inside, she was boiling with rage, mainly at herself for letting her guard down.

'Smart woman. Now stay that way.'

Kneeling on her back, the man bound her wrists together. Now her anger gave way to fear. What on earth was going on? Who was this man and why attack her? She suddenly had a vision of those warning texts and photos, and she froze. Ashcroft! She had seen first-hand what Alistair Ashcroft was capable of — the carnage he left in his wake. People under Ashcroft's control were capable of unspeakable acts. Was her captor one of those people?

'Okay. I'm going to sit you up, but no fighting me, or you'll regret it.'

He took hold of her, dragged her along the floor and pushed her into a seating position with her back against a wall.

'You may not believe it, Ella, but you're the lucky one. Stephen, he remembers you, says you're feisty. Seems you were prepared to fight back to protect two little boys. So he has chosen you to be the messenger.'

Stephen? From his reference to the boys, she realised he must be talking about Ashcroft. She waited.

'But first, so as to prove I'm telling the truth, I'll tell you something about yourself.'

He began to recite: 'Ella Carmel Jarvis, born eleventh July 1985, to James Jarvis and Lucy Jarvis, nee Campbell, in the village of Fendyke in Lincolnshire. Father worked as . . .' He droned on. '. . . Nanny, employed by James and Sarah Jackman to care for their sons, Ryan and Miles. After leaving their employ, you went on to train as a scene of crime officer and worked for Fenland Constabulary, until a case of child abuse caused you to abandon your career. For a short time you returned to the Jackman house to care for the aforementioned boys after their mother took her own life, but later you returned to scene of crime forensics, becoming photographer to Professor Rory Wilkinson . . . All correct so far?'

Ella coughed, unable to speak.

The man laughed. 'Oh, we know everything about you, Ella Carmel Jarvis, even down to your habit of touching that St Christopher medallion that hangs in your car every time you go to drive off. Keeps you safe, does it? Well, by the look of you right now, it doesn't seem to be working too well.'

Ella writhed in outrage.

'And you're just a minor player. Imagine what we know about the others, the leading characters.'

This . . . this intrusion. It was all too much. Ella exploded. 'Just cut the crap, Mr Know-it-all. Okay, so I'm your messenger. Then give me the fucking message!'

'Feisty! Stephen was right. All right, Ella Jarvis, I'll give you your message. Listen now, and listen good.'

She felt him lean closer to her and shrank back against the wall, suddenly regretting having shouted at him like that.

'I'll be leaving something with you when I go. As soon as you've got yourself untied, you go straight to DI Jackman with what I've given you, and you tell him this: *This is how easy it is. No one is safe. Not one of you can even breathe without me knowing. Understand that no matter what you do, you cannot stop me.*'

'Repeat what I said!'

Stammering, she did so.

'Word perfect. Good.'

The weight of his presence lessened. She had been expecting, at the very least, that he would hit her. Instead, she heard the sound of something heavy fall to the floor a little way in front of her.

'I'll be leaving in a minute. You'll find your wrists aren't bound tightly. By the time I've gone, you should have been able to get yourself free. You still have your mobile phone, so you call DI Jackman immediately. Got that?'

She mumbled a 'yes.'

'You've been spared for now, Ella Jarvis. Deliver that message or you won't be so lucky next time.'

A few moments later she heard the door slam. Silence descended over the house. Ella struggled to free her wrists and for a moment she panicked.

As the sound of the car engine died away, she felt the cords slacken. Tears coursing down her cheeks, she ripped off the hood and flung it to the ground, muttering, 'The bastard! The bastard!' She glanced at the large manilla envelope that her captor had left for Jackman, then pulled her phone from her pocket.

* * *

The others had left, but Marie and Jackman were still working when he received the call from Ella. Telling her to stay where she was, he and Marie ran to his car.

As they drove, he said, 'Will you drive her home in her car if she's still shaky?'

'Of course,' said Marie. 'Poor Ella. She must be beside herself.' She glanced at Jackman. 'This has taken a turn for the worse, hasn't it? Sure, he's no longer stalking the streets with a rifle like he did before, but there's someone out there, and they're doing it for him. Who? Another psycho?'

'Well one thing's for sure, no sane person would work for Alistair Ashcroft. By the way, Ella said he'd left something for me, a parcel.'

'You're not going to open it, are you, boss? Suppose it contains explosives?'

Jackman laughed dryly. 'There'd be no fun for him in that. No, it'll be something to taunt us with, something that'll have us running round in circles.'

'I hope Ella is all right,' said Marie. 'I wonder if Robbie knows yet? He'll be tearing his hair out if he does.'

'Which is exactly what Ashcroft would want,' growled Jackman. 'But so far she's only told us. Robbie still believes she's had a call out to a break-in. She didn't want him running around like a headless chicken in a total panic.'

'She sounds pretty together. After a scary experience like that, I'd have thought the first thing she would do would be to fling herself into his arms,' Marie said.

'Well, she's shocked, naturally, but she's angry too. It will most likely hit her later, and then she'll need Robbie's arms.'

Jackman slowed down and turned onto a lane that led out of the town and meandered past a series of isolated villages. 'It's along here somewhere,' he muttered, squinting at the houses they passed.

'There's Ella's car!' Marie pointed to a little red Honda, parked just inside the drive of a rather elegant property.

They hurried inside and found Ella sitting on the hall stairs. She looked shocked, but was holding it together.

She stood up as they came in. Marie hugged her tightly. 'You okay, hon? Are you hurt?'

'Only my pride,' said Ella ruefully. 'Why didn't I suspect that something was off about that call-out? I could kick myself!'

'Are you up to telling us what happened?' asked Jackman, closing the front door behind him. 'And whose house is this?'

'I've no idea who owns the place but, yes, I'm fine. I need to tell you what that man said before I forget. He said I must pass on a message, word for word.'

'Go ahead, Ella.'

She closed her eyes. '*This is how easy it is. No one is safe. Not one of you can even breathe without me knowing. And what you must*

243

understand . . . what you must understand is that no matter what you do, you cannot stop me.'

'We'll see about that,' Jackman muttered.

'And he left this for you.' Ella pointed to a large package lying on the floor near the stairs. 'It looks like paperwork. I didn't open it of course. I didn't even touch it.' She looked around. 'I was called to a crime scene, so I've got all my equipment here. Do you want me to—'

'No, Ella,' Jackman said. 'No way are you going to start working after what you've been through. Now, since we're here, we might as well take advantage of this unknown person's home and go through what occurred.'

'If it's okay with you, boss,' Marie said, 'I'll ring this in while you talk to Ella. If I get the SOCOs to come in while we're here, Ella can tell them where her assailant was standing and what he might have touched, where his car was parked and so on. We might get some trace evidence, you never know.'

Jackman agreed. He took Ella into the lounge and sat her down. 'Now, in your own time . . .'

Ella told him about receiving the call-out. 'There have been similar break-ins recently. The control officer told me that a pool detective called DC Jones would meet me here.' Ella looked pained. 'She gave me the address, just like always, sir. Even the police-speak was the same. There was nothing at all suspicious about it.'

'I'm sure it was,' said Jackman. 'These people are professionals, and they will have done their homework.'

'Even the man who attacked me sounded totally convincing, though — and I only realised it afterwards — he made sure I never saw his face. And I've never heard of a DC Jones. When control said he was a pool detective I just thought we hadn't met. What an idiot I was!'

Ella finished her account by saying how intimidating the man had sounded.

'His voice was really cold, sir. I got the feeling that if he had been sent to kill me, he wouldn't have hesitated for a moment.'

This sounded to Jackman like a professional hitman, and those people cost money — big money. How much did Ashcroft have squirrelled away? 'Try not to think about it, Ella. You've done exactly as he asked, so I'd say you are off the hook.'

'But what about everyone else?'

Good question, thought Jackman. 'That's why we are throwing everything at this. Every waking hour, we'll be engaged in the hunt for the person carrying out Ashcroft's dirty work for him.' He stood up. 'Are you up to seeing what this parcel contains? If you are, after I've had a look, I'll get you to seal it up for me in one of your evidence bags. I daren't contaminate it, but I have to know what it is.'

'Of course. I want to know too, even if I'm terrified of what it might be.'

They went back into the hall and met Marie coming in.

'All organised, boss. A crew's on its way, along with a SOCO.' Her eyes went to the parcel. 'Prezzie-opening time then, is it?'

'Well, I'm not saving it for Christmas,' Jackman said with a grim smile. He pulled on some nitrile gloves and, taking a deep breath, bent over the package. He accepted the sharp knife Ella held out to him and slit it open.

He pulled out a thick file with a see-through pocket on the front cover, holding a photograph of himself, labelled 'Jackman'.

As he stared at it, Marie squeezed his shoulder and whispered, 'Do you want to do this here, or shall we take it straight to the forensics lab and get them to tackle it in sterile conditions?'

He knew this was what he should do. Nonetheless, he *had* to open that file. 'I'll take one look inside, and then Ella can seal it up. Rory will fast-track it, I know, but I must know what Ashcroft's intentions are.'

He opened the file at a table of contents: '*Childhood. Early Years. School Years. University. Career. Family. Hobbies. Habits. Colleagues. Friends.*' The last heading read, '*Weaknesses,*' followed by '*Summary*'.

'Jesus,' muttered Marie. 'That's going to take some reading.'

Jackman stared at the file in his hands. How long had it taken to compile this dossier? Years? Ashcroft had probably started working on it after he had been confined to a wheelchair. He must have begun it in person, then had others continue. As Jackman knew, Ashcroft often described himself as a patient man, but this was the work of a man obsessed.

Jackman shivered at the thought of being the object of so single-minded a passion.

He leafed through it and saw his own biography, presented like a manuscript ready for publication, complete with photographs, copies of original documents, newspaper reports and magazine articles.

His hand shaking, he turned to the last page. As he had feared, there was an 'Epilogue', and below it, 'In Memorium,' above a photograph of himself, taken very recently. He even recalled where he'd been and what he was wearing. Taken less than twenty-four hours ago. Beneath the photograph were the words, 'Rest in Peace.'

'Oh, come on!' exclaimed Marie, who had been reading over his shoulder. 'This is the limit, really.'

But Jackman was elsewhere, overcome by a wave of intense sorrow. Those same words had been the epitaph for his beloved Laura.

Marie touched his shoulder. 'Don't let him win, Jackman. That,' and she waved her hand over the document, 'is just another of his mind games, and a very expensive one at that. Well, he's wasted his time and his money, because we are going to nail him. Just keep remembering that nice quiet cell beneath Britain's most dangerous high-security prison.'

Jackman swallowed. 'Sorry, Marie, just a minor wobble.' He turned to Ella. 'Get this garbage out of my sight, will you?'

She nodded briskly. 'Got it, sir. I'll seal it and sign it and we'll get it straight into the system. Like you said, the prof will fast-track it for you.'

'Thanks, Ella, and then we should get you home. Marie will drive you. I don't want you behind the wheel after the shock you've had.'

'I'm okay, sir. My biggest fear right now is telling Robbie!' She rolled her eyes. 'He's going to go ballistic. Especially because I didn't ring him.'

Jackman took his phone from his pocket. 'Well, we can't have that. I'll tell him I needed to debrief you immediately and wouldn't let you contact anyone until I'd assessed the situation.'

Still wearing her protective suit, Ella processed the bagged dossier. 'The SOCO that comes out might find something where my assailant attacked me. The sacking that was pulled over my head is still there, and there's also the kitchen door. He might have left a print on it you never know.'

Jackman doubted they'd find anything at all. This person was a professional and would leave no trace.

By the time Ella had gathered up her equipment, the room was lit up by a flashing blue light and a crew was making its way to the front door. Marie went out and briefed them, instructing them to wait for forensics before anyone went in.

Well, something positive has come out of this, thought Jackman. Now they knew for certain that it was Ashcroft behind the messages. Going by what Ella's assailant had told her, there could be little doubt. Therefore, his first task would be to get the madman removed from the Aegis Unit, for which he needed official sanction.

'Okay, Marie. You and Ella get off, I'll follow as soon as the SOCO gets here and pick you up at Robbie and Ella's place. Then, my friend, we have work to do.'

CHAPTER TWENTY-NINE

Ruth Crooke slammed down the receiver and glared at it. The superintendent wasn't used to not getting her own way. Worse, she would have to tell Jackman and Marie that she'd failed.

It was now after ten in the evening. She had returned to the station after Rowan called to inform her of the assault on the forensic photographer and the message she had been forced to deliver. Ruth was tired but it had nothing to do with the lateness of the hour and everything to do with Ashcroft's new assault. He was back, dangerous as ever, without even setting foot out of his cell. It was soul-destroying.

She rubbed at her temples, trying to assuage the headache that had troubled her ever since Ashcroft's involvement was confirmed. Still, it was no good procrastinating. She pushed her chair back and strode to the door.

She found Jackman and Marie, together with Gary Pritchard and PCs Stacey Smith and Jay Acharya, seated in front of the whiteboard. She dragged up a chair and joined them.

'We were just updating the board, and trying to assimilate what we know to date, Super,' said Jackman. 'Gary's just offered to go and get drinks, can we interest you in one?'

'The strongest coffee that rubbish machine can produce, please, Gary,' she said, holding out a couple of pound coins.

'Put it away, ma'am,' said Gary. 'This is my round.'

As he went off to get the drinks, Jackman said, 'We are dying to hear what news you have for us.'

She sighed. 'Not what we were hoping for, I'm afraid. But I'm not done trying, believe me. I just have to raise the right people. Few are available at this time of night.'

Jackman's face fell. 'Aren't they even listening? Surely, the prison must realise what a volatile situation we have here?'

'I'll explain in detail when Gary gets back with the coffee,' she said. 'In the meantime, are there any updates?'

'Stacey and Jay have heard a few rather disturbing snippets from some of their contacts on the streets.' He turned to her. 'Stacey?'

'I'm afraid we have no names yet, ma'am, but it appears that there's a new underground organisation causing considerable concern among the criminal community. The locals are worried because this new set-up seems to be infiltrating all their various shady activities. They're pretty ruthless, it seems. Step out of line and . . .' Stacey pulled a face. 'It's even been said that people have disappeared.'

'Not the best news, I admit, but how does that tie in with Ashcroft?' Ruth said.

'Because it's been hinted,' Jackman explained, 'that these new guys were behind the murder of Lance Newport, meaning they must be behind the snuff movies as well. And that puts them firmly in the frame for killing our two former colleagues, Frank and Dougie. I know we've handed that case over to DI Jenny Deane for now, but it's something we should bear in mind. We don't need this other crew muddying the waters while we're busy hunting down Ashcroft's henchmen.'

'Point taken.' Apart from anything else, Ruth didn't need a new set of criminals moving into their patch, things were bad enough already. She made a mental note to talk to Jenny Deane first thing in the morning and tell her to come directly to Ruth if anything occurred, rather than bothering Rowan.

'Coffee's up,' declared Gary, backing into the room with a tray of drinks.

When they all had their plastic cups, Jackman turned to the super. 'So, you'd better hit us with that bad news.'

There was little for it but to tell them. 'They have refused to move Alistair Ashcroft from the Aegis Unit.'

Jackman stared at her, incredulous. 'I can't believe it. What are they thinking? What sodding planet are they on? Can't they see he's playing the whole system?'

'Rowan,' she said calmly, 'I did everything in my power to have him put into segregation, and I've hit a brick wall. The governor assured me they have a fail-safe — a separate structure within the unit designed specifically to respond to this type of event. The governor called it a prison within a prison, a form of lockdown. More than that he couldn't say. Theo Carmichael wasn't available, so I'm speaking to him first thing in the morning. If necessary, I'll go there in person. Tonight, I can do no more.' Ruth picked up her coffee and took a long, thirsty swallow.

'It's not enough, though, is it? Not for a man like Ashcroft,' said Marie despondently.

'No, Marie, it isn't,' she said, bitterly, 'but for now we'll have to hope that their system is as good as he claims it to be. Tomorrow, I'll take up the struggle again, find my way through the red tape and the rest of the bureaucratic crap and force them to see Ashcroft for what he really is. He needs to be moved, taken far from here and put into isolation, maybe somewhere like Full Sutton, where they know how to handle truly dangerous criminals.'

'You've done your best, Ruth,' said Jackman. 'If anyone could have sorted it, it would have been you. All we can do is keep up the hunt for his minions and leave you to deal with the people at Aegis. Every single link with the outside must be vetted, all the staff from the director down to the cleaners. Someone is facilitating this vendetta of his.'

'If it was down to me, I'd replace everyone in that unit,' said Marie. 'I'd keep him in his room, cut him off from everyone, both other prisoners and staff. It's the only way.'

'I'll do all I can,' Ruth said. 'I want this over and done with as much as you.' What else could she say? They hadn't heard the patronising tone of the prison governor when she'd asked for Ashcroft to be transferred. "My good woman," he'd said, as if she were a fool. "It simply isn't possible for one of our prisoners to conduct any form of business, criminal or otherwise, from within the Aegis Unit." Telling Jackman and his people to get some rest, she drained her coffee and stood up.

Jackman agreed. 'You heard the super. We'll call it a day now, and in the morning, we'll be ready to work like Trojans.'

* * *

Apart from the faint hum of the computers, all was silent in Orac's underground domain. She stared at her phone, and the message that had just appeared:

Tell Jackman to keep his head. He is not alone in this fight.

Orac frowned. Whoever had sent it was highly skilled at circumventing the usual methods of tracing the sender of a call or message, so Orac gave up. She didn't have the time.

It was after eleven p.m., and Jackman and Marie would have left. Before she went home to snatch a few hours' rest, she fired off a text asking them to contact her first thing in the morning. Her eyes remained on her phone. How had the sender of that message gained access to her personal number?

Could it be coincidence that the ex-detective, Frank Rosen, had received an anonymous call warning him to get away from the TV shoot? Orac didn't believe in coincidence. Someone else was out there, watching Saltern-le-Fen's detectives and what they were doing. And how could they follow their every move unless they were close by?

Were they here then, inside the police station? She looked again at the message. '*Tell Jackman.*' Not tell DI Jackman, or tell the officer in charge, no, they'd called him Jackman. People who knew him said that. People who worked with him.

Hmm. Maybe she should trace the sender. Sleep never had been very high on her list of priorities. Two hours would be enough. Then she'd have the rest of the night to track down the anonymous protector.

* * *

Jackman received Orac's message just as he was nearing Cartoft village, and decided to call her the following day. It was cryptic, but Orac's communications usually were. She had some news that she would give him in the morning. He was tempted to ring her now, but it was approaching midnight and she might be asleep — though he couldn't imagine Orac ever sleeping!

When he got home, Sam's door was open. As soon as he switched off the engine, his old friend came hurrying across.

'I hate to do this to you, Jackman,' Sam said. 'I'm sure you are out on your feet, but could you spare Julia and me a few minutes before you turn in?'

Jackman was indeed exhausted but he gave Sam a smile. 'So long as you throw in a glass of your delicious single malt.'

He locked his car and followed Sam inside. Although this would always be Laura's special place, Jackman noticed that it hurt less to be here, now that Sam had filled it with his presence.

Julia was curled up, cat-like, on one of the couches, nursing a glass of what Jackman suspected to be Sam's favourite cognac. It looked like he wasn't the only one to have had a stressful day.

Sam poured him the promised whisky and sat down.

'The thing is, Jackman, you asked Julia to look for potential weaknesses in the Aegis set-up, and she's found a couple of possible candidates for closer inspection among the staff. As for myself, you wanted me to find out all I could about Theo Carmichael, and I have dug up a few nuggets that might interest you.'

'Before we get onto that, something happened tonight that you ought to know about.' Jackman told them about the attack on Ella, and the message she was made to deliver, along with the dossier, which proved unequivocally that Ashcroft was the man behind the chaos. 'However, Ruth's request to have him returned to the main prison and into segregation was vetoed. He stays put. Apparently, they have some lockdown procedure for emergencies, which they believe to be entirely adequate.'

Julia sighed, evidently frustrated. 'I thought something like that would happen. Theo built that unit around Ashcroft, and I'm pretty sure he would fight tooth and nail to keep him there.' She grimaced. 'In fact, I wouldn't be surprised if Theo had foreseen this very thing happening, hence the governor's "infallible" security procedure.'

Jackman nodded. 'Ruth suggested as much. It just goes to show the importance of what you two are doing to the investigation.'

'And to that end,' said Sam, 'Julia and I have an appointment with Theo at Aegis tomorrow morning at ten. We are hoping the reservations expressed by two of the most respected psychologists in his field will at least give him pause for thought.'

'It's fortuitous that you've told us about the dossier and that the attacker mentioned Stephen by name,' Julia added. 'We now have something concrete to confront him with.'

Jackman looked warily at Sam, remembering the effect his previous visit had had on him. 'Are you up for this, Sam? Be honest.'

'The situation requires me to grow a little more backbone,' said Sam drily. 'Or so Julia would tell me. But since I'll have her with me, I'll be able to cope, I'm sure.'

Jackman glanced at Julia, who nodded. 'He'll be fine. Neither of us will be visiting the man himself. It's Carmichael we'll be concentrating on, along with his second in command. I got the distinct feeling that Dr Casey Naylor is not Stephen's greatest fan, even if he is the main attraction.'

'Then I wish you luck, both of you. Will you ring me when you're through?' Jackman said.

'Of course,' said Sam. 'And we might need that luck. This is Theo's life's work we are about to lay siege to.'

'Maybe you should warn Theo that even he is not immune? If "his" Stephen gets irritated or bored with them, they could finish up on his hit list along with all the rest.' He sat back. 'But you haven't told me about those weak links, Julia, or the dirt you've dug up about Theo.'

'I think I'll save it until we've made our visit,' said Julia. 'We should know more after that. Besides, you look out on your feet, Jackman. Time to call it a day.'

He drank the last of the malt. 'Thank you for the nightcap, and I wish you well for tomorrow.'

Making his way to his own front door, Jackman thought about Sam and Julia, and how comfortable they were together. Maybe after this horrible case was over . . .? *After it's over.* He sighed. Until then, not one of them could move on with their lives. Once again, Ashcroft had them all frozen in place, like rabbits caught in the headlights.

Jackman went inside and made himself ready for bed. His last thought as sleep overtook him was, *Well, this is where it ends.*

* * *

Hazel Palgrave unlocked her door and went in, straight to the kitchen, where she cast a sorrowful glance at the empty cat basket. 'Miss you, you little stinker.'

Buffy the Vermin-Slayer was with a friend, on an extended holiday. Knowing that this part of the operation would call for long hours at the office, Hazel had thought it wise to have him fed and cared for elsewhere for the time being. But whenever she did go home, the big house seemed suddenly empty, and the cat wasn't the only one that she missed.

She pushed the thoughts aside and turning her eyes from the cat basket, she went to the freezer and took out a ready meal. These days her precious Aga went unused. Life had undergone a sea change when Stephen had come into it. Sometimes she wondered what her obsession with him was doing to her, but she always dismissed the thought. It didn't matter anyway, all that mattered was Stephen and ensuring that this operation worked perfectly.

While she waited for her meal to heat, she opened a drawer and removed a thick spiral-bound notebook. It was her personal account of the mission, filled with information, dates, times, names, though the bulk of the information had to do with backgrounds and personal histories. These, some hand-written, others printed, she had inserted into clear sleeves between the pages.

She removed her supper from its plastic tray and spooned it into a pasta dish. Along with a dessert of raspberries, blueberries, and a carton of Greek yoghurt, it would keep her going.

In between mouthfuls, she completed her entry for the day.

She finished at around one thirty in the morning and made her way upstairs to bed. She set her alarm for five, and lay, staring into the darkness, contemplating the tasks for the following morning. It was important that she get everything just right. One wrong timing and the whole operation could turn from success to disaster in the blink of an eye.

She went through everything in her head. Yes, it was all in place. She closed her eyes but her mind wouldn't stop working. It was John. She was fully aware that he was attracted to her, though he tried not to show it, but it was still a concern.

Hazel turned on her side and drew the covers over her head. Unbeknownst to John, she knew exactly what had happened to her predecessor, and she was equally aware of the danger she would be in if he were ordered to take the same

255

steps again. But she knew her worth to Stephen. He would want to keep her onboard.

Yes, she was safe, as long as she steered the ship safely to its final destination. The day to come was pivotal. The entire operation hinged on her getting it right. And so, as sleep finally claimed her, she was still whispering, 'I have to get it right, I have to.'

CHAPTER THIRTY

Marie woke early, seized with a premonition that the day ahead was somehow crucial. She eased herself out of bed, trying not to disturb Ralph, but a sleepy voice issued from under the covers. 'Oh God! It can't be morning already.'

''Fraid so, and I need to get moving. Big day today.'

Ralph sat up and swung his legs over the side of the bed. 'In that case, you have a shower and I'll get you some breakfast. Big days need to start with a full stomach.'

'One of those traditional Enderby family sayings?' she asked, stretching.

'No, just me being sensible. I'm a copper too, and I've missed more lunches and dinners than I care to mention.' He gave her a hug. 'I love you, and I don't want you fading away with hunger.' He nipped her ear playfully. 'So, one big breakfast coming up.'

Marie laughed. 'Can you honestly see me fading away? On second thoughts, forget what I said, I could do with one of your breakfasts — just in case.'

Three quarters of an hour later she was sitting in her car, filled to the brim with eggs, bacon, tomatoes and fried bread. She waved Ralph goodbye and drove off, wondering what the day would bring. The feeling of anticipation, almost of foreboding, was still with her, and she knew not to ignore it. All she could do was try to prepare herself.

Jackman's car was already outside the station when she arrived. She wondered if he too was feeling the same almost fearful anticipation. She found him in the CID room talking to the two detectives who'd been manning the night shift.

Marie got two coffees and took them to Jackman's office. 'So, boss, where do we start?'

'With the call I'm just about to make to Orac.'

She stared at him. '*You* are going to call Orac? Like talk to her personally? Good Lord.'

With a withering look at her, he handed her his phone.

She looked at the screen. 'Oh, that. I had a message too, and I'm itching to know what she'll tell us.'

His smile was smug. 'In which case, *you* can ring her — and put her on loudspeaker.'

'Coward,' she muttered, taking her phone from her pocket.

Orac answered almost immediately. 'Ah, Marie! Overslept, have we?'

'It's six thirty in the morning, Orac! And I've already had a cooked breakfast, I'll have you know.'

'Huh! If you worked in my department, you'd know what long hours really are. Anyway, down to business. I'm guessing my good friend Jackman is with you, so here's what I have to say.'

'Go ahead.'

Orac read out the message, mentioning the use of the name 'Jackman', suggesting the sender was someone he knew. 'But here's the odd thing. Naturally, I started a trace, and after following it halfway round the world, found myself back where I started.'

'Where's that?' asked Jackman.

'Right here in Saltern. To within the triangulation of the masts that serve the police station.'

Marie and Jackman were silent. Finally, Marie said, 'You mean it could come from in here? *Shit.*'

'Here, or close by,' said Orac. 'It's no longer an active IP address but still . . . All I can say is that someone seems to be paying very careful attention to what you detectives are up to. The best thing is that they appear to be on your side.'

'Or are trying to make us believe they are.' Jackman was clearly not convinced.

'I think this person really does have your back, Jackman,' said Orac. 'Call it the sixth sense of the Irish but if you want to know who it is, I'd look into the past. Someone connected to you in some way hates him as much as you guys do.'

He nodded. 'You're right, Orac, we too think the answer lies there. Ashcroft has to have set this up ages ago, before he was caught, and now he has people carrying out his orders. Right now, we're looking for the accountant, the man in control of the financing of this campaign of his.'

'Oh, I can help with that,' said Orac immediately. 'Marie sent me a nice bedtime storybook to while away the nights: "From abused child to serial killer: My Journey, by Alistair Ashcroft," or something like that. I've already identified a few juicy items to chase up from here — possibly illegally, though, of course, you never heard that.'

'We just went deaf,' chuckled Marie.

'But . . . before I dive in there, you asked for information on the messages we all, myself included, received. Well, I don't usually admit defeat, but I can only say that they originated in this country. So, I suggest my time would be better spent helping you follow the money trail.'

'Absolutely,' said Jackman. 'And perhaps if we go through that dossier and pick out the names of people who might fit the bill for this anonymous vigilante who appears to be on our side, you might be able to check them out for us?'

'I certainly can, and in half the time it would take you lot,' she said smugly. 'Send them down, and I'll tell you where they are and what they are doing right now — maybe even what they had for breakfast.'

'Then we better crack on,' said Jackman. 'We only have a week.'

'I'll be waiting.' Orac ended the call.

Marie bit back the urge to laugh at the confused look on Jackman's face; the one he always wore after talking to the enigmatic Orac. 'So, boss, what have you got for me?' Marie said.

'Grab that dossier,' said Jackman. 'You and I are going to take a painful walk down memory lane and weed out every single person who may have had call to hate Ashcroft. We'll start with the bereaved relatives and loved ones of Ashcroft's victims. When the others get in, I'll put them onto sourcing Ashcroft's photographer — the "ordinary" man who spoke to my mother — as well as whoever is handling the finances.'

'Gotcha, boss. I'll go and get my copy.'

Marie hurried to her workstation, gritting her teeth. This was not going to be fun.

* * *

Alistair Ashcroft lay in his bed with his eyes closed, contemplating the day to come. He had been preparing himself for this moment for years now, and it had taken all his courage to bring it to fruition. All channels of communication with the outside world had been severed, including those connecting him with Christos and Hazel Palgrave. From now on, Phase Two would run its course without him.

In his head, four words repeated themselves in a loop: *'Nothing can stop it.'*

His timing had been flawless, for a mere two hours after he had isolated himself, lockdown was announced. It appeared that fate was on his side, favouring the achievement of his lifelong ambition: to take the past and cleanse it of all the filth and suffering he had endured.

He opened his eyes and wondered what was for breakfast.

* * *

Theo Carmichael looked at the painting his father had given him. For the first time, his contemplation of it gave him no solace. Sadly, he shook his head and prepared for the coming day at Aegis.

He had been planning to go on one of his short trips into the countryside. However, it had become clear that this wouldn't be happening. Instead, he had allowed himself a much shorter break, finishing work at lunchtime and taking a long walk along the sea-bank from Stone Quay to the Wash. When he arrived home in the evening he found an urgent message from Casey Naylor. Apparently, the police had contacted the prison governor with concerns about Ashcroft. In Theo's absence, he had requested her to instigate the lockdown procedure. She had done as he asked, but had left it to Theo to implement the full protocol first thing the following morning. They were to meet at seven thirty to discuss the matter. He was also expecting a visit from Julia Tennant and, rather surprisingly, Professor Sam Page. It was the worst moment for them to have chosen for it.

Ever since Julia Tennant's first visit, he had been wondering why this eminent psychologist, well, why *two* eminent psychologists, should be so interested in his work. He had had many other professionals visit, and be excited about the work he was doing in Aegis, but Julia and Sam seemed to be operating on a different level altogether, and it bothered him.

He walked the short distance to the prison, trying to get his thoughts in order. They had often rehearsed the lockdown procedure, which was effected in three stages. Casey had already activated stage one, and today, the two of them would decide whether to bring the second into force, or launch stage three immediately. This would depend on what the police had said to the governor.

Once he was in his office, Casey recounted everything that had been said in his absence, emphasising the possibility that Stephen had coerced someone in the unit into helping him. It hadn't taken Theo long to realise the seriousness of the situation.

'We know these people!' he exclaimed for the second time. 'Every single individual who sets foot in this unit has been vetted to the nth degree. Stephen *cannot* be using them to make contact with anyone. It's just not possible.'

Casey received his outburst in silence.

'You're not having doubts, are you? I mean about our work here.'

'No, of course not,' Casey said, loudly. 'I believe as much as you that studying the thought processes of dangerous killers will provide important precedents for their future treatment. My only worry, as I've already said, is with the choice of subject: Stephen. Although why we have to call him that beats me. It's just another of his games. He is Alistair Ashcroft, a very dangerous psychopath who has murdered multiple people. We shouldn't pander to him this way.'

Theo stared at her. He'd never before heard Casey even raise her voice, now she was almost shouting.

'Sorry,' she said. 'That was out of order. But the fact remains — Ashcroft has something going on in that evil mind of his. I'm not the only one who thinks so, either, Patrick Galway does too. Honestly, Theo, I think we really do need to listen to what Julia Tennant says when she comes to see us. I'm certain she has the measure of him.' Theo opened his mouth to speak, but Casey held up a hand. 'As far as security goes, no one could have done more than you to make it absolutely watertight, but you know Ashcroft. I wouldn't put it past him to have ferreted out the single flaw in the system. They say that everyone has their price, maybe that weak spot lies in the vetting procedure.'

For the first time since he'd launched his dream project, Theo Carmichael wondered if his faith in Aegis was misplaced. Maybe his pride in his creation had given him tunnel vision. 'All right, Casey, I'll listen to our guests with an open mind.'

Casey's look at him was full of compassion. 'If he has found a way to undermine your project after all you've put into it, I warn you, I may not be responsible for my actions.'

Theo believed in the work he was doing, believed it to be a ground-breaking method for understanding, and even treating, psychopathy. If it were all to come to nothing, he didn't think he would be able to bear it.

* * *

Marie and Jackman spent over an hour poring over Jackman's biography and had discovered a number of possibilities. When Jackman was called up to Ruth's office, Marie continued to work on it at her desk.

The door to the CID room opened and Stacey and Jay came hurrying in.

'We've just had a bit of luck, Sarge,' said Stacey.

'And it's the good sort for once,' added Jay with a grin. 'We went to the stables to see Jackman's mother, and she brought together everyone who had been around when that nondescript looking man appeared, supposedly looking for a missing dog.'

'It so happened,' continued Stacey, 'that a youngster who was exercising one of the ponies took some photos of it on her phone. Guess who was in the background?'

'Not the "ordinary" man?' asked Marie.

'None other, and Harriet has confirmed it. Here.' Stacey pulled out her phone and showed Marie the photo.

The man certainly was ordinary-looking. No wonder Harriet Jackman hadn't been able to describe him. But now they knew who they were looking for. It was a major break-through.

Marie zoomed in on the figure. He was standing sideways on, obviously unaware of the girl with the phone. As the face became clearer, Marie experienced a brief flash of recognition. She knew this man! But wait, did she? He could easily just resemble someone she knew. So she dismissed it for the time being.

'We need to get that to IT and see if they can enhance it,' she said. 'Great work, you two. Jackman will be well chuffed.'

'We'll run it down there now, Sarge, if you like,' said Stacey.

'That would be good, thanks,' said Marie. 'Oh, and any luck with his car?'

Jay shook his head. 'He must have left it outside in the lane and walked in. Harriet said the fact that he appeared on foot made his story sound more plausible. She was furious with herself at being taken in.'

'Do you think DI Jackman would like us to help Robbie and Gary follow up on that mystery photographer, Sarge?' asked Stacey. 'After all, this man might have nothing to do with taking the pictures, he could be the delivery man.'

'Good idea. Liaise with them after you've taken that camera downstairs. Checking out all those photos is a huge task, so I'm sure they'll appreciate your help. It could be that the guy in the picture does both things, but we have to make sure.'

Stacey and Jay headed off to IT, and Marie returned to her task. As she noted the names, events she'd considered long forgotten resurfaced in her mind. The havoc Ashcroft had wreaked remained horribly distressing, and reading about it reopened all the old wounds.

She had divided the names into three columns. One listed only marginal candidates. A second had the names of people who were more likely to have held a grudge against Ashford. The third was a list of people who had made actual threats against him. Some among them would never have received consolation from the fact that the monster had been locked up for life. These had wished him dead.

'Sarge.'

'Oh, hi, Max, Got something?'

'Maybe . . . Um, if I threw a name at Orac, do you think she'd fast-track it for me? I've got a weird feeling about this bloke. He's cropped up a few times in connection with the Ashcroft estate. I'm taking about Daddy Ashcroft totalling his vehicle in a drainage ditch and conveniently snapping his neck. Little Alistair inherited everything, if you recall, but the money disappeared.'

'Who's this man?' asked Marie.

'Some posh git called Farnham — Crispin Farnham, but I'm buggered if I can find anything else about him. I've seen his name three times now.'

'Orac will help you. She's actually waiting for us to give her some names, so ring her now. Better still, go and visit her in her den.'

Max's eyes lit up. 'I hoped you'd say that. Blimey, that woman is so fascinating!'

He almost skipped out of the room, much to Marie's amusement.

Her smile soon faded when she returned to her lists. Name upon name of innocent people torn apart by Alistair Ashcroft's terrible deeds.

CHAPTER THIRTY-ONE

The minute he walked into the flat, John was aware of the difference in Hazel. Even the air around her was charged, as if he were standing near a high voltage pylon hearing the insulators crackle and hiss.

He went to the kitchen, made her a drink and set it down by her computer. He waited for her to speak.

After a while she sat back and looked up at him. 'God, this is intense.'

'But you've nailed it,' he said.

'So long as no one changes their routine or does something unexpected. Though even if they do, I have a Plan B ready. You wait — we'll be seeing some fireworks at the end of the day.' She paused, regarding him. 'We are on our own now, John. We reached the tipping point last night. The end game has begun.'

He said nothing, while in his mind the cruise ship sailed towards him, no longer a faint silhouette on the horizon.

'Now, here's what you have to do,' said Hazel. 'You will leave here in twenty-five minutes, complete the assignment I'm about to give you and be back here by twelve at the very latest.'

'Absolutely.' He swallowed. 'End game,' she had said.

Hazel handed him a printout. 'The details are here. Task number one will require some acting on your part. It's up to you how you play it.'

John skimmed through the instructions. 'It all seems straightforward enough, so long as the Baker Street Irregulars have done their bit.'

'I can't foresee any problems, the boys and girls are being very diligent, especially at this stage of the game.'

The 'Baker Street Irregulars' were a small gang of indigent youths whom Hazel paid to operate as her eyes and ears on the streets. Hazel had named them after the gang of street urchins Sherlock Holmes employed to "Go everywhere, see everything, and overhear everyone." The money she gave them had turned out to be a most worthwhile investment.

John checked his watch. He already had everything he might need packed in his car, and he was ready to go. 'I will need to assess the situation, of course, and if I can, I'll use the path of least resistance. Unlike HG Wells, I rarely find it the path of the loser.'

Hazel smiled. 'You're right. Keep it simple is what I say.'

Simple? Nothing about Hazel was simple, neither her person nor her work. John looked at her. They could be approaching the end of their working relationship. He desperately wanted to talk to her, broach the subject of the cruise, ask her if she would join him. Ask her if she would sail away with him and never come back.

He turned to go. This was not the time. If he were to say anything, it would have to be after their work for Stephen was done. Meanwhile, he had work to do.

* * *

Sam and Julia entered the Aegis Unit and were greeted by Casey Naylor. Sam had been anticipating this visit with a great deal of trepidation, and at one point only Julia's determined expression had prevented him from turning tail. He reminded himself of the importance of the meeting they were about to hold. How they dealt with Theo Carmichael could be key to ending Ashcroft's criminal activities once and for all. Unless that man was finally denied all form of contact with others, he, Sam, his friends and countless others would spend the rest of their lives looking over their shoulders.

'Theo asked me to assure you that all the prisoners are locked in at present,' Casey said to Sam. 'There is absolutely no chance of you running into Ashcroft.'

She ushered them into Theo Carmichael's office, where they were served with coffee. Casey then closed the door. A silence descended. When it became uncomfortable, Julia said, 'Perhaps I should start by explaining the reason for our visit this morning.'

'Please . . . go ahead,' Theo said uneasily.

Seeing his disquiet, Sam couldn't help feeling sorry for him. The fate of his pioneering experimental unit hung in the balance.

'I should start by saying that on my last visit, Mr Ashcroft revealed a great deal of knowledge about me and my personal history, above and beyond what he might have picked up from official sources,' Julia said. 'He also alleged that he had inside information on the current state of affairs at Saltern-le-Fen police station, including the threats to the officers and their families. He said I could not stop him.'

Theo remained silent.

'Yesterday,' Julia continued, 'a man who openly admit-ted to working for "Stephen" attacked a scene of crime pho-tographer, held her hostage and gave her a message to pass on to Detective Inspector Jackman. It was another death threat, although he didn't specify who it was directed at. He also left a dossier, a life history of DI Jackman from his childhood to the present day. It ended with the words, "In Memoriam." I think this makes Alistair Ashcroft's intentions abundantly clear.'

To his surprise, Sam found himself speaking without a tremor in his voice. 'The photographs were all taken very recently. Along with the messages, they make it abundantly clear that Alistair Ashcroft has been conducting his campaign of revenge against the people responsible for his arrest and subsequent incarceration from within this unit. There can be no doubt about it.'

'None whatsoever,' added Julia.

Theo, who had been staring into his cup while they spoke, raised his eyes. 'Our lockdown procedure operates in three stages. We have already implemented stage one. Having heard your concerns, I will now proceed to stage three.'

Sam raised his eyebrows. 'Meaning?'

'All prisons operate a lockdown regime,' Theo said slowly. 'Ours is similar but because we are such a small unit and are based within a high-security prison, we have tailored it to suit our particular situation. Initially, the rooms will be stripped and searched, and the prisoners then confined to their rooms for twenty-three hours a day. They will be allowed out to shower and to exercise for fifty minutes within a specially designed caged area designed to allow fresh air to enter. Prior to leaving their rooms they will be searched and then shackled for the duration of their exercise period. These will be removed on returning to their rooms. There will be no association during that time. Ashcroft will be accompanied by a minimum of four guards whenever he leaves his room. I also have authority to temporarily move some of the other prisoners back into the main prison until the current situation is resolved.'

Theo said all this in a monotone, as if he were reciting the words from a rule book.

'And the staff, Theo?' asked Julia.

'All will be temporarily replaced with others, until we discover how Ashcroft has managed to circumvent the system.'

She nodded.

'You say that you are at stage one,' Sam added. 'What exactly does that involve?'

'We are cut off from the main prison and have no contact with the outside world,' Casey said. 'The prisoners are not allowed visitors or phone calls. They are confined to their rooms except to have their meals and for one hour of exercise with a small group of other inmates. The staff presence is doubled whenever the prisoners leave their cells. It is an emergency security procedure, designed to prevent people, information or objects leaving the unit.'

'In a small unit like ours, stage one is usually all that is required,' added Theo. 'All the men in units like this are eager to conform to the regulations. They do not want to lose their privileges, believe me! So, the situation is usually resolved pretty quickly.' Theo looked deflated. 'But after hearing what you have told me, I'll obtain authorisation to move to the highest stage of security.'

'And this procedure takes how long?' Julia asked.

Theo shrugged. 'It's all down to the governor. He will accept my recommendation, but there is a protocol to be followed. Before now we have never had to activate the highest stage.'

Sam felt a little disappointed to hear of this delay. At least Theo had agreed to act — which had been their biggest potential obstacle — and if he set it in motion immediately, it was a good result.

'This is a big decision for Theo to make,' Casey added, 'and I think it's a brave one. Everything he has done here has been for the good of future generations. It will take years of study to identify the trigger that sets a damaged young person onto the path of murder. All the good he has done now hangs in the balance.'

'We do understand, you know,' Julia said. 'Important work is being carried out here, and we want it to continue. It is simply not the place for an Ashcroft. He belongs in total isolation, it's the only way to prevent him doing further damage.' She smiled at Casey. 'You already know this, don't you, my dear? You've seen it in him, that unstoppable force.'

Casey hung her head and whispered, 'Yes.'

Suddenly there came a knock at the door.

A tall prison guard filled the doorway with his bulk. 'Excuse me, sir. One of the prisoners wants to see you. He said it's urgent.'

'Which one?' asked Theo.

'Ashcroft, sir, and he said you might like to bring Professor Page with you. He'd like to chat to him again.'

Sam felt his chest tighten. No one but the police team knew of this visit. How had Ashcroft found out he was here?

'Sod that!' Julia looked daggers at Theo. 'If you are going to talk to that monster, you can damned well take *me*. Sam goes nowhere near him! And you, Sam Page,' she turned to face him, 'can apply a bit of common sense. Ashcroft is not all-seeing. He's just bloody clever. He knows he's in lockdown and he's just noticed the extra activity that indicates visitors from outside. No more than that.'

Sam smiled sheepishly. 'Point taken.'

'Right.' She turned to Theo. 'If you must acquiesce to the demands of the star of your show, I guess we'd better be off.'

Theo, too, looked a little abashed. 'Is that what it looks like? That I'm at his beck and call?'

'If the cap fits,' said Julia, raising an eyebrow. 'But if I were you, I'd make him wait. He'll be thinking we are desperate to hear what he has to say, so let's not give him the satisfaction.'

'You're right,' said Theo. 'We'll let him stew for a while.'

* * *

'You are going to love this!' DI Jenny Deane almost fell into Jackman's office, her eyes bright with enthusiasm. 'We are *this* far away from knowing who was behind the snuff movies, *and* a lot of other unsavoury enterprises. Holland have had a man on the inside of a suspect group for a while now, and today, thanks to the two songbirds in our custody suite, they are raiding their headquarters.' She threw herself into a chair next to Marie and beamed at Jackman. 'Not only that, but our two men, Andrew Shaw and Rick Grace, have furnished us with enough information to really make the charges against them stick. Even the CPS won't be able to knock holes in what we've accrued in the last twelve hours.'

271

She exhaled. 'So, you'll soon have the satisfaction of knowing that your Adonis murder victims will receive justice.'

Jackman heaved a sigh of relief. Another worry defused for the time being. 'Thanks, Jenny, we really owe you one for that.'

She shrugged, 'It's no big deal, I've just being tying in everything you gave us with what we already knew about the Netherlands.' She grinned at him. 'The Dutch police are all over it now, and very grateful for your input.' She yawned. 'I've been up all night waiting for news, but I'm damned if I'm going home until I hear from them.' She stood up. 'I'll let you get on, but I'll be back as soon as I know more.'

After she had gone, Jackman gave Marie a satisfied nod. 'So, we're one step closer to nailing whoever is responsible for the deaths of Dougie and Frank.'

'Thank God for that.' She sighed. 'Anyway, in the meantime, it's back to these lists.' She picked up a sheet of A4 paper that had been sitting in her lap.

Jackman ran his eyes down his copy. It was a long list, and it gave him something of a shock to see his own name among the priorities. But it was a fact. He had more reason to hate Ashcroft than anyone else on that list. After all, Ashcroft had murdered his sister-in-law and caused physical and mentally harm to the people he loved most. Below his name was Marie's. Ashcroft had injured her badly.

'Looking at it logically, it must be one of the principal victims' loved ones,' mused Marie. 'But another part of me can't help but wonder if someone lower down the list has been harbouring thoughts of revenge that have festered over time.'

'Or maybe one of our own people was so affected by his actions that they're determined to finish him off. After all, Ashcroft dispatched his victims in nightmarish ways. Look what it did to our Rosie.'

'Whoever our mysterious crusader is,' said Marie, 'he or she is somewhere in this list, but which one is it? More to the point, what the devil are they planning?'

'And how can they achieve their aim when their objective is locked away in a high-security prison?' Jackman added.

Marie screwed up her face. 'Unless they are there too. What if someone has been planning this for so long they've managed to get themselves into that Aegis Unit?'

Well, it was a possibility. 'I think we need Orac,' Jackman said. 'Get that list downstairs, Marie. Tell her to start with the likeliest candidates, the bereaved relatives and loved ones, and work down. I'll request access to Aegis's staff list and she can check that too. If anyone appears on both, your supposition is correct.' At least it was something. It might not be the answer but it was a thread that needed following. Any action was better than none.

Jackman picked up the phone and called the prison governor.

* * *

John knew that his mark would be on her guard, she more than any of the other targets. Any mother with young children to protect was a potential time-bomb. She was also a former detective, and apparently, a very good one. Hazel had said he would need his acting skills and, as always, she was right.

He had two choices if he wanted to play his part convincingly. He could either deal with her solo, or with the aid of a helper. He preferred to work alone, but since this particular piece of acting was to be staged in a supermarket car park, he opted to use Mouse. Mouse was one of the Baker Street Irregulars, a clever kid who was good at fooling the law-abiding citizenry. He had arranged to meet her at the supermarket, and had no doubt that she would be there. Like the rest of the Baker Street gang, she needed the money.

John drove into the massive car park and found a spot that seemed perfect for his needs. He checked his watch, locked the car, took a handful of plastic bags from behind the driver's seat and made his way to the entrance.

Carefully watching the time, he made his purchases and took them to the self-service checkouts. As he loaded his bags, he spotted Mouse, her hands thrust deep into the pockets of a shabby parka, hanging around outside the exit.

He smiled to himself. Her timing was impeccable.

Pushing the trolley containing his shopping, he left the store and ambled towards his car, looking like any bored shopper.

His mark, too, stuck to a regular timetable when she dashed out to do her shopping. She relied on her sister to care for her twins, and this sister had to leave work to do so.

He wondered absently what car parks revealed about people. Some liked to park as close as possible to the shop, others liked to be far away from others. Some didn't care where they parked and others had a particular spot.

Luckily for John, his target was one of the latter, and always parked in the back row, beneath a row of shrubs and trees. The bays were a bit wider there, and in summer the trees gave the car some shelter from the sun. And there it was, just as he knew it would be: Rosie Cohen's car.

John had parked two spaces away. He pushed the trolley up to his old nondescript vehicle and lifted the boot lid.

He had seen her in the store and had followed her at a distance. He estimated that in around three or four minutes, she would come hurrying across the tarmac towards her new silver Volkswagen.

He glanced around and saw Mouse, already in position. Any minute now.

John rummaged around in his boot, making room for his shopping bags. She was a bit late, probably due to a slow checkout girl, or an item that wouldn't scan properly. Then she appeared, looking flustered.

He finished loading his shopping and closed the boot. He gave a slight nod to Mouse, who started to move towards Rosie Cohen. As Mouse approached, John returned his trolley and sauntered back, timing his return perfectly to coincide with the confrontation between Rosie and Mouse.

Like any gentleman would, he stopped, hesitated as if wondering if he should interfere, and called out, 'Hey, you! Leave the lady alone! Go and beg somewhere else.'

Mouse stood her ground. She only wanted a few bob to get a hot drink.

In no uncertain terms, Rosie told her to bugger off, clearly not in need of any knight in shining armour. However, she was at a disadvantage, hampered by her shopping bags and a half-packed boot.

Mouse tried again to cadge some money, at which John stepped forward and ushered her away, saying, 'Okay, kid, if you'll just leave the lady, I'll give you something for a drink.' He fished in his pocket and produced a five-pound note. 'Here, now do as the lady said and bugger off.'

As Mouse shambled away, John shook his head and sighed. 'That sort of thing shouldn't happen. Kids like that ought to have a better life than begging.' He looked at Rosie. 'Are you okay?'

'You do know that will go on drugs, don't you?'

He smiled sadly. 'Yeah, most likely. But better I give it to her than she grabs some old lady's handbag.'

He turned and started to walk away, then he heard the boot close and Rosie call out, 'But thank you, I appreciate what you did. Sorry it cost you a fiver.'

He stopped and turned back. 'You know, when I see a girl like that, I sometimes see my own kids and I give thanks they turned out okay. It can be a fine line, especially with teenagers.'

Rosie nodded. 'Sorry, I must seem pretty hard, but I've seen too much of what drugs can do to young people.'

John stepped forward. 'As a copper, I'm sure you have.' He took the knife from his pocket. 'One move, one word, one scream or shout, and your twins will be motherless.'

Confusion, fear, surprise and anger followed one another in rapid succession across Rosie Cohen's face. For a brief moment he thought she would ignore the knife and lunge at him. Then the reality of his words obviously sunk in as she

275

thought of what it would do to her children and her husband, Max, if she were to die.

'Good. I see we understand each other. Now, we are going to have a friendly chat. You are going to lean against the driver's door and you are going to smile. It's a friendly chat, remember?'

Rosie did as he said, her smile a rictus, though she still found the courage to hiss, 'Bastard! What do you want?'

'Before I tell you, consider this. Apart from endangering your own life, think about your sister. She too has a visitor, because I'm not the only soldier in Stephen's army. She will be listening to a very similar conversation but she will be told that unless she remains calm and does as she's told, *you* will never return home.' He gave her a broad smile, as if they were indeed chatting amicably. 'And that when he leaves the house, no one in it will remain alive. No one.'

The full horror of what he was suggesting had evidently hit her hard, and he gave her full marks for trying not to show it. Yes, they had been right. She must have been a very good police officer.

'I asked you what you wanted,' she repeated, this time a little shakily.

'You were supposed to die, but luckily for you, my orders were revised. So now, like your friend Ella Jarvis, you are to be a messenger.' He narrowed his eyes. 'Use that sharp brain of yours to remember this, and when I leave, you ring Jackman and repeat it to him, word for word. Stephen likes people to be accurate.' His cold gaze lingered on her. 'This is what you'll say to Jackman: "*Nothing you do will make the slightest difference. The machine is in motion, and no matter what happens to me, you cannot stop it. You will pay. And you won't be alone.*" Repeat it.'

She stared at him, then spoke in a monotone. He repeated the message, more slowly, and this time she got it right.

'Good. Now, when I've gone, you are going to get into your car and sit there for five minutes. Then you make the call.' He dropped the amiable smile. 'And before you do anything stupid, think on this. My colleague is still with your sister and I need to check in with him at particular times. If

276

my vehicle is apprehended by the police and those calls do not take place . . . well, let's just say he isn't a patient man and killing comes easy to him. Do I make myself clear?'

She swallowed and nodded, so he turned to walk away, hissing over his shoulder, 'Good. Then do it.'

He climbed into his car and drove away, chuckling to himself. There was no sinister, murderous, colleague at her home. Her sister was probably playing games with the children right now, but even if Rosie Cohen suspected he was lying, she would not take the risk.

He had three meetings today. One down, two to go.

CHAPTER THIRTY-TWO

Julia had been ready to tear Ashcroft's head from his shoulders when she saw the effect of his message on Sam. Having calmed down, she admitted to herself that she too was reluctant to meet him again.

As agreed they took their time in responding and continued their discussion while they waited.

'If you obtain absolute proof that Ashcroft has used his time here to pursue his own agenda, will you see him removed from the unit immediately, Theo?' Sam asked.

'Initially he'll be assessed here, while we're in stage three lockdown,' said Theo, rather miserably. 'Then I will personally see to it that the governor has him shipped out to another high-security prison and into isolation. He will have betrayed our trust and made a mockery of all our years of work. I will never want to set eyes on him again, that's for sure.'

Poor man, thought Julia. 'This unit has done some amazing work, Theo. And I'm sure that if he was in touch with his people on the outside, it's nothing new. I'm willing to bet he's been doing so ever since he was first sent down. And all your observations are still valid. Ashcroft is what he is, Theo, and you'll take everything you've learned from him, and use that knowledge to study others.'

Casey Naylor gave a reassuring smile. 'She's right, Theo. You haven't wasted your time, nothing is lost. I'm sure that when we study his actions, we can learn a lot from them.'

Though obviously still doubtful, Theo looked a little brighter. 'I'm still trying to get my head around it all, but let's hope that you are right. Meanwhile, it's been well over half an hour, shall we go and see what he has to say?'

Julia was just about to agree when Sam held up his hand.

'I'd like to go with you.' He looked directly at her. 'It was a shock at first, but I think I need to see him one more time, even if it's just to prove to myself that he can't always be the winner. I need to see him for what he really is, just a man, not some evil genius.'

Julia exhaled. 'I really wouldn't advise it, but—'

'It's all right, Julia, honestly. I need to move on, and to do that, I must get my feelings about him into perspective.'

Returning his look, Julia saw all the damage Ashcroft had done to this dear, dear man. Sam had become a shell of his former self. Ashcroft had injured him, almost fatally, and then he had lost his prize student and friend, Laura, who had been like a daughter to him. Yes, he needed to move on and take his power back. He needed a life free of the spectre of Ashcroft.

Julia stood up, painting a confident expression onto her features, 'Okay. Let's get this over with, shall we?'

* * *

Sam walked alongside Julia, a few steps behind Theo and Casey. The sound of their footsteps was accompanied by the rattle of locks and the clang of doors closing behind them. It was a far cry from the austerity of a main prison block, but there was still a feeling of claustrophobia about the place. Julia remarked that the atmosphere in the unit was quite different to the one that prevailed during her last visit.

'Lockdown does that,' said Casey. 'It's a reminder that this is still a prison, despite the apparent freedom.'

With every step they took, Sam became more tense. He was certain he had done the right thing in coming, even though the thought of seeing Ashcroft again terrified him.

They passed through the lounge, where three men sat and talked together quietly. They fell silent when the group drew near.

'They're permitted a limited period for association,' explained Theo. 'In a few minutes they will be returning to their rooms.'

He led them along a wide corridor with doors on either side. Ashcroft's room was the last on the right. Sam took a deep breath.

They had agreed that Theo should go in first, while the others waited in the doorway. The room was bigger than an average prison cell, but it was still too small to hold all of them comfortably.

Theo knocked on the door, somewhat to Sam's amusement. Fancy the unit director politely requesting a prisoner for leave to enter!

'You wanted to see me, Stephen? Professor Page too, I understand. Well, here we are.'

The man inside remained lying on his bed, silent.

'Come on, Stephen! We don't have time for games.' Theo strode across to the bed and called his name again, louder.

Sam felt Julia stiffen beside him.

Theo bent over the recumbent form, shook it and started back in horror.

Julia was the first to react. She pushed past Theo and pulled back the covers, recoiling for a moment at the sight. She laid a finger on the side of his neck, feeling for a pulse. 'He's dead,' she whispered.

Sam moved to stand beside her and looked down.

The man in the bed had been strangled, with such vehemence that the ligature was embedded into the flesh, leaving a deep groove. His tongue protruded grotesquely and the eyes bulged.

Theo suddenly found his voice. 'Everyone out! This is a crime scene.'

Casey ran back down the corridor, calling for a warder. Two came running.

'Lock everyone in their rooms immediately!' she barked. 'Outer doors locked. No one in or out, and make sure this room stays locked. No one, I repeat no one must have access.' She spun back to face Theo. 'Instigate total emergency lockdown. Call security, the police and the prison governor. We need help here, fast.'

'Indeed, we do,' said Julia calmly. 'Because whoever killed Alistair Ashcroft, is locked in here with us, and I, for one, am curious to know who it is.'

* * *

Jackman listened to Rosie recite the message.

She was crying but not in fear; her tears were the product of rage and utter frustration. 'The bastard lied to me, sir. There was no one at the house. Just before the five minutes were up, my phone rang and it was my sister asking me to pick up some dog biscuits! Oh, sir, I thought they had the children! I didn't dare tackle him because of my babies. I'm so sorry.'

'Rosie!' he replied, firmly. 'Of course you couldn't take that risk, no one could. I'd have done exactly the same.'

She described what had happened, the girl begging for money, who had obviously been put there to provide the man with an excuse to speak to Rosie. 'His licence plates were smeared with mud, sir, no chance of getting his number. All I know is that the car was one of those older five door models, a Citroen Berlingo or a Peugeot Partner, a dirty grey colour. There must be CCTV at the supermarket so he should be on film. We were both parked in the back row on the left-hand side as you look away from the shop. He left at eleven seventeen hours.'

With a wry smile he noted that she was still thinking like a police officer.

'Sir, you must stop him,' she said urgently. 'He told me he had three what he called meetings today. I was the first. He said I was supposed to die but his instructions had been changed and I was to be like Ella, a messenger. But the others, sir! He intends to kill them, I know it. He had a wicked blade on him. You need to contact everyone who received those texts, sir, especially your family.'

Despite his mounting anxiety, Jackman kept his voice calm. 'Don't worry, Rosie, we'll contact them all. Just tell me, what did he look like?'

'Oh, just like some ordinary, rather sad bloke doing his shopping alone. Drab clothes, old brown jacket, medium brown hair going grey at the temples.'

The man who had spoken to his mother and attacked Ella. 'We have a photo, Rosie. I'll WhatsApp it to you and you can tell me if it's him. Now, are you up to getting yourself home, or shall I send a car out for you?'

She assured him she was okay and all she wanted was get straight back home.

'If you're sure then, I'll get someone to meet you there. Go back to your sister and the children but drive carefully. You've had one hell of a shock.'

Call ended, he hurried out into the CID room. 'Max!' he called. 'Get home, your wife needs you. Rosie's okay, but she's had a run in with the "ordinary man". Debrief her, take her statement, stay with her. Ring me when you're sure everything is all right there. Got it?'

Max was already on his feet and heading for the door. 'On my way.' For once, he failed to leave them with one of his famous Cockney quips.

'Marie! Gary! Robbie!' Jackman barked out. 'Ring all the people who received the original texts. Tell them to change their routines for today and make sure someone's with them at all times. They must be vigilant. Don't scare the shit out of them, but we have been warned that our "ordinary man" intends to kill two people, and we don't know who they are.'

Marie and Gary turned pale, and Robbie swallowed. It seemed to Jackman that Ashcroft really had set his infernal mechanism in motion, and like a snowball rolling down a hill, it was gathering momentum. Somehow, he had to stop it. He looked around and his gaze lit on Charlie and Kevin. 'Get over to the big Tesco on the outskirts of the town. You need to check their CCTV for a vehicle leaving the car park at eleven seventeen this morning.' He gave him the description of the car. 'And any footage you can see of Rosie Cohen talking with a man, and possibly a street kid, a girl. Check the camera over the main door as well. You might find him either entering or leaving the store. Maybe you'll get a better picture than the one we have.'

'On our way, boss,' Charlie said. 'We'll ring in with anything we find.'

Now all that remained was for Jackman to go and warn Ruth to keep her niece safe. Oh, and ring his mother. This nightmare just went on and on.

* * *

John had just parked the old vehicle in the double garage and moved everything in it to his other car, a small, equally unimpressive SUV, when his batphone rang. Hazel's was the only number on it, and it was used only for urgent messages about their missions, or for emergencies.

Hazel's tone was clipped and business-like. 'John. A status report immediately, please.'

'Instructions carried out to the letter, Hazel. No problems at all. Why? What's the matter?'

'You are certain there were no complications of any kind?' she demanded.

'None whatsoever, it went off flawlessly.' His tone now matched hers. 'If there is a glitch, it isn't my fault, Hazel, neither is it Mouse's. She was a class act.'

She grunted. 'Well, there's been a setback somewhere. We've been told to stand down until further notice. Your next target has suddenly altered her routine, as has the third victim. It might be coincidence but we need to rethink our plan. Christos has sent a warning to hold fire until he knows more. This is not good, John.'

'I'll get back to base straightaway,' he said. 'I'll be fifteen minutes.'

'No. Go directly to the safe house. We might have to quit this place. I have no idea what has happened, but it's going to go one of two ways. You might have to act very quickly, with new instructions, or we might . . . We might have to abandon the project.'

John was thunderstruck. 'But it's been going so smoothly! I don't understand.'

'Neither do I,' she retorted. 'But if this fails . . .' She left the sentence hanging.

John was well aware of how important this plan was to her, and how she idolised Stephen. He pitied her, but he wished she wouldn't unload all her frustration on him when, as far as he knew, he was blameless. 'It won't fail. Whatever has happened, it's not a failure on our part. Christos will isolate the problem, I'm sure, and we can forge ahead again. I'm ready for your next instructions, Hazel, and I won't let you down.'

'Just go to the safe house and await my call.'

'I will, and you can trust me, Hazel. I'll do whatever it takes to get this back on track.'

Apparently pacified, she said, 'Thank you, John. You know how important this is.'

He ended the call and hurriedly finished transferring his things from one car to the other. That done, he drove across town, wondering what could possibly have happened to make Christos suspend a mission that was going so well. Whatever it was, it had to be very serious. He frowned. Would he still receive his next pay cheque?

* * *

'I once happened to be inside a maximum-security psychiatric hospital when it went into lockdown over a suspicious death,' said Julia, sipping a mug of tea Casey had handed her. 'It was bedlam — literally. Everyone kicked off. They rioted. They were beyond control. I was terrified.' She shook her head at the memory. 'Thank heavens this is nothing like that.'

It was true. As soon as the lockdown had been put into effect, the unit fell silent. The atmosphere became hushed, as if everyone there was waiting. Which, of course, they were.

Annoyingly, this meant that they couldn't immediately inform Jackman of what had happened. The restrictions included not spreading the word beyond the prison walls, even to a senior law enforcement officer.

Finally, when everything was in place, Casey said they might contact the detective inspector.

Julia raised an eyebrow at Sam. 'I think this one is down to you.'

Sam drew in a breath. He hardly knew what to say to his friend. The shock of what they had seen in that room had not yet worn off, the sight of that horrible, distorted face remained burned into his retina.

'I can do it if you'd rather,' Julia said gently.

'No, I think it should come from me, but could we just talk for a moment before I call him?' He knew it sounded strange. Most people would be itching to get on the phone. After all, it was probably the best news that Jackman would ever hear but, somehow, he felt terribly confused by his own feelings.

'Of course,' said Julia. 'Drink your tea and tell me what's worrying you, then you can call.' She looked around the room. 'In any case, it looks like we'll be here for quite some time.'

Sam had a good idea that Julia knew exactly what was worrying him, but he was grateful for a few minutes' reprieve. 'The thing is,' he said, staring into his tea, 'why, when I should be experiencing massive relief that he's dead, do I feel sorry for him? I never did before.'

'Go on,' Julia said softly.

'It's just . . . seeing him there like that, instead of seeing a monster, I saw a little boy, abused and lonely, desperate for love. A child who was given one chance at freedom by his sister, who promised to take him away from his evil father and instead was murdered.' He shook his head. 'I should have been dancing with joy that this killer had been brutally murdered, just like he'd killed so many others. All I could feel was sadness, for the man on the bed had become what he was through the actions of another.'

Julia looked at him thoughtfully for a while, then she gave him a little smile. 'That's because you are a good man, Sam Page, and you know what can make a person take the dark road to either insanity or murder. You still have compassion in your heart, no matter what has happened to you and your friends. Of course you feel sad that circumstance took an unfortunate child and moulded him into a killer.' She touched his arm. 'You'll feel differently as time goes by. One day, you'll experience that relief, and you'll finally walk out from under his shadow.' She smiled again. 'And don't be surprised if your friends in the police feel differently about it. I can hear their comments already, for it's the answer to all their prayers.'

'Then I'd better ring Jackman, hadn't I? And stop being a prat.'

'That's a very good idea.'

CHAPTER THIRTY-THREE

Jackman spent the rest of the afternoon fielding calls and messages.

Later, Marie came in bringing some much-needed coffee. 'Everyone who received one of those texts has been notified, boss, and so far everyone is accounted for. Whatever the ordinary man was planning has yet to materialise.'

'Talking of him,' said Jackman, 'I just had a call from Max. Rosie has had a look at the photo taken at my mother's stable and has confirmed that it's the same man. Max also says that now she's over the initial shock of what happened, she thinks she recognises him from somewhere.'

'Really? Now that's interesting,' said Marie. 'I thought I did too when I saw that picture.'

'Apparently it's driving her mad, she's absolutely certain she has seen him somewhere.'

'We've all been there, haven't we?' Marie said, stirring her coffee. 'It's so annoying.'

'Apart from that, Charlie and Kevin have sent some stills from the CCTV at Tesco, and they have him, and his car. Unfortunately, the vehicle disappeared into one of those new housing estates close to the supermarket, they're like rabbit warrens, and it's not been picked up since.'

'Par for the course,' grumbled Marie, when, suddenly, Orac burst into the office.

Jackman was mildly — no, he was very shocked. He had no idea that Orac even knew her way out of her underground kingdom.

'You have to see this!' She thrust her phone under his nose.

He read the text aloud, so that Marie could hear. 'Tell Jackman to open the document in his inbox immediately, and act without delay. This is vital.'

'Do it,' said Orac. 'I've scanned it, and there's no virus. Go on.'

Jackman found his inbox, and in the list of new messages he saw one headed *This is vital*.

Marie went around the desk to look over his shoulder and the three of them read:

> *Jackman. I am going to give you two names. If you stop these two, you will end Ashcroft's game forever. But right now, just one of them is the real danger. You have to arrest him immediately, or people will die — your people, Jackman. The other is his controller. That one is dangerous in a different way and can wait, the one I'm about to give you is your main target. He is at 112 Stapleford Lane, Saltern. The owners are ostensibly a retired couple called Sweeting who spend a lot of their time globe-trotting. Its real function is to provide a safe house from which Ashcroft's organisation can operate. Right now, your man is alone there — but be careful: he carries a knife. Arrest him and you'll have the cold-blooded killer you have been looking for, but you must act fast, he's already getting nervous. His code name is John.*
>
> *Apprehend him now, and when he's locked up in your custody suite, read the attached file.*
>
> *Trust me and, please, act now.*

Jackman held his breath and then let it go slowly. Was this a trap?

'This message comes from your anonymous crusader, Jackman,' said Orac softly. 'I should know, I've spent most of my life as an undercover agent and I can tell that he's speaking the truth. This is no hoax. John is your ordinary man.'

Jackman jumped up. What did he have to lose? 'Marie, round up Robbie and Gary, grab stabbies for us all and get the duty sergeant to give us two crews. Explain the situation and the kind of man we could be dealing with, and that we want a silent approach. Now!'

As Marie ran from the room, he turned to Orac. 'Have you looked at the attachment?'

'Not the content, but it's safe to open,' she assured him.

'Will you read it now, while we're out, and tell me what it says if you think it's important? I don't want any nasty surprises when we get to this safe house.'

'Of course. Can I use your office?'

'Be my guest.'

'And, Jackman.' With a metallic gleam, her disconcerting eyes rested a moment on him. 'Be careful.'

He stopped mid-stride and smiled at her, touched by this enigmatic woman's sudden concern. 'We will.'

* * *

While Jackman and Marie swung into action, Orac sat down at Jackman's desk and opened the attachment.

'My oh my! Will you look at that!' she breathed. 'Someone has been busy.'

She stared at the document on the screen, the official personnel file for 'John'. Then she saw his real name.

'And I thought you were dead!' she whispered. 'We *all* did.'

She leafed through the document, and every page overturned one of their assumptions. It detailed his career in the police force, to which was appended an analysis of his mental state at the time of his departure, in an attempt to discover what had happened to make him throw away a promising career and — as they erroneously concluded — his life.

She moved on to the next section and let out a low whistle. 'Shit! What *is* this?'

The following paragraphs consisted of a document, much like an official secret file, detailing, in chronological order, every one of John's activities over the past five years. Reading through it, she came across the word *terminated*, phrases like, *assessment shows mop-up successful.*

It was clear to Orac that John had become a paid trouble-shooter, the man sent in to clean up. He was also an assassin. Jackman had said he didn't want any nasty surprises and this was very nasty indeed. There was nothing worse than a cop gone bad, and from reading this, they didn't come any worse than John. Over the years he had turned into the antithesis of the highly decorated detective sergeant he had formerly been. And now Jackman was going after him.

Orac swallowed and picked up her mobile phone.

Jackman told her they were five minutes away from their target. Their plan was to rendezvous in a layby some 500 metres from the house and proceed on foot, in a pincer movement, closing in on the front and the back doors simultaneously. Luckily, the nearest neighbours were some way off, separated from them by two small fields.

He sounded confident enough, but Orac had not yet told him who their target was. Rather than give Jackman his real name, she said only that he was ex-police, and therefore would know what to look out for, so Jackman should be extra wary.

'Does the document mention firearms, or just that he uses a knife?' Jackman asked.

'I haven't seen any mention of a gun but I haven't read it thoroughly, it's massive.'

She scrolled down to his more recent missions, and a name stopped her in her tracks.

Assignment . . . Dungeness, Kent. Assess successful termination of Douglas Marshall and ensure no witnesses or possible hot-spots remain . . . There followed a long summary, so she jumped to the next entry:

290

Assignment . . . Old Oaks Rectory. To pinpoint possible troublemakers and notify relevant operatives on site for them to deal with it appropriately. Conclusion. John stated that a situation arose that required immediate attention. No time to contact other operatives. He made the decision to act at once. Mark terminated . . . target's name: Frank Rosen.

'Orac, are you still there?' Jackman was asking.

'Sorry, yes. I'm just trying to get my head around what the document says next. Apparently, you are dealing with ex-Detective Sergeant Russell Copeland, code name John.'

There followed a short silence. 'But I thought he was dead!'

'So did practically everyone else,' Orac said. His car was found abandoned on a clifftop in Cornwall, as I recall, Russell missing without trace.'

'*He's* Ashcroft's hitman? But he was a hero! A bit of a tearaway, sure, but . . . Orac, are you certain?'

'Without a doubt. But there's worse to come, Jackman. As I said, I haven't gone through all the details but there are two familiar names on his hit list: Douglas Marshall, and Frank Rosen.'

Another silence. Orac could hear him breathing. 'I'm so sorry, Jackman, but you needed to know before you went in there.'

Briefly, almost absently, he thanked her and ended the call.

Orac returned to the document. Whoever was watching over them knew what they were doing. She re-read the original message and wondered who John's accomplice was. According to the message, they were John's handler. A major player then, someone operating from the wings, relaying messages, organising dates and times, and who probably liaised with whoever ran the organisation, maybe even with Ashcroft himself.

She stood up and paced the office, feeling like a caged animal. Sometimes she longed to be back in the field as in the old days.

She sat back down and spun the captain's chair around, trying to make sense of what this document had told them. It was clear that Ashcroft's organisation had been involved in the crimes that had taken place at the film set. Otherwise why kill Frank Rosen? Perhaps crimes such as the snuff films financed Ashcroft's campaign of revenge against Jackman and his team. She wondered how much he paid John.

Snuff movies. They were a rare commodity, one for which perverts would pay extortionate amounts of money.

But who was their champion? Who would make it their life's work to watch every move that Ashcroft and his underlings made? And why?

* * *

Jackman and Marie arrived at the rendezvous both still puzzling over Orac's strange revelation. Was John really the ex-copper, Russell Copeland, turned assassin, murderer of Frank and Dougie?

As he undid his seat belt, Jackman's phone vibrated in his pocket. He glanced at the screen. He didn't have time for anything else right now, they had a killer to apprehend. But it was Sam, and he and Julia were at the Aegis Unit. Something told him to answer it.

He spoke quickly. 'Sam, must be quick, we're just about to go after Ashcroft's hitman. I really can't talk now.'

'Jackman, this is important. Aegis is in total lockdown and all calls have been restricted until now. Something has happened and I wanted you to be the first to know.'

'What, Sam? What should I know?

'It's Ashcroft, Jackman. He's dead. Murdered.'

Beside him in the passenger seat, Marie gasped and put her hand to her mouth.

Stunned, Jackman was unable to speak. Dead? It was almost too much to take in.

'Look, I'm sorry, Jackman. Not the best time to land this on you. Ring me when you're done with the raid and I'll give you the details, such as they are. As I said, the Aegis Unit is in lockdown, us with it. We could be here for some time.'

Jackman mumbled a thanks and ended the call. He saw that his hand was shaking. He looked to Marie.

'I know, boss,' she said, reading his expression. 'But we have a job to do, and it can't wait. We'll take this John guy down, *then* we'll decide how many bottles of champagne to order, okay?'

He smiled. 'Exactly. Let's get this over with. And don't tell the others until we've collared our man.'

They hurried over to where the two uniformed crews, along with Robbie and Gary, were waiting for them.

'Listen up, everyone,' Jackman began. 'Change of plan. Having seen the location, I realise there's not enough cover to approach on foot without being seen. Instead, we use the vehicles, then decamp and go in hard and fast. Four take the front, the other four take the back.' He looked at the four uniforms. 'You've got enforcers?'

They nodded. A burly constable called Baz nodded to the heavy battering ram that lay on the ground beside him. 'The big red key, sir, and I'm all set to go.'

'Good. So, no messing, okay? Take those doors down and get in there. And remember, he has a knife and he's not afraid to use it. We have the advantage of surprise and we outnumber him eight to one, but don't underestimate him. He knows the layout of that house and we don't, and most of all, he's dangerous. Don't give him an inch.'

All nodded.

'Okay. Everyone in stab-proof vests?' More nods. 'And one of you has a Taser?'

'Yes, sir, an X26,' said a PC, known to everyone as 'Flash.' 'I'm Taser trained.'

'You'll have to react fast if he produces a knife, constable.' Jackman looked at his watch. 'Time to go. So, Flash, you and your crewmate come with Marie and me and we'll take the front door. Robbie, Gary, Baz and Joel, you're in through the back. Good luck, everyone. Let's make this textbook, shall we?'

A few moments later, their four cars screamed to a halt outside the safe house. The doors flew open and they ran to their designated points of entry and both doors, front and back, caved in almost simultaneously.

Then they were inside, boots thundering through the house, up the stairs, officers shouting to each other from the various rooms. It was only minutes before the call went up: 'In here!'

Jackman charged into the room and saw a man lying face down on the floor, his arms behind his back. To his right, Robbie was already fastening the cuffs, and to the left, with a satisfied smile on his face, the constable called Baz.

'This gentleman was attempting to exit through the window, boss,' said Robbie. 'Baz dissuaded him. And I removed that from his person.' A vicious-looking blade lay just out of reach. He grinned broadly. 'Textbook enough for you, sir?'

Robbie and Baz hauled their prisoner to his feet and Jackman stood facing the former ace detective.

'Russell Copeland, I'm arresting you for the murder of Frank Rosen. You do not have to say anything but it may harm your defence . . .' Such an ordinary man, he thought. An ordinary man and an assassin.

Russell Copeland looked utterly shocked. 'How did you know I'd be here? How did you *know* about this place?'

'Someone doesn't like you, mate, or the company you keep,' said Robbie. 'And I can't say I disagree with him. You were stitched up, good and proper.'

'Right. Into the car with him,' Jackman said, keen to get the man into custody. 'But, then, you're used to police cars, aren't you, Copeland? Though you won't be in the driving seat this time.'

Russell Copeland glared at Jackman. 'I wouldn't get too cocky if I was you, Jackman. You may have got me but you won't stop this. Stephen has seen to that. Your days are numbered, *sir*! Yours and your people. Like your two charming little nephews.'

Enraged, Jackman went to step forward but Marie quickly spoke up, defusing the tension.

'*This* is our hitman, boss? Our dangerous killer?' She let out a mocking laugh, then turned to Baz. 'Get this piece of shit into the back of that police car. And remember to disinfect it afterwards.'

'Thanks,' breathed Jackman, as Russell Copeland was dragged from the room.

Marie shrugged. 'Sorry I had to step in then. All I really wanted to do was tell him his sainted Stephen was brown bread.'

Jackman grimaced. 'Me too. And thinking about that, we must leave uniform to seal this place up. We need to get back fast. Don't forget, our informer said that to finally put an end to Ashcroft's campaign, we needed to apprehend another person, someone whose name he would give us after we'd dealt with John.'

'And we have to know what happened at the Aegis Unit,' added Marie. 'You must talk to Sam and Julia. I'm still struggling to believe Sam's news. Who the hell could have killed Ashcroft?'

Jackman, who was wondering the same thing, said, 'That can wait. He's dead, that's good enough for now. Let's get out of here, Marie. Things are going our way for once. Let's get this last name, then we can shut down Ashcroft's organisation for good.'

CHAPTER THIRTY-FOUR

The full impact of what had happened only hit John when he found himself locked in a tiny cell somewhere in the depths of the police station. Partly, he was angry at himself — he should have seen the raid coming. It was a safe house, for fuck's sake, and he had sat there, a sitting duck, believing that at any moment he'd get a call from Hazel telling him to resume his work. This couldn't be happening, not to them.

John got up, paced the small area, kicked out at the raised cell bench, which only served to hurt his foot. While the officers arresting him were bundling him into the police car, they had mentioned going after his controller next. There was nothing he could do to warn Hazel. If they succeeded, it would destroy her. Her one mission in life was to see Stephen's plan through to the end and now she had been thwarted.

John sank down onto the hard prison cot and groaned. In his mind, he saw a ship growing smaller and smaller until it finally disappeared over the horizon.

* * *

Ruth Crooke and Jackman were poring over the dossier that had been sent to him.

'I just can't get my head around it,' Ruth muttered. 'Russell Copeland was a dedicated detective with a glittering career ahead of him, the man had received commendations. Then something happened — who knows what — and he left and went to work for a private agency. Years later, another calamity. It was hushed up at the time, and I never got to know the real story. Then, when his car was found abandoned on a cliff edge, most, including me, assumed he'd taken his own life, although some thought he staged it in order to start a new life somewhere else.'

'Just goes to prove that it never pays to assume anything,' said Jackman. 'He came back with a vengeance — on the opposing side.'

'When you've got time, Rowan, read the section that explains what occurred, and why Russell went off the rails.' Ruth drew in a long breath. 'But right now, he's where he belongs, and your job is to try and find out just who has put this incredible document together, while you wait for him to send you the name of John's controller.'

'Marie and Orac are going through the names of all the people whose lives were damaged by Ashcroft's actions,' said Jackman. 'As soon as we get the word, we'll hit the controller. Hopefully, it'll go as smoothly as it did with John.'

'Yes, that was good work, Rowan.' She frowned and massaged her temple. 'I've got the headache from hell. By the way, have you heard anything from the Aegis Unit?'

Jackman shook his head. 'As far as I know, both Julia and Sam are being interviewed by the police and prison service investigation team. Sam did tell me, though, that they seem very interested in a couple of people who left the unit in the half hour between Ashcroft asking to see Theo Carmichael and when they went in and found him dead. Sam is doing his best to find out who they are. It's a good thing that Sam and Julia are being detained there so long. I get the feeling that without them picking up whatever information they can get, we might never know what went on.'

'All the media attention it'll get will do the prison no favours, that's for sure,' said Ruth.

At that moment, Marie hurried in. 'Boss, Orac just had another text. It says you should check your inbox in ten minutes' time.' She looked at him, her eyes sparkling. 'And we've eliminated a whole lot of names from our list. It's now down to two. Orac is trying to locate their present whereabouts right now. We're close, boss, very close.'

'Who are they?' asked Jackman.

'One is a close relative of one of Ashcroft's earliest victims, and the other is someone who may have been romantically attached to him somewhere along the line. We're not quite there yet, so if you don't mind, I'll get back downstairs. The minute we have something worth chasing, I'll be back.'

'Off you go. I'll head for my office and wait for the email.'

The ten minutes were endless. Ruth looked gaunt with worry, and Jackman reckoned he probably didn't look much better.

Finally, the message arrived.

Well, Jackman, it's been a long haul, but worth it. Everything I set out to do has been achieved. You only have to clean up after me now. If you follow the leads I am about to give you, you will bring some truly evil people to justice. A courier will be bringing you a small package. It is safe to open. The contents will serve to guide you, and if you follow it, you will make a number of very satisfying arrests. Thank you for never giving up. I was only moved to help you when I realised you would need a lot more resources than you had at your disposal if you were to bring this nightmare to a close. In the end, my way was the only way. Now we'll all sleep at night, and Ashcroft's victims will finally rest in peace.

Christos

Note: You might want to call at 12b, Ruskin Street, Saltern. It's a flat above a shop and the nerve centre for Ashcroft's organisation. John's controller operates from there. Her name is Hazel Palgrave.

Jackman scribbled down the address and, with a quick glance at Ruth, hurried outside, calling for Robbie and Charlie.

He handed the piece of paper with the name and address to Robbie. 'Repeat performance, please. A woman called Hazel Palgrave, and don't underestimate her just because she's a woman. Most of all, if you find any computer equipment there, seize it. I'll ring down and get some uniforms organised. It's local, so it shouldn't take long to get there.'

'You're not coming with us this time, boss?' asked Robbie, pulling on his stab-proof vest.

'No, I have other things to chase up. I think you and Charlie, along with a handful of uniforms, can handle this one. Ring me when you've sewn it up.'

'You got it, sir,' called Robbie and Charlie, already halfway through the door.

'Gary, do a search. Everything you can find on Hazel Palgrave.'

'I'm on it, sir,' said Gary, and swung his chair round to face his screen.

From his office, Jackman rang downstairs to organise back-up for Robbie and Charlie, and asked the desk sergeant to let him know when a package arrived for him by courier.

Ruth, who had been reading the message again, looked at him thoughtfully. 'A book to guide us, eh? This message says a lot, doesn't it?'

'Whoever this is they've been planning to bring Ashcroft down for a very long time.' Jackman scratched his head. 'Almost as long as Ashcroft himself has been in action.'

'Which points to the loved one of an early victim . . . just where Orac and Marie are heading. Does the name he gave — Christos — mean anything to you?'

'Nothing at all,' Jackman said.

Ruth walked towards the door. 'While we wait for the delivery of your "guidebook," we might pay a visit to the IT department. Maybe a Christos has popped up in their searches.'

Calling to Tim to ring him the minute a delivery arrived, Jackman followed Ruth out of the office.

* * *

Julia regarded Theo Carmichael speculatively. 'It doesn't make sense. Ashcroft wasn't free to move about during lockdown, was he?'

Theo paced the office. 'He . . . well, he shouldn't have been. Now I'm beginning to wonder.'

'Yes?' Julia prompted.

Theo looked pained. 'Look, this is just supposition, but when I spoke to the security guards, they said Ashcroft wanted to remain in his room during the association period. Apparently his legs were hurting and he'd rather lie down. They left his door unlocked in case he changed his mind. So his killer could have gone into his room then. When the guards locked the door again they would have seen him in bed, apparently asleep.'

'That can't be right,' said Sam. 'He asked to see us, didn't he, just at that time.'

'Uh, not exactly, Professor.' Theo looked miserable. 'Even that's not clear. It appears that one of the other prisoners passed on the message, and he had been given it by someone else. Ashcroft never spoke directly with the guard.'

Julia mulled this over. 'Might I ask if anyone left the unit during the time between Ashcroft deciding to stay in bed and us finding his body?'

'Three people passed through security. One prison officer, a nurse, and the chaplain, Patrick Galway. The police tell me they have all been contacted and are on their way back here now.'

'And the nurse and the prison officer are people who you vetted personally?' Sam asked.

'Absolutely. The nurse has been with us from day one, in fact she came to us specifically to look after Ashcroft. The injuries to his legs were so severe that they gave rise to other problems, and he needed regular medical treatment. The prison officer has also been with us right through. He's totally reliable and, like everyone, is subjected to continual assessment.'

'And the chaplain?' asked Julia.

'What? Patrick? He's one of the most fair-minded and dedicated men I've had the privilege to work with. No, Patrick is a man of God, an ordained priest. As such, he is naturally above suspicion.'

Julia said nothing. Some people, she thought to herself, would consider Ashcroft's death an example of divine retribution. In her book, no one was above suspicion.

'This murder must have been committed by one of the other prisoners,' insisted Theo. 'After all, they are all convicted killers. I just don't know which one, or how he managed it.'

'You are probably right,' said Julia, 'but just as a matter of interest, is it normal for a chaplain to spend so much time with the inmates? I was under the impression that they are usually only called upon in times of crisis, a natural death or something.'

Theo shrugged. 'I guess he does spend more time here than in other parts of the prison, but that's because he is an excellent counsellor. He has a remarkable ability to draw out the prisoners' innermost thoughts and feelings. Dr Naylor and I both saw this quality in him, and so we involve him in our discussions. He has become an invaluable member of the Aegis team.'

Julia simply nodded. Meanwhile, she was running through the list of Aegis staff, which she now knew by heart. There was only one regular nurse: Monica Rush, SRN. So, along with Patrick Galway, all she needed was the name of the guard who had delivered the message. Then, the moment she was able to, she would pass them on to Jackman. 'And who was the prison officer, Theo? And was he going off shift when he left?'

Theo looked rattled. 'Yes, James had worked well over his normal hours. He was going home.'

301

'James?'

'James Roper. Completely trustworthy, and — well, you've seen all their records, haven't you? They didn't just walk in here! I defy anyone to have been more thorough than we were in vetting them.'

'I'm not trying to upset you, Theo,' she said. 'I'm playing devil's advocate here. And anyway, it's no more than the police will ask, if they haven't already.'

'That's just it,' Theo said, and sighed. 'They have. I hated being questioned about these good people. We've worked so closely together, I felt I was being disloyal.'

Julia decided to cut him some slack. She had what she needed. 'I'm sorry. It must be hard for you.'

Theo, too, apologised. 'It's an awful situation, and I'm over-wrought, but that's no excuse for being rude, especially to you.' He smiled ruefully. 'It was such a shock, pulling back that cover and seeing his face . . .'

'It was a shock to us all, Theo,' said Sam quietly. 'Even us, who are trained to confront the unexpected.'

They all fell silent. Julia thought about the police officers who had discovered some of Ashcroft's victims. All of whom were still affected by it.

'Have you any idea how long we'll be kept here?' asked Sam.

'I'll see if I can find out for you,' said Theo, standing up and going to the door. 'You've both spoken to the investigating officers, so hopefully not too much longer. I'll have a word with the officer in charge.' With a weak smile, he added, 'I'll try and arrange your release from custody.'

As soon as he was out of the room, Julia rang Jackman. 'Three names, Jackman: Monica Rush, who was Ashcroft's nurse here, Patrick Galway, prison chaplain, and a security prison warder called James Roper. All work in Aegis. Maybe that incredible woman, Orac, could find out whether any of them are connected to one of Ashcroft's victims.'

Jackman said he was in IT at the moment, and he'd pass the names on at once. Did she believe that one of them was the killer? Julia shook her head. 'I'm not sure about anything right now, Jackman, except that it's more complicated than it seems.'

* * *

Orac looked at the names. 'I already have my elves working on these, along with all the others on the Aegis staff list. I've told them to check for any affiliation with Ashcroft's victims, especially the early ones, no matter how tenuous the connection.' She stood up. 'I'll see that they prioritise these names, if they haven't finished with them already.'

Jackman walked over to Marie, who sat thumbing through papers, handing some of them to Ruth Crooke to read.

'It's like we thought, boss, our list really is down to two people.'

'I suppose one isn't called Christos by any chance?'

'Not exactly, sir,' Marie said, 'but the first is called Christopher. Christopher Mark Sheffield was unofficially engaged to one of his first victims. The other is also a Chris, a woman called Helen Christine Winter, the first victim, Pauline's sister. Both went off the radar over a year ago, and even Orac can find no trace of them.'

The death of Pauline Grover had been a cause of some distress to Jackman. She had been his sister-in-law's best friend. He was about to comment when he received a call from Robbie.

'Sorry, boss, the bird had flown. No sign of Hazel or anyone else here.'

'Damn it!'

'However, it's not all bad news. I was about to pick up the computer you asked us to seize and a message flashed up on the screen. Hang on. I'll read it. It says:

"Here you are, Jackman! A present from me to you. Use this alongside your guide, and you will have the opportunity to close down Ashcroft's entire organisation from top to bottom, along

with some of the dirtiest rackets you have ever encountered. It's not encrypted — I dealt with that — and you will need no passwords, so I'm handing it to you on a plate. One last thing before I leave, there are a number of people mixed up in this who are totally innocent . . . I'll tell you now, all were coerced or used by me. This entire long-running operation is entirely my brainchild. No one else is to blame. Sorry we won't be able to meet, and thank you once again. Christos."'

Jackman swallowed hard. 'Can you send me that, Robbie? I need to see it for myself.'

'I'm sending it to your mobile now, sir. I'll stay here and wait for forensics to arrive and pack up the computer equipment. They shouldn't be long.'

'Fine. Then get back as soon as you can, Robbie.' Jackman ended the call and let out a long whistle. 'Whoever this Christos is, he'll go down in police history annals as the most helpful criminal ever! *If* what he's telling us is true, of course.' He showed Marie and Ruth the message on his phone. 'What part does, or did, Christos play in Ashcroft's organisation, I wonder?'

'He's the second in command,' said Orac, striding back into the room. 'I saw him mentioned in that file on John. He's Ashcroft's man on the outside, answerable only to Ashcroft himself and the mysterious accountant, a Crispin Farnham, though I doubt that's his real name.'

'I can't see a man as closely involved as Christos says he is wanting to bring the whole organisation down,' said Ruth. 'I mean, if we ever caught up with him he'd never see daylight again.'

Jackman's phone rang. This time it was Gary.

'I've got an address for Hazel Palgrave, sir. Shall I take Stacey and Jay and pay a call?'

'Where is it, Gary?'

'On the road to Fenchester, about a mile out of town. A place called Stonehouse Mews. It looks like a kind of bun-galow estate.'

'Yes, go now, but take Kevin as well. We have no idea how dangerous this woman might be, so wear your stabbies, okay?'

After this last call, Jackman sat down. 'Is it me, or is this all getting a bit weird?'

'You can say that again, boss,' muttered Marie. 'This Christos bloke drops hitman John in the shit, gives us the address of their HQ and then a computer that isn't even password protected. What on earth is it all about? And where is this Hazel woman, the controller? Do you think he's abducted her? Or worse?'

'Maybe she got wind of what was happening and did a runner,' suggested Ruth.

'It'll be interesting to see what Gary finds at her home,' added Marie. She turned to Orac. 'Any luck with those names yet?'

'Give my little elf, Leon, a few more minutes and he'll be out, hopefully with some rather useful information.' Those strange metallic orbs flashed suddenly, as if they'd caught the light. 'It'll be worth the wait, you'll see.'

Waiting. Jackman hated waiting at the best of times, and right now he seemed to be doing nothing else. Waiting for Christos's 'guide' to arrive. Waiting for Gary to call in from Hazel Palgrave's home. For anyone within the Aegis Unit with a connection to one of Ashcroft's victims. And now Leon with his information.

A silence fell over them. In the background, the gentle whirring of a printer, fingers tapping on a keyboard and the occasional quiet bleep denoting an incoming message. Time stood still while Jackman waited.

CHAPTER THIRTY-FIVE

'Blimey, I wasn't expecting this,' said Gary, staring at the neat little bungalow. 'It looks like a retirement village!'

'There's a TV on in the front room,' said Stacey. 'I can see it through the window.'

'And a wheelchair access ramp to the front door?' Jay pulled a face. 'This is the oddest raid I've ever been on.'

'This is all wrong, Gary,' said Kevin. 'There couldn't be two Hazel Palgraves, could there?'

'Well, there's only one way to find out,' said Gary. 'Though we'd better not go in mob-handed like we planned. We'll knock on the door, okay?'

'What?' said Jay, 'You mean like, "*Excuse me, can we come in*"?'

'Bit like that,' said Gary. 'But be on your guard. This could still be a set-up. Let's go.'

Gary rang the bell. They heard the sound of footsteps approach the door, and then a woman's voice. 'Who is it?'

'Police. We are looking for a Hazel Palgrave,' Gary answered.

They heard a security chain being unlatched, and the door opened. A woman looked at them, suspiciously at first, then offered up a weak smile. 'Yes, that's me.'

They held up their warrant cards and Gary asked if they might go inside and talk to her for a minute.

'I suppose so,' she said, and turned her back, leaving them to follow her inside.

Gary had noted the resignation in her tone. All, he was certain, was not as it seemed.

She switched off the television and turned to face them. She wasn't, as he had thought, old, probably in her mid-forties and quite attractive. And her pale face wore a very strange expression.

'You *are* Hazel Palgrave, aren't you?' said Gary. 'And correct me if I'm wrong, but you know why we are here, don't you?'

The woman smiled sadly. 'Yes. You know, I never really believed that this day would come. Part of me is . . . well, thankful in a way, and another part is rather frightened.'

She turned from them and went to a small writing desk on the other side of the room from which she took out an envelope. This she held out to Gary.

The label on the front read *Detective Inspector Rowan Jackman*.

'That's the first thing I have to do.' She glanced at a clock on the mantlepiece. 'And considering the time, I've been asked to tell you to get it to DI Jackman as speedily as possible.'

Gary handed the envelope to Jay. 'Get this back to the station, will you? And ring Jackman and tell him it's on its way, okay?'

'Of course.' Jay took the envelope and left immediately.

'May we sit down, Hazel?' asked Gary. 'I think you may have an interesting story to tell us.'

'Possibly, but it's very short. I'm afraid I'm a very small cog in the wheel. But, yes, please do sit.'

Gary sank into an armchair. 'I suggest that you were actually a very important cog, since you allowed someone else to use your name in order to perform her role. She could never have done it so well under her own.'

Hazel Palgrave shrugged. 'You seem to know it all already.'

Gary shook his head. 'No. As a matter of fact we know very little. Basically, I'm watching your body language, and the fact that you were entrusted with a letter for our DI, which means you are a trusted friend of its author.'

'True.'

'I'm sorry, Hazel, but I'm afraid we are going to have to take you to the station. You are clearly involved.'

'No,' she said flatly. 'I can't do that.'

'I'm afraid you have to.'

'You don't understand, Detective. It's not that I don't want to, I *can't*. I suffer from severe agoraphobia. I don't leave the house.' She twisted her hands together. 'I will talk to you, I'll tell you whatever you want to know, but, please, we have to do it here.'

Gary looked at Kevin. 'Under the circumstances, I'm inclined to say yes, but we need to clear it with the office. Would you ring it in, Kevin?'

While Kevin made the call, Gary turned back to Hazel Palgrave. 'Who took your name, and when did you last see her?'

'Her name is Helen Winter, nee Helen Grover, the younger sister of Pauline Grover — Alistair Ashcroft's first victim — and I last saw her two hours before you rang my bell.'

* * *

Jackman ripped open the envelope that Jay Acharya had handed him and read it out to Marie:

'Sorry to send you after a red herring but I needed to buy myself time to get away. Notwithstanding, you will now have everything you need to bring down a powerful criminal network. Ashcroft is dead, and you have his hired killer, John. My computer will lead you to Christos, so find him as fast

308

as you can. My only regret is that I have no idea who the accountant is, or where he's hiding. However, Christos does, so it's down to you from this point onwards. I have instructed the real Hazel Palgrave to give you the whole story, the full details of which you will find in my guidebook. You deserve that much. I hope you understand that Ashcroft had to be stopped, something prison could never do. Thus, it was up to me to draw the final line. Bear in mind my position as controller. As such, I knew what he had planned for his grand finale, the overwhelming destruction he was about to bring down on you and those close to you. I could not let that happen.

I did this for my darling sister, Pauline, for your sister-in-law, Sarah, and all the other innocent victims and their families. May they now find peace.

Helen Winter, nee Grover.'

'Well, we almost got there, didn't we?' said Orac with a glance at Marie. 'Anyway, I believe I now have a new directive. Isn't that right, Jackman? You want me to find out where she's going. Because I have a strong feeling she's heading out of the country.'

'Yes, Orac. Track her for me if you can.'

At that moment, Leon hurried in, waving a printout.

'Here's your list of people from the Aegis Unit who have connections to Ashcroft's victims.'

He hesitated for a moment or two, unsure of which one of them to give it to, so Marie took it and read the names. 'Oh my! Will you listen to this.'

Only Orac, whose fingers were a blur as she typed, didn't have her gaze fixed on her.

'We have three names, all with some type of connection to Ashcroft's victims. A prison officer called Sean Waller, the chaplain, Patrick Galway, and one of the other prisoners, named Jeremy Shaler.' She looked up from the page. 'Is this some kind of lethal syndicate?'

Jackman shook his head resignedly. 'Well, Julia reckoned it wasn't a simple murder.'

'Helen Winter said that this whole thing was her brain-child, didn't she?' said Ruth. 'She must have been planning it for years.'

'With the assistance of others whose lives had been torn apart by Ashcroft,' added Jackman. 'My God, she must have hated him.'

'Almost as much as we did,' muttered Marie. 'Only we tried to get him lawfully.'

For a while they all stood rooted to the spot while they came to terms with the enormity of just what Helen Winter had achieved, not least in wheedling her way into Ashcroft's confidence.

The sound of Jackman's phone startled them into life.

'Yes, Kevin?' barked Jackman and listened. 'Okay, stay right where you are. Marie and I will be with you as soon we can.' He ended the call and looked at Ruth. 'He says the real Hazel Palgrave has agoraphobia. Should we go to her? We badly need to hear what she has to say. If we do need to arrest her, we can think again.'

'Just go, Rowan,' said Ruth. 'I'll take over here.'

'And I'll find her for you,' added a voice from the nearby workstation, 'whether she's leaving by land, sea or air.'

Hurrying after Jackman, Marie had her doubts. If she was clever enough to fool the master manipulator Ashcroft, surely escaping the country would be no problem at all.

As they ran up the stairs, they met Tim on his way down. 'That parcel's arrived, sir. I thought you might need it urgently.'

Jackman took it from him. 'You drive, Marie. I need to have a look at this "guidebook" of hers.'

As they drove, Jackman carefully unwrapped the parcel. Marie glanced across and saw a thick spiral-bound notebook bulging with loose sheets of paper in transparent sleeves.

'It's a kind of diary, Marie, but stuffed with additional documents. It goes back years.' He flicked through the pages. 'I can see Helen's personal thoughts here too. Listen to this: "*he scares me enough to make my blood turn to ice in my veins, but then I think of how afraid of him my sister must have been. It enables me to*

310

master my fear and hatred and continue persuading him of how much I idolise him. I do this abominable thing, and I smile. For the sake of my beloved Pauline."'

Hearing this, Marie put her foot down.

The small room they walked into seemed full to capacity already. Jackman introduced himself and Marie to Hazel Palgrave and explained that if it was found that she had aided an offender, he would have to place her under arrest and caution her. However, they would take her condition into consideration.

Hazel Palgrave nodded and said she understood.

'Then we will begin. How did you come to know Helen Winter?'

'We met right here. Helen and her husband, Reuben, lived next door to my late mother's best friend, Nancy. I was my mother's carer, you see. When old Nancy's arthritis got too bad for the bus, Helen used to drop her off here to have a cuppa with my mum, and we struck up a friendship. There was an instant rapport between us. When Mum died, Helen was an enormous help given my problem with going out. Then over lunch one day she gave me her whole sad history. And I gave her mine.' She sighed.

'I'm sorry this is so painful for you,' Jackman said, 'but—'

She waved this aside. 'No matter. It has to be said. I wouldn't bother you with my story as it's not really relevant, but you should know the basics so you can understand why I agreed to help Helen.' She drew in a breath. 'When I was younger, I was mugged and badly beaten. There were no CCTV cameras then, so they never found who did it. You might say I was one of those cases no one wants to know about. The man who attacked me got away scot-free, and my life was ruined. Shortly after that, the agoraphobia kicked in and I started having panic attacks.'

Marie began to understand Hazel's compassion for this woman, whose sister had fallen victim to a manipulating killer.

'When Helen told me about the atrocities Ashcroft had committed, and of her plan to avenge her sister's killing,

311

along with the deaths of others, I offered my help. Aside from the fact that Helen is a wonderful person, we have a great deal in common. We both work in the computer industry, as systems analysts and software designers. It's a job that allows me to work from home.'

She went on to describe how Helen had spent six months visiting the relatives and loved ones of Ashcroft's many victims. Having seen the destruction he had wreaked, she determined to come face to face with this killer. Since she couldn't present herself as the sister of one of his victims, she required an alias. Which was where Hazel came in. For once, her agoraphobia proved to be a blessing. Helen Winter would become Hazel Palgrave, furnished with all the appropriate background details. Hazel had never driven, so Helen took a driving test under Hazel's name, passed, and received a very useful photo driving licence. Since Hazel hadn't been abroad, Helen applied for a passport, thereby arming herself with another official proof of identity. Armed with these documents she opened a bank account. To all intents and purposes, Helen was now Hazel Palgrave. As Hazel, she applied to become an official prison visitor, which was where fate intervened in the person of the prison chaplain, Patrick Galway, who interviewed her.

How patient she had been, marvelled Marie, as she listened to the story of how Helen, now Hazel Palgrave, wormed her way into Alistair Ashcroft's life.

'. . . Finally, just in case Ashcroft didn't trust her enough, Helen's devoted husband too began to insinuate himself into the killer's life and gain his confidence. In her role as prison visitor, Ashcroft wasn't the only inmate she saw. Through the victim's group, she discovered a young man called Jeremy Shaler. She spent a great deal of time with Jeremy.'

It dawned on Marie that of course, she needed an assassin who was on the inside, and who better than a convicted killer who was already serving a life sentence. Marie saw Jackman's grim smile. He, too, had worked that one out.

By this time Hazel Palgrave was beginning to flag. Jackman brought the interview to a close. 'There is a lot more that we need to know, but not now. Considering your candour and your condition, Hazel, I'm going to leave it there, but I need your assurance that you will stay here, and wait for me or one of my detectives to contact you.'

'You have my word, DI Jackman. If I did want to run, I'd probably only make it a few steps from the front door.' She stared at them thoughtfully. 'Helen admired you both immensely.' She looked at Marie. 'She said that you did more than anyone to try and put a stop to his activities. She was aware that you had reached the limit of what you could do, while she wasn't bound by the same ties. In her words, "the final blow must come from a free spirit."'

'Two last questions, although I don't really expect an answer,' Jackman said. 'Where is Helen Winter now? And where is she going?'

'She refused to tell me,' Hazel said. 'She said it was best I didn't know.' She swallowed. 'I will miss her terribly. She was an angel.'

Angel of death more like, thought Marie.

* * *

Sam put his phone back in his pocket and looked wide-eyed at Julia. 'That was Marie. They've had a major breakthrough.' He told her the story of Helen Winter and how she had inveigled herself into Ashcroft's confidence. 'And she said to tell you that there are *three* people on your list with connections to victims of Ashcroft. And Patrick Galway is one of them.'

Surprisingly, Julia merely sighed. 'And let me guess. Another is a member of staff who has access to the keys, and the third is one of the prisoners.'

Sam shook his head in wonder. 'Julia, you never cease to amaze me. So, this is what you meant by far from simple, is it?'

'There were far too many grey areas, my dear. Besides, Ashcroft had damaged so many people it was like a pebble dropped in a pond — the ripples spread. And the ripples encompassed others. All it took was someone sufficiently dedicated to their quest for justice to bring those others together. They may not have acted in accordance with the law but the people whose lives Ashcroft destroyed will consider justice to have been served.'

'Well, I can't argue with that,' Sam said. 'Now the initial shock has started to wear off, I'm beginning to experience a renewed sense of freedom, something that has been missing from my life far too long.'

Just then, Dr Casey Naylor walked in. 'This is so weird,' she said without preamble. 'The investigating team are in total disarray.'

'How come?' asked Sam.

'It's the prisoner interviews. They all, to a man, claim to have killed Ashcroft! Especially the obnoxious Fleming, who would like nothing better than to be acclaimed for taking down the notorious Alistair Ashcroft. It's just bizarre.'

Julia beamed at her. 'What a delightful spanner in the works! Did you sit in on the interviews, Casey?'

'Theo was there for all of them. I, er, was only there for one.'

'Jeremy Shaler, by any chance?' Julia raised an eyebrow.

'Well, yes, as it happens. He's always interested me, possibly even more than Ashcroft — though in a different way, of course. I wondered how he would deal with the questions, so I asked permission to observe.'

Julia said simply, 'I understand.'

Sam watched the two women. Something had passed between them, but what?

'I was wondering,' said Julia slowly, 'if I might be allowed to speak to him myself? With or without a police presence.'

'Well, I'm due to go on my rounds shortly,' said Casey, 'and I have no objection to you accompanying me.'

'Perfect,' said Julia. 'And perhaps we could make Shaler our first port of call?' When Casey agreed, Julia asked, 'By the way, how *did* he cope with his interview?'

'I'd like to say it was just like the way he deals with any questioning, which is to say detached and emotionless, but . . . but it wasn't. The difference was very subtle, but because I spend so much time with him, I was able to pick up indications of underlying tension.' She shrugged. 'Or maybe it was excitement. Yes, that was more like it.'

Excitement. Not a normal response to the news of the death and the ensuing lockdown. Was it Shaler, then, who had killed Ashcroft? Sam looked at Julia, but her expression was unreadable. It seemed he'd have to wait until she had seen the man for herself.

Sam smiled to himself. No matter what face Shaler chose to present, Julia would see through it.

Once again, he realised just how much he had missed her prescience. He and Laura had had a different kind of relationship, like that of father and daughter. They had shared a great deal in their long conversations about their subjects. Julia, however, was very different, perhaps because she was older. She was more incisive. He remembered a student once saying of her that Prof Tennant was a mastermind at cutting the crap.

Well, if ever that skill was badly needed, it was now.

Sam watched them leave the room and decided there was nothing for it but to make himself another cup of tea.

* * *

Jeremy Shaler had seen this older woman in the unit before, as well as the esteem in which her colleagues held her. Even he found her interesting, and not a little imposing. She reminded him of an aunt of his, a headmistress-like woman he usually did his best to avoid. This woman had the same air of calm authority. The doctor had asked him if he had any objection to her presence. He hadn't. Why should he? But he wondered what her position was, and why she was here with Dr Naylor.

'I know you killed him.'

The woman's tone was matter of fact, almost casual, but the words came as a bolt from the blue.

Then he laughed. Shaler never laughed, and it sounded weird, even to him. Dr Naylor looked completely taken aback, which made him laugh all the harder.

Julia Tennant, however, continued to regard him with the same calm expression.

After a while, he said, 'You do know that every single con in the unit has coughed to killing him?'

'Oh yes,' she said blithely, 'but that's par for the course, isn't it? They want the kudos. There's only one man who really did finish Alistair Ashcroft, isn't there? The only man with a good reason for doing so.' She looked at him with something like sympathy. 'We always say there are many more victims than just the person killed. One untimely death can leave countless other lives damaged beyond repair. Lives like yours, Jeremy.'

The veneer of toughness fell away and suddenly he felt like a little boy. He wanted to cry.

Julia's voice was infinitely gentle. 'Tell me? If you can.'

'He ripped my family apart. It wasn't a high-profile murder, just a diversion for Ashcroft, something to pass the time. When he got bored with it, he walked away and left the mess behind. My sister finished up on so many drugs that she overdosed — whether accidental or deliberate didn't really matter. She was gone.'

'And how was your brother involved, Jeremy?' Julia asked. 'I know you killed him but I'm sure your reason had to do with Ashcroft.'

Jesus, this woman was astute. It was like she'd been involved with Ashcroft herself. Maybe she had.

'It was my brother who introduced us to Ashcroft. He was the first to be brainwashed.'

'And you?' asked Julia. 'How did Ashcroft affect you, Jeremy?'

'I never even met him. I was working abroad, in Africa, and by the time I got home, my family had been destroyed and Ashcroft was long gone.' He swallowed. 'Imagine it. I came home to what had been a normal loving family to find a sister like a zombie, parents in pieces, and a brother who did nothing but spout garbage about his new friend Alistair, and how he hated his parents and sister for driving him away.' He heaved a sigh. 'When he then kicked off at my sister's funeral, I flipped. You know the rest. I killed him, and I'll never regret it.'

'And after a spell in HMP Lincoln, you found yourself in Gartree, along with Ashcroft,' added Casey Naylor.

'Where it all began,' added Julia. 'Where you met Helen Winter.'

'Where it all began,' he repeated. 'And here is where it all ended. Full circle, at last.'

He closed his eyes and was back in that morning, when the door of his room had been opened and a voice had said, 'It's time. He's alone and his door is unlocked.' Like an automaton, he got up, found the length of electrical cable that he had secreted away in preparation for this moment, and walked out into the corridor.

Ashcroft's expression, when he entered his room, was at first annoyed, then mildly interested.

'Well well, it's our own dark horse, Mr Shaler. Come in, sit, let's talk. One thing about this lockdown is that we have plenty of time to get to know each other.'

He was sitting up in bed, his damaged legs stretched out in front of him, with the air of a king holding court.

'The time for talking has passed, Ashcroft.'

He had been as fast as a cat pouncing on a mouse. In seconds, he had the ligature around Ashcroft's neck and twisted tightly behind his head. Ashcroft's scream was cut short. He flailed. He fought, but Jeremy had every single one of Ashcroft's victims giving him strength.

Then, before he finished the job, he loosened his grip, just enough to keep Ashcroft alive and conscious, then he started to talk. Ashcroft must die with the names of those whose lives he had ruined ringing in his ears:

'Heather Miller, later Sarah Jackman; Pauline Grover, known as Suri Forrester; Brendan Symons, Victoria Whitman, Isaac Whitman . . .' He had memorised every single one of their names. When he reached his own, he twisted the cord so tightly that it cut into the flesh. The eyes bulged, the tongue protruded. It was over.

He laid him down, covered him up and turned his back on him.

Jeremy returned to his own room, washed his hands again and again, scrubbing them until they were raw.

Back in the present, Jeremy Shaler blinked a few times and looked from Julia Tennant to Dr Casey Naylor. 'I'll tell you and the police everything, but believe me, I did this alone. No one else was involved. No one but me is to blame.'

'You might not believe this, Jeremy,' said Julia, 'but I blame no one at all.'

CHAPTER THIRTY-SIX

Jackman's car echoed with the sound of Orac's clear voice. 'I've found her — well, sort of.'

Having just pulled away from Hazel Palgrave's bungalow, he and Marie were on their way back to the station. 'Sort of?' Jackman said. 'What do you mean?'

'I'd spent the evening going through the passenger lists of flights out of the country and came up with nothing, so I widened my search,' said Orac. 'I've identified a Mr and Mrs Reuben Winter booked on a flight out of Orly Airport, Paris, tonight, destination Geneva.'

'Paris? But . . .' Jackman's mind raced. 'How on earth will they make it to France in time?'

'Well, here's the thing. Leon has been checking our Helen's background. I'll fill you in on the details when we have more time but suffice it to say that Reuben has been living with his brother since Helen took on the persona of Hazel Palgrave. The brother runs a private hire helicopter company, and he so happens to live not far from where you are now. If you like, I can tell you exactly where they'll be leaving from. The downside is that the pilot has asked for clearance to take off in less than twenty minutes.'

Jackman brought the car to a halt. 'Where?'

'White Horse Lane, a house named Belmont Lodge. It has a private helicopter pad.'

'Let's go!' urged Marie. 'We are only five or ten minutes from there.'

'Thank you, Orac, we're on our way.' Jackman ended the call, turned the car around and sped off back the way they had come.

'I'll call this in,' said Marie, 'get a crew to meet us.'

Jackman thought for a moment or two. 'Hold up on that, Marie. I think we might do better if we keep a low profile. You and I can handle this on our own.'

Marie glanced at him and frowned.

'It was Helen who tried to save Frank, wasn't it? It was her that sent that warning message,' Jackman said, replying to her unspoken question.

'It had to be her, all things considered,' said Marie. 'And I suggest that it was also her that changed John's directive regarding Rosie. If you remember, he told Rosie he had received new instructions. I reckon that was Helen's doing too.'

Jackman knew White Horse Lane. It was on the very outskirts of the Saltern area, in a remote spot surrounded by acres of arable fields. The only way from where they were now was along a long straight drove bordered by a deep drain. He was halfway down the drove when the car began to slow.

'What's the matter?' asked Marie.

'Engine trouble, an intermittent fault. It's been doing this for a few days now but I haven't had time to get it checked out.'

He pulled into a passing place and turned off the engine.

'I have to ring in now, or they'll get away!' Marie exclaimed. When he said nothing, she murmured: 'Ah, I see . . .' She turned and looked at him. 'And I suppose we are in a dead spot with no signal, would that be right?'

''Fraid so, Marie.' He shrugged. 'We just aren't going to make it in time.'

'No, we're not.' She said nothing for a moment or two. 'Let me check I've got this right: you want to give her a chance to get away, don't you?'

'Helen Winter pulled the plug on a killing spree that would have started with my family and friends, including you, Marie, and most likely your Ralph as well. Frankly, I've had enough death in my life, thank you. The least I can do is give Helen a sporting chance.'

'There's still Orac, though. She knows what flight they're booked on. By helicopter, they could be in Paris in under an hour and half. The French police could easily apprehend Helen and her husband at the airport.'

'Not if they don't know about it.'

They sat in silence, both looking out of the windscreen at the long road ahead. Jackman was just about to speak when he heard the racket of propeller blades turning. From behind a clump of trees some half a mile away, a helicopter rose. It dipped, turned, and roared away towards the coast.

Jackman started the car. 'Well I never! Like I said, an intermittent fault, so annoying.'

'And will you look at that, my phone has signal again,' added Marie dryly.

'Then if you'd be so kind, use my phone and ring Orac. I need to have a quiet word with her.'

Orac answered immediately. 'Would I be right in thinking that you missed the boat — or copter, to be precise?'

He wasn't expecting that one! 'Er, sadly no, we didn't make it.'

'I thought that might be the case. All right, DI Jackman, talk to me. I have a feeling you might be needing a sympathetic ear.'

'Sounds like I'm not the only witch around here,' muttered Marie. 'She knew exactly what you'd do.'

'I heard that, Marie Evans,' said Orac. 'I'm flattered you think that way.'

Marie chuckled.

'So, Orac, in that case you probably already know what I'm going to ask you. You have every right to refuse, and even report me if you wish.'

'Oh, Jackman, really!' Orac scoffed. 'What do you take me for? I've already told Leon to forget Reuben's brother for the time being. It can come out later. Right now, I can tell you that there is no record of the Winters being booked on any flights, or ships, leaving the UK tonight or tomorrow. Your all-points warning will throw up nothing. They are obviously lying low somewhere. Sorry, but for now, it seems we've lost them.'

Overcome with gratitude, Jackman was hard put to it to know what to say.

'We owe you, Orac,' said Marie. 'Big style.'

Jackman found his voice. 'I'll second that. We certainly do.'

'Glad to hear it. I'll spend many a happy hour thinking of ways for you to repay me. Meanwhile, *Oiche mhaith codladh samh*. For you ignorant heathens that means, "Good night and sweet dreams."' And Orac ended the call.

Marie said, 'Sorry, I baulked earlier. On reflection, you had no option, did you? Without Helen Winter — say if Ashcroft had used a different controller — we could all be dead by the end of the week.' They sat and listened to the smoothly running engine. 'I'm so glad your car developed that, what was it, intermittent fault?'

'That's the one.' He drew in a breath. 'Mind you, there's no guarantee that she won't be found when the official hunt gets underway, but at least we've given her a head start. Hopefully she's smart enough to change her name again. It'd be asking for trouble if she attempted to travel under her own.'

Marie smiled. 'I bet if you check that flight to Geneva, there'll be two passengers who didn't show. You said it yourself, she's smart. A pound to a penny that was a false trail. That helicopter we saw could have been going anywhere.'

'Oh, I hope so, Marie. I really do.'

322

CHAPTER THIRTY-SEVEN

One month later

After four weeks of trawling through countless interviews and documentation, Marie suddenly shut down her computer. She stood up and strode into Jackman's office.

'Okay, boss. I've had it up to here with sodding paper-work. And you, if you don't mind me saying so, look bug-eyed.' She took a set of keys from her pocket and dangled them in the air. 'We are going out. Get your jacket, I'm driving.'

'Have I just been hijacked?' asked Jackman, as they headed north on the main road out of Saltern.

'I prefer to think I'm saving your sanity, but hijacking will do.'

'Where are we going?' he asked.

'Wait and see, and in the meantime, relax. Try and think about something other than work if you can — well, at least until we get there.'

Soon, a signpost indicated that they were approaching the village of Corley Eaudyke. This was it. This was her new home.

'Here we are. And if I'm not mistaken, that's Ralph's car heading our way. Perfect timing.'

Marie pulled up outside the old police house. 'Jackman, meet Peelers End! I've been given the keys for the day, to come and measure up for curtains and stuff like that.'

Jackman looked at the old property and a smile spread across his face. 'This is yours?'

'All mine — oh, and his of course.' She indicated to Ralph, now strolling towards them.

'We've been dying to show you, but with work as bloody manic as it is, I decided I'd have to take drastic measures.'

Jackman shook the hand Ralph was holding out to him. 'Good to see you again, Ralph, and will you look at this place! It couldn't be better, could it?'

'Wait till you see inside,' said Ralph enthusiastically.

Once indoors, Jackman wandered around for a while, meeting the others in the kitchen. 'I cannot believe it still has the original cells!'

Marie grinned. 'I'm tempted to put one to use incarcerating cold callers. Oh, and when Ralph went up in the attic, he found some old boxes. They had some brilliant photos in them showing the place as it used to be. It's so nice to get a feel for how it was then.' She decided not to mention the old murder. Jackman had most likely had enough of death for a while.

'So, when do you move in?' asked Jackman, admiring the old-style range.

Marie glanced at Ralph, who nodded to her. They both smiled broadly.

'In three weeks' time,' she said. 'On the day after our wedding.'

Jackman blinked a few times, then laughed. 'You really are going for it! That's wonderful, both of you!' Hugging Marie, he said, 'I'm *so* happy for you.'

He turned and hugged Ralph too. 'And as for you . . . I can't make up my mind whether you deserve a medal for taking Marie on, or if you're the luckiest man alive!'

'I'm going for the latter,' said Ralph. 'But most importantly, would you consider being my best man?'

'Surely you have a close friend you should ask? I'd hate to tread on toes or spoil friendships.'

'You are my first choice, Jackman, and it has nothing to do with the ultimatum Marie has given me either!'

'Then it would be an honour and a privilege,' Jackman said, smiling.

'Sorted!' exclaimed Marie in delight. 'Now, I have some measuring up to do, then we'll have to get back to the grind.'

'I must get off too,' added Ralph. 'I'm supposed to be interviewing someone in twenty minutes' time. Great to see you again, Jackman. I'll ring you in a day or so and we can discuss the plans for the wedding.'

Marie kissed him lightly and watched him go. Then she turned to Jackman. 'You really do like this place?'

'I love it, Marie. You are going to be so happy here.'

'I know. I felt it the moment I set foot inside.' She gave him a hug. 'And you, my dearest friend, are welcome to visit — any time, any day.'

They clung together, while a lifetime of shared experiences and intense emotions passed between them. Marie said into his shoulder, 'And don't forget, I'm your sergeant and your friend, and nothing will ever change that.'

Jackman released her, wiping away what looked suspiciously like a tear. 'Message received and understood. Now off you go and measure your curtains.'

On the way back to the station, they discussed the case and the way it appeared to be heading. It was proving to be a legal minefield, finding proof of almost everything practically impossible. Marie had been right in saying the Winters wouldn't turn up for the flight from Paris to Geneva, and no trace had been seen of them since. Jackman had found a sealed envelope in the file Helen had sent him, containing a written confession, signed and witnessed by two upstanding professional people. It stated that she had brought coercion, threat and mental and physical pressure to bear on everyone involved in the plan to bring down Ashcroft's organisation

325

and end his life. So, in the absence of the principal offender, the case would remain open until Helen Winter was found.

'I reckon the weirdest part of the whole affair,' said Marie, 'was something completely spontaneous. It's turned out to be the biggest stumbling block in the case for the prosecution.'

'You're talking about Jeremy Shaler, I presume,' said Jackman, 'and the "Great Admission Game".'

'Absolutely. Six men, six convicted killers to boot, all swear they killed Ashcroft. The ligature was never found, even though the place was turned upside down. DNA and finger-prints from all those prisoners was found in Ashcroft's room and on his body. We know Ashcroft had all but destroyed Shaler's family but there is no way now to prove that he was the murderer.' She let out a long breath. 'I wonder where that ligature did go?'

'It's my belief that it was taken off the body and smug-gled out by one of the three people who left the unit shortly after Ashcroft died. My bet would be on the prison officer, James Roper, another man with a connection to a victim.'

'Or the nurse, Monica Rush. The guards would have been accustomed to her going in and out all the time, so her bag wasn't thoroughly searched. You know what they say about familiarity.'

'That's possible too,' Jackman said. 'I guess we'll never know for sure.'

'And then,' Marie said, slowing at the approach to a roundabout, 'there's DI Jenny Deane and her team who, along with the Dutch police, succeeded in foiling Ashcroft's criminal organisation. To my mind that's the best outcome of all.'

'You're right,' said Jackman. 'They've decimated the illegal blue film industry and managed to get every single villain involved in the snuff movies behind bars. Jenny is over the moon, since it's helped her tie up several of her old cases. Without a doubt, it's the biggest crackdown on vice-related crime that Saltern-le-Fen has ever seen.'

'Even Christos is banged up on remand. And all thanks to Helen Winter's journal and that file she left you.' Marie turned onto the road to the station. 'The only unsolved mystery is Ashcroft's nameless accountant. Do you think Christos will sing?'

'Jenny Deane reckons so,' said Jackman. 'Christos is in it up to his neck and giving us the accountant will go in his favour. He has nothing to lose, there are no gang members left to make sure he keeps his mouth shut.'

'Just think,' Marie said. 'All those horrific crimes committed with the sole purpose of funding Ashcroft's plan to eradicate us. Gives you the shivers just to think about it, doesn't it?'

'It's scary indeed to be so hated,' admitted Jackman, 'even if it was by a twisted psychopath.'

'I still can't believe that a formerly respected copper, no matter what he had suffered, could have brought himself to murder innocents and police officers,' Marie said.

'He murdered the man who saved his life! Our friend Frank Rosen. Be under no illusion, Marie, Russell Copeland would have killed us without a second thought. You read his history: a senior officer's wife pestered him continually, and when Russell, who was happily married, turned her down, she told her husband he had forced himself on her. It was a blatant lie, but no way could Russell prove it. It got so nasty that he left the force and went to work for a security firm as a bodyguard but bad luck found him there too. A job went wrong and a man died, all the fault of Russell's colleague, but he blamed Russell. Russell started procedures to fight the accusation but by way of a warning, his wife was run down in the street and killed. It was more than he could cope with mentally. He went completely off the rails at that point.'

Marie turned off the main road. 'Helen Winter suggested that something else happened to him, didn't she? Whatever it was, it seemed to obliterate every remaining vestige of decency and morality and left him with a single love: money.'

'Yeah. I saw the note in her journal where she writes that she was fully aware of what he had become but she still regretted handing him over to us. However, there was no way she could allow him to carry out Ashcroft's plan.'

'And now he'll spend the rest of his life in prison,' Marie said. 'That's one aspect of this case where a prosecution will stick. Russell Copeland, aka John, will go down for life.'

On arriving back in the CID room, they were met by Sam and Julia.

'We've just driven back from Cambridge,' said Sam, 'and we thought you might like to know the latest on the Aegis Unit.'

'Come into the office,' said Jackman.

'I'll go get some drinks,' said Marie. 'Coffee, everyone?'

They all said yes, so she headed for the vending machine, wondering whether the unit would be shut down following the murder of their principal subject.

When they were all settled, coffee in hand, Julia said, 'We've just come from speaking to Dr Casey Naylor. Apparently, the unit's fate hung in the balance for a while. Casey told us that Theo Carmichael underwent a serious personal crisis after Ashcroft died and was insisting the unit be closed. It was Casey Naylor who convinced the powers that be that it should remain open.'

'Casey was certain Theo just needed time to come to terms with it,' Sam added, 'and would come to realise that the work they had done there and the results achieved were worthwhile. It turns out that she was right.'

'He took himself off for a couple of weeks,' continued Julia. 'Went trekking in Morocco, and it seems the Atlas Mountains gave him the perspective he needed. He rang Casey and told her he wanted to discuss a new direction for Aegis.'

'And that's getting underway as from next week.' Sam sipped his coffee. 'Oh, and while we were there we met the chaplain, Patrick Galway. He came to say goodbye to Casey. Unsurprisingly, he's resigned his post at the prison and moving to our neck of the woods — Fenfleet, would you believe? He'll be working with the homeless from now on.'

'I felt rather sorry for him,' said Julia. 'He did amazing work with the prisoners, and I still can't make up my mind whether he had anything to do with Ashcroft's demise. Yes, he approved Helen Winters's application to be an official visitor, but at that point he had no idea of her agenda. We've agreed to meet up for a chat once he's settled in the Fens. Maybe he'll tell me more one day.'

'You'll be glad to know that all the original prisoners have been returned to the main prison to continue their sentences,' said Sam, 'including Jeremy Shaler.'

'The real murderer,' added Julia. 'Although if I had my way . . .'

Marie understood her to mean that considering the damage Ashcroft had inflicted on his family, in a perfect world Julia would have given him a free pardon and a vote of thanks for his services to humanity. Suddenly a thought hit her. 'Why didn't Ashcroft recognise Jeremy Shaler's name? Shaler isn't exactly common, and apparently, he spent quite a lot of time with Jeremy's family.'

'Because the family name was Smith,' Julia said. 'It was his mother's second marriage. Her first husband died of a heart attack not long after Jeremy was born — he was just a toddler when she remarried — and she didn't change his name. Jeremy was working abroad when Ashcroft came into their lives and he never met him, so Ashcroft would never have known that he had a different surname.'

Satisfied with the answer, Marie sat back, drank her coffee and fell into a reverie. She wondered how long it would take for it to really sink in that Ashcroft was gone, never to harm anyone again. Thankfully, he died before he could realise his plan and take the life of someone in the team or their loved ones. He had failed, thanks to the tenacity of one woman. Best of all, Helen Winter had turned the tables on him, the master, wormed her way into his organisation and brought him down. The icing on the cake was the manner of his death. No final blaze of glory for Ashcroft, he had died an obscure inmate in a tiny prison room, snuffed out like the last weak flame of a candle.

Thinking of icing on a cake reminded her of a forthcoming special occasion. She cleared her throat. 'On a very different subject, Sam. Julia. Please keep Saturday the twenty-third free, invitations to follow, *when* Jackman finally allows me a day off. Ralph and I want you to join us for what they call a wedding breakfast, though I've never understood that one.'

Sam and Julia were delighted to hear her news. When the congratulations had died down, Sam said, 'Just for your edification, the British call it a wedding breakfast because traditionally the wedding ceremony was held after mass. That meant the whole party would fast before mass, and for the bride and groom, this was their first meal together as they broke the fast.'

'Oh my!' said Marie. 'I'm afraid we won't be doing much fasting. Anyway, it will be in the early afternoon. Details to follow. We'll be married in a registry office, just Ralph and me and our witnesses, but afterwards we are going to party! All the team and their families, and all our wonderful friends, like Rory and Orac.' All the survivors of Ashcroft's reign of terror, she thought to herself.

After Sam and Julia had left, she and Jackman sat together for a while in companionable silence. Finally, Jackman said, 'I know the paperwork will go on for months, Marie, but I think we can at least clean the whiteboard, don't you?'

Marie nodded. 'Can I do the honours, boss?'

He stood up. 'You're welcome to.'

Out in the CID room, he beckoned to the team and they gathered around the whiteboard.

Marie took down all the memos and photographs, picked up the rubber and wiped the board clean. Then, in the centre of the empty board, she wrote the following four words:

ALISTAIR ASHCROFT
CASE CLOSED

THE END

THE JOFFE BOOKS STORY

We began in 2014 when Jasper agreed to publish his mum's much-rejected romance novel and it became a bestseller.

Since then we've grown into the largest independent publisher in the UK. We're extremely proud to publish some of the very best writers in the world, including Joy Ellis, Faith Martin, Caro Ramsay, Helen Forrester, Simon Brett and Robert Goddard. Everyone at Joffe Books loves reading and we never forget that it all begins with the magic of an author telling a story.

We are proud to publish talented first-time authors, as well as established writers whose books we love introducing to a new generation of readers.

We have been shortlisted for Independent Publisher of the Year at the British Book Awards three times, in 2020, 2021 and 2022, and for the Diversity and Inclusivity Award at the Independent Publishing Awards in 2022.

We built this company with your help, and we love to hear from you, so please email us about absolutely anything bookish at feedback@joffebooks.com

If you want to receive free books every Friday and hear about all our new releases, join our mailing list: www.joffebooks. com/contact

And when you tell your friends about us, just remember: it's pronounced Joffe as in coffee or toffee!

ALSO BY JOY ELLIS

JACKMAN & EVANS SERIES
Book 1: THE MURDERER'S SON
Book 2: THEIR LOST DAUGHTER
Book 3: THE FOURTH FRIEND
Book 4: THE GUILTY ONES
Book 5: THE STOLEN BOYS
Book 6: THE PATIENT MAN
Book 7: THEY DISAPPEARED
Book 8: THE NIGHT THIEF
Book 9: SOLACE HOUSE
Book 10: THE RIVER'S EDGE

THE NIKKI GALENA SERIES
Book 1: CRIME ON THE FENS
Book 2: SHADOW OVER THE FENS
Book 3: HUNTED ON THE FENS
Book 4: KILLER ON THE FENS
Book 5: STALKER ON THE FENS
Book 6: CAPTIVE ON THE FENS
Book 7: BURIED ON THE FENS
Book 8: THIEVES ON THE FENS
Book 9: FIRE ON THE FENS
Book 10: DARKNESS ON THE FENS
Book 11: HIDDEN ON THE FENS
Book 12: SECRETS ON THE FENS
Book 13: FEAR ON THE FENS
Book 14: GRAVES ON THE FENS

DETECTIVE MATT BALLARD
Book 1: BEWARE THE PAST
Book 2: FIVE BLOODY HEARTS
Book 3: THE DYING LIGHT
Book 4: MARSHLIGHT
Book 5: TRICK OF THE NIGHT